❝ What a very, very
LUCKY
person you are.

Spread out before you are the
FINEST and FUNNIEST
words from the finest and funniest writer
the past century ever knew. **❞**

Stephen Fry

Pelham Grenville Wodehouse (always known as 'Plum') wrote more than ninety novels and some three hundred short stories over 73 years. He is widely recognised as the greatest 20th century writer of humour in the English language.

Wodehouse mixed the high culture of his classical education with the popular slang of the suburbs in both England and America, becoming a 'cartoonist of words'. Drawing on the antics of a near-contemporary world, he placed his Drones, Earls, Ladies (including draconian aunts and eligible girls) and Valets, in a recently vanished society, whose reality is transformed by his remarkable imagination into something timeless and enduring.

Perhaps best known for the escapades of Bertie Wooster and Jeeves, Wodehouse also created the world of Blandings Castle, home to Lord Emsworth and his cherished pig, the Empress of Blandings. His stories include gems concerning the irrepressible and disreputable Ukridge; Psmith, the elegant socialist; the ever-so-slightly-unscrupulous Fifth Earl of Ickenham, better known as Uncle Fred; and those related by Mr Mulliner, the charming raconteur of The Angler's Rest, and the Oldest Member at the Golf Club.

Wodehouse collaborated with a variety of partners on straight plays and worked principally alongside Guy Bolton on providing the lyrics and script for musical comedies with such composers as George Gershwin, Irving Berlin and Cole Porter. He liked to say that the royalties for 'Just My Bill', which Jerome Kern incorporated into Showboat, were enough to keep him in tobacco and whisky for the rest of his life.

In 1936 he was awarded The Mark Twain Medal for 'having made an outstanding and lasting contribution to the happiness of the world'. He was made a Doctor of Letters by Oxford University in 1939 and in 1975, aged 93, he was knighted by Queen Elizabeth II. He died shortly afterwards, on St Valentine's Day.

To have created so many characters that require no introduction places him in a very select group of writers, lead by Shakespeare and Dickens.

'You don't analyse such sunlit
PERFECTION
you just bask in it warmth and splendour'

Stephen Fry

'Wodehouse is the
GREATEST
comic writer'

Douglas Adams

'**SUBLIME**
comic genius . . . light as a feather, but fabulous'

Ben Elton

'The
FUNNIEST
writer ever to put words on paper'

Hugh Laurie

'P.G. Wodehouse wrote
THE BEST
english comic novels of the century'

Sebastian Faulks

'**WITTY**
and effortlessly fluid. His books are laugh-out-loud funny'

Arabella Weir

'**THE HEAD**
of my profession'

Hilaire Belloc

'Wodehouse was quite simply
THE BEE'S KNEES.
And then some'

Joseph Connolly

'To pick up a Wodehouse novel is to find oneself in the presence of genius – no writer has ever given me so much **PURE ENJOYMENT**'

John Julius Norwich

'P. G. Wodehouse is **THE GOLD STANDARD OF ENGLISH WIT**'

Christopher Hitchens

'Wodehouse is so **UTTERLY, PROPERLY, SIMPLY FUNNY**'

Adele Parks

'To dive into a Wodehouse novel is to swim in some of the most **ELEGANTLY TURNED PHRASES** in the english language'

Ben Schott

'P.G. Wodehouse should be prescribed to treat depression. Cheaper, more effective than valium and far, far more **ADDICTIVE**'

Olivia Williams

'My only problem with Wodehouse is deciding which of his **ENCHANTING** books to take to my desert island'

Ruth Dudley Edwards

'Quite simply, **THE MASTER OF COMIC WRITING** at work'

Jane Moore

P.G. WODEHOUSE'S

BLANDINGS

arrow books

Published by Arrow Books 2012

3 5 7 9 10 8 6 4 2

First published in the United Kingdom in 1935 by Herbert Jenkins Ltd

Arrow Books
The Random House Group Limited
20 Vauxhall Bridge Road, London, SW1V 2SA

www.randomhouse.co.uk
www.wodehouse.co.uk

Addresses for companies within The Random House Group Limited can be found at:
www.randomhouse.co.uk/offices.htm

The Random House Group Limited Reg. No. 954009

A CIP catalogue record for this book
is available from the British Library

ISBN 9780099580690

The Random House Group Limited supports The Forest
Stewardship Council (FSC®), the leading international forest
certification organisation. Our books carrying the FSC label are
printed on FSC® certified paper. FSC is the only forest certification
scheme endorsed by the leading environmental organisations,
including Greenpeace. Our paper procurement policy can be found at:
www.randomhouse.co.uk/environment

Printed and bound by CPI Group (UK) Ltd, Croydon, CR0 4YY

P.G. WODEHOUSE'S

BLANDINGS

CONTENTS

THANKS to the publicity given to the matter by *The Bridg-north, Shifnal, and Albrighton Argus* (with which is incorporated *The Wheat-Growers' Intelligencer and Stock Breeders' Gazetteer*), the whole world to-day knows that the silver medal in the Fat Pigs class at the eighty-seventh annual Shropshire Agricultural Show was won by the Earl of Emsworth's black Berkshire sow, Empress of Blandings.

Very few people, however, are aware how near that splendid animal came to missing the coveted honour.

Now it can be told.

This brief chapter of Secret History may be said to have begun on the night of the eighteenth of July, when George Cyril Wellbeloved (twenty-nine), pig-man in the employ of Lord Emsworth, was arrested by Police-Constable Evans of Market Blandings for being drunk and disorderly in the tap-room of the Goat and Feathers. On July the nineteenth, after first offering to apologize, then explaining that it had been his birthday, and finally attempting to prove an alibi, George Cyril was very properly jugged for fourteen days without the option of a fine.

On July the twentieth, Empress of Blandings, always hitherto a hearty and even a boisterous feeder, for the first time on record declined all nourishment. And on the morning of July the twenty-first, the veterinary surgeon called in to diagnose and deal with this strange asceticism, was compelled to confess to Lord Emsworth that the thing was beyond his professional skill.

Let us just see, before proceeding, that we have got these dates correct:

July 18. – Birthday Orgy of Cyril Wellbeloved.

July 19. – Incarceration of Ditto.

July 20. – Pig Lays off the Vitamins.

July 21. – Veterinary Surgeon Baffled.

Right.

The effect of the veterinary surgeon's announcement on Lord Emsworth was overwhelming. As a rule, the wear and tear of our complex modern life left this vague and amiable peer unscathed. So long as he had sunshine, regular meals, and complete freedom from the society of his younger son Frederick, he was placidly happy. But there were chinks in his armour, and one of these had been pierced this morning. Dazed by the news he had received, he stood at the window of the great library of Blandings Castle, looking out with unseeing eyes.

As he stood there, the door opened. Lord Emsworth turned; and having blinked once or twice, as was his habit when confronted suddenly with anything, recognized in the handsome and imperious-looking woman who had entered his sister, Lady Constance Keeble. Her demeanour, like his own, betrayed the deepest agitation.

'Clarence,' she cried, 'an awful thing has happened!'

Lord Emsworth nodded dully.

'I know. He's just told me.'

'What! Has he been here?'

'Only this moment left.'

'Why did you let him go? You must have known I would want to see him.'

'What good would that have done?'

'I could at least have assured him of my sympathy,' said Lady Constance stiffly.

'Yes, I suppose you could,' said Lord Emsworth, having considered the point. 'Not that he deserves any sympathy. The man's an ass.'

'Nothing of the kind. A most intelligent young man, as young men go.'

'Young? Would you call him young? Fifty, I should have said, if a day.'

'Are you out of your senses? Heacham fifty?'

'Not Heacham. Smithers.'

As frequently happened to her when in conversation with her brother, Lady Constance experienced a swimming sensation in the head.

'Will you kindly tell me, Clarence, in a few simple words, what you imagine we are talking about?'

'I'm talking about Smithers. Empress of Blandings is refusing her food, and Smithers says he can't do anything about it. And he calls himself a vet!'

'Then you haven't heard? Clarence, a dreadful thing has happened. Angela has broken off her engagement to Heacham.'

'And the Agricultural Show on Wednesday week!'

'What on earth has that got to do with it?' demanded Lady Constance, feeling a recurrence of the swimming sensation.

'What has it got to do with it?' said Lord Emsworth warmly. 'My champion sow, with less than ten days to prepare herself for a most searching examination in competition with all the finest pigs in the county, starts refusing her food—'

'Will you stop maundering on about your insufferable pig and give your attention to something that really matters? I tell you that Angela – your niece Angela – has broken off her engagement to Lord Heacham and expresses her intention of marrying that hopeless ne'er-do-well, James Belford.'

'The son of old Belford, the parson?'

'Yes.'

'She can't. He's in America.'

'He is not in America. He is in London.'

'No,' said Lord Emsworth, shaking his head sagely. 'You're wrong. I remember meeting his father two years ago out on the road by Meeker's twenty-acre field, and he distinctly told me the boy was sailing for America next day. He must be there by this time.'

'Can't you understand? He's come back.'

'Oh? Come back? I see. Come *back?*'

'You know there was once a silly sentimental sort of affair between him and Angela; but a year after he left she became engaged to Heacham and I thought the whole thing was over and done with. And now it seems that she met this young man Belford when she was in London last week, and it has started all over again. She tells me she has written to Heacham and broken the engagement.'

There was a silence. Brother and sister remained for a space plunged in thought. Lord Emsworth was the first to speak.

'We've tried acorns,' he said. 'We've tried skim milk. And we've tried potato-peel. But, no, she won't touch them.'

Conscious of two eyes raising blisters on his sensitive skin, he came to himself with a start.

'Absurd! Ridiculous! Preposterous!' he said, hurriedly. 'Breaking the engagement? Pooh! Tush! What nonsense! I'll have a word with that young man. If he thinks he can go about the place playing fast and loose with my niece and jilting her without so much as a—'

'Clarence!'

Lord Emsworth blinked. Something appeared to be wrong, but he could not imagine what. It seemed to him that in his last speech he had struck just the right note – strong, forceful, dignified.

'Eh?'

'It is Angela who has broken the engagement.'

'Oh, Angela?'

'She is infatuated with this man Belford. And the point is, what are we to do about it?'

Lord Emsworth reflected.

'Take a strong line,' he said firmly. 'Stand no nonsense. Don't send 'em a wedding-present.'

There is no doubt that, given time, Lady Constance would have found and uttered some adequately corrosive comment on this imbecile suggestion; but even as she was swelling preparatory to giving tongue, the door opened and a girl came in.

She was a pretty girl, with fair hair and blue eyes which in their softer moments probably reminded all sorts of people of twin lagoons slumbering beneath a southern sky. This, however, was not one of those moments. To Lord Emsworth, as they met his, they looked like something out of an oxy-acetylene blow-pipe; and, as far as he was capable of being disturbed by anything that was not his younger son Frederick, he was disturbed. Angela, it seemed to him, was upset about something; and he was sorry. He liked Angela.

To ease a tense situation, he said:

'Angela, my dear, do you know anything about pigs?'

The girl laughed. One of those sharp, bitter laughs which are so unpleasant just after breakfast.

'Yes, I do. You're one.'

'Me?'

'Yes, you. Aunt Constance says that, if I marry Jimmy, you won't let me have my money.'

'Money? Money?' Lord Emsworth was mildly puzzled. 'What money? You never lent me any money.'

Lady Constance's feelings found vent in a sound like an overheated radiator.

'I believe this absent-mindedness of yours is nothing but a ridiculous pose, Clarence. You know perfectly well that when poor Jane died she left you Angela's trustee.'

'And I can't touch my money without your consent till I'm twenty-five.'

'Well, how old are you?'

'Twenty-one.'

'Then what are you worrying about?' asked Lord Emsworth, surprised. 'No need to worry about it for another four years. God bless my soul, the money is quite safe. It is in excellent securities.'

Angela stamped her foot. An unladylike action, no doubt, but how much better than kicking an uncle with it, as her lower nature prompted.

'I have told Angela,' explained Lady Constance, 'that, while we naturally cannot force her to marry Lord Heacham, we can at least keep her money from being squandered by this wastrel on whom she proposes to throw herself away.'

'He isn't a wastrel. He's got quite enough money to marry me on, but he wants some capital to buy a partnership in a—'

'He is a wastrel. Wasn't he sent abroad because—'

'That was two years ago. And since then—'

'My dear Angela, you may argue until—'

'I'm not arguing. I'm simply saying that I'm going to marry Jimmy, if we both have to starve in the gutter.'

'What gutter?' asked his lordship, wrenching his errant mind away from thoughts of acorns.

'Any gutter.'

'Now, please listen to me, Angela.'

It seemed to Lord Emsworth that there was a frightful amount of conversation going on. He had the sensation of having become a mere bit of flotsam upon a tossing sea of female voices. Both his sister and his niece appeared to have much to say, and they were saying it simultaneously and fortissimo. He looked wistfully at the door.

It was smoothly done. A twist of the handle, and he was where beyond those voices there was peace. Galloping gaily down the stairs, he charged out into the sunshine.

His gaiety was not long-lived. Free at last to concentrate itself on the really serious issues of life, his mind grew sombre and grim. Once more there descended upon him the cloud which had been oppressing his soul before all this Heacham-Angela-Belford business began. Each step that took him nearer to the sty where the ailing Empress resided seemed a heavier step than the last. He reached the sty; and, draping himself over the rails, peered moodily at the vast expanse of pig within.

For, even though she had been doing a bit of dieting of late, Empress of Blandings was far from being an ill-nourished animal. She resembled a captive balloon with ears and a tail, and was as nearly circular as a pig can be without bursting. Nevertheless, Lord Emsworth, as he regarded her, mourned and would not be comforted. A few more square meals under her belt, and no pig in all Shropshire could have held its head up in the Empress's presence. And now, just for lack of those few meals, the supreme animal would probably be relegated to the mean obscurity of an 'Honourably Mentioned.' It was bitter, bitter.

He became aware that somebody was speaking to him; and, turning, perceived a solemn young man in riding breeches.

'I say,' said the young man.

Lord Emsworth, though he would have preferred solitude, was relieved to find that the intruder was at least one of his own sex. Women are apt to stray off into side-issues, but men are practical and can be relied on to stick to the fundamentals. Besides, young Heacham probably kept pigs himself and might have a useful hint or two up his sleeve.

'I say, I've just ridden over to see if there was anything I could do about this fearful business.'

'Uncommonly kind and thoughtful of you, my dear fellow,' said Lord Emsworth, touched. 'I fear things look very black.'

'It's an absolute mystery to me.'

'To me, too.'

'I mean to say, she was all right last week.'

'She was all right as late as the day before yesterday.'

'Seemed quite cheery and chirpy and all that.'

'Entirely so.'

'And then this happens – out of a blue sky, as you might say.'

'Exactly. It is insoluble. We have done everything possible to tempt her appetite.'

'Her appetite? Is Angela ill?'

'Angela? No, I fancy not. She seemed perfectly well a few minutes ago.'

'You've seen her this morning, then? Did she say anything about this fearful business?'

'No. She was speaking about some money.'

'It's all so dashed unexpected.'

'Like a bolt from the blue,' agreed Lord Emsworth. 'Such a thing has never happened before. I fear the worst. According to the Wolff-Lehmann feeding standards, a pig, if in health, should consume daily nourishment amounting to fifty-seven thousand eight hundred calories, these to consist of proteids four pounds five ounces, carbohydrates twenty-five pounds—'

'What has that got to do with Angela?'

'Angela?'

'I came to find out why Angela has broken off our engagement.'

Lord Emsworth marshalled his thoughts. He had a misty idea that he had heard something mentioned about that. It came back to him.

'Ah, yes, of course. She has broken off the engagement, hasn't she? I believe it is because she is in love with someone else. Yes, now that I recollect, that was distinctly stated. The whole thing comes back to me quite clearly. Angela has decided to marry someone else. I knew there was some satisfactory explanation. Tell me, my dear fellow, what are your views on linseed meal.'

'What do you mean, linseed meal?'

'Why, linseed meal,' said Lord Emsworth, not being able to find a better definition. 'As a food for pigs.'

'Oh, curse all pigs!'

'What!' There was a sort of astounded horror in Lord Emsworth's voice. He had never been particularly fond of young

Heacham, for he was not a man who took much to his juniors, but he had not supposed him capable of anarchistic sentiments like this. 'What did you say?'

'I said, "Curse all pigs!" You keep talking about pigs. I'm not interested in pigs. I don't want to discuss pigs. Blast and damn every pig in existence!'

Lord Emsworth watched him, as he strode away, with an emotion that was partly indignation and partly relief – indignation that a landowner and a fellow son of Shropshire could have brought himself to utter such words, and relief that one capable of such utterance was not going to marry into his family. He had always in his woollen-headed way been very fond of his niece Angela, and it was nice to think that the child had such solid good sense and so much cool discernment. Many girls of her age would have been carried away by the glamour of young Heacham's position and wealth; but she, divining with an intuition beyond her years that he was unsound on the subject of pigs, had drawn back while there was still time and refused to marry him.

A pleasant glow suffused Lord Emsworth's bosom, to be frozen out a few moments later as he perceived his sister Constance bearing down upon him. Lady Constance was a beautiful woman, but there were times when the charm of her face was marred by a rather curious expression; and from nursery days onward his lordship had learned that this expression meant trouble. She was wearing it now.

'Clarence,' She said, 'I have had enough of this nonsense of Angela and young Belford. The thing cannot be allowed to go drifting on. You must catch the two o'clock train to London.'

'What! Why?'

'You must see this man Belford and tell him that, if Angela insists on marrying him, she will not have a penny for four years.

I shall be greatly surprised if that piece of information does not put an end to the whole business.'

Lord Emsworth scratched meditatively at the Empress's tank-like back. A mutinous expression was on his mild face.

'Don't see why she shouldn't marry the fellow,' he mumbled.

'Marry James Belford?'

'I don't see why not. Seems fond of him and all that.'

'You never have had a grain of sense in your head, Clarence. Angela is going to marry Heacham.'

'Can't stand that man. All wrong about pigs.'

'Clarence, I don't wish to have any more discussion and argument. You will go to London on the two o'clock train. You will see Mr Belford. And you will tell him about Angela's money. Is that quite clear?'

'Oh, all right,' said his lordship moodily. 'All right, all right, all right.'

The emotions of the Earl of Emsworth, as he sat next day facing his luncheon-guest, James Bartholomew Belford, across a table in the main dining-room of the Senior Conservative Club, were not of the liveliest and most agreeable. It was bad enough to be in London at all on such a day of golden sunshine. To be charged, while there, with the task of blighting the romance of two young people for whom he entertained a warm regard was unpleasant to a degree.

For, now that he had given the matter thought, Lord Emsworth recalled that he had always liked this boy Belford. A pleasant lad, with, he remembered now, a healthy fondness for that rural existence which so appealed to himself. By no means the sort of fellow who, in the very presence and hearing of Empress of Blandings, would have spoken disparagingly and with oaths of pigs as a class. It occurred to Lord Emsworth, as it has occurred to so many people, that the distribution of money in this world is all wrong. Why should a man like pig-despising Heacham have a rent roll that ran into the tens of thousands, while this very deserving youngster had nothing?

These thoughts not only saddened Lord Emsworth – they embarrassed him. He hated unpleasantness, and it was suddenly borne in upon him that, after he had broken the news that Angela's bit of capital was locked up and not likely to get loose, conversation with his young friend during the remainder of lunch would tend to be somewhat difficult.

He made up his mind to postpone the revelation. During the meal, he decided, he would chat pleasantly of this and that; and then, later, while bidding his guest good-bye, he would spring the thing on him suddenly and dive back into the recesses of the club.

Considerably cheered at having solved a delicate problem with such adroitness, he started to prattle.

'The gardens at Blandings,' he said, 'are looking particularly attractive this summer. My head-gardener, Angus McAllister, is a man with whom I do not always find myself seeing eye to eye, notably in the matter of hollyhocks, on which I consider his views subversive to a degree; but there is no denying that he understands roses. The rose garden—'

'How well I remember that rose garden,' said James Belford, sighing slightly and helping himself to brussels sprouts. 'It was there that Angela and I used to meet on summer mornings.'

Lord Emsworth blinked. This was not an encouraging start, but the Emsworths were a fighting clan. He had another try.

'I have seldom seen such a blaze of colour as was to be witnessed there during the month of June. Both McAllister and I adopted a very strong policy with the slugs and plant lice, with the result that the place was a mass of flourishing Damasks and Ayrshires and—'

'Properly to appreciate roses,' said James Belford, 'You want to see them as a setting for a girl like Angela. With her fair hair gleaming against the green leaves she makes a rose garden seem a veritable Paradise.'

'No doubt,' said Lord Emsworth. 'No doubt. I am glad you liked my rose garden. At Blandings, of course, we have the natural advantage of loamy soil, rich in plant food and humus; but, as I often say to McAllister, and on this point we have never had the slightest disagreement, loamy soil by itself is not enough. You must have manure. If every autumn a liberal mulch of stable manure is spread upon the beds and the coarser parts removed in the spring before the annual forking—'

'Angela tells me,' said James Belford, 'that you have forbidden our marriage.'

Lord Emsworth choked dismally over his chicken. Directness of this kind, he told himself with a pang of self-pity, was the sort of thing young Englishmen picked up in America. Diplomatic circumlocution flourished only in a more leisurely civilization, and in those energetic and forceful surroundings you learned to Talk Quick and Do It Now, and all sorts of uncomfortable things.

'Er – well, yes, now you mention it, I believe some informal decision of that nature was arrived at. You see, my dear fellow, my sister Constance feels rather strongly—'

'I understand. I suppose she thinks I'm a sort of prodigal.'

'No, no, my dear fellow. She never said that. Wastrel was the term she employed.'

'Well, perhaps I did start out in business on those lines. But you can take it from me that when you find yourself employed on a farm in Nebraska belonging to an applejack-nourished patriarch with strong views on work and a good vocabulary, you soon develop a certain liveliness.'

'Are you employed on a farm?'

'I was employed on a farm.'

'Pigs?' said Lord Emsworth in a low, eager voice.

'Among other things.'

Lord Emsworth gulped. His fingers clutched at the table-cloth.

'Then perhaps, my dear fellow, you can give me some advice. For the last two days my prize sow, Empress of Blandings, has declined all nourishment. And the Agricultural Show is on Wednesday week. I am distracted with anxiety.'

James Belford frowned thoughtfully.

'What does your pig-man say about it?'

'My pig-man was sent to prison two days ago. Two days!' For the first time the significance of the coincidence struck him. 'You don't think that can have anything to do with the animal's loss of appetite?'

'Certainly. I imagine she is missing him and pining away because he isn't there.'

Lord Emsworth was surprised. He had only a distant acquaintance with George Cyril Wellbeloved, but from what he had seen of him he had not credited him with this fatal allure.

'She probably misses his afternoon call.'

Again his lordship found himself perplexed. He had had no notion that pigs were such sticklers for the formalities of social life.

'His call?'

'He must have had some special call that he used when he wanted her to come to dinner. One of the first things you learn on a farm is hog-calling. Pigs are temperamental. Omit to call them, and they'll starve rather than put on the nose-bag. Call them right, and they will follow you to the ends of the earth with their mouths watering.'

'God bless my soul! Fancy that.'

'A fact, I assure you. These calls vary in different parts of America. In Wisconsin, for example, the words "Poig, Poig, Poig" bring home – in both the literal and the figurative sense – the bacon. In Illinois, I believe they call "Burp, Burp, Burp," while in Iowa the phrase "Kus, Kus, Kus" is preferred. Proceeding to Minnesota, we find "Peega, Peega, Peega" or, alternatively, "Oink, Oink, Oink," whereas in Milwaukee, so largely inhabited by those of German descent, you will hear the good old Teuton "Komm Schweine, Komm Schweine." Oh, yes, there are all sorts of pig-calls, from the Massachusetts "Phew, Phew, Phew" to the "Loo-ey, Loo-ey, Loo-ey" of Ohio, not counting various local devices such as beating on tin cans with axes or rattling pebbles in a suit-case. I knew a man out in Nebraska who used to call his pigs by tapping on the edge of the trough with his wooden leg.'

'Did he, indeed?'

'But a most unfortunate thing happened. One evening, hearing a woodpecker at the top of a tree, they started shinning up it; and when the man came out he found them all lying there in a circle with their necks broken.'

'This is no time for joking,' said Lord Emsworth, pained.

'I'm not joking. Solid fact. Ask anybody out there.'

Lord Emsworth placed a hand to his throbbing forehead.

'But if there is this wide variety, we have no means of knowing which call Wellbeloved ...'

'Ah,' said James Belford, 'but wait. I haven't told you all. There is a master-word.'

'A what?'

'Most people don't know it, but I had it straight from the lips of Fred Patzel, the hog-calling champion of the Western States. What a man! I've known him to bring pork chops leaping from their plates. He informed me that, no matter whether an animal has been trained to answer to the Illinois "Burp" or the Minnesota "Oink," it will always give immediate service in response to this magic combination of syllables. It is to the pig world what the Masonic grip is to the human. "Oink" in Illinois or "Burp" in Minnesota, and the animal merely raises its eyebrows' and stares coldly. But go to either state and call "Pig-hoo-oo-ey!" ...'

The expression on Lord Emsworth's face was that of a drowning man who sees a lifeline.

'Is that the master-word of which you spoke?'

'That's it.'

'Pig –?'

'– hoo-oo-ey.'

'Pig-hoo-o-ey?'

'You haven't got it quite right. The first syllable should be short and staccato, the second long and rising into a falsetto, high but true.'

'Pig-hoo-o-o-ey.'

'Pig-hoo-o-o-ey.'

'Pig-hoo-o-o-ey!' yodelled Lord Emsworth, flinging his head back and giving tongue in a high, penetrating tenor which caused ninety-three Senior Conservatives, lunching in the vicinity, to congeal into living statues of alarm and disapproval.

'More body to the "hoo,"' advised James Belford.

The Senior Conservative Club is one of the few places in London where lunchers are not accustomed to getting music with their meals. White-whiskered financiers gazed bleakly at bald-headed politicians, as if asking silently what was to be done about this. Bald-headed politicians stared back at white-whiskered financiers, replying in the language of the eye that they did not know. The general sentiment prevailing was a vague determination to write to the Committee about it.

'Pig-hoo-o-o-o-ey!' carolled Lord Emsworth. And, as he did so, his eye fell on the clock over the mantelpiece. Its hands pointed to twenty minutes to two.

He started convulsively. The best train in the day for Market Blandings was the one which left Paddington station at two sharp. After that there was nothing till the five-five.

He was not a man who often thought; but, when he did, to think was with him to act. A moment later he was scudding over the carpet, making for the door that led to the broad staircase.

Throughout the room which he had left, the decision to write in strong terms to the Committee was now universal; but from the mind, such as it was, of Lord Emsworth the past, with the single exception of the word 'Pig-hoo-o-o-o-ey!' had been completely blotted.

Whispering the magic syllables, he sped to the cloak-room and retrieved his hat. Murmuring them over and over again, he sprang into a cab. He was still repeating them as the train moved out of the station; and he would doubtless have gone on repeating them all the way to Market Blandings, had he not, as was his invariable practice when travelling by rail, fallen asleep after the first ten minutes of the journey.

The stopping of the train at Swindon Junction woke him with a start. He sat up, wondering, after his usual fashion on these occasions, who and where he was. Memory returned to him, but a memory that was, alas, incomplete. He remembered his name. He remembered that he was on his way home from a visit to London. But what it was that you said to a pig when inviting it to drop in for a bite of dinner he had completely forgotten.

It was the opinion of Lady Constance Keeble, expressed verbally during dinner in the brief intervals when they were alone, and by means of silent telepathy when Beach, the butler, was adding his dignified presence to the proceedings, that her brother Clarence, in his expedition to London to put matters plainly to James Belford, had made an outstanding idiot of himself.

There had been no need whatever to invite the man Belford to lunch; but, having invited him to lunch, to leave him sitting, without having clearly stated that Angela would have no money for four years, was the act of a congenital imbecile. Lady Constance had been aware ever since their childhood days that her brother had about as much sense as a—

Here Beach entered, superintending the bringing-in of the savoury, and she had been obliged to suspend her remarks.

This sort of conversation is never agreeable to a sensitive man, and his lordship had removed himself from the danger zone as soon as he could manage it. He was now seated in the library, sipping port and straining a brain which Nature had never intended for hard exercise in an effort to bring back that word of magic of which his unfortunate habit of sleeping in trains had robbed him.

'Pig—'

He could remember as far as that; but of what avail was a single syllable? Besides, weak as his memory was, he could recall that the whole gist or nub of the thing lay in the syllable that followed. The 'pig' was a mere preliminary.

Lord Emsworth finished his port and got up. He felt restless, stifled. The summer night seemed to call to him like some silver-voiced swineherd calling to his pig. Possibly, he thought, a breath of fresh air might stimulate his brain-cells. He wandered downstairs; and, having dug a shocking old slouch hat out of the cupboard where he hid it to keep his sister Constance from impounding and burning it, he strode heavily out into the garden.

He was pottering aimlessly to and fro in the parts adjacent to the rear of the castle when there appeared in his path a slender female form. He recognized it without pleasure. Any unbiased judge would have said that his niece Angela, standing there in the soft, pale light, looked like some dainty spirit of the Moon. Lord Emsworth was not an unbiased judge. To him Angela merely looked like Trouble. The march of civilization has given the modern girl a vocabulary and an ability to use it which her grandmother never had. Lord Emsworth would not have minded meeting Angela's grandmother a bit.

'Is that you, my dear?' he said nervously.

'Yes.'

'I didn't see you at dinner.'

'I didn't want any dinner. The food would have choked me. I can't eat.'

'It's precisely the same with my pig,' said his lordship. 'Young Belford tells me—'

Into Angela's queenly disdain there flashed a sudden animation.

'Have you seen Jimmy? What did he say?'

'That's just what I can't remember. It began with the word "Pig"—'

'But after he had finished talking about you, I mean. Didn't he say anything about coming down here?'

'Not that I remember.'

'I expect you weren't listening. You've got a very annoying habit, Uncle Clarence,' said Angela maternally, 'of switching your mind off and just going blah when people are talking to you. It gets you very much disliked on all sides. Didn't Jimmy say anything about me?'

'I fancy so. Yes, I am nearly sure he did.'

'Well, what?'

'I cannot remember.'

There was a sharp clicking noise in the darkness. It was caused by Angela's upper front teeth meeting her lower front teeth; and was followed by a sort of wordless exclamation. It seemed only too plain that the love and respect which a niece should have for an uncle were in the present instance at a very low ebb.

'I wish you wouldn't do that,' said Lord Emsworth plaintively.

'Do what?'

'Make clicking noises at me.'

'I will make clicking noises at you. You know perfectly well, Uncle Clarence, that you are behaving like a bohunkus.'

'A what?'

'A bohunkus,' explained his niece coldly, 'is a very inferior sort of worm. Not the kind of worm that you see on lawns, which you can respect, but a really degraded species.'

'I wish you would go in, my dear,' said Lord Emsworth. 'The night air may give you a chill.'

'I won't go in. I came out here to look at the moon and think of Jimmy. What are you doing out here, if it comes to that?'

'I came here to think. I am greatly exercised about my pig, Empress of Blandings. For two days she has refused her food, and young Belford says she will not eat until she hears the proper call or cry. He very kindly taught it to me, but unfortunately I have forgotten it.'

'I wonder you had the nerve to ask Jimmy to teach you pig-calls, considering the way you're treating him.'

'But—'

'Like a leper, or something. And all I can say is that, if you remember this call of his, and it makes the Empress eat, you ought to be ashamed of yourself if you still refuse to let me marry him.'

'My dear,' said Lord Emsworth earnestly, 'if through young Belford's instrumentality Empress of Blandings is induced to take nourishment once more, there is nothing I will refuse him – nothing.'

'Honour bright?'

'I give you my solemn word.'

'You won't let Aunt Constance bully you out of it?'

Lord Emsworth drew himself up.

'Certainly not,' he said proudly. 'I am always ready to listen to your Aunt Constance's views, but there are certain matters where I claim the right to act according to my own judgment.' He paused and stood musing. 'It began with the word "Pig—"'

From somewhere near at hand music made itself heard. The servants' hall, its day's labours ended, was refreshing itself with the housekeeper's gramophone. To Lord Emsworth the strains were merely an additional annoyance. He was not fond of music.

It reminded him of his younger son Frederick, a flat but persevering songster both in and out of the bath.

'Yes, I can distinctly recall as much as that. Pig – Pig—'

'WHO—'

Lord Emsworth leaped in the air. It was as if an electric shock had been applied to his person.

'WHO stole my heart away?' howled the gramophone. 'WHO—?'

The peace of the summer night was shattered by a triumphant shout.

'Pig-HOO-o-o-o-ey!'

A window opened. A large, bald head appeared. A dignified voice spoke.

'Who is there? Who is making that noise?'

'Beach!' cried Lord Emsworth. 'Come out here at once.'

'Very good, your lordship.'

And presently the beautiful night was made still more lovely by the added attraction of the butler's presence.

'Beach, listen to this.'

'Very good, your lordship.'

'Pig-hoo-o-o-o-ey!'

'Very good, your lordship.'

'Now you do it.'

'I, your lordship?'

'Yes. It's a way you call pigs.'

'I do not call pigs, your lordship,' said the butler coldly.

'What do you want Beach to do it for?' asked Angela.

'Two heads are better than one. If we both learn it, it will not matter should I forget it again.'

'By Jove, yes! Come on, Beach. Push it over the thorax,' urged the girl eagerly. 'You don't know it, but this is a matter of life and death. At-a-boy, Beach! Inflate the lungs and go to it.'

It had been the butler's intention, prefacing his remarks with the statement that he had been in service at the castle for eighteen years, to explain frigidly to Lord Emsworth that it was not his place to stand in the moonlight practising pig-calls. If, he would have gone on to add, his lordship saw the matter from a different angle, then it was his, Beach's, painful duty to tender his resignation, to become effective one month from that day.

But the intervention of Angela made this impossible to a man of chivalry and heart. A paternal fondness for the girl, dating from the days when he had stooped to enacting – and very convincingly, too, for his was a figure that lent itself to the impersonation – the *rôle* of a hippopotamus for her childish amusement, checked the words he would have uttered. She was looking at him with bright eyes, and even the rendering of pig-noises seemed a small sacrifice to make for her sake.

'Very good, your lordship,' he said in a low voice, his face pale and set in the moonlight. 'I shall endeavour to give satisfaction. I would merely advance the suggestion, your lordship, that we move a few steps farther away from the vicinity of the servants' hall. If I were to be overheard by any of the lower domestics, it would weaken my position as a disciplinary force.'

'What chumps we are!' cried Angela, inspired. 'The place to do it is outside the Empress's sty. Then, if it works, we'll see it working.'

Lord Emsworth found this a little abstruse, but after a moment he got it.

'Angela,' he said, 'you are a very intelligent girl. Where you get your brains from, I don't know. Not from my side of the family.'

The bijou residence of the Empress of Blandings looked very snug and attractive in the moonlight. But beneath even the beautiful things of life there is always an underlying sadness. This was supplied in the present instance by a long, low trough, only too plainly full to the brim of succulent mash and acorns. The fast, obviously, was still in progress.

The sty stood some considerable distance from the castle walls, so that there had been ample opportunity for Lord Emsworth to rehearse his little company during the journey. By the time they had ranged themselves against the rails, his two assistants were letter-perfect.

'Now,' said his lordship.

There floated out upon the summer night a strange composite sound that sent the birds roosting in the trees above shooting off their perches like rockets. Angela's clear soprano rang out like the voice of the village blacksmith's daughter. Lord Emsworth contributed a reedy tenor. And the bass notes of Beach probably did more to startle the birds than any other one item in the programme.

They paused and listened. Inside the Empress's boudoir there sounded the movement of a heavy body. There was an inquiring grunt. The next moment the sacking that covered the doorway was pushed aside, and the noble animal emerged.

'Now!' said Lord Emsworth again.

Once more that musical cry shattered the silence of the night. But it brought no responsive movement from Empress of Blandings. She stood there motionless, her nose elevated, her ears hanging down, her eyes everywhere but on the trough where, by rights, she should now have been digging in and getting hers. A chill disappointment crept over Lord Emsworth, to be succeeded by a gust of petulant anger.

'I might have known it,' he said bitterly. 'That young scoundrel was deceiving me. He was playing a joke on me.'

'He wasn't,' cried Angela indignantly. 'Was he, Beach?'

'Not knowing the circumstances, miss, I cannot venture an opinion.'

'Well, why has it no effect, then?' demanded Lord Emsworth.

'You can't expect it to work right away. We've got her stirred up, haven't we? She's thinking it over, isn't she? Once more will do the trick. Ready, Beach?'

'Quite ready, miss.'

'Then when I say three. And this time, Uncle Clarence, do please for goodness' sake not yowl like you did before. It was enough to put any pig off. Let it come out quite easily and gracefully. Now, then. One, two – three!'

The echoes died away. And as they did so a voice spoke.

'Community singing?'

'Jimmy!' cried Angela, whisking round.

'Hullo, Angela. Hullo, Lord Emsworth. Hullo, Beach.'

'Good evening, sir. Happy to see you once more.'

'Thanks. I'm spending a few days at the Vicarage with my father. I got down here by the five-five.'

Lord Emsworth cut peevishly in upon these civilities.

'Young man,' he said, 'what do you mean by telling me that my pig would respond to that cry? It does nothing of the kind.'

'You can't have done it right.'

'I did it precisely as you instructed me. I have had, moreover, the assistance of Beach here and my niece Angela—'

'Let's hear a sample.'

Lord Emsworth cleared his throat.

'Pig-hoo-o-o-o-ey!'

James Belford shook his head.

'Nothing like it,' he said. 'You want to begin the "Hoo" in a low minor of two quarter notes in four-four time. From this build gradually to a higher note, until at last the voice is soaring in full crescendo, reaching F sharp on the natural scale and dwelling for two retarded half-notes, then breaking into a shower of accidental grace-notes.'

'God bless my soul!' said Lord Emsworth, appalled. 'I shall never be able to do it.'

'Jimmy will do it for you,' said Angela. 'Now that he's engaged to me, he'll be one of the family and always popping about here. He can do it every day till the show is over.'

James Belford nodded.

'I think that would be the wisest plan. It is doubtful if an amateur could ever produce real results. You need a voice that has been trained on the open prairie and that has gathered richness and strength from competing with tornadoes. You need a manly, sunburned, wind-scorched voice with a suggestion in it of the crackling of corn husks and the whisper of evening breezes in the fodder. Like this!'

Resting his hands on the rail before him, James Belford swelled before their eyes like a young balloon. The muscles on his cheekbones stood out, his forehead became corrugated, his ears seemed to shimmer. Then, at the very height of the tension, he let it go like, as the poet beautifully puts it, the sound of a great Amen.

'Pig-HOOOOO-OOO-OOO-O-O-ey!'

They looked at him, awed. Slowly, fading off across hill and dale, the vast bellow died away. And suddenly, as it died, another, softer sound succeeded it. A sort of gulpy, gurgly, plobby, squishy, wofflesome sound, like a thousand eager men drinking soup in a foreign restaurant. And, as he heard it, Lord Emsworth uttered a cry of rapture.

The Empress was feeding.

THE day was so warm, so fair, so magically a thing of sunshine and blue skies and bird-song that anyone acquainted with Clarence, ninth Earl of Emsworth, and aware of his liking for fine weather, would have pictured him going about the place on this summer morning with a beaming smile and an uplifted heart. Instead of which, humped over the breakfast-table, he was directing at a blameless kippered herring a look of such intense bitterness that the fish seemed to sizzle beneath it. For it was August Bank Holiday, and Blandings Castle on August Bank Holiday became, in his lordship's opinion, a miniature Inferno.

This was the day when his park and grounds broke out into a noisome rash of swings, roundabouts, marquees, toy balloons and paper bags; when a tidal wave of the peasantry and its squealing young engulfed those haunts of immemorial peace. On August Bank Holiday he was not allowed to potter pleasantly about his gardens in an old coat: forces beyond his control shoved him into a stiff collar and a top hat and told him to go out and be genial. And in the cool of the quiet evenfall they put him on a platform and made him make a speech. To a man with a day like that in front of him fine weather was a mockery.

His sister, Lady Constance Keeble, looked brightly at him over the coffee-pot.

'What a lovely morning!' she said.

Lord Emsworth's gloom deepened. He chafed at being called upon — by this woman of all others — to behave as if everything was for the jolliest in the jolliest of all possible worlds. But for his sister Constance and her hawk-like vigilance, he might, he thought, have been able at least to dodge the top-hat.

'Have you got your speech ready?'

'Yes.'

'Well, mind you learn it by heart this time and don't stammer and dodder as you did last year.'

Lord Emsworth pushed plate and kipper away. He had lost his desire for food.

'And don't forget you have to go to the village this morning to judge the cottage gardens.'

'All right, all right, all right,' said his lordship testily. 'I've not forgotten.'

'I think I will come to the village with you. There are a number of those Fresh Air London children staying there now, and I must warn them to behave properly when they come to the Fête this afternoon. You know what London children are. McAllister says he found one of them in the gardens the other day, picking his flowers.'

At any other time the news of this outrage would, no doubt, have affected Lord Emsworth profoundly. But now, so intense was his self-pity, he did not even shudder. He drank coffee with the air of a man who regretted that it was not hemlock.

'By the way, McAllister was speaking to me again last night about that gravel path through the yew alley. He seems very keen on it.'

'Glug!' said Lord Emsworth — which, as any philologist will

tell you, is the sound which peers of the realm make when stricken to the soul while drinking coffee.

Concerning Glasgow, that great commercial and manufacturing city in the county of Lanarkshire in Scotland, much has been written. So lyrically does the Encyclopædia Britannica deal with the place that it covers twenty-seven pages before it can tear itself away and go on to Glass, Glastonbury, Glatz and Glauber. The only aspect of it, however, which immediately concerns the present historian is the fact that the citizens it breeds are apt to be grim, dour, persevering, tenacious men; men with red whiskers who know what they want and mean to get it. Such a one was Angus McAllister, head-gardener at Blandings Castle.

For years Angus McAllister had set before himself as his earthly goal the construction of a gravel path through the Castle's famous yew alley. For years he had been bringing the project to the notice of his employer, though in anyone less whiskered the latter's unconcealed loathing would have caused embarrassment. And now, it seemed, he was at it again.

'Gravel path!' Lord Emsworth stiffened through the whole length of his stringy body. Nature, he had always maintained, intended a yew alley to be carpeted with a mossy growth. And, whatever Nature felt about it, he personally was dashed if he was going to have men with Clydeside accents and faces like dissipated potatoes coming along and mutilating that lovely expanse of green velvet. 'Gravel path, indeed! Why not asphalt? Why not a few hoardings with advertisements of liver pills and a filling-station? That's what the man would really like.'

Lord Emsworth felt bitter, and when he felt bitter he could be terribly sarcastic.

'Well, I think it is a very good idea,' said his sister. 'One could walk there in wet weather then. Damp moss is ruinous to shoes.'

Lord Emsworth and the Girlfriend

Lord Emsworth rose. He could bear no more of this. He left the table, the room and the house and, reaching the yew alley some minutes later, was revolted to find it infested by Angus McAllister in person. The head-gardener was standing gazing at the moss like a high priest of some ancient religion about to stick the gaff into the human sacrifice.

'Morning, McAllister,' said Lord Emsworth coldly.

'Good morrrrning, your lorrudsheep.'

There was a pause. Angus McAllister, extending a foot that looked like a violin-case, pressed it on the moss. The meaning of the gesture was plain. It expressed contempt, dislike, a generally anti-moss spirit: and Lord Emsworth, wincing, surveyed the man unpleasantly through his pince-nez. Though not often given to theological speculation, he was wondering why Providence, if obliged to make head-gardeners, had found it necessary to make them so Scotch. In the case of Angus McAllister, why, going a step farther, have made him a human being at all? All the ingredients of a first-class mule simply thrown away. He felt that he might have liked Angus McAllister if he had been a mule.

'I was speaking to her leddyship yesterday.'

'Oh?'

'About the gravel path I was speaking to her leddyship.'

'Oh?'

'Her leddyship likes the notion fine.'

'Indeed! Well...'

Lord Emsworth's face had turned a lively pink, and he was about to release the blistering words which were forming themselves in his mind when suddenly he caught the head-gardener's eye and paused. Angus McAllister was looking at him in a peculiar manner, and he knew what that look meant. Just one crack, his eye was saying – in Scotch, of course – just one crack

31

out of you and I tender my resignation. And with a sickening shock it came home to Lord Emsworth how completely he was in this man's clutches.

He shuffled miserably. Yes, he was helpless. Except for that kink about gravel paths, Angus McAllister was a head-gardener in a thousand, and he needed him. He could not do without him. That, unfortunately, had been proved by experiment. Once before, at the time when they were grooming for the Agricultural Show that pumpkin which had subsequently romped home so gallant a winner, he had dared to flout Angus McAllister. And Angus had resigned, and he had been forced to plead – yes, plead – with him to come back. An employer cannot hope to do this sort of thing and still rule with an iron hand. Filled with the coward rage that dares to burn but does not dare to blaze, Lord Emsworth coughed a cough that was undisguisedly a bronchial white flag.

'I'll – er – I'll think it over, McAllister.'

'Mphm.'

'I have to go to the village now. I will see you later.'

'Mphm.'

'Meanwhile, I will – er – think it over.'

'Mphm.'

The task of judging the floral displays in the cottage gardens of the little village of Blandings Parva was one to which Lord Emsworth had looked forward with pleasurable anticipation. It was the sort of job he liked. But now, even though he had managed to give his sister Constance the slip and was free from her threatened society, he approached the task with a downcast spirit. It is always unpleasant for a proud man to realize that he is no longer captain of his soul; that he is to all intents and purposes ground beneath the number twelve heel of a Glaswegian head-gardener; and, brooding on this, he judged the cottage gardens with a distrait eye. It was only when he came to the last on his list that anything like animation crept into his demeanour.

This, he perceived, peering over its rickety fence, was not at all a bad little garden. It demanded closer inspection. He unlatched the gate and pottered in. And a dog, dozing behind a water-butt, opened one eye and looked at him. It was one of those hairy, nondescript dogs, and its gaze was cold, wary and suspicious, like that of a stockbroker who thinks someone is going to play the confidence trick on him.

Lord Emsworth did not observe the animal. He had pottered to a bed of wallflowers and now, stooping, he took a sniff at them.

As sniffs go, it was an innocent sniff, but the dog for some reason appeared to read into it criminality of a high order. All the indignant householder in him woke in a flash. The next moment the world had become full of hideous noises, and Lord Emsworth's preoccupation was swept away in a passionate desire to save his ankles from harm.

As these chronicles of Blandings Castle have already shown, he was not at his best with strange dogs. Beyond saying 'Go away, sir!' and leaping to and fro with an agility surprising in one of his years, he had accomplished little in the direction of a reasoned plan of defence when the cottage door opened and a girl came out.

'Hoy!' cried the girl.

And on the instant, at the mere sound of her voice, the mongrel, suspending hostilities, bounded at the new-comer and writhed on his back at her feet with all four legs in the air.

The spectacle reminded Lord Emsworth irresistibly of his own behaviour when in the presence of Angus McAllister.

He blinked at his preserver. She was a small girl, of uncertain age – possibly twelve or thirteen, though a combination of London fogs and early cares had given her face a sort of wizened motherliness which in some odd way caused his lordship from the first to look on her as belonging to his own generation. She was the type of girl you see in back streets carrying a baby nearly as large as herself and still retaining sufficient energy to lead one little brother by the hand and shout recrimination at another in the distance. Her cheeks shone from recent soaping, and she was dressed in a velveteen frock which was obviously the pick of her wardrobe. Her hair, in defiance of the prevailing mode, she wore drawn tightly back into a short pigtail.

'Er – thank you,' said Lord Emsworth.

'Thank you, sir,' said the girl.

For what she was thanking him, his lordship was not able to gather. Later, as their acquaintance ripened, he was to discover that this strange gratitude was a habit with his new friend. She thanked everybody for everything. At the moment, the mannerism surprised him. He continued to blink at her through his pince-nez.

Lack of practice had rendered Lord Emsworth a little rusty in the art of making conversation to members of the other sex. He sought in his mind for topics.

'Fine day.'

'Yes, sir. Thank you, sir.'

'Are you' – Lord Emsworth furtively consulted his list – 'are you the daughter of – ah – Ebenezer Sprockett?' he asked, thinking, as he had often thought before, what ghastly names some of his tenantry possessed.

'No, sir. I'm from London, sir.'

'Ah? London, eh? Pretty warm it must be there.' He paused. Then, remembering a formula of his youth: 'Er – been out much this Season?'

'No, sir.'

'Everybody out of town now, I suppose? What part of London?'

'Drury Line, sir.'

'What's your name? Eh, what?'

'Gladys, sir. Thank you, sir. This is Ern.'

A small boy had wandered out of the cottage, a rather hard-boiled specimen with freckles, bearing surprisingly in his hand a large and beautiful bunch of flowers. Lord Emsworth bowed courteously and with the addition of this third party to the *tête-à-tête* felt more at his ease.

'How do you do,' he said. 'What pretty flowers.'

With her brother's advent, Gladys, also, had lost diffidence and gained conversational aplomb.

'A treat, ain't they?' she agreed eagerly. 'I got 'em for 'im up at the big 'ahse. Coo! The old josser the plice belongs to didn't arf chase me. 'E found me picking 'em and 'e sharted somefin at me and come runnin' after me, but I copped 'im on the shin wiv a stone and 'e stopped to rub it and I come away.'

Lord Emsworth might have corrected her impression that Blandings Castle and its gardens belonged to Angus McAllister, but his mind was so filled with admiration and gratitude that he refrained from doing so. He looked at the girl almost reverently. Not content with controlling savage dogs with a mere word, this super-woman actually threw stones at Angus McAllister – a thing which he had never been able to nerve himself to do in an association which had lasted nine years – and, what was more, copped him on the shin with them. What nonsense, Lord Emsworth felt, the papers talked about the Modern Girl. If this was a specimen, the Modern Girl was the highest point the sex had yet reached.

'Ern,' said Gladys, changing the subject, 'is wearin' 'air-oil todiy.'

Lord Emsworth had already observed this and had, indeed, been moving to windward as she spoke.

'For the Feet,' explained Gladys.

'For the feet?' It seemed unusual.

'For the Feet in the pork this afternoon.'

'Oh, you are going to the Fête?'

'Yes, sir, thank you, sir.'

For the first time, Lord Emsworth found himself regarding that grisly social event with something approaching favour.

'We must look out for one another there,' he said cordially. 'You will remember me again? I shall be wearing' – he gulped – 'a top hat.'

'Ern's going to wear a stror penamaw that's been give 'im.'

Lord Emsworth regarded the lucky young devil with frank envy. He rather fancied he knew that panama. It had been his constant companion for some six years and then had been torn from him by his sister Constance and handed over to the vicar's wife for her rummage-sale.

He sighed.

'Well, good-bye.'

'Good-bye, sir. Thank you, sir.'

Lord Emsworth walked pensively out of the garden and, turning into the little street, encountered Lady Constance.

'Oh, there you are, Clarence.'

'Yes,' said Lord Emsworth, for such was the case.

'Have you finished judging the gardens?'

'Yes.'

'I am just going into this end cottage here. The vicar tells me there is a little girl from London staying there. I want to warn her to behave this afternoon. I have spoken to the others.'

Lord Emsworth drew himself up. His pince-nez were slightly askew, but despite this his gaze was commanding and impressive.

'Well, mind what you say,' he said authoritatively. 'None of your district-visiting stuff, Constance.'

'What do you mean?'

'You know what I mean. I have the greatest respect for the young lady to whom you refer. She behaved on a certain recent occasion – on two recent occasions – with notable gallantry and resource, and I won't have her ballyragged. Understand that!'

The technical title of the orgy which broke out annually on the first Monday in August in the park of Blandings Castle was the Blandings Parva School Treat, and it seemed to Lord Emsworth, wanly watching the proceedings from under the shadow of his top hat, that if this was the sort of thing schools looked on as pleasure he and they were mentally poles apart. A function like the Blandings Parva School Treat blurred his conception of Man as Nature's Final Word.

The decent sheep and cattle to whom this park normally belonged had been hustled away into regions unknown, leaving the smooth expanse of turf to children whose vivacity scared Lord Emsworth and adults who appeared to him to have cast aside all dignity and every other noble quality which goes to make a one hundred per cent. British citizen. Look at Mrs Rossiter over there, for instance, the wife of Jno. Rossiter,

Provisions, Groceries and Home-Made Jams. On any other day of the year, when you met her, Mrs Rossiter was a nice, quiet, docile woman who gave at the knees respectfully as you passed. To-day, flushed in the face and with her bonnet on one side, she seemed to have gone completely native. She was wandering to and fro drinking lemonade out of a bottle and employing her mouth, when not so occupied, to make a devastating noise with what he believed was termed a squeaker.

The injustice of the thing stung Lord Emsworth. This park was his own private park. What right had people to come and blow squeakers in it? How would Mrs Rossiter like it if one afternoon he suddenly invaded her neat little garden in the High Street and rushed about over her lawn, blowing a squeaker?

And it was always on these occasions so infernally hot. July might have ended in a flurry of snow, but directly the first Monday in August arrived and he had to put on a stiff collar out came the sun, blazing with tropic fury.

Of course, admitted Lord Emsworth, for he was a fair-minded man, this cut both ways. The hotter the day, the more quickly his collar lost its starch and ceased to spike him like a javelin. This afternoon, for instance, it had resolved itself almost immediately into something which felt like a wet compress. Severe as were his sufferings, he was compelled to recognize that he was that much ahead of the game.

A masterful figure loomed at his side.

'Clarence!'

Lord Emsworth's mental and spiritual state was now such that not even the advent of his sister Constance could add noticeably to his discomfort.

'Clarence, you look a perfect sight.'

'I know I do. Who wouldn't in a rig-out like this? Why in the name of goodness you always insist . . .'

'Please don't be childish, Clarence. I cannot understand the fuss you make about dressing for once in your life like a reasonable English gentleman and not like a tramp.'

'It's this top hat. It's exciting the children.'

'What on earth do you mean, exciting the children?'

'Well, all I can tell you is that just now, as I was passing the place where they're playing football – Football! In weather like this! – a small boy called out something derogatory and threw a portion of a coco-nut at it.'

'If you will identify the child,' said Lady Constance warmly, 'I will have him severely punished.'

'How the dickens,' replied his lordship with equal warmth, 'can I identify the child? They all look alike to me. And if I did identify him, I would shake him by the hand. A boy who throws coco-nuts at top hats is fundamentally sound in his views. And stiff collars . . .'

'Stiff! That's what I came to speak to you about. Are you aware that your collar looks like a rag? Go in and change it at once.'

'But, my dear Constance . . .'

'At once, Clarence. I simply cannot understand a man having so little pride in his appearance. But all your life you have been like that. I remember when we were children . . .'

Lord Emsworth's past was not of such a purity that he was prepared to stand and listen to it being lectured on by a sister with a good memory.

'Oh, all right, all right, all right,' he said. 'I'll change it, I'll change it.'

'Well, hurry. They are just starting tea.'

Lord Emsworth quivered.

'Have I got to go into that tea-tent?'

'Of course you have. Don't be so ridiculous. I do wish you would realize your position. As master of Blandings Castle...'

A bitter, mirthless laugh from the poor peon thus ludicrously described drowned the rest of the sentence.

It always seemed to Lord Emsworth, in analysing these entertainments, that the August Bank Holiday Saturnalia at Blandings Castle reached a peak of repulsiveness when tea was served in the big marquee. Tea over, the agony abated, to become acute once more at the moment when he stepped to the edge of the platform and cleared his throat and tried to recollect what the deuce he had planned to say to the goggling audience beneath him. After that, it subsided again and passed until the following August.

Conditions during the tea hour, the marquee having stood all day under a blazing sun, were generally such that Shadrach, Meshach and Abednego, had they been there, could have learned something new about burning fiery furnaces. Lord Emsworth, delayed by the revision of his toilet, made his entry when the meal was half over and was pleased to find that his second collar almost instantaneously began to relax its iron grip. That, however, was the only gleam of happiness which was to be vouchsafed him. Once in the tent, it took his experienced eye but a moment to discern that the present feast was eclipsing in frightfulness all its predecessors.

Young Blandings Parva, in its normal form, tended rather to the stolidly bovine than the riotous. In all villages, of course, there must of necessity be an occasional tough egg – in the case of Blandings Parva the names of Willie Drake and Thomas

(Rat-Face) Blenkiron spring to the mind – but it was seldom that the local infants offered anything beyond the power of a curate to control. What was giving the present gathering its striking resemblance to a reunion of *sans-culottes* at the height of the French Revolution was the admixture of the Fresh Air London visitors.

About the London child, reared among the tin cans and cabbage stalks of Drury Lane and Clare Market, there is a breezy insouciance which his country cousin lacks. Years of back-chat with annoyed parents and relatives have cured him of any tendency he may have had towards shyness, with the result that when he requires anything he grabs for it, and when he is amused by any slight peculiarity in the personal appearance of members of the governing classes he finds no difficulty in translating his thoughts into speech. Already, up and down the long tables, the curate's unfortunate squint was coming in for hearty comment, and the front teeth of one of the school-teachers ran it a close second for popularity. Lord Emsworth was not, as a rule, a man of swift inspirations, but it occurred to him at this juncture that it would be a prudent move to take off his top hat before his little guests observed it and appreciated its humorous possibilities.

The action was not, however, necessary. Even as he raised his hand a rock cake, singing through the air like a shell, took it off for him.

Lord Emsworth had had sufficient. Even Constance, unreasonable woman though she was, could hardly expect him to stay and beam genially under conditions like this. All civilized laws had obviously gone by the board and Anarchy reigned in the marquee. The curate was doing his best to form a provisional government consisting of himself and the two school-teachers, but there was only one man who could have coped adequately with the situation and that was King Herod, who – regrettably – was not among those present. Feeling like some aristocrat of the old *régime* sneaking away from the tumbril, Lord Emsworth edged to the exit and withdrew.

Outside the marquee the world was quieter, but only comparatively so. What Lord Emsworth craved was solitude, and in all the broad park there seemed to be but one spot where it was to be had. This was a red-tiled shed, standing beside a small pond, used at happier times as a lounge or retiring-room for cattle. Hurrying thither, his lordship had just begun to revel in the cool, cow-scented dimness of its interior when from one of the dark corners, causing him to start and bite his tongue, there came the sound of a subdued sniff.

He turned. This was persecution. With the whole park to mess about in, why should an infernal child invade this one sanctuary of his? He spoke with angry sharpness. He came of a line of warrior ancestors and his fighting blood was up.

'Who's that?'

'Me, sir. Thank you, sir.'

Only one person of Lord Emsworth's acquaintance was capable of expressing gratitude for having been barked at in such a tone. His wrath died away and remorse took its place. He felt like a man who in error has kicked a favourite dog.

'God bless my soul!' he exclaimed. 'What in the world are you doing in a cow-shed?'

'Please, sir, I was put.'

'Put? How do you mean, put? Why?'

'For pinching things, sir.'

'Eh? What? Pinching things? Most extraordinary. What did you – er – pinch?'

'Two buns, two jem-sengwiches, two apples and a slicer cake.'

The girl had come out of her corner and was standing correctly at attention. Force of habit had caused her to intone the list of the purloined articles in the singsong voice in which she was wont to recite the multiplication-table at school, but Lord Emsworth could see that she was deeply moved. Tear-stains glistened on her face, and no Emsworth had ever been able to watch unstirred a woman's tears. The ninth Earl was visibly affected.

'Blow your nose,' he said, hospitably extending his handkerchief.

'Yes, sir. Thank you, sir.'

'What did you say you had pinched? Two buns ...'

'... Two jem-sengwiches, two apples and a slicer cake.'

'Did you eat them?'

'No, sir. They wasn't for me. They was for Ern.'

'Ern? Oh, ah, yes. Yes, to be sure. For Ern, eh?'

'Yes, sir.'

'But why the dooce couldn't Ern have – er – pinched them for himself? Strong, able-bodied young feller, I mean.'

Lord Emsworth, a member of the old school, did not like this disposition on the part of the modern young man to shirk the dirty work and let the woman pay.

'Ern wasn't allowed to come to the treat, sir.'

'What! Not allowed? Who said he mustn't?'

'The lidy, sir.'

'What lidy?'

'The one that come in just after you'd gorn this morning.'

A fierce snort escaped Lord Emsworth. Constance! What the devil did Constance mean by taking it upon herself to revise his list of guests without so much as a ... Constance, eh? He snorted again. One of these days Constance would go too far.

'Monstrous!' he cried.

'Yes, sir.'

'High-handed tyranny, by Gad. Did she give any reason?'

'The lidy didn't like Ern biting 'er in the leg, sir.'

'Ern bit her in the leg?'

'Yes, sir. Pliying 'e was a dorg. And the lidy was cross and Ern wasn't allowed to come to the treat, and I told 'im I'd bring 'im back somefing nice.'

Lord Emsworth breathed heavily. He had not supposed that in these degenerate days a family like this existed. The sister copped Angus McAllister on the shin with stones, the brother bit Constance in the leg ... It was like listening to some grand old saga of the exploits of heroes and demigods.

'I thought if I didn't 'ave nothing myself it would make it all right.'

'Nothing?' Lord Emsworth started. 'Do you mean to tell me you have not had tea?'

'No, sir. Thank you, sir. I thought if I didn't 'ave none, then it would be all right Ern 'aving what I would 'ave 'ad if I 'ad 'ave 'ad.'

His lordship's head, never strong, swam a little. Then it resumed its equilibrium. He caught her drift.

'God bless my soul!' said Lord Emsworth. 'I never heard anything so monstrous and appalling in my life. Come with me immediately.'

'The lidy said I was to stop 'ere, sir.'

Lord Emsworth gave vent to his loudest snort of the afternoon.

'Confound the lidy!'

'Yes, sir. Thank you, sir.'

Five minutes later Beach, the butler, enjoying a siesta in the housekeeper's room, was roused from his slumbers by the unexpected ringing of a bell. Answering its summons, he found his employer in the library, and with him a surprising young person in a velveteen frock, at the sight of whom his eyebrows quivered and, but for his iron self-restraint, would have risen.

'Beach!'

'Your lordship?'

'This young lady would like some tea.'

'Very good, your lordship.'

'Buns, you know. And apples, and jem – I mean jam-sandwiches, and cake, and that sort of thing.'

'Very good, your lordship.'

'And she has a brother, Beach.'

'Indeed, your lordship?'

'She will want to take some stuff away for him.' Lord Emsworth turned to his guest. 'Ernest would like a little chicken, perhaps?'

'Coo!'

'I beg your pardon?'

'Yes, sir. Thank you, sir.'

'And a slice or two of ham?'

'Yes, sir. Thank you, sir.'

'And – he has no gouty tendency?'

'No, sir. Thank you, sir.'

'Capital! Then a bottle of that new lot of port, Beach. It's some stuff they've sent me down to try,' explained his lordship. 'Nothing special, you understand,' he added apologetically, 'but quite drinkable. I should like your brother's opinion of it. See that all that is put together in a parcel, Beach, and leave it on the table in the hall. We will pick it up as we go out.'

A welcome coolness had crept into the evening air by the time Lord Emsworth and his guest came out of the great door of the castle. Gladys, holding her host's hand and clutching the parcel, sighed contentedly. She had done herself well at the tea-table. Life seemed to have nothing more to offer.

Lord Emsworth did not share this view. His spacious mood had not yet exhausted itself.

'Now, is there anything else you can think of that Ernest would like?' he asked. 'If so, do not hesitate to mention it. Beach, can you think of anything?'

The butler, hovering respectfully, was unable to do so.

'No, your lordship. I ventured to add – on my own responsibility, your lordship – some hard-boiled eggs and a pot of jam to the parcel.'

'Excellent! You are sure there is nothing else?'

A wistful look came into Gladys's eyes.

'Could he 'ave some flarze?'

'Certainly,' said Lord Emsworth. 'Certainly, certainly, certainly. By all means. Just what I was about to suggest my – er – what *is* flarze?'

Beach, the linguist, interpreted.

'I think the young lady means flowers, your lordship.'

'Yes, sir. Thank you, sir. Flarze.'

'Oh?' said Lord Emsworth. 'Oh? Flarze?' he said slowly. 'Oh, ah, yes. Yes. I see. H'm!'

He removed his pince-nez, wiped them thoughtfully, replaced them, and gazed with wrinkling forehead at the gardens that stretched gaily out before him. Flarze! It would be idle to deny that those gardens contained flarze in full measure. They were bright with Achillea, Bignonia Radicans, Campanula, Digitalis, Euphorbia, Funkia, Gypsophila, Helianthus, Iris, Liatris, Monarda, Phlox Drummondi, Salvia, Thalictrum, Vinca and Yucca. But the devil of it was that Angus McAllister would have a fit if they were picked. Across the threshold of this Eden the ginger whiskers of Angus McAllister lay like a flaming sword.

As a general rule, the procedure for getting flowers out of Angus McAllister was as follows. You waited till he was in one of his rare moods of complaisance, then you led the conversation gently round to the subject of interior decoration, and then, choosing your moment, you asked if he could possibly spare a few to be put in vases. The last thing you thought of doing was to charge in and start helping yourself.

'I – er – . . .' said Lord Emsworth.

He stopped. In a sudden blinding flash of clear vision he had seen himself for what he was – the spineless, unspeakably unworthy descendant of ancestors who, though they may have had their faults, had certainly known how to handle employees. It was 'How now, varlet!' and 'Marry come up, thou malapert knave!' in the days of previous Earls of Emsworth. Of course, they had possessed certain advantages which he lacked. It undoubtedly helped a man in his dealings with the domestic staff to have, as they had had, the rights of the high, the middle and the low justice – which meant, broadly, that if you got annoyed with your head-gardener you could immediately divide him into four head-gardeners with a battle-axe and no questions asked – but even so, he realized that they were better men than he was and that, if he allowed craven fear of Angus McAllister to stand in the way of this delightful girl and her charming brother getting all the flowers they required, he was not worthy to be the last of their line.

Lord Emsworth wrestled with his tremors.

'Certainly, certainly, certainly,' he said, though not without a qualm. 'Take as many as you want.'

And so it came about that Angus McAllister, crouched in his potting-shed like some dangerous beast in its den, beheld a sight which first froze his blood and then sent it boiling through his veins. Flitting to and fro through his sacred gardens, picking his sacred flowers, was a small girl in a velveteen frock. And – which brought apoplexy a step closer – it was the same small girl who two days before had copped him on the shin with a stone. The stillness of the summer evening was shattered by a roar that sounded like boilers exploding, and Angus McAllister came out of the potting-shed at forty-five miles per hour.

Gladys did not linger. She was a London child, trained from infancy to bear herself gallantly in the presence of alarms and excursions, but this excursion had been so sudden that it momentarily broke her nerve. With a horrified yelp she scuttled to where Lord Emsworth stood and, hiding behind him, clutched the tails of his morning-coat.

'Oo-er!' said Gladys.

Lord Emsworth was not feeling so frightfully good himself. We have pictured him a few moments back drawing inspiration from the nobility of his ancestors and saying, in effect, 'That for McAllister!' but truth now compels us to admit that this hardy attitude was largely due to the fact that he believed the head-gardener to be a safe quarter of a mile away among the swings and roundabouts of the Fête. The spectacle of the man charging vengefully down on him with gleaming eyes and bristling whiskers made him feel like a nervous English infantryman at the Battle of Bannockburn. His knees shook and the soul within him quivered.

And then something happened, and the whole aspect of the situation changed.

It was, in itself, quite a trivial thing, but it had an astoundingly stimulating effect on Lord Emsworth's morale. What happened was that Gladys, seeking further protection, slipped at this moment a small, hot hand into his.

It was a mute vote of confidence, and Lord Emsworth intended to be worthy of it.

'He's coming,' whispered his lordship's Inferiority Complex agitatedly.

'What of it?' replied Lord Emsworth stoutly.

'Tick him off,' breathed his lordship's ancestors in his other ear.

'Leave it to me,' replied Lord Emsworth.

He drew himself up and adjusted his pince-nez. He felt filled with a cool masterfulness. If the man tendered his resignation, let him tender his damned resignation.

'Well, McAllister?' said Lord Emsworth coldly.

He removed his top hat and brushed it against his sleeve.

'What is the matter, McAllister?'

He replaced his top hat.

'You appear agitated, McAllister.'

He jerked his head militantly. The hat fell off. He let it lie. Freed from its loathsome weight he felt more masterful than ever. It had just needed that to bring him to the top of his form.

'This young lady,' said Lord Emsworth, 'has my full permission to pick all the flowers she wants, McAllister. If you do not see eye to eye with me in this matter, McAllister, say so and we will discuss what you are going to do about it, McAllister. These gardens, McAllister, belong to me, and if you do not – er – appreciate that fact you will, no doubt, be able to find another employer – ah – more in tune with your views. I value your services highly, McAllister, but I will not be dictated to in my own garden, McAllister. Er – dash it,' added his lordship, spoiling the whole effect.

A long moment followed in which Nature stood still, breathless. The Achillea stood still. So did the Bignonia Radicans. So did the Campanula, the Digitalis, the Euphorbia, the Funkia, the Gypsophila, the Helianthus, the Iris, the Liatris, the Monarda, the Phlox Drummondi, the Salvia, the Thalictrum, the Vinca and the Yucca. From far off in the direction of the park there sounded the happy howls of children who were probably breaking things, but even these seemed hushed. The evening breeze had died away.

Angus McAllister stood glowering. His attitude was that of one sorely perplexed. So might the early bird have looked if the worm ear-marked for its breakfast had suddenly turned and snapped at it. It had never occurred to him that his employer would voluntarily suggest that he sought another position, and now that he had suggested it Angus McAllister disliked the idea very much. Blandings Castle was in his bones. Elsewhere, he would feel an exile. He fingered his whiskers, but they gave him no comfort.

He made his decision. Better to cease to be a Napoleon than be a Napoleon in exile.

'Mphm,' said Angus McAllister.

'Oh, and by the way, McAllister,' said Lord Emsworth, 'that matter of the gravel path through the yew alley. I've been thinking it over, and I won't have it. Not on any account. Mutilate my beautiful moss with a beastly gravel path? Make an eyesore of the loveliest spot in one of the finest and oldest gardens in the United Kingdom? Certainly not. Most decidedly not. Try to remember, McAllister, as you work in the gardens of Blandings Castle, that you are not back in Glasgow, laying out recreation grounds. That is all, McAllister. Er – dash it – that is all.'

'Mphm,' said Angus McAllister.

He turned. He walked away. The potting-shed swallowed him up. Nature resumed its breathing. The breeze began to blow again. And all over the gardens birds who had stopped on their high note carried on according to plan.

Lord Emsworth took out his handkerchief and dabbed with it at his forehead. He was shaken, but a novel sense of being a man among men thrilled him. It might seem bravado, but he almost wished – yes, dash it, he almost wished – that his sister Constance would come along and start something while he felt like this.

He had his wish.

'Clarence!'

Yes, there she was, hurrying towards him up the garden path. She, like McAllister, seemed agitated. Something was on her mind.

'Clarence!'

'Don't keep saying "Clarence!" as if you were a dashed parrot,' said Lord Emsworth haughtily. 'What the dickens is the matter, Constance?'

'Matter? Do you know what the time is? Do you know that everybody is waiting down there for you to make your speech?'

Lord Emsworth met her eye sternly.

'I do not,' he said. 'And I don't care. I'm not going to make any dashed speech. If you want a speech, let the vicar make it. Or make it yourself. Speech! I never heard such dashed nonsense in my life.' He turned to Gladys. 'Now, my dear,' he said, 'if you will just give me time to get out of these infernal clothes and this ghastly collar and put on something human, we'll go down to the village and have a chat with Ern.'

THE Hon. Freddie Threepwood, married to the charming daughter of Donaldson's Dog-Biscuits of Long Island City, N.Y., and sent home by his father-in-law to stimulate the sale of the firm's products in England, naturally thought right away of his aunt Georgiana. There, he reasoned, was a woman who positively ate dog-biscuits. She had owned, when he was last in the country, a matter of four Pekes, two Poms, a Yorkshire terrier, five Sealyhams, a Borzoi and an Airedale: and if that didn't constitute a promising market for Donaldson's Dog-Joy ('Get your dog thinking the Donaldson way'), he would like to know what did. The Alcester connection ought, he considered, to be good for at least ten of the half-crown cellophane-sealed packets a week.

A day or so after his arrival, accordingly, he hastened round to Upper Brook Street to make a sales-talk: and it was as he was coming rather pensively out of the house at the conclusion of the interview that he ran into Beefy Bingham, who had been up at Oxford with him. Several years had passed since the other, then a third year Blood and Trial Eights man, had bicycled along tow-paths saying rude things through a megaphone about Freddie's stomach, but he recognized him instantly. And this in spite of the fact that the passage of time appeared to have turned old

Beefers into a clergyman. For the colossal frame of this Bingham was now clad in sober black, and he was wearing one of those collars which are kept in position without studs, purely by the exercise of will-power.

'Beefers!' cried Freddie, his slight gloom vanishing in the pleasure of this happy reunion.

The Rev. Rupert Bingham, though he returned his greeting with cordiality, was far from exuberant. He seemed subdued, gloomy, as if he had discovered schism among his flock. His voice, when he spoke, was the voice of a man with a secret sorrow.

'Oh, hullo, Freddie. I haven't seen you for years. Keeping pretty fit?'

'As a fiddle, Beefers, old man, as a fiddle. And you?'

'Oh, I'm all right,' said the Rev. Rupert, still with that same strange gloom. 'What were you doing in that house?'

'Trying to sell dog-biscuits.'

'Do you sell dog-biscuits?'

'I do when people have sense enough to see that Donaldson's Dog-Joy stands alone. But could I make my fatheaded aunt see that? No, Beefers, not though I talked for an hour and sprayed her with printed matter like a—'

'Your aunt? I didn't know Lady Alcester was your aunt.'

'Didn't you, Beefers? I thought it was all over London.'

'Did she tell you about me?'

'What about you? Great Scott! Are you the impoverished bloke who wants to marry Gertrude?'

'Yes.'

'Well, I'm dashed.'

'I love her, Freddie,' said the Rev. Rupert Bingham. 'I love her as no man . . .'

'Rather. Quite. Absolutely. I know. All the usual stuff. And she loves you, what?'

'Yes. And now they've gone and sent her off to Blandings, to be out of my way.'

'Low. Very low. But why are you impoverished? What about tithes? I always understood you birds made a pot out of tithes.'

'There aren't any tithes where I am.'

'No tithes?'

'None.'

'H'm. Not so hot. Well, what are you going to do about it, Beefers?'

'I thought of calling on your aunt and trying to reason with her.'

Freddie took his old friend's arm sympathetically and drew him away.

'No earthly good, old man. If a woman won't buy Donaldson's Dog-Joy, it means she has some sort of mental kink and it's no use trying to reason with her. We must think of some other procedure. So Gertrude is at Blandings, is she? She would be. The family seem to look on the place as a sort of Bastille. Whenever the young of the species make a floater like falling in love with the wrong man, they are always shot off to Blandings to recover. The guv'nor has often complained about it bitterly. Now, let me think.'

They passed into Park Street. Some workmen were busy tearing up the paving with pneumatic drills, but the whirring of Freddie's brain made the sound almost inaudible.

'I've got it,' he said at length, his features relaxing from the terrific strain. 'And it's a dashed lucky thing for you, my lad, that I went last night to see that super-film, "Young Hearts Adrift," featuring Rosalie Norton and Otto Byng. Beefers, old man, you're legging it straight down to Blandings this very afternoon.'

'What!'

'By the first train after lunch. I've got the whole thing planned out. In this super-film, "Young Hearts Adrift," a poor but deserving young man was in love with the daughter of rich and haughty parents, and they took her away to the country so that she could forget, and a few days later a mysterious stranger turned up at the place and ingratiated himself with the parents and said he wanted to marry their daughter, and they gave their consent, and the wedding took place, and then he tore off his whiskers and it was Jim!'

'Yes, but...'

'Don't argue. The thing's settled. My aunt needs a sharp lesson. You would think a woman would be only too glad to put business in the way of her nearest and dearest, especially when shown samples and offered a fortnight's free trial. But no! She insists on sticking to Peterson's Pup-Food, a wholly inferior product – lacking, I happen to know, in many of the essential vitamins – and from now on, old boy, I am heart and soul in your cause.'

'Whiskers?' said the Rev. Rupert doubtfully.

'You won't have to wear any whiskers. My guv'nor's never seen you. Or has he?'

'No, I've not met Lord Emsworth.'

'Very well, then.'

'But what good will it do me, ingratiating myself, as you call it, with your father? He's only Gertrude's uncle.'

'What good? My dear chap, are you aware that the guv'nor owns the country-side for miles around? He has all sorts of livings up his sleeve – livings simply dripping with tithes – and can distribute them to whoever he likes. I know, because at one time there was an idea of making me a parson. But I would have none of it.'

The Rev. Rupert's face cleared.

'Freddie, there's something in this.'

'You bet there's something in it.'

'But how can I ingratiate myself with your father?'

'Perfectly easy. Cluster round him. Hang on his every word. Interest yourself in his pursuits. Do him little services. Help him out of chairs.... Why, great Scott, I'd undertake to ingratiate myself with Stalin if I gave my mind to it. Pop off and pack the old toothbrush, and I'll go and get the guv'nor on the 'phone.'

At about the time when this pregnant conversation was taking place in London, W.1, far away in distant Shropshire Clarence, ninth Earl of Emsworth, sat brooding in the library of Blandings Castle. Fate, usually indulgent to this dreamy peer, had suddenly turned nasty and smitten him a grievous blow beneath the belt.

They say Great Britain is still a first-class power, doing well and winning respect from the nations: and, if so, it is, of course, extremely gratifying. But what of the future? That was what Lord Emsworth was asking himself. Could this happy state of things last? He thought not. Without wishing to be pessimistic, he was dashed if he saw how a country containing men like Sir Gregory Parsloe-Parsloe of Matchingham Hall could hope to survive.

Strong? No doubt. Bitter? Granted. But not, we think, too strong, not – in the circumstances – unduly bitter. Consider the facts.

When, shortly after the triumph of Lord Emsworth's pre-eminent sow, Empress of Blandings, in the Fat Pigs Class at the eighty-seventh annual Shropshire Agricultural Show, George Cyril Wellbeloved, his lordship's pig-man, had expressed a desire to hand in his portfolio and seek employment elsewhere, the amiable peer, though naturally grieved, felt no sense of outrage. He put the thing down to the old roving spirit of the Wellbeloveds. George Cyril, he assumed, wearying of Shropshire, wished to try a change of air in some southern or eastern country. A nuisance, undoubtedly, for the man, when sober, was beyond question a force in the piggery. He had charm and personality. Pigs liked him. Still, if he wanted to resign office, there was nothing to be done about it.

But when, not a week later, word was brought to Lord Emsworth that, so far from having migrated to Sussex or Norfolk or Kent or somewhere, the fellow was actually just round the corner in the neighbouring village of Much Matchingham, serving under the banner of Sir Gregory Parsloe-Parsloe of Matchingham Hall, the scales fell from his eyes. He realized that black treachery had been at work. George Cyril Wellbeloved had sold himself for gold, and Sir Gregory Parsloe-Parsloe, hitherto looked upon as a high-minded friend and fellow Justice of the Peace, stood revealed as that lowest of created things, a lurer-away of other people's pig-men.

And there was nothing one could do about it.

Monstrous!

But true.

So deeply was Lord Emsworth occupied with the consideration of this appalling state of affairs that it was only when the knock upon the door was repeated that it reached his consciousness.

'Come in,' he said hollowly.

He hoped it was not his niece Gertrude. A gloomy young woman. He could hardly stand Gertrude's society just now.

It was not Gertrude. It was Beach, the butler.

'Mr Frederick wishes to speak to your lordship on the telephone.'

An additional layer of greyness fell over Lord Emsworth's spirit as he toddled down the great staircase to the telephone closet in the hall. It was his experience that almost any communication from Freddie indicated trouble.

But there was nothing in his son's voice as it floated over the wire to suggest that all was not well.

'Hullo, guv'nor.'

'Well, Frederick?'

'How's everything at Blandings?'

Lord Emsworth was not the man to exhibit the vultures gnawing at his heart to a babbler like the Hon. Freddie. He replied, though it hurt him to do so, that everything at Blandings was excellent.

'Good-oh!' said Freddie. 'Is the old doss-house very full up at the moment?'

'If,' replied his lordship, 'you are alluding to Blandings Castle, there is nobody at present staying here except myself and your cousin Gertrude. Why?' he added in quick alarm. 'Were you thinking of coming down?'

'Good God, no!' cried his son with equal horror. 'I mean to say, I'd love it, of course, but just now I'm too busy with Dog-Joy.'

'Who is Popjoy?'

'Popjoy? Popjoy? Oh, ah, yes. He's a pal of mine and, as you've plenty of room, I want you to put him up for a bit. Nice chap.

You'll like him. Right-ho, then, I'll ship him off on the three-fifteen.'

Lord Emsworth's face had assumed an expression which made it fortunate for his son that television was not yet in operation on the telephone systems of England: and he had just recovered enough breath for the delivery of a blistering refusal to have any friend of Freddie's within fifty miles of the place when the other spoke again.

'He'll be company for Gertrude.'

And at these words a remarkable change came over Lord Emsworth. His face untwisted itself. The basilisk glare died out of his eyes.

'God bless my soul! That's true!' he exclaimed. 'That's certainly true. So he will. The three-fifteen, did you say? I will send the car to Market Blandings to meet it.'

Company for Gertrude? A pleasing thought. A fragrant, refreshing, stimulating thought. Somebody to take Gertrude off his hands occasionally was what he had been praying for ever since his sister Georgiana had dumped her down on him.

One of the chief drawbacks to entertaining in your home a girl who has been crossed in love is that she is extremely apt to go about the place doing good. All that life holds for her now is the opportunity of being kind to others, and she intends to be kind if it chokes them. For two weeks Lord Emsworth's beautiful young niece had been moving to and fro through the castle with a drawn face, doing good right and left: and his lordship, being handiest, had had to bear the brunt of it. It was with the first real smile he had smiled that day that he came out of the telephone-cupboard and found the object of his thoughts entering the hall in front of him.

'Well, well, well, my dear,' he said cheerily. 'And what have you been doing?'

There was no answering smile on his niece's face. Indeed, looking at her, you could see that this was a girl who had forgotten how to smile. She suggested something symbolic out of Maeterlinck.

'I have been tidying your study, Uncle Clarence,' she replied listlessly. 'It was in a dreadful mess.'

Lord Emsworth winced as a man of set habits will who has been remiss enough to let a Little Mother get at his study while his back is turned, but he continued bravely on the cheerful note.

'I have been talking to Frederick on the telephone.'

'Yes?' Gertrude sighed, and a bleak wind seemed to blow through the hall. 'Your tie's crooked, Uncle Clarence.'

'I like it crooked,' said his lordship, backing. 'I have a piece of news for you. A friend of Frederick's is coming down here to-night for a visit. His name, I understand, is Popjoy. So you will have some young society at last.'

'I don't want young society.'

'Oh, come, my dear.'

She looked at him thoughtfully with large, sombre eyes. Another sigh escaped her.

'It must be wonderful to be as old as you are, Uncle Clarence.'

'Eh?' said his lordship, starting.

'To feel that there is such a short, short step to the quiet tomb, to the ineffable peace of the grave. To me, life seems to stretch out endlessly, like a long, dusty desert. Twenty-three! That's all I am. Only twenty-three. And all our family live to sixty.'

'What do you mean, sixty?' demanded his lordship, with the warmth of a man who would be that next birthday. 'My poor father was seventy-seven when he was killed in the hunting-field. My uncle Robert lived till nearly ninety. My cousin Claude was eighty-four when he broke his neck trying to jump a five-barred gate. My mother's brother, Alistair...'

'Don't!' said the girl with a little shudder. 'Don't! It makes it all seem so awful and hopeless.'

Yes, that was Gertrude: and in Lord Emsworth's opinion she needed company.

The reactions of Lord Emsworth to the young man Popjoy, when he encountered him for the first time in the drawing-room shortly before dinner, were in the beginning wholly favourable. His son's friend was an extraordinarily large and powerful person with a frank, open, ingenuous face about the colour of the inside of a salmon, and he seemed a little nervous. That, however, was in his favour. It was, his lordship felt, a pleasant surprise to find in one of the younger generation so novel an emotion as diffidence.

He condoned, therefore, the other's trick of laughing hysterically even when the subject under discussion was the not irresistibly ludicrous one of green-fly in the rose-garden. He excused him for appearing to find something outstandingly comic in the statement that the glass was going up. And when, springing to his feet at the entrance of Gertrude, the young man performed some complicated steps in conjunction with a table covered with china and photograph-frames, he joined in the mirth which the feat provoked not only from the visitor but actually from Gertrude herself.

Yes, amazing though it might seem, his niece Gertrude, on seeing this young Popjoy, had suddenly burst into a peal of happy laughter. The gloom of the last two weeks appeared to be gone. She laughed. The young man laughed. They proceeded down to dinner in a perfect gale of merriment, rather like a chorus of revellers exiting after a concerted number in an old-fashioned comic opera.

And at dinner the young man had spilt his soup, broken a wine-glass, and almost taken another spectacular toss when leaping up at the end of the meal to open the door. At which Gertrude had laughed, and the young man had laughed, and his lordship had laughed – though not, perhaps, quite so heartily as the young folks, for that wine-glass had been one of a set which he valued.

However, weighing profit and loss as he sipped his port, Lord Emsworth considered that the ledger worked out on the right side. True, he had taken into his home what appeared to be a half-witted acrobat: but then any friend of his son Frederick was bound to be weak in the head, and, after all, the great thing was that Gertrude seemed to appreciate the newcomer's society. He looked forward contentedly to a succession of sunshine days of peace, perfect peace with loved ones far away; days when he would be able to work in his garden without the fear, which had been haunting him for the last two weeks, of finding his niece drooping wanly at his side and asking him if he was wise to stand about in the hot sun. She had company now that would occupy her elsewhere.

His lordship's opinion of his guest's mental deficiencies was strengthened late that night when, hearing footsteps on the terrace, he poked his head out and found him standing beneath his window, blowing kisses at it.

At the sight of his host he appeared somewhat confused.

'Lovely evening,' he said, with his usual hyenaesque laugh. 'I – er – thought . . . or, rather . . . that is to say . . . Ha, ha, ha!'

'Is anything the matter?'

'No, no! No! No, thanks, no! No! No, no! I – er – ho, ho, ho! – just came out for a stroll, ha, ha!'

Lord Emsworth returned to his bed a little thoughtfully. Perhaps some premonition of what was to come afflicted his subconscious mind, for, as he slipped between the sheets, he shivered. But gradually, as he dozed off, his equanimity became restored.

Looking at the thing in the right spirit, it might have been worse. After all, he felt, the mists of sleep beginning to exert their usual beneficent influence, he might have been entertaining at Blandings Castle one of his nephews, or one of his sisters, or even – though this was morbid – his younger son Frederick.

In matters where shades of feeling are involved, it is not always easy for the historian to be as definite as he could wish. He wants to keep the record straight, and yet he cannot take any one particular moment of time, pin it down for the scrutiny of Posterity and say 'This was the moment when Lord Emsworth for the first time found himself wishing that his guest would tumble out of an upper window and break his neck.' To his lordship it seemed that this had been from the beginning his constant day-dream, but such was not the case. When, on the second morning of the other's visit, the luncheon-gong had found them chatting in the library and the young man, bounding up, had extended a hand like a ham and, placing it beneath his host's arm, gently helped him to rise, Lord Emsworth had been quite pleased by the courteous attention.

But when the fellow did the same thing day after day, night after night, every time he caught him sitting; when he offered him an arm to help him across floors; when he assisted him up stairs, along corridors, down paths, out of rooms and into rain-coats; when he snatched objects from his hands to carry them himself; when he came galloping out of the house on dewy evenings laden down with rugs, mufflers, hats and, on one occasion, positively a blasted respirator... why, then Lord Emsworth's proud spirit rebelled. He was a tough old gentleman and, like most tough old gentlemen, did not enjoy having his juniors look on him as something pathetically helpless that crawled the earth waiting for the end.

It had been bad enough when Gertrude was being the Little Mother. This was infinitely worse. Apparently having conceived for him one of those unreasoning, overwhelming devotions, this young Popjoy stuck closer than a brother; and for the first time Lord Emsworth began to appreciate what must have been the feelings of that Mary who aroused a similar attachment in the bosom of her lamb. It was as if he had been an Oldest Inhabitant fallen into the midst of a troop of Boy Scouts, all doing Good Deeds simultaneously, and he resented it with an indescribable bitterness. One can best illustrate his frame of mind by saying that, during the last phase, if he had been called upon to choose between his guest and Sir Gregory Parsloe-Parsloe as a companion for a summer ramble through the woods, he would have chosen Sir Gregory.

And then, on top of all this, there occurred the episode of the step-ladder.

The Hon. Freddie Threepwood, who had decided to run down and see how matters were developing, learned the details of this rather unfortunate occurrence from his cousin Gertrude. She met him at Market Blandings Station, and he could see there was something on her mind. She had not become positively Maeterlinckian again, but there was sorrow in her beautiful eyes: and Freddie, rightly holding that with a brainy egg like himself directing her destinies they should have contained only joy and sunshine, was disturbed by this.

'Don't tell me the binge has sprung a leak,' he said anxiously.

Gertrude sighed.

'Well, yes and no.'

'What do you mean, yes and no? Properly worked, the thing can't fail. This points to negligence somewhere. Has old Beefers been ingratiating himself?'

'Yes.'

'Hanging on the guv'nor's every word? Interesting himself in his pursuits? Doing him little services? And been at it two weeks? Good heavens! By now the guv'nor should be looking on him as a prize pig. Why isn't he?'

'I didn't say he wasn't. Till this afternoon I rather think he was. At any rate, Rupert says he often found Uncle Clarence staring at him in a sort of lingering, rather yearning way. But when that thing happened this afternoon, I'm afraid he wasn't very pleased.'

'What thing?'

'That step-ladder business. It was like this. Rupert and I sort of went for a walk after lunch, and by the time I had persuaded him that he ought to go and find Uncle Clarence and ingratiate himself with him, Uncle Clarence had disappeared. So Rupert hunted about for a long time and at last heard a snipping noise and found him miles away standing on a step-ladder, sort of pruning some kind of tree with a pair of shears. So Rupert said, "Oh, there you are!" And Uncle Clarence said, Yes, there he was, and Rupert said, "Ought you to tire yourself? Won't you let me do that for you?"'

'The right note,' said Freddie approvingly. 'Assiduity. Zeal. Well?'

'Well, Uncle Clarence said, "No, thank you! – Rupert thinks it was "Thank you" – and Rupert stood there for a bit, sort of talking, and then he suddenly remembered and told Uncle Clarence that you had just 'phoned that you were coming down this evening, and I think Uncle Clarence must have got a touch of cramp or something, because he gave a kind of sudden sharp groan, Rupert says, and sort of quivered all over. This made the steps wobble, of course, so Rupert dashed forward to steady them, and he doesn't know how it happened, but they suddenly seemed to sort of shut up like a pair of scissors, and the next thing he knew Uncle Clarence was sitting on the grass, not seeming to like it much, Rupert says. He had ricked his ankle a bit and shaken himself up a bit, and altogether, Rupert says, he wasn't fearfully sunny. Rupert says he thinks he may have lost ground a little.'

Freddie pondered with knit brows. He was feeling something of the chagrin of a general who, after sweating himself to a shadow planning a great campaign, finds his troops unequal to carrying it out.

'It's such a pity it should have happened. One of the vicars near here has just been told by the doctor that he's got to go off to the south of France, and the living is in Uncle Clarence's gift. If only Rupert could have had that, we could have got married. However, he's bought Uncle Clarence some lotion.'

Freddie started. A more cheerful expression came into his sternly careworn face.

'Lotion?'

'For his ankle.'

'He couldn't have done better,' said Freddie warmly. 'Apart from showing the contrite heart, he has given the guv'nor medicine, and medicine to the guv'nor is what catnip is to the cat. Above all things he dearly loves a little bit of amateur doctoring. As a rule he tries it on somebody else – two years ago he gave one of the housemaids some patent ointment for chilblains and she went screaming about the house – but, no doubt, now that the emergency has occurred, he will be equally agreeable to treating himself. Old Beefers has made the right move.'

In predicting that Lord Emsworth would appreciate the gift of lotion, Freddie had spoken with an unerring knowledge of his father's character. The master of Blandings was one of those fluffy-minded old gentlemen who are happiest when experimenting with strange drugs. In a less censorious age he would have been a Borgia. It was not until he had retired to bed that he discovered the paper-wrapped bottle on the table by his side. Then he remembered that the pest Popjoy had mumbled something at dinner about buying him something or other for his injured ankle. He tore off the paper and examined the contents of the bottle with a lively satisfaction. The liquid was a dingy grey and sloshed pleasantly when you shook it. The name on the label – Blake's Balsam – was new to him, and that in itself was a recommendation.

His ankle had long since ceased to pain him, and to some men this might have seemed an argument against smearing it with balsam; but not to Lord Emsworth. He decanted a liberal dose into the palm of his hand. He sniffed it. It had a strong, robust, bracing sort of smell. He spent the next five minutes thoughtfully rubbing it in. Then he put the light out and went to sleep.

It is a truism to say that in the world as it is at present constituted few things have more far-reaching consequences than the accident of birth. Lord Emsworth had probably suspected this. He was now to receive direct proof. If he had been born a horse instead of the heir to an earldom, that lotion would have been just right for him. It was for horses, though the Rev. Rupert Bingham had omitted to note the fact, that Blake had planned his balsam; and anyone enjoying even a superficial acquaintance with horses and earls knows that an important difference between them is that the latter have the more sensitive skins. Waking at a quarter to two from dreams of being burned at the stake by Red Indians, Lord Emsworth found himself suffering acute pain in the right leg.

He was a little surprised. He had not supposed that that fall from the ladder had injured him so badly. However, being a good amateur doctor, he bore up bravely and took immediate steps to cope with the trouble. Having shaken the bottle till it foamed at the mouth, he rubbed in some more lotion. It occurred to him that the previous application might have been too sketchy, so this time he did it thoroughly. He rubbed and kneaded for some twenty minutes. Then he tried to go to sleep.

Nature has made some men quicker thinkers than others. Lord Emsworth's was one of those leisurely brains. It was not till nearly four o'clock that the truth came home to him. When it did, he was just on the point of applying a fifth coating of the balsam to his leg. He stopped abruptly, replaced the cork, and, jumping out of bed, hobbled to the cold-water tap and put as much of himself under it as he could manage.

The relief was perceptible, but transitory. At five he was out again, and once more at half-past. At a quarter to six, succeeding in falling asleep, he enjoyed a slumber, somewhat disturbed by the intermittent biting of sharks, which lasted till a few minutes past eight. Then he woke as if an alarm clock had rung, and realized that further sleep was out of the question.

He rose from his bed and peered out of the window. It was a beautiful morning. There had been rain in the night and a world that looked as if it had just come back from the cleaner's sparkled under a beaming sun. Cedars cast long shadows over the smooth green lawns. Rooks cawed soothingly: thrushes bubbled in their liquid and musical way: and the air was full of a summer humming. Among those present of the insect world, Lord Emsworth noticed several prominent gnats.

Beyond the terrace, glittering through the trees, gleamed the waters of the lake. They seemed to call to him like a bugle. Although he had neglected the practice of late, there was nothing Lord Emsworth enjoyed more than a before-breakfast dip: and to-day anything in the nature of water had a particularly powerful appeal for him. The pain in his ankle had subsided by now to a dull throbbing, and it seemed to him that a swim might remove it altogether. Putting on a dressing-gown and slippers, he took his bathing-suit from its drawer and went downstairs.

The beauties of a really fine English summer day are so numerous that it is excusable in a man if he fails immediately to notice them all. Only when the sharp agony of the first plunge had passed and he was floating out in mid-water did Lord Emsworth realize that in some extraordinary way he had overlooked what was beyond dispute the best thing that this perfect morning had to offer him. Gazing from his bedroom window, he had observed the sun, the shadows, the birds, the trees, and the insects, but he had omitted to appreciate the fact that nowhere in this magic world that stretched before him was there a trace of his young guest, Popjoy. For the first time in two weeks he appeared to be utterly alone and free from him.

Floating on his back and gazing up into the turquoise sky, Lord Emsworth thrilled at the thought. He kicked sportively in a spasm of pure happiness. But this, he felt, was not enough. It failed to express his full happiness. To the ecstasy of this golden moment only music – that mystic language of the soul – could really do justice. The next instant there had cut quiveringly into the summer stillness that hung over the gardens of Blandings Castle a sudden sharp wail that seemed to tell of a human being in mortal distress. It was the voice of Lord Emsworth, raised in song.

It was a gruesome sound, calculated to startle the stoutest: and two bees, buzzing among the lavender, stopped as one bee and looked at each other with raised eyebrows. Nor were they alone affected. Snails withdrew into their shells: a squirrel doing calisthenics on the cedar nearly fell off its branch: and – moving a step up in the animal kingdom – the Rev. Rupert Bingham, standing behind the rhododendron bushes and wondering how long it would be before the girl he loved came to keep her tryst, started violently, dropped his cigarette and, tearing off his coat, rushed to the water's edge.

Out in the middle of the lake, Lord Emsworth's transports continued undiminished. His dancing feet kicked up a flurry of foam. His short-sighted, but sparkling, eyes stared into the blue. His voice rose to a pulsing scream.

'Love me,' sang Lord Emsworth, 'and the wo-o-o-o-rld is – ah – mi-yun!'

'It's all right,' said a voice in his ear. 'Keep cool. Keep quite cool.'

The effect of a voice speaking suddenly, as it were out of

the void, is always, even in these days of wireless, disconcerting to a man. Had he been on dry land Lord Emsworth would have jumped. Being in ten feet of water, he went under as if a hand had pushed him. He experienced a momentary feeling of suffocation, and then a hand gripped him painfully by the fleshy part of the arm and he was on the surface again, spluttering.

'Keep quite cool,' murmured the voice. 'There's no danger.'

And now he recognized whose voice it was.

There is a point beyond which the human brain loses its kinship with the Infinite and becomes a mere seething mass of deleterious passions. Malays, when pushed past this point, take down the old *kris* from its hook and go out and start carving up the neighbours. Women have hysterics. Earls, if Lord Emsworth may be taken as a sample, haul back their right fists and swing them as violently as their age and physique will permit. For two long weeks Lord Emsworth had been enduring this pestilential young man with outward nonchalance, but the strain had told. Suppressed emotions are always the most dangerous. Little by little, day by day, he had been slowly turning into a human volcano, and this final outrage blew the lid off him.

He raged with a sense of intolerable injury. Was it not enough that this porous plaster of a young man should adhere to him on shore? Must he even pursue him out into the waste of waters and come fooling about and pawing at him when he was enjoying the best swim he had had that summer? In all their long and honourable history no member of his ancient family had ever so far forgotten the sacred obligations of hospitality as to plug a guest in the eye. But then they had never had guests like this. With a sharp, passionate snort, Lord Emsworth extracted his right hand from the foam, clenched it, drew it back and let it go.

He could have made no more imprudent move. If there was one thing the Rev. Rupert Bingham, who in his time had swum for Oxford, knew, it was what to do when drowning men struggled. Something that might have been a very hard and knobbly leg of mutton smote Lord Emsworth violently behind the ear: the sun was turned off at the main: the stars came out, many of them of a singular brightness: there was a sound of rushing waters: and he knew no more.

When Lord Emsworth came to himself, he was lying in bed. And, as it seemed a very good place to be, he remained there. His head ached abominably, but he scarcely noticed this, so occupied was he with the thoughts which surged inside it. He mused on the young man Popjoy: he meditated on Sir Gregory Parsloe-Parsloe: and wondered from time to time which he disliked the more. It was a problem almost too nice for human solution. Here, on the one hand, you had a man who pestered you for two weeks and wound up by nearly murdering you as you bathed, but who did not steal pig-men: there, on the other, one who stole pig-men but stopped short of actual assault on the person. Who could hope to hold the scales between such a pair?

He had just remembered the lotion and was wondering if this might not be considered the deciding factor in this contest for the position of the world's premier blot, when the door opened and the Hon. Freddie Threepwood insinuated himself into the room.

'Hullo, guv'nor.'

'Well, Frederick?'

'How are you feeling?'

'Extremely ill.'

'Might have been worse, you know.'

'Bah!'

'Watery grave and all that.'

'Tchah!' said Lord Emsworth.

There was a pause. Freddie, wandering about the room, picked up and fidgeted with a chair, a vase, a hair-brush, a comb, and a box of matches: then, retracing his steps, fidgeted with them all over again in the reverse order. Finally, he came to the foot of his father's bed and dropped over it like, it seemed to that sufferer's prejudiced eye, some hideous animal gaping over a fence.

'I say, guv'nor.'

'Well, Frederick?'

'Narrow squeak, that, you know.'

'Pah!'

'Do you wish to thank your brave preserver?'

Lord Emsworth plucked at the coverlet.

'If that young man comes near me,' he said, 'I will not be answerable for the consequences.'

'Eh?' Freddie stared. 'Don't you like him?'

'Like him! I think he is the most appalling young man I ever met.'

It is customary when making statements of this kind to except present company, but so deeply did Lord Emsworth feel on the subject that he omitted to do so. Freddie, having announced that he was dashed, removed himself from the bed-rail and, wandering once more about the room, fidgeted with a toothbrush, a soap-dish, a shoe, a volume on spring bulbs, and a collar-stud.

'I say, guv'nor.'

'Well, Frederick?'

'That's all very well, you know, guv'nor,' said the Hon. Freddie, returning to his post and seeming to draw moral support from the feel of the bed-rail, 'but after what's happened it looks to me as if you were jolly well bound to lend your countenance to the union, if you know what I mean.'

'Union? What are you talking about? What union?'

'Gertrude and old Beefers.'

'Who the devil is old Beefers?'

'Oh, I forgot to tell you about that. This bird Popjoy's name isn't Popjoy. It's Bingham. Old Beefy Bingham. You know, the fellow Aunt Georgie doesn't want to marry Gertrude.'

'Eh?'

'Throw your mind back. They pushed her off to Blandings to keep her out of his way. And I had the idea of sending him down here *incog* to ingratiate himself with you. The scheme being that, when you had learned to love him, you would slip him a vacant vicarage, thus enabling them to get married. Beefers is a parson, you know.'

Lord Emsworth did not speak. It was not so much the shock of this revelation that kept him dumb as the astounding discovery that any man could really want to marry Gertrude, and any girl this Popjoy. Like many a thinker before him, he was feeling that there is really no limit to the eccentricity of human tastes. The thing made his head swim.

But when it had ceased swimming he perceived that this was but one aspect of the affair. Before him stood the man who had inflicted Popjoy on him, and with something of King Lear in his demeanour Lord Emsworth rose slowly from the pillows. Words trembled on his lips, but he rejected them as not strong enough and sought in his mind for others.

'You know, guv'nor,' proceeded Freddie, 'there's nothing to prevent you doing the square thing and linking two young hearts in the bonds of the Love God, if you want to. I mean to say, old

Braithwaite at Much Matchingham has been ordered to the south of France by his doctor, so there's a living going that you've got to slip to somebody.'

Lord Emsworth sank back on the pillows.

'Much Matchingham!'

'Oh, dash it, you must know Much Matchingham, guv'nor. It's just round the corner. Where old Parsloe lives.'

'Much Matchingham!'

Lord Emsworth was blinking, as if his eyes had seen a dazzling light. How wrong, he felt, how wickedly mistaken and lacking in faith he had been when he had said to himself in his folly that Providence offers no method of retaliation to the just whose pig-men have been persuaded by Humanity's dregs to leave their employment and seek advanced wages elsewhere. Conscience could not bring remorse to Sir Gregory Parsloe-Parsloe, and the law, in its present imperfect state, was powerless to punish. But there was still a way. With this young man Popjoy – or Bingham – or whatever his name was, permanently established not a hundred yards from his park gates, would Sir Gregory Parsloe-Parsloe ever draw another really care-free breath? From his brief, but sufficient, acquaintance with the young man Bingham – or Popjoy – Lord Emsworth thought not.

The punishment was severe, but who could say that Sir Gregory had not earned it?

'A most admirable idea,' said Lord Emsworth cordially. 'Certainly I will give your friend the living of Much Matchingham.'

'You will?'

'Most decidedly.'

'At-a-boy, guv'nor!' said Freddie. 'Came the Dawn!'

4 THE GO-GETTER

On the usually unruffled brow of the Hon. Freddie Threepwood, as he paced the gardens of Blandings Castle, there was the slight but well-marked frown of one whose mind is not at rest. It was high summer and the gardens were at their loveliest, but he appeared to find no solace in their splendour. Calceolarias, which would have drawn senile yips of ecstasy from his father, Lord Emsworth, left him cold. He eyed the lobelias with an unseeing stare, as if he were cutting an undesirable acquaintance in the paddock at Ascot.

What was troubling this young man was the continued sales-resistance of his Aunt Georgiana. Ever since his marriage to the only daughter of Donaldson's Dog-Biscuits, of Long Island City, N. Y., Freddie Threepwood had thrown himself heart and soul into the promotion of the firm's wares. And, sent home to England to look about for likely prospects, he had seen in Georgiana, Lady Alcester, as has been already related, a customer who approximated to the ideal. The owner of four Pekingese, two Poms, a Yorkshire terrier, five Sealyhams, a Borzoi and an Airedale, she was a woman who stood for something in dog-loving circles. To secure her patronage would be a big thing for him. It would stamp him as a live wire and a go-getter. It would please his father-in-law hugely. And the proprietor of Donaldson's Dog-Joy was a man who, when even slightly pleased, had a habit of spraying five thousand dollar cheques like a geyser.

And so far, despite all his eloquence, callously oblivious of the ties of kinship and the sacred obligations they involve, Lady Alcester had refused to sign on the dotted line, preferring to poison her menagerie with some degraded garbage called, if he recollected rightly, Peterson's Pup-Food.

A bitter snort escaped Freddie. It was still echoing through the gardens, when he found that he was no longer alone. He had been joined by his cousin Gertrude.

'What-ho!' said Freddie amiably. He was fond of Gertrude, and did not hold it against her that she had a mother who was incapable of spotting a good dog-biscuit when she saw one. Between him and Gertrude there had long existed a firm alliance. It was to him that Gertrude had turned for assistance when the family were trying to stop her getting engaged to good old Beefy Bingham: and he had supplied assistance in such good measure that the engagement was now an accepted fact and running along nicely.

'Freddie,' said Gertrude, 'may I borrow your car?'

'Certainly. Most decidedly. Going over to see old Beefers?'

'No,' said Gertrude, and a closer observer than her cousin might have noted in her manner a touch of awkwardness. 'Mr Watkins wants me to drive him to Shrewsbury.'

'Oh? Well, carry on, as far as I'm concerned. You haven't seen your mother anywhere, have you?'

'I think she's sitting on the lawn.'

'Ah? Is she? Right-ho. Thanks.'

Freddie moved off in the direction indicated, and presently came in sight of his relative, seated as described. The Airedale was lying at her feet. One of the Pekes occupied her lap. And she was gazing into the middle distance in a preoccupied manner, as if she, like her nephew, had a weight on her mind.

Nor would one who drew this inference from her demeanour have been mistaken. Lady Alcester was feeling disturbed.

A woman who stands in *loco parentis* to fourteen dogs must of necessity have her cares, but it was not the dumb friends that were worrying Lady Alcester now. What was troubling her was the disquieting behaviour of her daughter Gertrude.

Engaged to the Rev. Rupert Bingham, Gertrude seemed to her of late to have become infatuated with Orlo Watkins, the Crooning Tenor, one of those gifted young men whom Lady Constance Keeble, the chatelaine of Blandings, was so fond of inviting down for lengthy visits in the summer-time.

On the subject of the Rev. Rupert Bingham, Lady Alcester's views had recently undergone a complete change. In the beginning, the prospect of having him for a son-in-law had saddened and distressed her. Then, suddenly discovering that he was the nephew and heir of as opulent a shipping magnate as ever broke bread at the Adelphi Hotel, Liverpool, she had soared from the depths to the heights. She was now strongly pro-Bingham. She smiled upon him freely. Upon his appointment to the vacant Vicarage of Much Matchingham, the village nearest to Market Blandings, she had brought Gertrude to the Castle so that the young people should see one another frequently.

And, instead of seeing her betrothed frequently, Gertrude seemed to prefer to moon about with this Orlo Watkins, this Crooning Tenor. For days they had been inseparable.

Now, everybody knows what Crooning Tenors are. Dangerous devils. They sit at the piano and gaze into a girl's eyes and sing in a voice that sounds like gas escaping from a pipe about

Love and the Moonlight and You: and, before you know where you are, the girl has scrapped the deserving young clergyman with prospects to whom she is affianced and is off and away with a man whose only means of livelihood consist of intermittent engagements with the British Broadcasting Corporation.

If a mother is not entitled to shudder at a prospect like that, it would be interesting to know what she is entitled to shudder at.

Lady Alcester, then, proceeded to shudder: and was still shuddering when the drowsy summer peace was broken by a hideous uproar. The Peke and the Airedale had given tongue simultaneously, and, glancing up, Lady Alcester perceived her nephew Frederick approaching.

And what made her shudder again was the fact that in Freddie's eye she noted with concern the familiar go-getter gleam, the old dog-biscuit glitter.

However, as it had sometimes been her experience, when cornered by her nephew, that she could stem the flood by talking promptly on other subjects, she made a gallant effort to do so now.

'Have you seen Gertrude, Freddie?' she asked.

'Yes. She borrowed my car to go to Shrewsbury.'

'Alone?'

'No. Accompanied by Watkins. The Yowler.'

A further spasm shook Lady Alcester.

'Freddie,' she said, 'I'm terribly worried.'

'Worried?'

'About Gertrude.'

Freddie dismissed Gertrude with a gesture.

'No need to worry about her,' he said. 'What you want to worry about is these dogs of yours. Notice how they barked at me? Nerves. They're a mass of nerves. And why? Improper feeding. As long as you mistakenly insist on giving them Peterson's Pup-Food – lacking, as it is, in many of the essential vitamins – so long will they continue to fly off the handle every time they see a human being on the horizon. Now, pursuant on what we were talking about this morning, Aunt Georgiana, there is a little demonstration I would like . . . '

'Can't you give her a hint, Freddie?'

'Who?'

'Gertrude.'

'Yes, I suppose I could give her a hint. What about?'

'She is seeing far too much of this man Watkins.'

'Well, so am I, for the matter of that. So is everybody who sees him more than once.'

'She seems quite to have forgotten that she is engaged to Rupert Bingham.'

'Rupert Bingham, did you say?' said Freddie with sudden animation. 'I'll tell you something about Rupert Bingham. He has a dog named Bottles who has been fed from early youth on Donaldson's Dog-Joy, and I wish you could see him. Thanks to the bone-forming properties of Donaldson's Dog-Joy, he glows with health. A fine, upstanding dog, with eyes sparkling with the joy of living and both feet on the ground. A credit to his master.'

'Never mind about Rupert's dog!'

'You've got to mind about Rupert's dog. You can't afford to ignore him. He is a dog to be reckoned with. A dog that counts. And all through Donaldson's Dog-Joy.'

'I don't want to talk about Donaldson's Dog-Joy.'

'I do. I want to give you a demonstration. You may not know it, Aunt Georgiana, but over in America the way we advertise this product, so rich in bone-forming vitamins, is as follows: We instruct our demonstrator to stand out in plain view before the many-headed and, when the audience is of sufficient size, to take a biscuit and break off a piece and chew it. By this means we prove that Donaldson's Dog-Joy is so superbly wholesome as actually to be fit for human consumption. Our demonstrator not only eats the biscuit – he enjoys it. He rolls it round his tongue. He chews it and mixes it with his saliva . . .'

'Freddie, please!'

'With his saliva,' repeated Freddie firmly. 'And so does the dog. He masticates the biscuit. He enjoys it. He becomes a bigger and better dog. I will now eat a Donaldson's Dog-Biscuit.'

And before his aunt's nauseated gaze he proceeded to attempt this gruesome feat.

It was an impressive demonstration, but it failed in one particular. To have rendered it perfect, he should not have choked. Want of experience caused the disaster. Long years of training go to the making of the seasoned demonstrators of Donaldson's Dog-Joy. They start in a small way with carpet-tacks and work up through the flat-irons and patent breakfast cereals till they are ready for the big effort. Freddie was a novice. Endeavouring to roll the morsel round his tongue, he allowed it to escape into his windpipe.

The sensation of having swallowed a mixture of bricks and sawdust was succeeded by a long and painful coughing fit. And when at length the sufferer's eyes cleared, no human form met their gaze. There was the Castle. There was the lawn. There were the gardens. But Lady Alcester had disappeared.

However, it is a well-established fact that good men, like Donaldson's Dog-Biscuits, are hard to keep down. Some fifty minutes later, as the Rev. Rupert Bingham sat in his study at Matchingham Vicarage, the parlourmaid announced a visitor. The Hon. Freddie Threepwood limped in, looking shop-soiled.

'What-ho, Beefers,' he said. 'I just came to ask if I could borrow Bottles.'

He bent to where the animal lay on the hearth-rug and prodded it civilly in the lower ribs. Bottles waved a long tail in brief acknowledgment. He was a fine dog, though of uncertain breed. His mother had been a popular local belle with a good deal of sex-appeal, and the question of his paternity was one that would have set a Genealogical College pursing its lips perplexedly.

'Oh, hullo, Freddie,' said the Rev. Rupert.

The young Pastor of Souls spoke in an absent voice. He was frowning. It is a singular fact – and one that just goes to show what sort of a world this is – that of the four foreheads introduced so far to the reader of this chronicle, three have been corrugated with care. And, if girls had consciences, Gertrude's would have been corrugated, too – giving us a full hand.

'Take a chair,' said the Rev. Rupert.

'I'll take a sofa,' said Freddie, doing so. 'Feeling a bit used up. I had to hoof it all the way over.'

'What's happened to your car?'

'Gertrude took it to drive Watkins to Shrewsbury.'

The Rev. Rupert sat for a while in thought. His face, which was large and red, had a drawn look. Even the massive body which had so nearly won him a Rowing Blue at Oxford gave the illusion of having shrunk. So marked was his distress that even Freddie noticed it.

'Something up, Beefers?' he inquired.

For answer the Rev. Rupert Bingham extended a ham-like hand which held a letter. It was written in a sprawling, girlish handwriting.

'Read that.'

'From Gertrude?'

'Yes. It came this morning. Well?'

Freddie completed his perusal and handed the document back. He was concerned.

'I think it's the bird,' he said.

'So do I.'

'It's long,' said Freddie, 'and it's rambling. It is full of stuff about "Are we sure?" and "Do we know our own minds?" and "Wouldn't it be better, perhaps?" But I think it is the bird.'

'I can't understand it.'

Freddie sat up.

'I can,' he said. 'Now I see what Aunt Georgiana was drooling about. Her fears were well founded. The snake Watkins has stolen Gertrude from you.'

'You think Gertrude's in love with Watkins?'

'I do. And I'll tell you why. He's a yowler, and girls always fall for yowlers. They have a glamour.'

'I've never noticed Watkins's glamour. He has always struck me as a bit of a weed.'

'Weed he may be, Beefers, but, none the less, he knows how to do his stuff. I don't know why it should be, but there is a certain type of tenor voice which acts on girls like catnip on a cat.'

The Rev. Rupert breathed heavily.

'I see,' he said.

'The whole trouble is, Beefers,' proceeded Freddie, 'that Watkins is romantic and you're not. Your best friend couldn't call you romantic. Solid worth, yes. Romance, no.'

'So it doesn't seem as if there was much to be done about it?' Freddie reflected.

'Couldn't you manage to show yourself in a romantic light?'

'How?'

'Well – stop a runaway horse.'

'Where's the horse?'

''Myes,' said Freddie. 'That's by way of being the difficulty, isn't it? The horse – where is it?'

There was silence for some moments.

'Well, be that as it may,' said Freddie. 'Can I borrow Bottles?'

'What for?'

'Purposes of demonstration. I wish to exhibit him to my Aunt Georgiana, so that she may see for herself to what heights of robustness a dog can rise when fed sedulously on Donaldson's Dog-Joy. I'm having a lot of trouble with that woman, Beefers. I try all the artifices which win to success in salesmanship, and they don't. But I have a feeling that if she could see Bottles and poke him in the ribs and note the firm, muscular flesh, she might drop. At any rate, it's worth trying. I'll take him along, may I?'

'All right.'

'Thanks. And, in regard to your little trouble, I'll be giving it my best attention. You're looking in after dinner to-night?'

'I suppose so,' said the Rev. Rupert moodily.

The information that her impressionable daughter had gone off to roam the country-side in a two-seater car with the perilous Watkins had come as a grievous blow to Lady Alcester. As she sat on the terrace, an hour after Freddie had begun the weary homeward trek from Matchingham Vicarage, her heart was sorely laden.

The Airedale had wandered away upon some private ends, but the Peke lay slumbering in her lap. She envied it its calm detachment. To her the future looked black and the air seemed heavy with doom.

Only one thing mitigated her depression. Her nephew Frederick had disappeared. Other prominent local pests were present, such as flies and gnats, but not Frederick. The grounds of Blandings Castle appeared to be quite free from him.

And then even this poor consolation was taken from the stricken woman. Limping a little, as if his shoes hurt him, the Hon. Freddie came round the corner of the shrubbery, headed in her direction. He was accompanied by something having the outward aspect of a dog.

'What-ho, Aunt Georgiana!'

'Well, Freddie?' sighed Lady Alcester resignedly.

The Peke, opening one eye, surveyed the young man for a moment, seemed to be debating within itself the advisability of barking, came apparently to the conclusion that it was too hot, and went to sleep again.

'This is Bottles,' said Freddie.

'Who?'

'Bottles. The animal I touched on some little time back. Note the well-muscled frame.'

'I never saw such a mongrel in my life.'

'Kind hearts are more than coronets,' said Freddie. 'The point at issue is not this dog's pedigree, which, I concede, is not all Burke and Debrett, but his physique. Reared exclusively on a diet of Donaldson's Dog-Joy, he goes his way with his chin up, frank and fearless. I should like you, if you don't mind, to come along to the stables and watch him among the rats. It will give you some idea.'

He would have spoken further, but at this point something occurred, as had happened during his previous sales talk, to mar the effect of Freddie's oratory.

The dog Bottles, during this conversation, had been roaming to and fro in the inquisitive manner customary with dogs who find themselves in strange territory. He had sniffed at trees. He had rolled on the turf. Now, returning to the centre of things, he observed for the first time that on the lap of the woman seated in the chair there lay a peculiar something.

What it was Bottles did not know. It appeared to be alive. A keen desire came upon him to solve this mystery. To keep the records straight, he advanced to the chair, thrust an inquiring nose against the object, and inhaled sharply.

The next moment, to his intense surprise, the thing had gone off like a bomb, had sprung to the ground, and was moving rapidly towards him.

Bottles did not hesitate. A rough-and-tumble with one of his peers he enjoyed. He, as it were, rolled it round his tongue and mixed it with his saliva. But this was different. He had never met a Pekingese before, and no one would have been more surprised than himself if he had been informed that this curious, fluffy thing was a dog. Himself, he regarded it as an Act of God, and, thoroughly unnerved, he raced three times round the lawn and tried to climb a tree. Failing in this endeavour, he fitted his ample tail if possible more firmly into its groove and vanished from the scene.

The astonishment of the Hon. Freddie Threepwood was only equalled by his chagrin. Lady Alcester had begun now to express her opinion of the incident, and her sneers, her jeers, her unveiled innuendoes were hard to bear. If, she said, the patrons of Donaldson's Dog-Joy allowed themselves to be chased off the map in this fashion by Pekingese, she was glad she had never been weak enough to be persuaded to try it.

'It's lucky,' said Lady Alcester in her hard, scoffing way, 'that Susan wasn't a rat. I suppose a rat would have given that mongrel of yours heart failure.'

'Bottles,' said Freddie stiffly, 'is particularly sound on rats. I think, in common fairness, you ought to step to the stables and give him a chance of showing himself in a true light.'

'I have seen quite enough, thank you.'

'You won't come to the stables and watch him dealing with rats?'

'I will not.'

'In that case,' said Freddie sombrely, 'there is nothing more to be said. I suppose I may as well take him back to the Vicarage.'

'What Vicarage?'

'Matchingham Vicarage.'

'Was that Rupert's dog?'

'Of course it was.'

'Then have you seen Rupert?'

'Of course I have.'

'Did you warn him? About Mr Watkins?'

'It was too late to warn him. He had had a letter from Gertrude, giving him the raspberry.'

'What!'

'Well, she said Was he sure and Did they know their own minds, but you can take it from me that it was tantamount to the raspberry. Returning, however, to the topic of Bottles, Aunt Georgiana, I think you ought to take into consideration the fact that, in his recent encounter with the above Peke, he was undergoing a totally new experience and naturally did not appear at his best. I repeat once more that you should see him among the rats.'

'Oh, Freddie?'

'Hullo?'

'How can you babble about this wretched dog when Gertrude's whole future is at stake? It is simply vital that somehow she be cured of this dreadful infatuation...'

'Well, I'll have a word with her if you like, but, if you ask me, I think the evil has spread too far. Watkins has yowled himself into her very soul. However, I'll do my best. Excuse me, Aunt Georgiana.'

From a neighbouring bush the honest face of Bottles was protruding. He seemed to be seeking assurance that the All Clear had been blown.

It was at the hour of the ante-dinner cocktail that Freddie found his first opportunity of having the promised word with Gertrude. Your true salesman and go-getter is never beaten, and a sudden and brilliant idea for accomplishing the conversion of his Aunt Georgiana had come to him as he brushed his hair. He descended to the drawing-room with a certain jauntiness, and was reminded by the sight of Gertrude of his mission. The girl was seated at the piano, playing dreamy chords.

'I say,' said Freddie, 'a word with you, young Gertrude. What is all this bilge I hear about you and Beefers?'

The girl flushed.

'Have you seen Rupert?'

'I was closeted with him this afternoon. He told me all.'

'Oh?'

'He's feeling pretty low.'

'Oh?'

'Yes,' said Freddie, 'pretty low the poor old chap is feeling, and I don't blame him, with the girl he's engaged to rushing about the place getting infatuated with tenors. I never heard of such a thing, dash it! What do you see in this Watkins? Wherein lies his attraction? Certainly not in his ties. They're awful. And the same applies to his entire outfit. He looks as if he had bought his clothes off the peg at a second-hand gents' costumiers. And, as if that were not enough, he wears short, but distinct, side-whiskers. You aren't going to tell me that you're seriously considering chucking a sterling egg like old Beefers in favour of a whiskered warbler?'

There was a pause. Gertrude played more dreamy chords.

'I'm not going to discuss it,' she said. 'It's nothing to do with you.'

'Pardon me!' said Freddie. 'Excuse me! If you will throw your mind back to the time when Beefers was conducting his wooing, you may remember that I was the fellow who worked the whole thing. But for my resource and ingenuity you and the old bounder would never have got engaged. I regard myself, therefore, in the light of a guardian angel or something; and as such am entitled to probe the matter to its depths. Of course,' said Freddie, 'I know exactly how you're feeling. I see where you have made your fatal bloomer. This Watkins has cast his glamorous spell about you, and you're looking on Beefers as a piece of unromantic cheese. But mark this, girl . . .'

'I wish you wouldn't call me "girl."'

'Mark this, old prune,' amended Freddie. 'And mark it well. Beefers is tried, true and trusted. A man to be relied on. Whereas Watkins, if I have read those whiskers aright, is the sort of fellow who will jolly well let you down in a crisis. And then, when it's too late, you'll come moaning to me, weeping salt tears and saying, "Ah, why did I not know in time?" And I shall reply, "You unhappy little fathead...!"'

'Oh, go and sell your dog-biscuits, Freddie!'

Gertrude resumed her playing. Her mouth was set in an obstinate line. Freddie eyed her with disapproval.

'It's some taint in the blood,' he said. 'Inherited from female parent. Like your bally mother, you are constitutionally incapable of seeing reason. Pig-headed, both of you. Sell my dog-biscuits, you say? Ha! As if I hadn't boosted them to Aunt Georgiana till my lips cracked. And with what result? So far, none. But wait till to-night.'

'It is to-night.'

'I mean, wait till later on to-night. Watch my little experiment.'

'What little experiment?'

'Ah!'

'What do you mean, "Ah"?'

'Just "Ah!"' said Freddie.

The hour of the after-dinner coffee found Blandings Castle apparently an abode of peace. The superficial observer, peeping into the amber drawing-room through the French windows that led to the terrace, would have said that all was well with the inmates of this stately home of England. Lord Emsworth sat in a corner absorbed in a volume dealing with the treatment of pigs in sickness and in health. His sister, Lady Constance Keeble, was sewing. His other sister, Lady Alcester, was gazing at Gertrude. Gertrude was gazing at Orlo Watkins. And Orlo Watkins was gazing at the ceiling and singing in that crooning voice of his a song of Roses.

The Hon. Freddie Threepwood was not present. And that fact alone, if one may go by the views of his father, Lord

Emsworth, should have been enough to make a success of any party.

And yet beneath this surface of cosy peace troubled currents were running. Lady Alcester, gazing at Gertrude, found herself a prey to gloom. She did not like the way Gertrude was gazing at Orlo Watkins. Gertrude, for her part, as the result of her recent conversation with the Hon. Freddie, was experiencing twinges of remorse and doubt. Lady Constance was still ruffled from the effect of Lady Alcester's sisterly frankness that evening on the subject of the imbecility of hostesses who deliberately let Crooning Tenors loose in castles. And Lord Emsworth was in that state of peevish exasperation which comes to dreamy old gentlemen who, wishing to read of Pigs, find their concentration impaired by voices singing of Roses.

Only Orlo Watkins was happy. And presently he, too, was to join the ranks of gloom. For just as he started to let himself go and handle this song as a song should be handled, there came from the other side of the door the sound of eager barking. A dog seemed to be without. And, apart from the fact that he disliked and feared all dogs, a tenor resents competition.

The next moment the door had opened, and the Hon. Freddie Threepwood appeared. He carried a small sack, and was accompanied by Bottles, the latter's manner noticeably lacking in repose.

On the face of the Hon. Freddie, as he advanced into the room, there was that set, grim expression which is always seen on the faces of those who are about to put their fortune to the test, to win or lose it all. The Old Guard at Waterloo looked much the same. For Freddie had decided to stake all on a single throw.

Many young men in his position, thwarted by an aunt who resolutely declined to amble across to the stables and watch a dog redeem himself among the rats, would have resigned themselves sullenly to defeat. But Freddie was made of finer stuff.

'Aunt Georgiana,' he said, holding up the sack, at which Bottles was making agitated leaps, 'you refused to come to the stables this afternoon to watch this Donaldson's Dog-Joy-fed animal in action, so you have left me no alternative but to play the fixture on your own ground.'

Lord Emsworth glanced up from his book.

'Frederick, stop gibbering. And take that dog out of here.'

Lady Constance glanced up from her sewing.

'Frederick, if you are coming in, come in and sit down. And take that dog out of here.'

Lady Alcester, glancing up from Gertrude, exhibited in even smaller degree the kindly cordiality which might have been expected from an aunt.

'Oh, do go away, Freddie! You're a perfect nuisance. And take that dog out of here.'

The Hon. Freddie, with a noble look of disdain, ignored them all.

'I have here, Aunt Georgiana,' he said, 'a few simple rats. If you will kindly step out on to the terrace I shall be delighted to give a demonstration which should, I think, convince even your stubborn mind.'

The announcement was variously received by the various members of the company. Lady Alcester screamed. Lady Constance sprang for the bell. Lord Emsworth snorted. Orlo Watkins blanched and retired behind Gertrude. And Gertrude, watching him blench, seeing him retire, tightened her lips. A country-bred girl, she was on terms of easy familiarity with rats, and this evidence of alarm in one whom she had set on a pedestal disquieted her.

The door opened and Beach entered. He had come in pursuance of his regular duties to remove the coffee cups, but arriving, found other tasks assigned to him.

'Beach!' The voice was that of Lady Constance. 'Take away those rats.'

'Rats, m'lady?'

'Take that sack away from Mr Frederick!'

Beach understood. If he was surprised at the presence of the younger son of the house in the amber drawing-room with a sack of rats in his hand, he gave no indication of the fact. With a murmured apology, he secured the sack and started to withdraw. It was not, strictly, his place to carry rats, but a good butler is always ready to give and take. Only so can the amenities of a large country house be preserved.

'And don't drop the dashed things,' urged Lord Emsworth.

'Very good, m'lord.'

The Hon. Freddie had flung himself into a chair, and was sitting with his chin cupped in his hands, a bleak look on his face. To an ardent young go-getter these tyrannous actions in restraint of trade are hard to bear.

Lord Emsworth returned to his book.

Lady Constance returned to her sewing.

Lady Alcester returned to her thoughts.

At the piano Orlo Watkins was endeavouring to justify the motives which had led him a few moments before to retire prudently behind Gertrude.

'I hate rats,' he said. 'They jar upon me.'

'Oh?' said Gertrude.

'I'm not afraid of them, of course, but they give me the creeps.'

'Oh?' said Gertrude.

There was an odd look in her eyes. Of what was she thinking, this idealistic girl? Was it of the evening, a few short weeks before, when, suddenly encountering a beastly bat in the gloaming, she had found in the Rev. Rupert Bingham a sturdy and intrepid protector? Was she picturing the Rev. Rupert as she had seen him then – gallant, fearless, cleaving the air with long sweeps of his clerical hat, encouraging her the while with word and gesture?

Apparently so, for a moment later she spoke.

'How are you on bats?'

'Rats?'

'Bats.'

'Oh, bats?'

'Are you afraid of bats?'

'I don't like bats,' admitted Orlo Watkins.

Then, dismissing the subject, he reseated himself at the piano and sang of June and the scent of unseen flowers.

Of all the little group in the amber drawing-room, only one member has now been left unaccounted for.

An animal of slow thought-processes, the dog Bottles had not at first observed what was happening to the sack. At the moment of its transference from the custody of Freddie to that of Beach, he had been engaged in sniffing at the leg of a chair. It was only as the door began to close that he became aware of the bereavement that threatened him. He bounded forward with a passionate cry, but it was too late. He found himself faced by unyielding wood. And when he started to scratch vehemently on this wood, a sharp pain assailed him. A book on the treatment of Pigs in sickness and in health, superbly aimed, had struck him in the small of the back. Then, for a space, he, like the Hon. Freddie Threepwood, his social sponsor, sat down and mourned.

'Take that beastly, blasted, infernal dog out of here,' cried Lord Emsworth.

Freddie rose listlessly.

'It's old Beefers' dog,' he said. 'Beefers will be here at any moment. We can hand the whole conduct of the affair over to him.'

Gertrude started.

'Is Rupert coming here to-night?'

'Said he would,' responded Freddie, and passed from the scene. He had had sufficient of his flesh and blood and was indisposed to linger. It was his intention to pop down to Market Blandings in his two-seater, soothe his wounded sensibilities, so far as they were capable of being soothed, with a visit to the local motion-picture house, look in at the Emsworth Arms for a spot of beer, and then home to bed, to forget.

Gertrude had fallen into a reverie. Her fair young face was overcast. A feeling of embarrassment had come upon her. When she had written that letter and posted it on the previous night, she had not foreseen that the Rev. Rupert would be calling so soon.

'I didn't know Rupert was coming to-night,' she said.

'Oh, yes,' said Lady Alcester brightly.

'Like a lingering tune, my whole life through, 'twill haunt me for EV-ah, that night in June with you-oo,' sang Orlo Watkins.

And Gertrude, looking at him, was aware for the first time of a curious sensation of not being completely in harmony with this young whiskered man. She wished he would stop singing. He prevented her thinking.

Bottles, meanwhile, had resumed his explorations. Dogs are philosophers. They soon forget. They do not waste time regretting the might-have-beens. Adjusting himself with composure to the changed conditions, Bottles moved to and fro in a spirit of affable inquiry. He looked at Lord Emsworth, considered the idea of seeing how he smelt, thought better of it, and advanced towards the French windows. Something was rustling in the bushes outside, and it seemed to him that this might as well be looked into before he went and breathed on Lady Constance's leg.

He had almost reached his objective, when Lady Alcester's Airedale, who had absented himself from the room some time before in order to do a bit of bone-burying, came bustling in, ready, his business completed, to resume the social whirl.

Seeing Bottles, he stopped abruptly.

Both then began a slow and cautious forward movement, of a crab-like kind. Arriving at close quarters, they stopped again. Their nostrils twitched a little. They rolled their eyes. And to the ears of those present there came, faintly at first, a low, throaty sound, like the far-off gargling of an octogenarian with bronchial trouble.

This rose to a sudden crescendo. And the next moment hostilities had begun.

In underrating Bottles's qualities and scoffing at him as a fighting force, Lady Alcester had made an error. Capable though he was of pusillanimity in the presence of female Pekingese, there was nothing of the weakling about this sterling animal. He had cleaned up every dog in Much Matchingham and was spoken of on all sides – from the Blue Boar in the High Street to the distant Cow and Caterpillar on the Shrewsbury Road – as an ornament to the Vicarage and a credit to his master's Cloth.

On the present occasion, moreover, he was strengthened by the fact that he felt he had right on his side. In spite of a certain coldness on the part of the Castle circle and a soreness about the ribs where the book on Pigs and their treatment had found its billet, there seems to be no doubt that Bottles had by this time become thoroughly convinced that this drawing-room was his official home. And, feeling that all these delightful people were relying on him to look after their interests and keep alien and subversive influences at a distance, he advanced with a bright willingness to the task of ejecting this intruder.

Nor was the Airedale disposed to hold back. He, too, was no stranger to the ring. In Hyde Park, where, when at his London residence, he took his daily airing, he had met all comers and acquitted himself well. Dogs from Mayfair, dogs from Bays-water, dogs from as far afield as the Brompton Road and West Kensington had had experience of the stuff of which he was made. Bottles reminded him a little of an animal from Pont Street, over whom he had once obtained a decision on the banks of the Serpentine; and he joined battle with an easy confidence,

The reactions of a country-house party to an after-dinner dog-fight in the drawing-room always vary considerably accord-ing to the individual natures of its members. Lady Alcester, whose long association with the species had made her a sort of honorary dog herself, remained tranquil. She surveyed the proceedings with unruffled equanimity through a tortoise-shell-rimmed lorgnette. Her chief emotion was one of surprise at the fact that Bottles was unquestionably getting the better of the exchanges. She liked his footwork. Impressed, she was obliged to admit that, if this was the sort of battler it turned out, there must be something in Donaldson's Dog-Joy after all.

The rest of the audience were unable to imitate her noncha-lance. The two principals were giving that odd illusion, custom-ary on these occasions, of being all over the place at the same time: and the demeanour of those in the ring-side seats was frankly alarmed. Lady Constance had backed against the wall, from which position she threw a futile cushion. Lord Emsworth, in his corner, was hunting feebly for ammunition and wishing that he had not dropped the pince-nez, without which he was no sort of use in a crisis.

And Gertrude? Gertrude was staring at Orlo Watkins, who, with a resource and presence of mind unusual in one so young, had just climbed on top of a high cabinet containing china.

His feet were on a level with her eyes, and she saw that they were feet of clay.

And it was at this moment, when a girl stood face to face with her soul, that the door opened.

'Mr Bingham,' announced Beach.

Men of the physique of the Rev. Rupert Bingham are not as a rule quick thinkers. From earliest youth, the Rev. Rupert had run to brawn rather than brain. But even the dullest-witted person could have told, on crossing that threshold, that there was a dog-fight going on. Beefy Bingham saw it in a flash, and he acted promptly.

There are numerous methods of stopping these painful affairs. Some advocate squirting water, others prefer to sprinkle pepper. Good results may be obtained, so one school of thought claims, by holding a lighted match under the nearest nose. Beefy Bingham was impatient of these subtleties.

To Beefy all this was old stuff. Ever since he had been given his Cure of Souls, half his time, it sometimes seemed to him, had been spent in hauling Bottles away from the throats of the dogs of his little flock. Experience had given him a technique. He placed one massive hand on the neck of the Airedale, the other on the neck of Bottles, and pulled. There was a rending sound, and they came apart.

'Rupert!' cried Gertrude.

Gazing at him, she was reminded of the heroes of old. And few could have denied that he made a strangely impressive figure, this large young man, standing there with bulging eyes and a gyrating dog in each hand. He looked like a statue of Right triumphing over Wrong. You couldn't place it exactly, because it was so long since you had read the book, but he reminded you of something out of 'Pilgrim's Progress.'

So, at least, thought Gertrude. To Gertrude it was as if the scales had fallen from her eyes and she had wakened from some fevered dream. Could it be she, she was asking herself, who had turned from this noble youth and strayed towards one who, though on the evidence he seemed to have a future before him as an Alpine climber, was otherwise so contemptible?

'Rupert!' said Gertrude.

Beefy Bingham had now completed his masterly campaign. He had thrown Bottles out of the window and shut it behind him. He had dropped the Airedale to the carpet, where it now sat, licking itself in a ruminative way. He had produced a handkerchief and was passing it over his vermilion brow.

'Oh, Rupert!' said Gertrude, and flung herself into his arms.

The Rev. Rupert said nothing. On such occasions your knowledgeable Vicar does not waste words.

Nor did Orlo Watkins speak. He had melted away. Perhaps, perched on his eyrie, he had seen in Gertrude's eyes the look which, when seen in the eyes of a girl by any interested party, automatically induces the latter to go to his room and start packing, in readiness for the telegram which he will receive on the morrow, summoning him back to London on urgent business. At any rate, he had melted.

It was late that night when the Hon. Freddie Threepwood returned to the home of his fathers. Moodily undressing, he was surprised to hear a knock on the door.

His Aunt Georgiana entered. On her face was the unmistakable look of a mother whose daughter has seen the light and will shortly be marrying a deserving young clergyman with a bachelor uncle high up in the shipping business.

'Freddie,' said Lady Alcester, 'you know that stuff you're always babbling about – I've forgotten its name...'

'Donaldson's Dog-Joy,' said Freddie. 'It may be obtained either in the small (or one-and-threepenny) packets or in the half-crown (or large) size. A guarantee goes with each purchase. Unique in its health-giving properties...'

'I'll take two tons to start with,' said Lady Alcester.

The day on which Lawlessness reared its ugly head at Blandings Castle was one of singular beauty. The sun shone down from a sky of cornflower blue, and what one would really like would be to describe in leisurely detail the ancient battlements, the smooth green lawns, the rolling parkland, the majestic trees, the well-bred bees and the gentlemanly birds on which it shone.

But those who read thrillers are an impatient race. They chafe at scenic rhapsodies and want to get on to the rough stuff. When, they ask, did the dirty work start? Who were mixed up in it? Was there blood, and, if so, how much? And – most particularly – where was everybody and what was everybody doing at whatever time it was? The chronicler who wishes to grip must supply this information at the earliest possible moment.

The wave of crime, then, which was to rock one of Shropshire's stateliest homes to its foundations broke out towards the middle of a fine summer afternoon, and the persons involved in it were disposed as follows:

Clarence, ninth Earl of Emsworth, the castle's owner and overlord, was down in the potting-shed, in conference with Angus McAllister, his head gardener, on the subject of sweet peas.

His sister, Lady Constance, was strolling on the terrace with a swarthy young man in spectacles, whose name was Rupert Baxter and who had at one time been Lord Emsworth's private secretary.

Beach, the butler, was in a deck-chair outside the back premises of the house, smoking a cigar and reading Chapter Sixteen of *The Man With The Missing Toe.*

George, Lord Emsworth's grandson, was prowling through the shrubbery with the airgun which was his constant companion.

Jane, his lordship's niece, was in the summer-house by the lake.

And the sun shone serenely down – on, as we say, the lawns, the battlements, the trees, the bees, the best type of bird and the rolling parkland.

Presently Lord Emsworth left the potting-shed and started to wander towards the house. He had never felt happier. All day his mood had been one of perfect contentment and tranquillity, and for once in a way Angus McAllister had done nothing to disturb it. Too often, when you tried to reason with that human mule, he had a way of saying 'Mphm' and looking Scotch and then saying 'Grmph' and looking Scotch again, and after that just fingering his beard and looking Scotch without speaking, which was intensely irritating to a sensitive employer. But this afternoon Hollywood yes-men could have taken his correspondence course, and Lord Emsworth had none of that uneasy feeling, which usually came to him on these occasions, that the moment his back was turned his own sound, statesmanlike policies would be shelved and some sort of sweet pea New Deal put into practice as if he had never spoken a word.

He was humming as he approached the terrace. He had his programme all mapped out. For perhaps an hour, till the day had cooled off a little, he would read a Pig book in the library. After that he would go and take a sniff at a rose or two and possibly do a bit of snailing. These mild pleasures were all his simple soul demanded. He wanted nothing more. Just the quiet life, with nobody to fuss him.

And now that Baxter had left, he reflected buoyantly, nobody did fuss him. There had, he dimly recalled, been some sort of trouble a week or so back – something about some man his niece Jane wanted to marry and his sister Constance didn't want her to marry – but that had apparently all blown over. And even when the thing had been at its height, even when the air had been shrill with women's voices and Connie had kept popping out at him and saying 'Do *listen*, Clarence!' he had always been able to reflect that, though all this was pretty unpleasant, there was nevertheless a bright side. He had ceased to be the employer of Rupert Baxter.

There is a breed of granite-faced, strong-jawed business man to whom Lord Emsworth's attitude towards Rupert Baxter would have seemed frankly inexplicable. To these Titans a private secretary is simply a Hey-you, a Hi-there, a mere puppet to be ordered hither and thither at will. The trouble with Lord Emsworth was that it was he and not his secretary who had been the puppet. Their respective relations had always been those of a mild reigning monarch and the pushing young devil who has taken on the dictatorship. For years, until he had mercifully tendered his resignation to join an American named Jevons, Baxter had worried Lord Emsworth, bossed him, bustled him, had always been after him to do things and remember things and sign things. Never a moment's peace. Yes, it was certainly delightful to think that Baxter had departed for ever. His going had relieved this Garden of Eden of its one resident snake.

Still humming, Lord Emsworth reached the terrace. A moment later, the melody had died on his lips and he was rocking back on his heels as if he had received a solid punch on the nose.

'God bless my soul!' he ejaculated, shaken to the core.

His pince-nez, as always happened when he was emotionally stirred, had leaped from their moorings. He recovered them and put them on again, hoping feebly that the ghastly sight he had seen would prove to have been an optical illusion. But no. However much he blinked, he could not blink away the fact that the man over there talking to his sister Constance was Rupert Baxter in person. He stood gaping at him with a horror which would have been almost excessive if the other had returned from the tomb.

Lady Constance was smiling brightly, as women so often do when they are in the process of slipping something raw over on their nearest and dearest.

'Here is Mr Baxter, Clarence.'

'Ah,' said Lord Emsworth.

'He is touring England on his motor-bicycle, and finding himself in these parts, of course, he looked us up.'

'Ah,' said Lord Emsworth.

He spoke dully, for his soul was heavy with foreboding. It was all very well for Connie to say that Baxter was touring England, thus giving the idea that in about five minutes the man would leap on his motor-bicycle and dash off to some spot a hundred miles away. He knew his sister. She was plotting. Always ardently pro-Baxter, she was going to try to get Blandings Castle's leading incubus back into office again. Lord Emsworth would have been prepared to lay the odds on this in the most liberal spirit. So he said 'Ah.'

The monosyllable, taken in conjunction with the sagging of her brother's jaw and the glare of agony behind his pince-nez, caused Lady Constance's lips to tighten. A disciplinary light came into her fine eyes. She looked like a female lion-tamer about to assert her personality with one of the troupe.

'Clarence!' she said sharply. She turned to her companion. 'Would you excuse me for a moment, Mr Baxter. There is something I want to talk to Lord Emsworth about.'

She drew the pallid peer aside, and spoke with sharp rebuke. 'Just like a stuck pig!'

'Eh?' said Lord Emsworth. His mind had been wandering, as it so often did. The magic word brought it back. 'Pigs? What about pigs?'

'I was saying that you were looking like a stuck pig. You might at least have asked Mr Baxter how he was.'

'I could see how he was. What's he doing here?'

'I told you what he was doing here.'

'But how does he come to be touring England on motor-bicycles? I thought he was working for an American fellow named something or other.'

'He has left Mr Jevons.'

'What!'

'Yes. Mr Jevons had to return to America, and Mr Baxter did not want to leave England.'

Lord Emsworth reeled. Jevons had been his sheet anchor. He had never met that genial Chicagoan, but he had always thought kindly and gratefully of him, as one does of some great doctor who has succeeded in insulating and confining a disease germ.

'You mean the chap's out of a job?' he cried aghast.

'Yes. And it could not have happened at a more fortunate time, because something has got to be done about George.'

'Who's George?'

'You have a grandson of that name,' explained Lady Constance with the sweet, frozen patience which she so often used when conversing with her brother. 'Your heir, Bosham, if you recollect, has two sons, James and George. George, the younger, is spending his summer holidays here. You may have noticed him about. A boy of twelve with auburn hair and freckles.'

'Oh, George? You mean George? Yes, I know George. He's my grandson. What about him?'

'He is completely out of hand. Only yesterday he broke another window with that airgun of his.'

'He needs a mother's care?' Lord Emsworth was vague, but he had an idea that that was the right thing to say.

'He needs a tutor's care, and I am glad to say that Mr Baxter has very kindly consented to accept the position.'

'What!'

'Yes. It is all settled. His things are at the Emsworth Arms, and I am sending down for them.'

Lord Emsworth sought feverishly for arguments which would quash this frightful scheme.

'But he can't be a tutor if he's galumphing all over England on a motor-bicycle.'

'I had not overlooked that point. He will stop galumphing over England on a motor-bicycle.'

'But—'

'It will be a wonderful solution of a problem which was becoming more difficult every day. Mr Baxter will keep George in order. He is so firm.'

She turned away, and Lord Emsworth resumed his progress towards the library.

It was a black moment for the ninth Earl. His worst fears had been realized. He knew just what all this meant. On one of his rare visits to London he had once heard an extraordinarily vivid phrase which had made a deep impression upon him. He had been taking his after-luncheon coffee at the Senior Conservative Club and some fellows in an adjoining nest of arm-chairs had started a political discussion, and one of them had said about something or other that, mark his words, it was the 'thin end of the wedge.' He recognized what was happening now as the thin end of the wedge. From Baxter as a temporary tutor to Baxter as a permanent secretary would, he felt, be so short a step that the contemplation of it chilled him to the bone.

A short-sighted man whose pince-nez have gone astray at the very moment when vultures are gnawing at his bosom seldom guides his steps carefully. Anyone watching Lord Emsworth totter blindly across the terrace would have foreseen that he would shortly collide with something, the only point open to speculation being with what he would collide. This proved to be a small boy with ginger hair and freckles who emerged abruptly from the shrubbery carrying an airgun.

'Coo!' said the small boy. 'Sorry, grandpapa.'

Lord Emsworth recovered his pince-nez and, having adjusted them on the old spot, glared balefully.

'George! Why the dooce don't you look where you're going?'

'Sorry, grandpapa.'

'You might have injured me severely.'

'Sorry, grandpapa.'

'Be more careful another time.'

'Okay, big boy.'

'And don't call me "big boy."'

'Right ho, grandpapa. I say,' said George, shelving the topic, 'who's the bird talking to Aunt Connie?'

He pointed – a vulgarism which a good tutor would have corrected – and Lord Emsworth, following the finger, winced as his eye rested once more upon Rupert Baxter. The secretary – already Lord Emsworth had mentally abandoned the qualifying 'ex' – was gazing out over the rolling parkland, and it seemed to his lordship that his gaze was proprietorial. Rupert Baxter, flashing his spectacles over the grounds of Blandings Castle, wore – or so it appeared to Lord Emsworth – the smug air of some ruthless monarch of old surveying conquered territory.

'That is Mr Baxter,' he replied.

'Looks a bit of a blister,' said George critically.

The expression was new to Lord Emsworth, but he recognized it at once as the ideal description of Rupert Baxter. His heart warmed to the little fellow, and he might quite easily at this moment have given him sixpence.

'Do you think so?' he said lovingly.

'What's he doing here?'

Lord Emsworth felt a pang. It seemed brutal to dash the sunshine from the life of this admirable boy. Yet somebody had got to tell him.

'He is going to be your tutor.'

'Tutor?'

The word was a cry of agony forced from the depths of the boy's soul. A stunned sense that all the fundamental decencies of life were being outraged had swept over George. His voice was thick with emotion.

'Tutor?' he cried. '*Tew*-tor? Ter-YEW-tor? In the middle of the summer holidays? What have I got to have a tutor for in the middle of the summer holidays? I do call this a bit off. I mean, in the middle of the summer holidays. Why do I want a tutor? I mean to say, in the middle of . . .'

He would have spoken at greater length, for he had much to say on the subject, but at this point Lady Constance's voice, musical but imperious, interrupted his flow of speech.

'Gee-orge.'

'Coo! Right in the middle—'

'Come here, George. I want you to meet Mr Baxter.'

'Coo!' muttered the stricken child again and, frowning darkly, slouched across the terrace. Lord Emsworth proceeded to the library, a tender pity in his heart for this boy who by his crisp summing-up of Rupert Baxter had revealed himself so kindred a spirit. He knew just how George felt. It was not always easy to get anything into Lord Emsworth's head, but he had grasped the substance of his grandson's complaint unerringly. George, about to have a tutor in the middle of the summer holidays, did not want one.

Sighing a little, Lord Emsworth reached the library and found his book.

There were not many books which at a time like this could have diverted Lord Emsworth's mind from what weighed upon it, but this one did. It was Whiffle on *The Care Of The Pig* and, buried in its pages, he forgot everything. The chapter he was reading was that noble one about swill and bran-mash, and it took him completely out of the world, so much so that when some twenty minutes later the door suddenly burst open it was as if a bomb had been exploded under his nose. He dropped Whiffle and sat panting. Then, although his pince-nez had followed routine by flying off, he was able by some subtle instinct to sense that the intruder was his sister Constance, and an observation beginning with the words 'Good God, Connie!' had begun to leave his lips, when she cut it short.

'Clarence,' she said, and it was plain that her nervous system, like his, was much shaken, 'the most dreadful thing has happened!'

'Eh?'

'That man is here.'

'What man?'

'That man of Jane's. The man I told you about.'

'What man did you tell me about?'

Lady Constance seated herself. She would have preferred to have been able to do without tedious explanations, but long association with her brother had taught her that his was a memory that had to be refreshed. She embarked, accordingly, on these explanations, speaking wearily, like a schoolmistress to one of the duller members of her class.

'The man I told you about – certainly not less than a hundred times – was a man Jane met in the spring, when she went to stay with her friends the Leighs in Devonshire. She had a silly flirtation with him, which, of course, she insisted on magnifying into a great romance. She kept saying they were engaged. And he hasn't a penny. Nor prospects. Nor, so I gathered from Jane, a position.'

Lord Emsworth interrupted at this point to put a question.

'Who,' he asked courteously, 'is Jane?'

Lady Constance quivered a little.

'Oh, Clarence! Your niece Jane.'

'Oh, my *niece* Jane? Ah! Yes. Yes, of course. My niece Jane. Yes, of course, to be sure. My—'

'Clarence, please! For pity's sake! Do stop doddering and listen to me. For once in your life I want you to be firm.'

'Be what?'

'Firm. Put your foot down.'

'How do you mean?'

'About Jane. I had been hoping that she had got over this ridiculous infatuation – she has seemed perfectly happy and contented all this time – but no. Apparently they have been corresponding regularly, and now the man is here.'

'Here?'

'Yes.'

'Where?' asked Lord Emsworth, gazing in an interested manner about the room.

'He arrived last night and is staying in the village. I found out by the merest accident. I happened to ask George if he had seen Jane, because I wanted Mr Baxter to meet her, and he said he had met her going towards the lake. So I went down to the lake, and there I discovered her with a young man in a tweed coat and flannel knickerbockers. They were kissing one another in the summer-house.'

Lord Emsworth clicked his tongue.

'Ought to have been out in the sunshine,' he said, disapprovingly.

Lady Constance raised her foot quickly, but instead of kicking her brother on the shin merely tapped the carpet with it. Blood will tell.

'Jane was defiant. I think she must be off her head. She insisted that she was going to marry this man. And, as I say, not only has he not a penny, but he is apparently out of work.'

'What sort of work does he do?'

'I gather that he has been a land-agent on an estate in Devonshire.'

'It all comes back to me,' said Lord Emsworth. 'I remember now. This must be the man Jane was speaking to me about yesterday. Of course, yes. She asked me to give him Simmons's job. Simmons is retiring next month. Good fellow,' said Lord Emsworth sentimentally. 'Been here for years and years. I shall be sorry to lose him. Bless my soul, it won't seem like the same place without old Simmons. Still,' he said, brightening, for he was a man who could make the best of things, 'no doubt this new chap will turn out all right. Jane seems to think highly of him.'

Lady Constance had risen slowly from her chair. There was incredulous horror on her face.

'Clarence! You are not telling me that you have promised this man Simmons's place?'

'Eh? Yes, I have. Why not?'

'Why not! Do you realize that directly he gets it he will marry Jane?'

'Well, why shouldn't he? Very nice girl. Probably make him a good wife.'

Lady Constance struggled with her feelings for a space.

'Clarence,' she said, 'I am going out now to find Jane. I shall tell her that you have thought it over and changed your mind.'

'What about?'

'Giving this man Simmons's place.'

'But I haven't.'

'Yes, you have.'

And so, Lord Emsworth discovered as he met her eye, he had. It often happened that way after he and Connie had talked a thing over. But he was not pleased about it.

'But, Connie, dash it all—'

'We will not discuss it any more, Clarence.'

Her eye played upon him. Then she moved to the door and was gone.

Alone at last, Lord Emsworth took up his Whiffle on *The Care Of The Pig* in the hope that it might, as had happened before, bring calm to the troubled spirit. It did, and he was absorbed in it when the door opened once more.

His niece Jane stood on the threshold.

Lord Emsworth's niece Jane was the third prettiest girl in Shropshire. In her general appearance she resembled a dewy rose, and it might have been thought that Lord Emsworth, who yielded to none in his appreciation of roses, would have felt his heart leap up at the sight of her.

This was not the case. His heart did leap, but not up. He was a man with certain definite views about roses. He preferred them without quite such tight lips and determined chins. And he did not like them to look at him as if he were something slimy and horrible which they had found under a flat stone.

The wretched man was now fully conscious of his position. Under the magic spell of Whiffle he had been able to thrust from his mind for awhile the thought of what Jane was going to say when she heard the bad news; but now, as she started to advance slowly into the room in that sinister, purposeful way characteristic of so many of his female relations, he realized what he was in for, and his soul shrank into itself like a salted snail.

Jane, he could not but remember, was the daughter of his sister Charlotte, and many good judges considered Lady Charlotte a tougher egg even than Lady Constance, or her younger sister, Lady Julia. He still quivered at some of the things Charlotte had said to him in her time; and, eyeing Jane apprehensively, he saw no reason for supposing that she had not inherited quite a good deal of the maternal fire.

The girl came straight to the point. Her mother, Lord Emsworth recalled, had always done the same.

'I should like an explanation, Uncle Clarence.'

Lord Emsworth cleared his throat unhappily.

'Explanation, my dear?'

'Explanation was what I said.'

'Oh, explanation? Ah, yes. Er – what about?'

'You know jolly well what about. That agent job. Aunt Constance says you've changed your mind. Have you?'

'Er...Ah...Well...'

'Have you?'

'Ah...Well...Er...'

'HAVE you?'

'Well...Er...Ah...Yes.'

'Worm!' said Jane. 'Miserable, crawling, cringing, gelatine-backboned worm!'

Lord Emsworth, though he had been expecting something along these lines, quivered as if he had been harpooned.

'That,' he said, attempting a dignity which he was far from feeling, 'is not a very nice thing to say...'

'If you only knew the things I would like to say! I'm holding myself in. So you've changed your mind, have you? Ha! Does a sacred promise mean nothing to you, Uncle Clarence? Does a girl's whole life's happiness mean nothing to you? I never would have believed that you could have been such a blighter.'

'I am not a blighter.'

'Yes, you are. You're a life-blighter. You're trying to blight my life. Well, you aren't going to do it. Whatever happens, I mean to marry George.'

Blandings Castle

Lord Emsworth was genuinely surprised.

'Marry George? But Connie told me you were in love with this fellow you met in Devonshire.'

'His name is George Abercrombie.'

'Oh, ah?' said Lord Emsworth, enlightened. 'Bless my soul, I thought you meant my grandson George, and it puzzled me. Because you couldn't marry him, of course. He's your brother or cousin or something. Besides, he's too young for you. What would George be? Ten? Eleven?'

He broke off. A reproachful look had hit him like a shell.

'Uncle Clarence!'

'My dear?'

'Is this a time for drivelling?'

'My dear!'

'Well, is it? Look in your heart and ask yourself. Here I am, with everybody spitting on their hands and dashing about trying to ruin my life's whole happiness, and instead of being kind and understanding and sympathetic you start talking rot about young George.'

'I was only saying—'

'I heard what you were saying, and it made me sick. You really must be the most callous man that ever lived. I can't understand you of all people behaving like this, Uncle Clarence. I always thought you were fond of me.'

'I am fond of you.'

'It doesn't look like it. Flinging yourself into this foul conspiracy to wreck my life.'

Lord Emsworth remembered a good one.

'I have your best interests at heart, my dear.'

It did not go very well. A distinct sheet of flame shot from the girl's eyes.

'What do you mean, my best interests? The way Aunt Constance talks, and the way you are backing her up, anyone would think that George was someone in a straw hat and a scarlet cummerbund that I'd picked up on the pier at Blackpool. The Abercrombies are one of the oldest families in Devonshire. They date back to the Conquest, and they practically ran the Crusades. When your ancestors were staying at home on the plea of war work of national importance and wangling jobs at the base, the Abercrombies were out fighting the Paynim.'

'I was at school with a boy named Abercrombie,' said Lord Emsworth musingly.

'I hope he kicked you. No, no, I don't mean that. I'm sorry. The one thing I'm trying to do is to keep this little talk free of – what's the word?'

Lord Emsworth said he did not know.

'Acrimony. I want to be calm and cool and sensible. Honestly, Uncle Clarence, you would love George. You'll be a sap if you give him the bird without seeing him. He's the most wonderful man on earth. He got into the last eight at Wimbledon this year.'

'Did he, indeed? Last eight what?'

'And there isn't anything he doesn't know about running an estate. The very first thing he said when he came into the park was that a lot of the timber wanted seeing to badly.'

'Blast his impertinence,' said Lord Emsworth warmly. 'My timber is in excellent condition.'

'Not if George says it isn't. George knows timber.'

'So do I know timber.'

'Not so well as George does. But never mind about that. Let's get back to this loathsome plot to ruin my life's whole happiness. Why can't you be a sport, Uncle Clarence, and stand up for me?

Can't you understand what this means to me? Weren't you ever in love?'

'Certainly I was in love. Dozens of times. I'll tell you a very funny story—'

'I don't want to hear funny stories.'

'No, no. Quite. Exactly.'

'All I want is to hear you saying that you will give George Mr Simmons's job, so that we can get married.'

'But your aunt seems to feel so strongly—'

'I know what she feels strongly. She wants me to marry that ass Roegate.'

'Does she?'

'Yes, and I'm not going to. You can tell her from me that I wouldn't marry Bertie Roegate if he were the only man in the world—'

'There's a song of that name,' said Lord Emsworth, interested. 'They sang it during the War. No, it wasn't "man." It was "girl." If you were the only...How did it go? Ah, yes. "If you were the only girl in the world and I was the only boy"...'

'Uncle Clarence!'

'My dear?'

'Please don't sing. You're not in the tap-room of the Emsworth Arms now.'

'I have never been in the tap-room of the Emsworth Arms.'

'Or at a smoking-concert. Really, you seem to have the most extraordinary idea of the sort of attitude that's fitting when you're talking to a girl whose life's happiness everybody is sprinting about trying to ruin. First you talk rot about young George, then you start trying to tell funny stories, and now you sing comic songs.'

'It wasn't a comic song.'

'It was, the way you sang it. Well?'

'Eh?'

'Have you decided what you are going to do about this?'

'About what?'

The girl was silent for a moment, during which moment she looked so like her mother that Lord Emsworth shuddered.

'Uncle Clarence,' she said in a low, trembling voice, 'you are not going to pretend that you don't know what we've been talking about all this time? Are you or are you not going to give George that job?'

'Well—'

'Well?'

'Well—'

'We can't stay here for ever, saying "Well" at one another. Are you or are you not?'

'My dear, I don't see how I can. Your aunt seems to feel so very strongly. . .'

He spoke mumblingly, avoiding his companion's eye, and he had paused, searching for words, when from the drive outside there arose a sudden babble of noise. Raised voices were proceeding from the great open spaces. He recognized his sister Constance's penetrating soprano, and mingling with it his grandson George's treble 'Coo.' Competing with both, there came the throaty baritone of Rupert Baxter. Delighted with the opportunity of changing the subject, he hurried to the window.

'Bless my soul! What's all that?'

The battle, whatever it may have been about, had apparently rolled away in some unknown direction, for he could see nothing from the window but Rupert Baxter, who was smoking a cigarette in what seemed a rather overwrought manner. He turned back, and with infinite relief discovered that he was alone. His niece had disappeared. He took up Whiffle on *The Care Of The Pig* and had just started to savour once more the perfect prose of that chapter about swill and bran-mash, when the door opened. Jane was back. She stood on the threshold, eyeing her uncle coldly.

'Reading, Uncle Clarence?'

'Eh? Oh, ah, yes. I was just glancing at Whiffle on *The Care Of The Pig*!'

'So you actually have the heart to read at a time like this? Well, well! Do you ever read Western novels, Uncle Clarence?'

'Eh? Western novels? No. No, never.'

'I'm sorry. I was reading one the other day, and I hoped that you might be able to explain something that puzzled me. What one cowboy said to another cowboy.'

'Oh, yes?'

'This cowboy – the first cowboy – said to the other cowboy – the second cowboy – "Gol dern ye, Hank Spivis, for a sneaking, ornery, low-down, double-crossing, hornswoggling skunk." Can you tell me what a sneaking, ornery, low-down, double-crossing, hornswoggling skunk is, Uncle Clarence?'

'I'm afraid I can't, my dear.'

'I thought you might know.'

'No.'

'Oh.'

She passed from the room, and Lord Emsworth resumed his Whiffle.

But it was not long before the volume was resting on his knee while he stared before him with a sombre gaze. He was reviewing the recent scene and wishing that he had come better out of it. He was a vague man, but not so vague as to be unaware that he might have shown up in a more heroic light.

How long he sat brooding, he could not have said. Some little time, undoubtedly, for the shadows on the terrace had, he observed as he glanced out of the window, lengthened quite a good deal since he had seen them last. He was about to rise and seek consolation from a ramble among the flowers in the garden below, when the door opened – it seemed to Lord Emsworth, who was now feeling a little morbid, that that blasted door had never stopped opening since he had come to the library to be alone – and Beach, the butler, entered.

He was carrying an airgun in one hand and in the other a silver salver with a box of ammunition on it.

Beach was a man who invested all his actions with something of the impressiveness of a high priest conducting an intricate service at some romantic altar. It is not easy to be impressive when you are carrying an airgun in one hand and a silver salver with a box of ammunition on it in the other, but Beach managed it. Many butlers in such a position would have looked like sportsmen setting out for a day with the birds, but Beach still looked like a high priest. He advanced to the table at Lord Emsworth's side and laid his cargo upon it as if the gun and the box of ammunition had been a smoked offering and his lordship a tribal god.

Lord Emsworth eyed his faithful servitor sourly. His manner was that of a tribal god who considers the smoked offering not up to sample.

'What the devil's all this?'

'It is an airgun, m'lord.'

'I can see that, dash it. What are you bringing it here for?'

'Her ladyship instructed me to convey it to your lordship – I gathered for safe keeping, m'lord. The weapon was until recently the property of Master George.'

'Why the dooce are they taking his airgun away from the poor boy?' demanded Lord Emsworth hotly. Ever since the lad had called Rupert Baxter a blister he had been feeling a strong affection for his grandson.

'Her ladyship did not confide in me on that point, m'lord. I was merely instructed to convey the weapon to your lordship.'

At this moment, Lady Constance came sailing in to throw light on the mystery.

'Ah, I see Beach has brought it to you. I want you to lock that gun up somewhere, Clarence. George is not to be allowed to have it any more.'

'Why not?'

'Because he is not to be trusted with it. Do you know what happened? He shot Mr Baxter!'

'What!'

'Yes. Out on the drive just now. I noticed that the boy's manner was sullen when I introduced him to Mr Baxter, and said that he was going to be his tutor. He disappeared into the shrubbery, and just now, as Mr Baxter was standing on the drive, George shot him from behind a bush.'

'Good!' cried Lord Emsworth, then prudently added the word 'gracious.'

There was a pause. Lord Emsworth took up the gun and handled it curiously.

'Bang!' he said, pointing it at a bust of Aristotle which stood on a bracket by the book-shelves.

'Please don't wave the thing about like that, Clarence. It may be loaded.'

'Not if George has just shot Baxter with it. No,' said Lord Emsworth, pulling the trigger, 'it's not loaded.' He mused awhile. An odd, nostalgic feeling was creeping over him. Far-off memories of his hot boyhood had begun to stir within him. 'Bless my soul,' he said. 'I haven't had one of these things in my hand since I was a child. Did you ever have one of these things, Beach?'

'Yes, m'lord, when a small lad.'

'Bless my soul, I remember my sister Julia borrowing mine to shoot her governess. You remember Julia shooting the governess, Connie?'

'Don't be absurd, Clarence.'

'It's not absurd. She did shoot her. Fortunately women wore bustles in those days. Beach, don't you remember my sister Julia shooting the governess?'

'The incident would, no doubt, have occurred before my arrival at the castle, m'lord.'

'That will do, Beach,' said Lady Constance. 'I do wish, Clarence,' she continued as the door closed, 'that you would not say that sort of thing in front of Beach.'

'Julia did shoot the governess.'

'If she did, there is no need to make your butler a confidant.'

'Now, what was that governess's name? I have an idea it began with—'

'Never mind what her name was or what it began with. Tell me about Jane. I saw her coming out of the library. Had you been speaking to her?'

'Yes. Oh, yes. I spoke to her.'

'I hope you were firm.'

'Oh, very firm. I said "Jane . . ." But listen, Connie, damn it, aren't we being a little hard on the girl? One doesn't want to ruin her whole life's happiness, dash it.'

'I knew she would get round you. But you are not to give way an inch.'

'But this fellow seems to be a most suitable fellow. One of the Abercrombies and all that. Did well in the Crusades.'

'I am not going to have my niece throwing herself away on a man without a penny.'

'She isn't going to marry Roegate, you know. Nothing will induce her. She said she wouldn't marry Roegate if she were the only girl in the world and he was the only boy.'

'I don't care what she said. And I don't want to discuss the matter any longer. I am now going to send George in, for you to give him a good talking-to.'

'I haven't time.'

'You have time.'

'I haven't. I'm going to look at my flowers.'

'You are not. You are going to talk to George. I want you to make him see quite clearly what a wicked thing he has done. Mr Baxter was furious.'

'It all comes back to me,' cried Lord Emsworth. 'Mapleton!'

'What *are* you talking about?'

'Her name was Mapleton. Julia's governess.'

'Do stop about Julia's governess. Will you talk to George?'

'Oh, all right, all right.'

'Good. I'll go and send him to you.'

And presently George entered. For a boy who had just stained the escutcheon of a proud family by shooting tutors with airguns, he seemed remarkably cheerful. His manner was that of one getting together with an old crony for a cosy chat.

'Hullo, grandpapa,' he said breezily.

'Hullo, my boy,' replied Lord Emsworth, with equal affability.

'Aunt Connie said you wanted to see me.'

'Eh? Ah! Oh! Yes.' Lord Emsworth pulled himself together.

'Yes, that's right. Yes, to be sure. Certainly I want to see you. What's all this, my boy, eh? Eh, what? What's all this?'

'What's all what, grandpapa?'

'Shooting people and all that sort of thing. Shooting Baxter and all that sort of thing. Mustn't do that, you know. Can't have that. It's very wrong and – er – very dangerous to shoot at people with a dashed great gun. Don't you know that, hey? Might put their eye out, dash it.'

'Oh, I couldn't have hit him in the eye, grandpapa. His back was turned and he was bending over, tying his shoelace.'

Lord Emsworth started.

'What! Did you get Baxter in the seat of the trousers?'

'Yes, grandpapa.'

'Ha, ha . . . I mean, disgraceful . . . I – er – I expect he jumped?'

'Oh, yes, grandpapa. He jumped like billy-o.'

'Did he, indeed? How this reminds me of Julia's governess. Your Aunt Julia once shot her governess under precisely similar conditions. She was tying her shoelace.'

'Coo! Did *she* jump?'

'She certainly did, my boy.'

'Ha, ha!'

'Ha, ha!'

'Ha, ha!'

'Ha, h – . . . Ah . . . Er – well, just so,' said Lord Emsworth, a belated doubt assailing him as to whether this was quite the tone. 'Well, George, I shall of course impound this – er – instrument.'

'Right ho, grandpapa,' said George, with the easy amiability of a boy conscious of having two catapults in his drawer upstairs.

'Can't have you going about the place shooting people.'

'Okay, Chief.'

Lord Emsworth fondled the gun. That nostalgic feeling was growing.

'Do you know, young man, I used to have one of these things when I was a boy.'

'Coo! Were guns invented then?'

'Yes, I had one when I was your age.'

'Ever hit anything, grandpapa?'

Lord Emsworth drew himself up a little haughtily.

'Certainly I did. I hit all sorts of things. Rats and things. I had a very accurate aim. But now I wouldn't even know how to load the dashed affair.'

'This is how you load it, grandpapa. You open it like this and shove the slug in here and snap it together again like that and there you are.'

'Indeed? Really? I see. Yes. Yes, of course, I remember now.'

'You can't kill anything much with it,' said George, with a wistfulness which betrayed an aspiration to higher things. 'Still, it's awfully useful for tickling up cows.'

'And Baxter.'

'Yes.'

'Ha, ha!'

'Ha, ha!'

Once more, Lord Emsworth forced himself to concentrate on the right tone.

'We mustn't laugh about it, my boy. It's no joking matter. It's very wrong to shoot Mr Baxter.'

'But he's a blister.'

'He is a blister,' agreed Lord Emsworth, always fairminded. 'Nevertheless. . . . Remember, he is your tutor.'

'Well, I don't see why I've got to have a tutor right in the middle of the summer holidays. I sweat like the dickens all through the term at school,' said George, his voice vibrant with self-pity, 'and then plumb spang in the middle of the holidays they slosh a tutor on me. I call it a bit thick.'

Lord Emsworth might have told the little fellow that thicker things than that were going on in Blandings Castle, but he refrained. He dismissed him with a kindly, sympathetic smile and resumed his fondling of the airgun.

Like so many men advancing into the sere and yellow of life, Lord Emsworth had an eccentric memory. It was not to be trusted an inch as far as the events of yesterday or the day before were concerned. Even in the small matter of assisting him to find a hat which he had laid down somewhere five minutes ago it was nearly always useless. But by way of compensation for this it was a perfect encyclopædia on the remote past. It rendered his boyhood an open book to him.

Lord Emsworth mused on his boyhood. Happy days, happy days. He could recall the exact uncle who had given him the weapon, so similar to this one, with which Julia had shot her governess. He could recall brave, windswept mornings when he had gone prowling through the stable yard in the hope of getting a rat – and many a fine head had he secured. Odd that the passage of time should remove the desire to go and pop at things with an airgun. . . .

Or did it?

With a curious thrill that set his pince-nez rocking gently on his nose, Lord Emsworth suddenly became aware that it did not. All that the passage of time did was to remove the desire to pop temporarily – say for forty years or so. Dormant for a short while – well, call it fifty years – that desire, he perceived, still lurked unquenched. Little by little it began to stir within him now.

Slowly but surely, as he sat there fondling the gun, he was once more becoming a potential popper.

At this point, the gun suddenly went off and broke the bust of Aristotle.

It was enough. The old killer instinct had awakened. Reloading with the swift efficiency of some hunter of the woods, Lord Emsworth went to the window. He was a little uncertain as to what he intended to do when he got there, except that he had a very clear determination to loose off at something. There flitted into his mind what his grandson George had said about tickling up cows, and this served to some extent to crystallize his aims. True, cows were not plentiful on the terrace of Blandings Castle. Still, one might have wandered there. You never knew with cows.

There were no cows. Only Rupert Baxter. The ex-secretary was in the act of throwing away a cigarette.

Most men are careless in the matter of throwing away cigarettes. The world is their ashtray. But Rupert Baxter had a tidy soul. He allowed the thing to fall to the ground like any ordinary young man, it is true, but immediately he had done so his better self awakened. He stooped to pick up the object that disfigured the smooth flagged stones, and the invitation of that beckoning trousers' seat would have been too powerful for a stronger man than Lord Emsworth to resist.

He pulled the trigger, and Rupert Baxter sprang into the air with a sharp cry. Lord Emsworth reseated himself and took up Whiffle on *The Care Of The Pig*.

Everybody is interested nowadays in the psychology of the criminal. The chronicler, therefore, feels that he runs no risk of losing his grip on the reader if he pauses at this point to examine and analyse the workings of Lord Emsworth's mind after the penetration of the black act which has just been recorded.

At first, then, all that he felt as he sat turning the pages of his Whiffle was a sort of soft warm glow, a kind of tremulous joy such as he might have experienced if he had just been receiving the thanks of the nation for some great public service.

It was not merely the fact that he had caused his late employee to skip like the high hills that induced this glow. What pleased him so particularly was that it had been such a magnificent shot. He was a sensitive man, and though in his conversation with his grandson George he had tried to wear the mask, he had not been able completely to hide his annoyance at the boy's careless assumption that in his airgun days he had been an indifferent marksman.

'Did you ever hit anything, grandpapa?' Boys say these things with no wish to wound, but nevertheless they pierce the armour. 'Did you ever hit anything, grandpapa?' forsooth! He would have liked to see George stop putting finger to trigger for forty-seven years and then, first crack out of the box, pick off a medium-sized secretary at a distance like that! In rather a bad light, too.

But after he had sat for awhile, silently glowing, his mood underwent a change. A gunman's complacency after getting his man can never remain for long an unmixed complacency. Sooner or later there creeps in the thought of Retribution. It did with Lord Emsworth. Quite suddenly, whispering in his ear, he heard the voice of Conscience say:

'What if your sister Constance learns of this?'

A moment before this voice spoke, Lord Emsworth had been smirking. He now congealed, and the smile passed from his lips like breath off a razor blade, to be succeeded by a tense look of anxiety and alarm.

Nor was this alarm unjustified. When he reflected how scathing and terrible his sister Constance could be when he committed even so venial a misdemeanour as coming down to dinner with a brass paper-fastener in his shirt front instead of the more conventional stud, his imagination boggled at the thought of what she would do in a case like this. He was appalled. Whiffle on *The Care Of The Pig* fell from his nerveless hand, and he sat looking like a dying duck. And Lady Constance, who now entered, noted the expression and was curious as to its cause.

'What is the matter, Clarence?'

'Matter?'

'Why are you looking like a dying duck?'

'I am not looking like a dying duck,' retorted Lord Emsworth with what spirit he could muster.

'Well,' said Lady Constance, waiving the point, 'have you spoken to George?'

'Certainly. Yes, of course I've spoken to George. He was in here just now and I – er – spoke to him.'

'What did you say?'

'I said' – Lord Emsworth wanted to make this very clear – 'I said that I wouldn't even know how to load one of those things.'

'Didn't you give him a good talking-to?'

'Of course I did. A very good talking-to. I said "Er – George, you know how to load those things and I don't, but that's no reason why you should go about shooting Baxter."'

'Was that all you said?'

'No. That was just how I began. I—'

Lord Emsworth paused. He could not have finished the sentence if large rewards had been offered to him to do so. For, as he spoke, Rupert Baxter appeared in the doorway, and he shrank back in his chair like some Big Shot cornered by G-men.

The secretary came forward limping slightly. His eyes behind their spectacles were wild and his manner emotional. Lady Constance gazed at him wonderingly.

'Is something the matter, Mr Baxter?'

'Matter?' Rupert Baxter's voice was taut and he quivered in every limb. He had lost his customary suavity and was plainly in no frame of mind to mince his words. 'Matter? Do you know what has happened? That infernal boy has shot me *again*!'

'What!'

'Only a few minutes ago. Out on the terrace.'

Lord Emsworth shook off his palsy.

'I expect you imagined it,' he said.

'Imagined it!' Rupert Baxter shook from spectacles to shoes. 'I tell you I was on the terrace, stooping to pick up my cigarette, when something hit me on the . . . something hit me.'

'Probably a wasp,' said Lord Emsworth. 'They are very plentiful this year. I wonder,' he said chattily, 'if either of you are aware that wasps serve a very useful purpose. They keep down the leather-jackets, which, as you know, inflict serious injury upon—'

Lady Constance's concern became mixed with perplexity.

'But it could not have been George, Mr Baxter. The moment you told me of what he had done, I confiscated his airgun. Look, there it is on the table now.'

'Right there on the table,' said Lord Emsworth, pointing helpfully. 'If you come over here, you can see it clearly. Must have been a wasp.'

'You have not left the room, Clarence?'

'No. Been here all the time.'

'Then it would have been impossible for George to have shot you, Mr Baxter.'

'Quite,' said Lord Emsworth. 'A wasp, undoubtedly. Unless, as I say, you imagined the whole thing.'

The secretary stiffened.

'I am not subject to hallucinations, Lord Emsworth.'

'But you are, my dear fellow. I expect it comes from exerting your brain too much. You're always getting them.'

'Clarence!'

'Well, he is. You know that as well as I do. Look at that time he went grubbing about in a lot of flower-pots because he thought you had put your necklace there.'

'I did not—'

'You did, my dear fellow. I dare say you've forgotten it, but you did. And then, for some reason best known to yourself, you threw the flower-pots at me through my bedroom window.'

Baxter turned to Lady Constance, flushing darkly. The episode to which his former employer had alluded was one of which he never cared to be reminded.

'Lord Emsworth is referring to the occasion when your diamond necklace was stolen, Lady Constance. I was led to believe that the thief had hidden it in a flower-pot.'

'Of course, Mr Baxter.'

'Well, have it your own way,' said Lord Emsworth agreeably. 'But bless my soul, I shall never forget waking up and finding all those flower-pots pouring in through the window and then looking out and seeing Baxter on the lawn in lemon-coloured pyjamas with a wild glare in his—'

'Clarence!'

'Oh, all right. I merely mentioned it. Hallucinations – he gets them all the time,' he said stoutly, though in an undertone.

Lady Constance was cooing to the secretary like a mother to her child.

'It really is impossible that George should have done this, Mr Baxter. The gun has never left this—'

She broke off. Her handsome face seemed to turn suddenly to stone. When she spoke again the coo had gone out of her voice and it had become metallic.

'Clarence!'

'My dear?'

Lady Constance drew in her breath sharply.

'Mr Baxter, I wonder if you would mind leaving us for a moment. I wish to speak to Lord Emsworth.'

The closing of the door was followed by a silence, followed in its turn by an odd, whining noise like gas escaping from a pipe. It was Lord Emsworth trying to hum carelessly.

'Clarence!'

'Yes? Yes, my dear?'

The stoniness of Lady Constance's expression had become more marked with each succeeding moment. What had caused it in the first place was the recollection, coming to her like a flash, that when she had entered this room she had found her brother looking like a dying duck. Honest men, she felt, do not look like dying ducks. The only man whom an impartial observer could possibly mistake for one of these birds *in extremis* is the man with crime upon his soul.

'Clarence, was it you who shot Mr Baxter?'

Fortunately there had been that in her manner which led Lord Emsworth to expect the question. He was ready for it.

'Me? Who, me? Shoot Baxter? What the dooce would I want to shoot Baxter for?'

'We can go into your motives later. What I am asking you now is – Did you?'

'Of course I didn't.'

'The gun has not left the room.'

'Shoot Baxter, indeed! Never heard anything so dashed absurd in my life.'

'And you have been here all the time.'

'Well, what of it? Suppose I have? Suppose I had wanted to shoot Baxter? Suppose every fibre in my being had egged me on, dash it, to shoot the feller? How could I have done it, not even knowing how to load the contrivance?'

'You used to know how to load an airgun.'

'I used to know a lot of things.'

'It's quite easy to load an airgun. I could do it myself.'

'Well, I didn't.'

'Then how do you account for the fact that Mr Baxter was shot by an airgun which had never left the room you were in?'

Lord Emsworth raised pleading hands to heaven.

'How do you know he was shot with this airgun? God bless my soul, the way women jump to conclusions is enough to. . . . How do you know there wasn't another airgun? How do you know the place isn't bristling with airguns? How do you know Beach hasn't an airgun? Or anybody?'

'I scarcely imagine that Beach would shoot Mr Baxter.'

'How do you know he wouldn't? He used to have an airgun when he was a small lad. He said so. I'd watch the man closely.'

'Please don't be ridiculous, Clarence.'

'I'm not being half as ridiculous as you are. Saying I shoot people with airguns. Why should I shoot people with airguns? And how do you suppose I could have potted Baxter at that distance?'

'What distance?'

'He was standing on the terrace, wasn't he? He specifically stated that he was standing on the terrace. And I was up here. It would take a most expert marksman to pot the fellow at a distance like that. Who do you think I am? One of those chaps who shoot apples off their son's heads?'

The reasoning was undeniably specious. It shook Lady Constance. She frowned undecidedly.

'Well, it's very strange that Mr Baxter should be so convinced that he was shot.'

'Nothing strange about it at all. There wouldn't be anything strange if Baxter was convinced that he was a turnip and had been bitten by a white rabbit with pink eyes. You know perfectly well, though you won't admit it, that the fellow's a raving lunatic.'

'Clarence!'

'It's no good saying "Clarence." The fellow's potty to the core, and always has been. Haven't I seen him on the lawn at five o'clock in the morning in lemon-coloured pyjamas, throwing flower-pots in at my window? Pooh! Obviously, the whole thing is the outcome of the man's diseased imagination. Shot, indeed! Never heard such nonsense. And now,' said Lord Emsworth, rising firmly, 'I'm going out to have a look at my roses. I came to this room to enjoy a little quiet reading and meditation, and ever since I got here there's been a constant stream of people in and out, telling me they're going to marry men named Abercrombie and saying they've been shot and saying I shot them and so on and so forth. . . . Bless my soul, one might as well try to read and meditate in the middle of Piccadilly Circus. Tchah!' said Lord Emsworth, who had now got near enough to the door to feel safe in uttering this unpleasant exclamation. 'Tchah!' he said, and adding 'Pah!' for good measure made a quick exit.

But even now his troubled spirit was not to know peace. To reach the great outdoors at Blandings Castle, if you start from the library and come down the main staircase, you have to pass through the hall. To the left of this hall there is a small writing-room. And outside this writing-room Lord Emsworth's niece Jane was standing.

'Yoo-hoo,' she cried. 'Uncle Clarence.'

Lord Emsworth was in no mood for yoo-hooing nieces. George Abercrombie might enjoy chatting with this girl. So might Herbert, Lord Roegate. But he wanted solitude. In the course of the afternoon he had had so much female society thrust upon him that if Helen of Troy had appeared in the doorway of the writing-room and yoo-hooed at him, he would merely have accelerated his pace.

He accelerated it now.

'Can't stop, my dear, can't stop.'

'Oh, yes you can, old Sure-Shot,' said Jane, and Lord Emsworth found that he could. He stopped so abruptly that he nearly dislocated his spine. His jaw had fallen and his pince-nez were dancing on their string like leaves in the wind.

'Two-Gun Thomas, the Marksman of the Prairie – He never misses. Kindly step this way, Uncle Clarence,' said Jane, 'I would like a word with you.'

Lord Emsworth stepped that way. He followed the girl into the writing-room and closed the door carefully behind him.

'You – you didn't see me?' he quavered.

'I certainly did see you,' said Jane. 'I was an interested eye-witness of the whole thing from start to finish.'

Lord Emsworth tottered to a chair and sank into it, staring glassily at his niece. Any Chicago business man of the modern school would have understood what he was feeling and would have sympathized with him.

The thing that poisons life for gunmen and sometimes makes them wonder moodily if it is worth-while going on is this tendency of the outside public to butt in at inconvenient moments. Whenever you settle some business dispute with a commercial competitor by means of your sub-machine gun, it always turns out that there was some officious witness passing at the time, and there you are, with a new problem confronting you.

And Lord Emsworth was in worse case than his spiritual brother of Chicago would have been, for the latter could always have solved his perplexities by rubbing out the witness. To him this melancholy pleasure was denied. A prominent Shropshire landowner, with a position to keep up in the county, cannot rub out his nieces. All he can do, when they reveal that they have seen him wallowing in crime, is to stare glassily at them.

'I had a front seat for the entire performance,' proceeded Jane. 'When I left you, I went into the shrubbery to cry my eyes out because of your frightful cruelty and inhumanity. And while I was crying my eyes out, I suddenly saw you creep to the window of the library with a hideous look of low cunning on your face and young George's airgun in your hand. And I was just wondering if I couldn't find a stone and bung it at you, because it seemed to me that something along those lines was what you had been asking for from the start, when you raised the gun and I saw that you were taking aim. The next moment there was a shot, a cry, and Baxter weltering in his blood on the terrace. And as I stood there, a thought floated into my mind. It was – What will Aunt Constance have to say about this when I tell her?'

Lord Emsworth emitted a low, gargling sound, like the death rattle of that dying duck to which his sister had compared him.

'You – you aren't going to tell her?'

'Why not?'

An aguelike convulsion shook Lord Emsworth.

'I implore you not to tell her, my dear. You know what she's like. I should never hear the end of it.'

'She would give you the devil, you think?'

'I do.'

'So do I. And you thoroughly deserve it.'

'My dear!'

'Well, don't you? Look at the way you've been behaving. Working like a beaver to ruin my life's happiness.'

'I don't want to ruin your life's happiness.'

'You don't? Then sit down at this desk and dash off a short letter to George, giving him that job.'

'But—'

'What did you say?'

'I only said, "But—"'

'Don't say it again. What I want from you, Uncle Clarence, is prompt and cheerful service. Are you ready? "Dear Mr Abercrombie . . ."'

'I don't know how to spell it,' said Lord Emsworth, with the air of a man who has found a way out satisfactory to all parties.

'I'll attend to the spelling. A-b, ab; e-r, er; c-r-o-m, crom; b-i-e, bie. The whole constituting the word "Abercrombie," which is the name of the man I love. Got it?'

'Yes,' said Lord Emsworth sepulchrally. 'I've got it.'

'Then carry on. "Dear Mr Abercrombie. Pursuant" – One p.,

two u's – spread 'em about a bit, an r., an s., and an ant – "Pursuant on our recent conversation—"'

'But I've never spoken to the man in my life.'

'It doesn't matter. It's just a form. "Pursuant on our recent conversation, I have much pleasure in offering you the post of land-agent at Blandings Castle, and shall be glad if you will take up your duties immediately. Yours faithfully Emsworth." E-m-s-w-o-r-t-h.'

Jane took the letter, pressed it lovingly on the blotting-pad and placed it in the recesses of her costume. 'Fine,' she said. 'That's that. Thanks most awfully, Uncle Clarence. This has squared you nicely for your recent foul behaviour in trying to ruin my life's happiness. You made a rocky start, but you've come through magnificently at the finish.'

Kissing him affectionately, she passed from the room, and Lord Emsworth, slumped in his chair, tried not to look at the vision of his sister Constance which was rising before his eyes. What Connie was going to say when she learned that in defiance of her direct commands he had given this young man . . .

He mused on Lady Constance, and wondered if there were any other men in the world so sister-pecked as he. It was weak of him, he knew, to curl up into an apologetic ball when assailed by a mere sister. Most men reserved such craven conduct for their wives. But it had always been so, right back to those boyhood days which he remembered so well. And too late to alter it now, he supposed.

The only consolation he was able to enjoy in this dark hour was the reflection that, though things were bad, they were unquestionably less bad than they might have been. At the least, his fearful secret was safe. That rash moment of recovered boyhood would never now be brought up against him. Connie would never know whose hand it was that had pulled the fatal trigger. She might suspect, but she could never know. Nor could Baxter ever know. Baxter would grow into an old, white-haired, spectacled pantaloon, and always this thing would remain an insoluble mystery to him.

Dashed lucky, felt Lord Emsworth, that the fellow had not been listening at the door during the recent conversation. . . .

It was at this moment that a sound behind him caused him to turn and, having turned, to spring from his chair with a convulsive leap that nearly injured him internally. Over the sill of the open window, like those of a corpse emerging from the tomb to confront its murderer, the head and shoulders of Rupert Baxter were slowly rising. The evening sun fell upon his spectacles, and they seemed to Lord Emsworth to gleam like the eyes of a dragon.

Rupert Baxter had not been listening at the door. There had been no necessity for him to do so. Immediately outside the writing-room window at Blandings Castle there stands a rustic garden seat, and on this he had been sitting from beginning to end of the interview which has just been recorded. If he had been actually in the room, he might have heard a little better, but not much.

When two men stand face to face, one of whom has recently shot the other with an airgun and the second of whom has just discovered who it was that did it, it is rarely that conversation flows briskly from the start. One senses a certain awkwardness – what the French call *gêne*. In the first half-minute of this encounter the only thing that happened in a vocal way was that Lord Emsworth cleared his throat, immediately afterwards becoming silent again. And it is possible that his silence might have prolonged itself for some considerable time, had not Baxter made a movement as if about to withdraw. All this while he had been staring at his former employer, his face an open book in which it was easy for the least discerning eye to read a number of disconcerting emotions. He now took a step backwards, and Lord Emsworth's asphasia left him.

'Baxter!'

There was urgent appeal in the ninth Earl's voice. It was not often that he wanted Rupert Baxter to stop and talk to him, but he was most earnestly desirous of detaining him now. He wished to soothe, to apologize, to explain. He was even prepared, should it be necessary, to offer the man his old post of private secretary as the price of his silence.

'Baxter! My dear fellow!'

A high tenor voice, raised almost to A in Alt by agony of soul, has a compelling quality which it is difficult even for a man in Rupert Baxter's mental condition to resist. Rupert Baxter had not intended to halt his backward movement, but he did so, and Lord Emsworth, reaching the window and thrusting his head out, was relieved to see that he was still within range of the honeyed word.

'Er – Baxter,' he said, 'could you spare me a moment?'

The secretary's spectacles flashed coldly.

'You wish to speak to me, Lord Emsworth?'

'That's exactly it,' assented his lordship, as if he thought it a very happy way of putting the thing. 'Yes, I wish to speak to you.' He paused, and cleared his throat again. 'Tell me, Baxter – tell me, my dear fellow – were you – er – were you sitting on that seat just now?'

'I was.'

'Did you, by any chance, overhear my niece and myself talking?'

'I did.'

'Then I expect – I fancy – perhaps – possibly – no doubt you were surprised at what you heard?'

'I was astounded,' said Rupert Baxter, who was not going to be fobbed off with any weak verbs at a moment like this.

Lord Emsworth cleared his throat for the third time.

'I want to tell you all about that,' he said.

'Oh?' said Rupert Baxter.

'Yes. I – ah – welcome this opportunity of telling you all about it,' said Lord Emsworth, though with less pleasure in his voice than might have been expected from a man welcoming an opportunity of telling somebody all about something. 'I fancy that my niece's remarks may – er – possibly have misled you.'

'Not at all.'

'They may have put you on the wrong track.'

'On the contrary.'

'But, if I remember correctly, she gave the impression – by what she said – my niece gave the impression by what she said – anybody overhearing what my niece said would have received the impression that I took deliberate aim at you with that gun.'

'Precisely.'

'She was quite mistaken,' said Lord Emsworth warmly. 'She had got hold of the wrong end of the stick completely. Girls say such dashed silly things . . . cause a lot of trouble . . . upset people. They ought to be more careful. What actually happened, my dear fellow, was that I was glancing out of the library window . . . with the gun in my hand . . . and without knowing it I must have placed my finger on the trigger . . . for suddenly . . .

without the slightest warning...you could have knocked me down with a feather...the dashed thing went off. By accident.'

'Indeed?'

'Purely by accident. I should not like you to think that I was aiming at you.'

'Indeed?'

'And I should not like you to tell – er – anybody about the unfortunate occurrence in a way that would give her...I mean them...the impression that I aimed at you.'

'Indeed?'

Lord Emsworth could not persuade himself that his companion's manner was encouraging. He had a feeling that he was not making headway.

'That's how it was,' he said, after a pause.

'I see.'

'Pure accident. Nobody more surprised than myself.'

'I see.'

So did Lord Emsworth. He saw that the time had come to play his last card. It was no moment for shrinking back and counting the cost. He must proceed to that last fearful extremity which he had contemplated.

'Tell me, Baxter,' he said, 'are you doing anything just now, Baxter?'

'Yes,' replied the other, with no trace of hesitation. 'I am going to look for Lady Constance.'

A convulsive gulp prevented Lord Emsworth from speaking for an instant.

'I mean,' he quavered, when the spasm had spent itself, 'I gathered from my sister that you were at liberty at the moment – that you had left that fellow what's-his-name – the American fellow – and I was hoping, my dear Baxter,' said Lord Emsworth, speaking thickly, as if the words choked him, 'that I might be able to persuade you to take up – to resume – in fact, I was going to ask you if you would care to become my secretary again.'

He paused and, reaching for his handkerchief, feebly mopped his brow. The dreadful speech was out, and its emergence had left him feeling spent and weak.

'You were?' cried Rupert Baxter.

'I was,' said Lord Emsworth hollowly.

A great change for the better had come over Rupert Baxter. It was as if those words had been a magic formula, filling with sweetness and light one who until that moment had been more like a spectacled thunder-cloud than anything human. He ceased to lower darkly. His air of being on the point of shooting out forked lightning left him. He even went so far as to smile. And if the smile was a smile that made Lord Emsworth feel as if his vital organs were being churned up with an egg-whisk, that was not his fault. He was trying to smile sunnily.

'Thank you,' he said. 'I shall be delighted.'

Lord Emsworth did not speak.

'I was always happy at the Castle.'

Lord Emsworth did not speak.

'Thank you very much,' said Rupert Baxter. 'What a beautiful evening.'

He passed from view, and Lord Emsworth examined the evening. As Baxter had said, it was beautiful, but it did not bring the balm which beautiful evenings usually brought to him. A blight seemed to hang over it. The setting sun shone bravely on the formal garden over which he looked, but it was the lengthening shadows rather than the sunshine that impressed themselves upon Lord Emsworth.

His heart was bowed down with weight of woe. Oh, says the poet, what a tangled web we weave when first we practise to deceive, and it was precisely the same, Lord Emsworth realized, when first we practise to shoot airguns. Just one careless, offhand pop at a bending Baxter, and what a harvest, what a retribution! As a result of that single idle shot he had been compelled to augment his personal staff with a land-agent, which would infuriate his sister Constance, and a private secretary, which would make his life once again the inferno it had been in the old, bad Baxter days. He could scarcely have got himself into more trouble if he had gone blazing away with a machine gun.

It was with a slow and distrait shuffle that he eventually took himself from the writing-room and proceeded with his interrupted plan of going and sniffing at his roses. And so preoccupied was his mood that Beach, his faithful butler, who came to him after he had been sniffing at them for perhaps half an hour, was obliged to speak twice before he could induce him to remove his nose from a Gloire de Dijon.

'Eh?'

'A note for you, m'lord.'

'A note? Who from?'

'Mr Baxter, m'lord.'

If Lord Emsworth had been less careworn, he might have noticed that the butler's voice had not its customary fruity ring. It had a dullness, a lack of tone. It was the voice of a butler who has lost the blue bird. But, being in the depths and so in no frame of mind to analyse the voice-production of butlers, he merely took the envelope from its salver and opened it listlessly, wondering what Baxter was sending him notes about.

The communication was so brief that he was enabled to discover this at a glance.

'LORD EMSWORTH,

'After what has occurred, I must reconsider my decision to accept the post of secretary which you offered me.

'I am leaving the Castle immediately.

'R. BAXTER.'

Simply that, and nothing more.

Lord Emsworth stared at the thing. It is not enough to say that he was bewildered. He was nonplussed. If the Gloire de Dijon at which he had recently been sniffing had snapped at his nose and bitten the tip off, he could scarcely have been more taken aback. He could make nothing of this.

As in a dream, he became aware that Beach was speaking.

'Eh?'

'My month's notice, m'lord.'

'Your what?'

'My month's notice, m'lord.'

'What about it?'

'I was saying that I wish to give my month's notice, m'lord.'

A weak irritation at all this chattering came upon Lord Emsworth. Here he was, trying to grapple with this frightful thing which had come upon him, and Beach would insist on weakening his concentration by babbling.

'Yes, yes, yes,' he said. 'I see. All right. Yes, yes.'

'Very good, m'lord.'

Left alone, Lord Emsworth faced the facts. He understood now what had happened. The note was no longer mystic. What it meant was that for some reason that trump card of his had proved useless. He had thought to stop Baxter's mouth with bribes, and he had failed. The man had seemed to accept the olive branch, but later there must have come some sharp revulsion of feeling, causing him to change his mind. No doubt a sudden twinge of pain in the wounded area had brought the memory of his wrongs flooding back upon him, so that he found himself preferring vengeance to material prosperity. And now he was going to blow the gaff. Even now the whole facts in the case might have been placed before Lady Constance. And even now, Lord Emsworth felt with a shiver, Connie might be looking for him.

The sight of a female form coming through the rose bushes brought him the sharpest shudder of the day, and for an instant he stood pointing like a dog. But it was not his sister Constance. It was his niece Jane.

Jane was in excellent spirits.

'Hullo, Uncle Clarence,' she said. 'Having a look at the roses? I've sent that letter off to George, Uncle Clarence. I got the boy who cleans the knives and boots to take it. Nice chap. His name is Cyril.'

'Jane,' said Lord Emsworth, 'a terrible, a ghastly thing has happened. Baxter was outside the window of the writing-room when we were talking, and he heard everything.'

'Golly! He didn't?'

'He did. Every word. And he means to tell your aunt.'

'How do you know?'

'Read this.'

Jane took the note.

'H'm,' she said, having scanned it. 'Well, it looks to me, Uncle Clarence, as if there was only one thing for you to do. You must assert yourself.'

'Assert myself?'

'You know what I mean. Get tough. When Aunt Constance comes trying to bully you, stick your elbows out and put your head on one side and talk back at her out of the corner of your mouth.'

'But what shall I say?'

'Good heavens, there are a hundred things you can say. "Oh, yeah?" "Is zat so?" "Hey, just a minute," "Listen baby," "Scram" . . .'

'Scram?'

'It means "Get the hell outa here."'

'But I can't tell Connie to get the hell outa here.'

'Why not? Aren't you master in your own house?'

'No,' said Lord Emsworth.

Jane reflected.

'Then I'll tell you what to do. Deny the whole thing.'

'Could I, do you think?'

'Of course you could. And then Aunt Constance will ask me, and I'll deny the whole thing. Categorically. We'll both deny it categorically. She'll have to believe us. We'll be two to one. Don't you worry, Uncle Clarence. Everything'll be all right.'

She spoke with the easy optimism of Youth, and when she passed on a few moments later seemed to be feeling that she was leaving an uncle with his mind at rest. Lord Emsworth could hear her singing a gay song.

He felt no disposition to join in the chorus. He could not bring himself to share her sunny outlook. He looked into the future and still found it dark.

There was only one way of taking his mind off this dark future, only one means of achieving a momentary forgetfulness of what lay in store. Five minutes later, Lord Emsworth was in the library, reading Whiffle on *The Care Of The Pig*.

But there is a point beyond which the magic of the noblest writer ceases to function. Whiffle was good – no question about that – but he was not good enough to purge from the mind such a load of care as was weighing upon Lord Emsworth's. To expect him to do so was trying him too high. It was like asking Whiffle to divert and entertain a man stretched upon the rack.

Lord Emsworth was already beginning to find a difficulty in concentrating on that perfect prose, when any chance he might have had of doing so was removed. Lady Constance appeared in the doorway.

'Oh, here you are, Clarence,' said Lady Constance.

'Yes,' said Lord Emsworth in a low, strained voice.

A close observer would have noted about Lady Constance's manner, as she came into the room, something a little nervous and apprehensive, something almost diffident, but to Lord Emsworth, who was not a close observer, she seemed pretty much as usual, and he remained gazing at her like a man confronted with a ticking bomb. A dazed sensation had come upon him. It was in an almost detached way that he found himself speculating as to which of his crimes was about to be brought up for discussion. Had she met Jane and learned of the fatal letter? Or had she come straight from an interview with Rupert Baxter in which that injured man had told all?

He was so certain that it must be one of these two topics that she had come to broach that her manner as she opened the conversation filled him with amazement. Not only did it lack ferocity, it was absolutely chummy. It was as if a lion had come into the library and started bleating like a lamb.

'All alone, Clarence?'

Lord Emsworth hitched up his lower jaw, and said Yes, he was all alone.

'What are you doing? Reading?'

Lord Emsworth said Yes, he was reading.

'I'm not disturbing you, am I?'

Lord Emsworth, though astonishment nearly robbed him of speech, contrived to say that she was not disturbing him. Lady Constance walked to the window and looked out.

'What a lovely evening.'

'Yes.'

'I wonder you aren't out of doors.'

'I was out of doors. I came in.'

'Yes. I saw you in the rose garden.' Lady Constance traced a pattern on the window-sill with her finger. 'You were speaking to Beach.'

'Yes.'

'Yes, I saw Beach come up and speak to you.'

There was a pause. Lord Emsworth was about to break it by asking his visitor if she felt quite well, when Lady Constance spoke again. That apprehension in her manner, that nervousness, was now well marked. She traced another pattern on the window-sill.

'Was it important?'

'Was what important?'

'I mean, did he want anything?'

'Who?'

'Beach.'

'Beach?'

'Yes. I was wondering what he wanted to see you about.'

Quite suddenly there flashed upon Lord Emsworth the recollection that Beach had done more than merely hand him Baxter's note. With it – dash it, yes, it all came back to him – with it he had given his month's notice. And it just showed, Lord Emsworth felt, what a morass of trouble he was engulfed in that the fact of this superb butler handing in his resignation had made almost no impression upon him. If such a thing had happened only as recently as yesterday, it would have constituted a major crisis. He would have felt that the foundations of his world were rocking. And he had scarcely listened. 'Yes, yes,' he had said, if he remembered correctly. 'Yes, yes, yes. All right.' Or words to that effect.

Bending his mind now on the disaster, Lord Emsworth sat stunned. He was appalled. Almost since the beginning of time, this super-butler had been at the Castle, and now he was about to melt away like snow in the sunshine – or as much like snow in the sunshine as was within the scope of a man who weighed sixteen stone in the buff. It was frightful. The thing was a nightmare. He couldn't get on without Beach. Life without Beach would be insupportable.

He gave tongue, his voice sharp and anguished.

'Connie! Do you know what's happened? Beach has given notice!'

'What!'

'Yes! His month's notice. He's given it. Beach has. And not a word of explanation. No reason. No—'

Lord Emsworth broke off. His face suddenly hardened. What seemed the only possible solution of the mystery had struck him. Connie was at the bottom of this. Connie must have been coming the *grande dame* on the butler, wounding his sensibilities.

Yes, that must be it. It was just the sort of thing she would do. If he had caught her being the Old English Aristocrat once, he had caught her a hundred times. That way of hers of pursing the lips and raising the eyebrows and generally doing the daughter-of-a-hundred-earls stuff. Naturally no butler would stand it.

'Connie,' he cried, adjusting his pince-nez and staring keenly and accusingly, 'what have you been doing to Beach?'

Something that was almost a sob burst from Lady Constance's lips. Her lovely complexion had paled, and in some odd way she seemed to have shrunk.

'I shot him,' she whispered.

Lord Emsworth was a little hard of hearing.

'You did what?'

'I shot him.'

'Shot him?'

'Yes.'

'You mean, *shot* him?'

'Yes, yes, yes! I shot him with George's airgun.'

A whistling sigh escaped Lord Emsworth. He leaned back in his chair, and the library seemed to be dancing old country dances before his eyes. To say that he felt weak with relief would be to understate the effect of this extraordinary communication. His relief was so intense that he felt absolutely boneless. Not once but many times during the past quarter of an hour he had said to himself that only a miracle could save him from the consequences of his sins, and now the miracle had happened. No one was more alive than he to the fact that women are abundantly possessed of crust, but after this surely even Connie could not have the crust to reproach him for what he had done.

'Shot him?' he said, recovering speech.

A fleeting touch of the old imperiousness returned to Lady Constance.

'Do stop saying "Shot him?" Clarence! Isn't it bad enough to have done a perfectly mad thing, without having to listen to you talking like a parrot? Oh, dear! Oh, dear!'

'But what did you do it for?'

'I don't know. I tell you I don't know. Something seemed suddenly to come over me. It was as if I had been bewitched.

After you went out, I thought I would take the gun to Beach—'

'Why?'

'I . . . I. . . . Well, I thought it would be safer with him than lying about in the library. So I took it down to his pantry. And all the way there I kept remembering what a wonderful shot I had been as a child—'

'What?' Lord Emsworth could not let this pass. 'What do you mean, you were a wonderful shot as a child? You've never shot in your life.'

'I have. Clarence, you were talking about Julia shooting Miss Mapleton. It wasn't Julia – it was I. She had made me stay in and do my rivers of Europe over again, so I shot her. I was a splendid shot in those days.'

'I bet you weren't as good as me,' said Lord Emsworth, piqued. 'I used to shoot rats.'

'So used I to shoot rats.'

'How many rats did you ever shoot?'

'Oh, Clarence, Clarence! Never mind about the rats.'

'No,' said Lord Emsworth, called to order. 'No, dash it. Never mind about the rats. Tell me about this Beach business.'

'Well, when I got to the pantry, it was empty, and I saw Beach outside by the laurel bush, reading in a deck-chair—'

'How far away?'

'I don't know. What does it matter? About six feet, I suppose.'

'Six feet? Ha!'

'And I shot him. I couldn't resist it. It was like some horrible obsession. There was a sort of hideous picture in my mind of how he would jump. So I shot him.'

'How do you know you did? I expect you missed him.'

'No. Because he sprang up. And then he saw me at the

window and came in, and I said "Oh, Beach, I want you to take this airgun and keep it," and he said, "Very good, m'lady."'

'He didn't say anything about your shooting him?'

'No. And I have been hoping and hoping that he had not realized what had happened. I have been in an agony of suspense. But now you tell me that he has given his notice, so he must have done. Clarence,' cried Lady Constance, clasping her hands like a persecuted heroine, 'you see the awful position, don't you? If he leaves us, he will spread the story all over the county and people will think I'm mad. I shall never be able to live it down. You must persuade him to withdraw his notice. Offer him double wages. Offer him anything. He must not be allowed to leave. If he does, I shall never . . . S'h!'

'What do you mean, S' . . . Oh, ah,' said Lord Emsworth, at last observing that the door was opening.

It was his niece Jane who entered.

'Oh, hullo, Aunt Constance,' she said. 'I was wondering if you were in here. Mr Baxter's looking for you.'

Lady Constance was distrait.

'Mr Baxter?'

'Yes. I heard him asking Beach where you were. I think he wants to see you about something,' said Jane.

She directed at Lord Emsworth a swift glance, accompanied by a fleeting wink. 'Remember!' said the glance. 'Categorically!' said the wink.

Footsteps sounded outside. Rupert Baxter strode into the room.

At an earlier point in this chronicle, we have compared the aspect of Rupert Baxter, when burning with resentment, to a thunder-cloud, and it is possible that the reader may have formed a mental picture of just an ordinary thunder-cloud, the kind that rumbles a bit but does not really amount to anything very much. It was not this kind of cloud that the secretary resembled now, but one of those which burst over cities in the Tropics, inundating countrysides while thousands flee. He moved darkly towards Lady Constance, his hand outstretched. Lord Emsworth he ignored.

'I have come to say good-bye, Lady Constance,' he said.

There were not many statements that could have roused Lady Constance from her preoccupation, but this one did. She ceased to be the sports-woman brooding on memories of shikari, and stared aghast.

'Good-bye?'

'Good-bye.'

'But, Mr Baxter, you are not leaving us?'

'Precisely.'

For the first time, Rupert Baxter deigned to recognize that the ninth Earl was present.

'I am not prepared,' he said bitterly, 'to remain in a house where my chief duty appears to be to act as a target for Lord Emsworth and his airgun.'

'What!'

'Exactly.'

In the silence which followed these words, Jane once more gave her uncle that glance of encouragement and stimulation – that glance which said 'Be firm!' To her astonishment, she perceived that it was not needed. Lord Emsworth was firm already. His face was calm, his eye steady, and his pince-nez were not even quivering.

'The fellow's potty,' said Lord Emsworth in a clear, resonant voice. 'Absolutely potty. Always told you he was. Target for my airgun? Pooh! Pah! What's he talking about?'

Rupert Baxter quivered. His spectacles flashed fire.

'Do you deny that you shot me, Lord Emsworth?'

'Certainly I do.'

'Perhaps you will deny admitting to this lady here in the writing-room that you shot me?'

'Certainly I do.'

'Did you tell me that you had shot Mr Baxter, Uncle Clarence?' said Jane. 'I didn't hear you.'

'Of course I didn't.'

'I thought you hadn't. I should have remembered it.'

Rupert Baxter's hands shot ceilingwards, as if he were calling upon heaven to see justice done.

'You admitted it to me personally. You begged me not to tell anyone. You tried to put matters right by engaging me as your secretary, and I accepted the position. At that time I was perfectly willing to forget the entire affair. But when, not half an hour later...'

Lord Emsworth raised his eyebrows. Jane raised hers.

'How very extraordinary,' said Jane.

'Most,' said Lord Emsworth.

He removed his pince-nez and began to polish them, speaking soothingly the while. But his manner, though soothing, was very resolute.

'Baxter, my dear fellow,' he said, 'there's only one explanation of all this. It's just what I was telling you. You've been having these hallucinations of yours again. I never said a word to you about shooting you. I never said a word to my niece about shooting you. Why should I, when I hadn't? And, as for what you say about engaging you as my secretary, the absurdity of the thing is manifest on the very face of it. There is nothing on earth that would induce me to have you as my secretary. I don't want to hurt your feelings, but I'd rather be dead in a ditch. Now, listen, my dear Baxter, I'll tell you what to do. You just jump on that motor-bicycle of yours and go on touring England where you left off. And soon you will find that the fresh air will do wonders for that pottiness of yours. In a day or two you won't know...'

Rupert Baxter turned and stalked from the room.

'Mr Baxter!' cried Lady Constance.

Her intention of going after the fellow and pleading with him to continue inflicting his beastly presence on the quiet home life of Blandings Castle was so plain that Lord Emsworth did not hesitate.

'Connie!'

'But, Clarence!'

'Constance, you will remain where you are. You will not stir a step.'

'But, Clarence!'

'Not a dashed step. You hear me? Let him scram!'

Lady Constance halted, irresolute. Then suddenly she met the full force of the pince-nez and it was as if she – like Rupert Baxter – had been struck by a bullet. She collapsed into a chair and sat there twisting her rings forlornly.

'Oh, and, by the way, Connie,' said Lord Emsworth, 'I've been meaning to tell you. I've given that fellow Abercrombie that job he was asking for. I thought it all over carefully, and decided to drop him a line saying that pursuant on our recent conversation I was offering him Simmons's place. I've been making inquiries, and I find he's a capital fellow.'

'He's a baa-lamb,' said Jane.

'You hear? Jane says he's a baa-lamb. Just the sort of chap we want about the place.'

'So now we're going to get married.'

'So now they're going to get married. An excellent match, don't you think, Connie?'

Lady Constance did not speak. Lord Emsworth raised his voice a little.

'DON'T YOU, CONNIE?'

Lady Constance leaped in her seat as if she had heard the Last Trump.

'Very,' she said. 'Oh, very.'

'Right,' said Lord Emsworth. 'And now I'll go and talk to Beach.'

In the pantry, gazing sadly out on the stable yard, Beach the butler sat sipping a glass of port. In moments of mental stress, port was to Beach what Whiffle was to his employer, or, as we must now ruefully put it, his late employer. He flew to it when Life had got him down, and never before had Life got him down as it had now.

Sitting there in his pantry, that pantry which so soon would know him no more, Beach was in the depths. He mourned like some fallen monarch about to say good-bye to all his greatness and pass into exile. The die was cast. The end had come. Eighteen years, eighteen happy years, he had been in service at Blandings Castle, and now he must go forth, never to return. Little wonder that he sipped port. A weaker man would have swigged brandy.

Something tempestuous burst open the door, and he perceived that his privacy had been invaded by Lord Emsworth. He rose, and stood staring. In all the eighteen years during which he had held office, his employer had never before paid a visit to the pantry.

But it was not simply the other's presence that caused

his gooseberry eyes to dilate to their full width, remarkable though that was. The mystery went deeper than that. For this was a strange, unfamiliar Lord Emsworth, a Lord Emsworth who glared where once he had blinked, who spurned the floor like a mettlesome charger, who banged tables and spilled port.

'Beach,' thundered this changeling, 'what the dooce is all this dashed nonsense?'

'M'lord?'

'You know what I mean. About leaving me. Have you gone off your head?'

A sigh shook the butler's massive frame.

'I fear that in the circumstances it is inevitable, m'lord.'

'Why? What are you talking about? Don't be an ass, Beach. Inevitable, indeed! Never heard such nonsense in my life. Why is it inevitable? Look me in the face and answer me that.'

'I feel it is better to tender my resignation than to be dismissed, m'lord.'

It was Lord Emsworth's turn to stare.

'Dismissed?'

'Yes, m'lord.'

'Beach, you're tight.'

'No, m'lord. Has not Mr Baxter spoken to you, m'lord?'

'Of course he's spoken to me. He's been gassing away half the afternoon. What's that got to do with it?'

Another sigh, seeming to start at the soles of his flat feet, set the butler's waistcoat rippling like corn in the wind.

'I see that Mr Baxter has not yet informed you, m'lord. I assumed that he would have done so before this. But it is a mere matter of time, I fear, before he makes his report.'

'Informed me of what?'

'I regret to say, m'lord, that in a moment of uncontrollable impulse I shot Mr Baxter.'

Lord Emsworth's pince-nez flew from his nose. Without them he could see only indistinctly, but he continued to stare at the butler, and in his eyes there appeared an expression which was a blend of several emotions. Amazement would have been the chief of these, had it not been exceeded by affection. He did not speak, but his eyes said 'My brother!'

'With Master George's airgun, m'lord, which her ladyship left in my custody. I regret to say, m'lord, that upon receipt of the weapon I went out into the grounds and came upon Mr Baxter walking near the shrubbery. I tried to resist the temptation, m'lord, but it was too keen. I was seized with an urge which I have not experienced since I was a small lad, and, in short, I—'

'Plugged him?'

'Yes, m'lord.'

Lord Emsworth could put two and two together.

'So that's what he was talking about in the library. That's what made him change his mind and send me that note. . . . How far was he away when you shot him?'

'A matter of a few feet, m'lord. I endeavoured to conceal myself behind a tree, but he turned very sharply, and I was so convinced that he had detected me that I felt I had no alternative but to resign my situation before he could make his report to you, m'lord.'

'And I thought you were leaving because my sister Connie shot you!'

'Her ladyship did not shoot me, m'lord. It is true that the weapon exploded accidentally in her ladyship's hand, but the bullet passed me harmlessly.'

Lord Emsworth snorted.

'And she said she was a good shot! Can't even hit a sitting butler at six feet. Listen to me, Beach. I want no more of this nonsense of you resigning. Bless my soul, how do you suppose I could get on without you? How long have you been here?'

'Eighteen years, m'lord.'

'Eighteen years! And you talk of resigning! Of all the dashed absurd ideas!'

'But I fear, m'lord, when her ladyship learns—'

'Her ladyship won't learn. Baxter won't tell her. Baxter's gone.'

'Gone, m'lord?'

'Gone for ever.'

'But I understood, m'lord—'

'Never mind what you understood. He's gone. A few feet away, did you say?'

'M'lord?'

'Did you say Baxter was only a few feet away when you got him?'

'Yes, m'lord.'

'Ah!' said Lord Emsworth.

He took the gun absently from the table and absently slipped a slug into the breach. He was feeling pleased and proud, as champions do whose pre-eminence is undisputed. Connie had missed a mark like Beach – practically a haystack – at six feet. Beach had plugged Baxter – true – and so had young George – but only with the muzzle of the gun almost touching the fellow. It had been left for him, Clarence, ninth Earl of Emsworth, to do the real shooting. . . .

A damping thought came to diminish his complacency. It was as if a voice had whispered in his ear the word 'Fluke!' His jaw dropped a little, and he stood for awhile, brooding. He felt flattened and discouraged.

Had it been merely a fluke, that superb shot from the library window? Had he been mistaken in supposing that the ancient skill still lingered? Would he – which was what the voice was hinting – under similar conditions miss nine times out of ten?

A stuttering, sputtering noise broke in upon his reverie. He raised his eyes to the window. Out in the stable yard, Rupert Baxter was starting up his motor-bicycle.

'Mr Baxter, m'lord.'

'I see him.'

An overwhelming desire came upon Lord Emsworth to put this thing to the test, to silence for ever that taunting voice.

'How far away would you say he was, Beach?'

'Fully twenty yards, m'lord.'

'Watch!' said Lord Emsworth.

Into the sputtering of the bicycle there cut a soft pop. It was followed by a sharp howl. Rupert Baxter, who had been leaning on the handle-bars, rose six inches with his hand to his thigh.

'There!' said Lord Emsworth.

Baxter had ceased to rub his thigh. He was a man of intelligence, and he realized that anyone on the premises of Blandings Castle who wasted time hanging about and rubbing thighs was simply asking for it. To one trapped in this inferno of a Blandings Castle instant flight was the only way of winning to safety. The sputtering rose to a crescendo, diminished, died away altogether. Rupert Baxter had gone on, touring England.

Lord Emsworth was still gazing out of the window, raptly, as if looking at the X which marked the spot. For a long moment Beach stood staring reverently at his turned back. Then, as if performing some symbolic rite in keeping with the dignity of the scene, he reached for his glass of port and raised it in a silent toast.

Crime Wave at Blandings

Peace reigned in the butler's pantry. The sweet air of the summer evening poured in through the open window. It was as if Nature had blown the All Clear.

Blandings Castle was itself again.

I

Of the two young men sharing a cell in one of New York's popular police stations Tipton Plimsoll, the tall thin one, was the first to recover, if only gradually, from the effect of the potations which had led to his sojourn in the coop. The other, Wilfred Allsop, pint-size and fragile and rather like the poet Shelley in appearance, was still asleep.

For some time after life had returned to the rigid limbs Tipton sat with his head between his hands, the better to prevent it floating away from the parent neck. He was still far from feeling at the peak of his form and would have given much for a cake of ice against which to rest his forehead, but he was deriving a certain solace from the thought that his betrothed, Veronica, only daughter of Colonel and Lady Hermione Wedge of Rutland Gate, London S.W.7, was three thousand miles away and would never learn of his doings this summer night. He was also reviewing the past, trying to piece together the events that had led up to the tragedy, and little by little they began to come back to him.

The party in the Greenwich Village studio. Quite a good party, with sculptors, *avant garde* playwrights and other local fauna dotted around, busy with their bohemian revels. There had occurred that morning on the New York Stock Exchange one of those slumps or crashes which periodically spoil the day for Stock Exchanges, but it had not touched the lives of residents in the Washington Square neighbourhood, where intellect reigns and little interest is taken in the fluctuations of the money market. Unmoved by the news in the evening papers that Amalgamated Cheese had closed twenty points off and Consolidated Hamburgers fifteen, the members of the party, most of whom would not have known a stock certificate from a greeting card, were all cutting up and having a good time, and so was Tipton. The large fortune he had recently inherited from a deceased uncle was invested in the shares of Tipton's Stores, which never varied more than a point or two, no matter what financial earthquakes might be happening elsewhere.

Over in a corner of this Greenwich Village studio he had perceived a pint-size character at the piano, tickling the ivories with a skill that commanded admiration. His compliments to this pint-size bozo on his virtuosity. The 'Oh, thanks awfully' which betrayed the other's English origin. The subsequent fraternisation. The exchange of names. The quick start of surprise on the bozo's part. Plimsoll, did you say? Not *Tipton* Plimsoll? Sure. Are you the chap who's engaged to Veronica Wedge? That's right. Do you know her? She's my cousin. She's what? My cousin. You mean you're Vee's *cousin*? Have been for years. Well, fry me for an oyster, I think this calls for a drink, don't you?

And that was how it had all begun. Circumstances, it came out in the course of conversation, had rendered Wilfred Allsop low-spirited, and when he sees a friend low-spirited, especially a friend linked by ties of blood to the girl he loves, the man of sensibility spares no effort or expense to alleviate his depression and bring the roses back to his cheeks. One beaker had led to another, the lessons learned at mother's knee had been temporarily forgotten, and here they were, behind bars.

Tipton had been nursing his throbbing head for perhaps a quarter of an hour and had just assured himself by delicate experiment that it was not, as he had at one time feared, going to explode like a high-powered shell, when a soft moan in his rear caused him to turn. Wilfred Allsop was sitting up, his face pale, his eyes glassy, his hair disordered. He looked like the poet Shelley after a big night out with Lord Byron.

'What's this place?' he asked in a faint whisper. 'Is it a jug of some description?'

'That's just about what it is, Willie. We call them hoosegows over here, but the general effect is the same. How's the boy?'

'What boy?'

'You.'

'Oh, me? I'm dying.'

'Of course you're not.'

'Yes, I am,' said Wilfred with some asperity. A man is entitled to know whether he is dying or not. 'And before I pass on there's something I want you to promise you'll do for me. If you're engaged to Vee, I take it you've visited Blandings Castle?'

'Sure. It was there I met her.'

'Well, did you happen, while there, to run into a girl called Monica Simmons?'

'The name doesn't ring a bell. Who is she?'

'She looks after Empress of Blandings, that pig of my Uncle Clarence's.'

'Ah, then I've seen her. Old Emsworth took me to the sty a couple of times and she was there, ladling out the bran mash. Girl who looks like an all-in wrestler.'

Wilfred's asperity became more marked. Their evening

together had filled him with a deep affection for Tipton Plimsoll, but even from a great friend he could not countenance loose talk of this sort.

'I am sorry you think she looks like an all-in wrestler,' he said stiffly. 'To me she seems to resemble one of those Norse goddesses. However, be that as it may, I love her, Tippy. I fell in love with her at first sight.'

Recalling the picture of Miss Simmons in smock and trousers with a good deal of mud on her face, Tipton found this difficult to believe, but he was sympathetic.

'Good for you. Peach of a girl, I should imagine. Did you tell her so?'

'I couldn't do it. I hadn't the nerve. She's so majestic, and I'm such a little squirt. You agree that I'm a little squirt, Tippy?'

'Well, I don't know I'd put it just that way, but I guess one's got to face it, there are taller guys around.'

'All I've done so far is look at her and talk about the weather.'

'Not much percentage in that.'

'No, the whole thing's quite hopeless. But here's what I was starting to say. I want you, when I am gone, to see that she gets my cigarette case. It's all I have to leave. Can I trust you to do this when I have passed beyond the veil?'

'You aren't going to pass beyond the veil.'

'I *am* going to pass beyond the veil,' said Wilfred petulantly. 'You've made a note of what I was saying. Cigarette case. To be given to Monica Simmons after my decease.'

'Does she smoke?'

'Of course she smokes.'

'She'll be able to blow smoke rings at the pig.'

Wilfred stiffened.

'There is no need to be flippant about it, Plimsoll. I am asking you as a friend to perform this small act of kindness for me. Can I rely on you?'

'Sure. I'll attend to it.'

'Tell her my last thoughts were of her and I expired with her name on my lips.'

'Okay.'

'Thank you, thank you, thank you,' said Wilfred, and went to sleep again.

II

Deprived of human companionship, Tipton felt sad and lonely. He was a gregarious soul and it always made him uneasy when he had no one to talk to. Throughout these exchanges with Wilfred Allsop he had been aware of a policeman pacing up and down the corridor on the other side of the bars, and policemen, while often not ideal as conversationalists, being inclined to confine themselves to monosyllables and those spoken out of the side of their mouths, are better than nothing. He went to the bars and, peering through them like some rare specimen in a zoo, uttered a husky 'Hey, officer.'

The policeman was a long, stringy policeman, who flowed out of his uniform at odd spots. His face was gnarled, his wrists knobbly and of a geranium hue, and he had those three or four extra inches of neck which disqualify a man for high honours in a beauty competition. But beneath this forbidding exterior there lay a kindly heart and he could make allowances for the indiscretions of youth. Muggers, stick-up men and hoodlums in general he disliked, but towards the Tipton type of malefactor he was able to be indulgent. So where to one of his ordinary clientele he would have replied with a brusque 'Pipe down, youse,' he now said 'Hi' in a not uncordial voice and joined Tipton at the bars, through which they proceeded to converse like a modern Pyramus and Thisbe.

'How's it coming?' he asked.

Tipton replied that he had a headache, and the policeman said that that occasioned him no surprise.

'You certainly earned it, Mac.'

'I guess I was kind of high.'

'You sure were,' said the policeman. 'The boys were saying it took three of them to get you into the paddy wagon.'

His manner had not been censorious and his voice had contained admiration rather than reproof, but nevertheless Tipton felt it incumbent on him to justify himself.

'You mustn't think I do this sort of thing often,' he said. 'At one time, yes, but not since I became engaged. I promised my fiancée I'd go easy on the nights of wine and roses. But this was a special case. I was trying to cheer up my friend over there and bring a little sunshine into his life.'

'Feeling low, was he?'

'In the depths, officer, and with reason. He was telling me the whole story. He's a musician. Plays the piano and composes things. He came here from England some months ago hoping to crash Tin Pan Alley or get taken on by one of the bands, but couldn't make the grade. Ran out of money and had to cable home for supplies.'

'And the folks wouldn't send him none?'

'Oh sure, they sent him enough to buy his passage to England. He leaves the day after tomorrow. But his Aunt Hermione said it was high time he stopped fooling around and settled down to a regular job, and she'd found one for him. And do you know what that job is? Teaching music in a girls' school. And that's not all. The woman who runs the school is a rabid Dry and won't let her staff so much as look at a snifter. It means that poor old Willie won't be able to take aboard the simplest highball except in vacation time.'

'What he had tonight ought to last him quite a while.'

'Don't mock, officer, don't scoff,' said Tipton, frowning. 'The thing's a tragedy. It has absolutely shattered Willie, and I don't wonder. There was a guy at the Drones Club in London, of which I am a member, who once got roped in to make a speech to a girls' school, and he never really recovered from the experience. To this day he trembles like a leaf if he sees anything in a straw hat and a blazer, with pigtails down its back. Teaching a bunch of girls music will be ten times worse. They'll put their heads together and whisper. They'll nudge each other and giggle. They'll probably throw spitballs at him. And nothing to strengthen him for the ordeal but lemonade and sarsaparilla. But I notice you're yawning. I'm not keeping you up, am I?'

The policeman said he was not. He was, he explained, on all-night duty and was glad of a chat to while the time away.

'Fine,' said Tipton, reassured. 'Yes, I can imagine you must find it pretty dull without anyone to shoot the breeze with. It can't be all jam being a cop.'

'You can say that again.'

'Still, you have compensations.'

'Name three.'

'Well, you meet such interesting people – bandits, porch climbers, dope pushers, sex fiends and what not. The whole boiling from deadbeats to millionaires.'

'We don't get a lot of millionaires.'

'You don't?'

'Never seen one myself.'

'Is that so? Well, you're seeing one now. Take a gander.'

The policeman stared.

'You?'

'Me.'

'No kidding?'

'None whatever. You know Tipton's Stores?'

'Sure. The wife does her marketing there.'

'Well, tell her when you get home that you were host tonight to the guy who owns the controlling interest in them. My Uncle Chet founded Tipton's Stores. He checked out not long ago and I inherited his block of shares, practically all there are. I'm rolling.'

'Then why don't you pay your ten bucks and get out of here?'

'What ten bucks?'

'For bail. I'd do it if it was me.'

A bitter laugh escaped Tipton, the sort of laugh a toad beneath the harrow might have uttered if some passer-by had asked it why it did not move from beneath the harrow, where conditions must be far from comfortable.

'I dare say you would,' he said, 'and so would I if I had the dough. But I've no funds of any description. Oh, I don't mean I've been wiped out in this Stock Exchange crash they've been having – I may be a chump, but I'm not chump enough to play the market – but I don't have a nickel on me at the moment. At some point in this evening's proceedings some child of unmarried parents got away with my entire wad, leaving me without a cent. I own a controlling interest in the country's largest supermarket, with branches in every town in the United States. I own a ranch out west. I own an apartment house on Park Avenue. I even own a music publishing business in London.

But I can't get out of this darned dungeon because I haven't ten
dollars in my kick. Can you beat that for irony?'

The policeman said he was unable to, but seemed to see no
cause for despair.

'You got friends, ain't you?'

'Lashings of them.'

'Well, why don't you phone one of them and get him to help
you out?'

Tipton was surprised.

'Do they let you phone from here?'

'You're allowed one call.'

'Is that the law?'

'That's the law.'

'Then ... Oh, finished your little nap, Willie?'

Wilfred Allsop had risen, blinked his eyes several times,
groaned, shuddered from head to foot and was now joining the
party. He seemed in slightly better shape than on the occasion
of his previous resurrection. His resemblance to a corpse that
had been in the water several days was still pronounced, but it
had become a cheerier corpse, one that had begun to look on the
bright side.

'Oh, Tippy,' he said, 'I thought you would be interested to
know that I'm not going to die. I'm feeling a little better.'

'That's the spirit.'

'Not much better, but a little. So never mind about the cigarette case. Who's that you're talking to? I can't see him very
distinctly, but isn't he a policeman?'

'That's right.'

'Do you think he could tell us how to get out of here?'

'The very point I was discussing with him when you came to

the surface. He says the hellhounds of the system will release us if we slip them ten bucks apiece.'

Wilfred's mind was still clouded, but he was capable of formulating an idea.

'Let's slip them ten bucks apiece,' he suggested.

'How? You haven't any dough, have you?'

'None.'

'Nor have I. Somebody swiped my roll. But this gentleman, Mr – ?'

'Garroway.'

'Mr Garroway here says I can phone a friend for some.'

Again Wilfred Allsop had a constructive proposal to put forward.

'Go and phone a friend for some.'

Tipton shook his head, and uttered a sharp howl. There are times when shaking the head creates the illusion that one has met Jael the wife of Heber, incurred her displeasure and started her going into her celebrated routine.

'It isn't as simple as all that. There's a catch. One's only allowed one call.'

'I don't get your point.'

'Then you must be still stewed. You get it, don't you, Mr Garroway?'

'Sure. Your buddy mightn't be there. Then you'll have used up your call and got nowheres.'

'Exactly. It's the middle of August and all the guys I know are out of town. They'll be coming back after Labour Day, but it won't be Labour Day for another three weeks, and we don't want to have to wait till then. Gosh, I wish you wouldn't do that,' said Tipton, wincing.

He was alluding to a sudden sharp barking sound which had

proceeded from his fellow prisoner's lips. It had affected his head unpleasantly, creating the passing impression that someone had touched off a stick or two of dynamite inside it.

'Sorry,' said Wilfred. 'I was thinking of Uncle Clarence.'

The statement did nothing to mollify Tipton. He said with a good deal of bitterness that that did credit to a nephew's heart. It was nice of him, he said, to think of his Uncle Clarence.

'He's in New York. He's at the Plaza. He came over here for my Aunt Constance's wedding. She was marrying a Yank called Schoonmaker.'

Tipton saw that he had judged his friend too hastily. What he had taken for an idle changing of the subject had been in reality most pertinent to the issue.

'That's right,' he exclaimed. 'I read about it in the papers. This begins to look good. You're sure he's at the Plaza?'

'Certain. Aunt Hermione told me to go and look him up there.'

'But can I wake him at this time of night?'

'If you explain that it's an emergency. You'll have to make it quite clear that your need is urgent. You know what a muddle-headed old ass he is.'

This was perfectly true. Clarence, ninth Earl of Emsworth, that vague and dreamy peer, was not one of England's keenest brains. The life he led made for slowness of the thinking processes. Except when he was attending sisters' weddings in America, he spent his time pottering about the gardens and messuages of Blandings Castle, his rural seat, his thoughts, such as they were, concentrated on his prize sow, Empress of Blandings. When indoors you could generally find him in his study engrossed in a book of porcine interest, most frequently that monumental work *On The Care Of The Pig* by Augustus

Whipple (Popgood and Grooly, thirty-five shillings), of which he never wearied.

Tipton's first enthusiasm had begun to wane. Like Hamlet, he had become irresolute. He chewed his lower lip dubiously.

'It's taking a big chance. Suppose he's out on a toot somewhere?'

'Is it likely that a staid old bird like Uncle Clarence would go on toots?'

'You never know.'

'If it was my Uncle Galahad, I wouldn't say, but surely not Uncle Clarence.'

'It's a possibility that has to be taken into consideration. The most respectable of Limeys get it up their noses and start stepping out when they come to New York. It's the air here. Very heady. What would you do in a case like this, Mr Garroway?'

The policeman fingered a chin modelled on the ram of a battleship. There was a rasping sound as he scratched it.

'Lemme get it straight. You want to make sure the guy's in?'

'The whole enterprise depends on that.'

'Well, how about me calling him first? If he answers, it'll mean he's there and I'll hang up. Then you give him a buzz.'

Tipton eyed him reverently. A Daniel come to judgment, he was feeling. If this was the normal level of intelligence in New York's police force, it was not to be wondered at that they were known as The Finest.

'God bless you, Garroway,' he said emotionally, 'you've solved the whole problem. Tell Mrs Garroway next time she shops at Tipton's Stores to mention my name and say I said she was to have anything she wants on the house, from certified butter to prime rib of beef and chicken noodle soup.'

'Very kind of you, sir. She'll be tickled pink. The Plaza I think you said, and your buddy's name is Clarence?'

'Emsworth.'

'My mistake.'

'Ask for the Earl of Emsworth. He's a lord.'

'Oh, one of those? Right.'

III

The officer hurried off, and Tipton gazed after him, awed.

'What malarkey people talk about the New York police being brutal,' he said. 'Brutal, my left eyeball. I never met a sweeter guy, did you?'

'Never.'

'You can hear the milk of human kindness sloshing about inside him.'

'Distinctly.'

'It wouldn't surprise me to find he'd started life as a Boy Scout.'

'Nor me.'

'It shows how silly it is to go by people's looks. It's not his fault that he's no oil painting.'

'Of course not.'

'And what is beauty, after all?'

'Exactly. Skin deep, I often say.'

'So do I, frequently.'

'It's the heart that counts.'

'Every time. And his is as big as the Yankee Stadium. Ah, Garroway. What's the score?'

'He's there.'

'Three – no, make it four – rousing cheers. How did he seem?'

'Sleepy.'

'I mean in what sort of mood? Amiable? Docile? Friendly? A likely prospect for the touch, did you feel?'

'Sure.'

'Then stand out of my way and let me get at that telephone,' said Tipton.

As he went, his head was still aching, but his heart was light. He was about to embark on a course of action which would fill the bosoms of several of his fellow creatures, notably Colonel and Lady Hermione Wedge, with alarm and despondency, but he did not know this. He was not clairvoyant.

CHAPTER 2

I

The Blandings Castle of which mention was made in the previous chapter of this chronicle stands on a knoll of rising ground at the southern end of the Vale of Blandings in the county of Shropshire. It came into existence towards the middle of the fifteenth century at a time when the landed gentry of England, who never knew when a besieging army might not be coming along, particularly if they lived close to the Welsh border, believed in building their little nests solid. Huge and grey and majestic, adorned with turrets and battlements in great profusion, it unquestionably takes the eye. Even Tipton Plimsoll, though not as a rule given to poetic rhapsodies, had become lyrical on first beholding it, making a noise with his tongue like the popping of a cork and saying 'Some joint!' The illustrated weeklies often print articles about it accompanied by photographs showing the park, the gardens, the yew alley and its other attractions. In these its proprietor, Clarence, ninth Earl of Emsworth, sometimes appears, looking like an absentminded member of the Jukes family, for he has always been a careless dresser and when in front of a camera is inclined to let his mouth hang open in rather a noticeable way.

On a fine morning a few days after the hand of the law had

fallen on Tipton and his fiancée's cousin Wilfred Allsop the beauty of the noble building was enhanced by the presence outside it of Sebastian Beach, the castle butler. He was standing beside a luggage-laden car which was drawn up at the front door, waiting to give an official send-off to Lord Emsworth's younger brother Galahad, who, with his niece Veronica Wedge, was about to drive to London to pick up the ninth Earl on his return from America.

As is so often the case with butlers, there was a good deal of Beach. Julius Caesar, who liked to have men about him that were fat, would have taken to him at once. He was a man who had made two chins grow where only one had been before, and his waistcoat swelled like the sail of a racing yacht. You would never have thought, to look at him, that forty years ago he had come in first in a choir boys' bicycle race, open to those whose voices had not broken by the first Sunday in Epiphany, and that only two days before the start of this story he had won the Market Blandings Darts Tournament, outshooting such seasoned experts as Jno. Robinson, who ran the station taxi cab, and Percy Bulstrode, the local chemist.

He had been standing there for some minutes, when a brisk, dapper little gentleman in the early fifties appeared in the doorway and came down the steps. This was the Hon. Galahad Threepwood, a man disapproved of by his numerous sisters but considered in the Servants' Hall to shed lustre on Blandings Castle.

Gally Threepwood was the only genuinely distinguished member of the family of which Lord Emsworth was the head. Lord Emsworth himself had once won a first prize for pumpkins at the Shropshire Agricultural Show and his pig, Empress of Blandings, had three times been awarded the silver medal for fatness at that annual festival, but you could not say that he had really risen to eminence in the public life of England. Gally, on the other hand, had made a name for himself. The passage of the years had put him more or less in retirement now, but in his youth he had been one of the lights of London, one of the great figures at whom the world of the stage, the racecourse and the rowdier restaurants had pointed with pride. There were men in London – bookmakers, skittle sharps, jellied eel sellers at race meetings and the like – who would have been puzzled to know whom you were referring to if you had spoken of Einstein, but they were all familiar with Gally.

He was soberly dressed now for his visit to London, but even in this decorous costume he seemed to bring with him a whiff of the paddock and the American bar. He still gave the impression that he was wearing a checked coat, tight trousers and a grey bowler hat and that there were race glasses bumping against his left hip. His bright eyes, one of them adorned with a black-rimmed monocle, seemed to be watching horses rounding into the straight, his neatly shod foot to be pawing in search of a brass rail.

He greeted Beach with the easy cordiality of a friend of long standing. There had existed between them a perfect *rapport* since they had both been slips of boys of forty. Each respected and admired the other for his many gifts.

'Hullo, Beach. Lovely morning.'

'Yes, sir.'

Gally looked at him sharply. The sombreness of his voice had surprised him. Scanning his face, he could see that it was a dull purple colour and that the lower of his two chins was quivering.

'Something the matter, Beach? You have the air of a man whose soul is not at rest. What's wrong?'

From anyone else the butler would have hidden his secret sorrow, but everybody confided in Gally. Barmaids poured out their troubles to him, and the humblest racecourse tout knew that he could rely on him for sympathy and understanding.

'I have been grossly insulted, Mr Galahad.'

'You have? Who by? Or by whom, as the case may be?'

'The young gentleman.'

'You don't mean Wilfred Allsop?'

'No, sir. Master Winkworth.'

'Oh, Huxley? Unpleasant brat, that. And yet his mother dotes on him, which just shows there's no accounting for tastes. What did he say?'

'He criticised my personal appearance.'

'He must be hard to please.'

'Yes, sir,' said Beach, prepared now to withhold nothing. He had been wanting a friendly shoulder to cry on ever since the affront to his dignity had occurred. 'He told me that I was fatter than Empress of Blandings.'

No vestige of a smile appeared on Gally's face. He was all kindly reassurance.

'You mustn't pay any attention to what a little wart like that says. He only does it to annoy, because he knows it teases. I hope you treated him with the contempt he deserved.'

'I am afraid I came within an ace of clipping him on the side of the head, Mr Galahad.'

'It would have done him all the good in the world, but I'm glad you didn't. It wouldn't have pleased his mother. But don't let his critique worry you. Admittedly you get your money's worth out of a weighing machine and if your body were fished out of the Thames it would be described as that of a well-nourished man of middle age, but what of it? I rather envy you.

I could do with a few more pounds myself. Odd,' said Gally thoughtfully, 'how sensitive people are about their weight. I am reminded of Chet Tipton. Did I ever tell you about Chet Tipton?'

'Not to my recollection, Mr Galahad.'

'Uncle of the chap who's marrying my niece Veronica. American, but spent a good deal of his time over here and I used to see a lot of him at the old Pelican Club. Enormously fat fellow. People used to chaff him about it, so at last he decided to buy one of those abdominal belts you see advertised. Rubber they're made of and you clamp them round your tummy and melt inside them. Well, naturally they have to be a pretty tight fit and Chet could hardly breathe in his and of course could take no solid nourishment, but he stuck to it because he knew how slim it was making him look, and he was having a buttered rum in the Criterion bar one morning instead of lunch, when a friend of his came in and said "Hullo, Chet", and he said "Hullo, George or Jack or Jimmy or whatever the name was", and they chatted for a while, and then the chap said "Aren't you rather stouter than when I saw you last? I'll tell you what you ought to do, Chet. You ought to get one of those abdominal belts". He gave it up after that. Sort of discouraged him. Dead now, poor fellow, as so many of the old crowd are. Yes, only a few of us left now. Well, is the luggage all in?'

'Yes, sir.'

'Then if I'm going to pick Clarence up for lunch, we ought to be starting. What's the time?'

Beach drew from the pocket of his spreading waistcoat the handsome silver watch bestowed on him as the prize in the Market Blandings Darts Tournament. It was his dearest possession and never failed to give him a thrill when he looked at it.

'Just on ten, Mr Galahad.'

'Well, dash in and tell that Wedge girl to get a move on. Ah, here she is. No, it's only Sandy Callender.'

II

The girl who was coming down the steps was in many respects a most agreeable sight for the eye to rest on. Her figure was trim, her nose and mouth above criticism and her hair that attractive red that Titian used to admire so much. But to a connoisseur of beauty like Gally the whole effect was spoiled by the tortoise-shell-rimmed spectacles she was wearing. They seemed to cover most of her face, and he wondered when she had taken to them. There had been no sign of them at their last meeting, though of course she may have had them tucked away in her bag.

'Hullo, young Sandy,' he said.

Alexandra ('Sandy') Callender and he were old friends. She had been working for the late Chet Tipton when he had first known her, and it was he who had obtained for her the post of secretary to his brother Clarence, a fact which he hoped would never come to his brother Clarence's knowledge, for his reproaches would have been hard to bear. Lord Emsworth was, and always had been, allergic to secretaries.

'You look very dusty, Sandy. Have you been rolling in something?'

'I've been cleaning out Lord Emsworth's study.'

'Poor devil.'

'Me?'

'Clarence. He hates having his study cleaned.'

'Does he like a mess?'

'He loves it. It's his idea of comfort. Well, you seem to have been putting in some strenuous work. Your appearance brings to mind a headline I saw in a paper once about Sons Of Toil Buried Beneath Tons Of Soil. Still, if it makes you happy.'

'Oh, I'm quite happy. Gally, I wonder if you would mind posting this parcel in London for me.'

'Of course.'

'Thank you,' said Sandy, and went back into the house.

Gally looked after her thoughtfully. There had been a certain something in her manner that gave him the impression that she was not as happy as she had stated herself to be, and it disturbed him. It was not the first time he had noticed this. She had been below par since her arrival. In the Chet Tipton days he had found her a merry little soul, always good for a couple of laughs, but Blandings Castle seemed to have depressed her. Brooding on something, unless he was very much mistaken. He scanned the parcel, noting the address.

'S. G. Bagshott, 4 Halsey Chambers, Halsey Court, London W.1. Unusual name. There can't be many Bagshotts around. I wonder if he's any relation to my old friend Boko. You remember Boko Bagshott, Beach?'

'I fear not, Mr Galahad. I do not think he was ever a visitor at the castle.'

'That's right, I don't believe he ever was. I used to see him in London and at a whacking big house he had down in Sussex near Petworth. Interesting personality. He made a practice every year of kidding some insurance company that he wanted to insure his life for a hundred thousand pounds or so and after the doctors had examined him telling them he had changed his mind. He thus got an annual medical check-up for nothing.'

'Ingenious, Mr Galahad.'

'Very. One of the brightest brains in the old Pelican. This chap might quite easily be his son. He had a son called Samuel Galahad. I recall that distinctly. He named him Samuel after Sam Bowles the jockey and Galahad because he was a bit superstitious and thought it might lead to the boy inheriting what he supposed to be my ability to spot winners. Not that I ever did spot many winners, but he always had a great respect for my judgment after I gave him a hundred to eight shot for the Jubilee Cup. He used to come to me before every important meeting and seek my advice. I wonder what young Sandy is sending him parcels about. There is a squashiness about this one that excites the interest. It feels as if—'

He would have spoken further of the parcel's squashiness and its possible contents, but at this moment an interruption occurred. A vision of beauty had appeared at the head of the steps, a girl of a radiant blonde loveliness that would have drawn a whistle from the least susceptible of the Armed Forces of the United States of America. Nature had not given Veronica Wedge more than about as much brain as would fit comfortably into an aspirin bottle, feeling no doubt that it was better not to overdo the thing, but apart from that she had everything and it is scarcely surprising that Tipton Plimsoll, when he spoke of her, did so with a catch in his throat and a tremolo in his voice.

She was followed by her mother, Lord Emsworth's sister Hermione, at whom not even Don Juan or Casanova would have whistled. Lady Hermione Wedge was the only one of the female members of the Emsworth family who was not statuesquely handsome. She was short and dumpy and looked like a cook – in her softer moods a cook well satisfied with her latest soufflé; when stirred to anger a cook about to give notice; but always a cook of strong character. Her husband, Colonel

Egbert Wedge, was as wax in her hands, as was her daughter Veronica.

The parcel attracted her attention.

'What have you got there, Galahad?'

'It's something squashy the Callender girl wants me to post for her in London. Amazing that she has time to pack parcels with all the charlady work she's doing in Clarence's study. She's certainly a competent secretary. Poor old Clarence!'

'What do you mean, poor old Clarence?'

'Well, you know how he dislikes competent secretaries. They bother him and get on his nerves. They keep him from evading his responsibilities.'

'What does evading his responsibilities mean, Mummee?' said Veronica.

It was the sort of question she frequently asked, and as a rule her mother was prompt with patient explanations, sometimes taking as much as ten minutes over them, but now she found herself ignored. Lady Hermione's thoughts were not on her off-spring. Gally's monocle had just flashed in the morning sun and she was thinking how much she disliked it. In common with all her sisters she considered Gally a disgrace to a proud family and a blot on the escutcheon, but she sometimes felt that she could have borne him with more fortitude if he had not worn a monocle. There were bookmakers and racecourse touts who held a similar view. Widely differing from Lady Hermione on almost every other point, they became, as she did, uncomfortable beneath the glare of Gally's black-rimmed eyeglass.

'Clarence must be made to realise that he cannot evade his responsibilities. The one thing he needs is a good secretary. Left to himself, he would never answer his letters.'

His letters! A blinding light flashed upon Gally.

'Excuse me a moment,' he said, and leaped lissomely up the steps and into the house. Lady Hermione looked after him frowningly, her lips set. She liked him least when he behaved like a pea on a hot shovel.

III

Sandy was in Lord Emsworth's study, more than ever encrusted with dust and deep in documents which should have been attended to weeks before. She looked up, surprised, as Gally came trotting in.

'Haven't you gone yet?'

'The start of the expedition has been postponed in order that I may have a word with you. Busy?'

'Very.'

'Wait till Clarence sees your handiwork. He'll have a fit. For God's sake don't ever let him know that it was I who got you the job. Well, young Sandy, so you're sending the boy friend back his letters, are you?'

She started, dislodging a bill for goods supplied which had managed to get entangled in her hair.

'I don't know what you mean!'

'No good trying to fool me, child. I know what's in this parcel. Correct me if I'm wrong, but this is the set-up as I see it. You were engaged to this S. G. Bagshott. For a time you thought him the only onion in the stew. Then you had a fight about something and relations deteriorated to the point where you told him those wedding bells would not ring out. Take back your ring, you said, take back the bottle of scent you gave me on my birthday, you said, and now you're returning his letters. Am I right?'

'More or less.'

'And you really want me to post this parcel?'

'Yes.'

'This is the end, is it?'

'Yes.'

'What did the poor fish do to make you mad? How do you know the girl you saw him kissing wasn't his aunt?'

'I did not see him kissing a girl.'

'Well, what put you off him? Did he step on your foot while dancing? Did he criticise your hair-do? Lose your umbrella? Take you out of a business double?'

'If you don't mind, Gally, I've a lot of work to do.'

'What you mean is, Don't be such a damned old Nosey Parker. All right, if you insist. But I'm going to find out what the trouble was. What does that S of his stand for?'

'Samuel.'

'I thought as much. It now becomes pretty certain that he's the son of an old friend of mine and has a claim on my interest. I shall call on him and deliver this parcel in person. He'll give me the facts, and the betting is that I shall bring you two young sundered hearts together again. Sundered hearts make me sick,' said Gally. 'I've been against them from boyhood.'

CHAPTER 3

I

Halsey Court, though situated in Mayfair and entitled to put 'London W.r' after its name, is not a fashionable locality. It is a small, dark, dingy cul-de-sac, far too full of prowling cats, fluttering newspapers and derelict banana skins to attract the *haut monde*. Dukes avoid it, marquises give it a wide berth, earls and viscounts would not settle there if you paid them. It consists of some seedy offices and a block of residential flats, Halsey Chambers, which are occupied mostly by young men of slender means who cannot afford to pick and choose and are thankful to have an inexpensive roof over their heads. Jeff Miller, the writer of novels of suspense, lived there at one time; so did Jerry Shoesmith, editor until his services were dispensed with of the weekly paper *Society Spice*; and now that they had married and gone elsewhere literature was represented by Sandy Callender's late betrothed, Samuel Galahad Bagshott.

Actually, when he had forms to fill up and information to give to an inquisitive bureaucracy, Sam described himself as a barrister, but it was his typewriter that enabled him to pay the rent and enjoy three moderately square meals a day. Like so many commencing barristers, he wrote assiduously while waiting for the briefs to start coming in. He wrote short, bright articles on fly fishing, healthy living, muscle development, great lovers through the ages and the modern girl. He wrote light verse, reviews of novels, interviews with celebrities, chatty Guides to the Brontë country and the Land of Dickens, stories for halfwitted adults, stories for retarded boys and stories for children with water on the brain. It was with the last-named section of his public in mind that he was toiling on the morning when Gally had started his drive to London. He was writing a short story about a kitten called Pinky-Poo which he hoped, if all went well and the editor's heart was in the right place, to sell to the Yuletide number of *Wee Tots*.

He did not look the sort of young man from whom one would have expected stories about kittens called Pinky-Poo or indeed about kittens whose godparents had been less fanciful in their choice of names, for his appearance was distinctly on the rugged side. Tough was the adjective a stylist like Gustave Flaubert would have applied to him, though being French he would have said *dur* or *coriace*. He was large and chunky, he had been one of the Possibles in an England international Rugby trial game, and a fondness for boxing had left his nose a little out of the straight and one of his ears twisted. If he had been your guide to the Brontë country or the Land of Dickens, you would probably have felt a qualm at the thought of being alone with him on a deserted moor or down a dark alley, but your apprehensions would have been needless, for despite his intimidating looks he was inwardly, like Tipton Plimsoll's Officer Garroway, all sweetness and light. Off the football field and outside the ring anything in the shape of mayhem would have been unthinkable to him.

He had written the words 'There never was a naughtier kitten than Pinky-Poo' and was leaning back in his chair with the feeling that he was off to a good start but wondering what twists and turns his narrative would now take, when the doorbell rang. Going to answer it, he found standing on the mat a small, dapper, elderly gentleman with an eyeglass who bade him a civil good morning.

'Good morning,' said Sam, not to be outdone in the courtesies. The thought occurred to him that this might be a solicitor bringing a brief, but he did not really hope. Solicitors, if they call on barristers, do so at their chambers in Lincoln's Inn or wherever it may be, and they seldom wear monocles and never beam as this visitor was doing. Nor are they as a rule so rosy and robust.

That was what struck Sam immediately about Galahad Threepwood, that he looked extraordinarily fit for his years. It was the impression Gally made on everyone who met him. After the life he had led he had no right to burst with health, but he did. Where most of his contemporaries had long ago thrown in the towel and retired to cure resorts to nurse their gout, he had gone blithely on, ever rising on stepping stones of dead whiskies and sodas to higher things. He had discovered the prime grand secret of eternal youth – to keep the decanter circulating, to stop smoking only when snapping the lighter for his next cigarette and never to retire to rest before three in the morning.

'Doesn't he look marvellous?' one of his nieces had once said of him. 'It really is extraordinary that anyone who has had as good a time as he has can be so amazingly healthy. Everywhere you look you see men leading model lives and pegging out in their prime, but good old Uncle Gally, who apparently never went to bed till he was fifty, is still breezing along as perky as ever.'

'Yes?' said Sam.

'Mr Bagshott?'

'Yes.'

'My name is Threepwood.'

'Oh yes?'

'Galahad Threepwood.'

The name touched a chord in Sam's memory. It was one the late Berkeley Bagshott had often mentioned when in reminiscent vein. The conversation of his intimates of the old days was always inclined to turn to Gally as they probed the past.

'Oh, really?' he said, beaming in his turn. 'I've heard my father speak of you.'

'So you *are* old Boko's son? I thought so.'

'You were great friends, weren't you?'

'Bosom.'

'That was why he had me christened Galahad, I suppose.'

'Yes, it was a pretty thought. He told me he would have asked me to be your godfather, only he didn't feel it would be safe. Starting you off under too much of a handicap.'

'Well, it's awfully nice of you to look me up. How did you find my address?'

'It was given me by Sandy Callender as I was leaving Blandings Castle this morning.'

'Oh?' Sam gulped. 'So you've met Sandy?'

'I've known her for quite a time. We first met in New York when she was working for Chet Tipton, a pal of mine. He, poor chap, handed in his dinner pail and she came to London, looking for a job. I ran into her just when my sister Hermione was wanting a secretary for my brother Clarence, so I recommended her and she was signed on. This morning, as I was leaving, she gave me this parcel to post. I saw your name, the S.G. struck me as significant and I decided to deliver it in person, just in case you were the fellow I thought you might be, if you see what I mean. I don't know what odds a bookie would have given me against your turning out to be Boko's son, but it seemed a fair speculative venture, and the long shot came off.'

'I see. Er – how is Sandy?'

'Physically fizzing, spiritually not so good. She has the air of one who is brooding on something, as it might be a broken engagement or something of that kind. Am I right in supposing that this parcel contains your letters?'

Sam nodded gloomily.

'I expect so. She told me she was going to send them back.'

There was a world of sympathy in the eye behind Gally's monocle. As many people did, he had taken an instant liking to this son of one with whom he had so often heard the chimes of midnight, and he longed to do something to lighten his gloom. Years of membership of the old Pelican Club, where somebody was always having trouble with duns or bookies or women, had taught him how comforting it was to tell your sad story to a compassionate listener.

'Would it,' he said, 'be impertinent of me, always bearing in mind that your father and I were old friends and that I may quite possibly have dandled you on my knee as a baby, if I asked what caused the rift between you and young Sandy?'

'Not at all. But it's rather a long story.'

'I have all the time in the world. I've got to meet my brother at Barribault's Hotel, but that's only just round the corner and he won't mind waiting. I'll trickle in, shall I?'

'Do. How about a drink?'

'If you have a spot of whisky?'

'The one thing I do have.'

'Excellent. But I'm afraid I'm interrupting your work.'

'Oh, that's all right. I'm only writing a story about a kitten, and I had got stuck when you arrived. What can I make a kitten do?'

'Chase its tail?'

'But after that? I need a strong story line and a couple of situations that'll knock the *Wee Tots* subscribers' eyes out.'

'Is it your aim to amuse the little blisters, or do you want to scare the pants off them?'

'Either. I'm not fussy.'

'I'm afraid I can't help you.'

'Then help yourself,' said Sam hospitably, placing bottle, glass and syphon at his side.

II

Gally took a restorative draught. Refreshed, he lit a cigarette.

'*Wee Tots*,' he said meditatively. 'I know a fellow who once edited that powerful sheet. Monty Bodkin. Ever meet him?'

'I've seen him at the Drones.'

'You are a member of the Drones Club?'

Sam gave a short, bitter laugh.

'Am I a member of the Drones Club! Yes, Mr Threepwood—'

'Call me Gally.'

'May I?'

'Of course. Everybody does. You were saying – ?'

'Yes, Gally, I am a member of the Drones Club. If I weren't, there wouldn't have been this trouble between Sandy and me.'

'She wanted you to resign?'

'No, it wasn't that. But I'd better begin at the beginning, hadn't I?'

'It sounds an excellent idea.'

Sam mused, marshalling his thoughts. Producing another glass, he mixed himself a whisky and soda. It stimulated him to speech.

'Well, the first thing that happened was that I was rather frank about her spectacles.'

'I don't follow you.'

'I mean that was what really started the unpleasantness. It got the conversation off on the wrong note. Is she wearing those damned spectacles?'

'Never without them. A pity she's had to take to them. They spoil her appearance.'

'That's what I told her. I said they made her look like a horror from outer space.'

'And what had she to say in response?'

'Oh, this and that,' said Sam. It was plain that the memory was not one on which he cared to dwell.

Gally pursed his lips. He was a chivalrous man. In his time he had said things equally or even more offensive to silver ring bookmakers and their like, but these had invariably been of the male sex. To women from youth upward he had always prided himself on being scrupulously polite. Even on the occasion in his early days when a ballet dancer of mixed Spanish and Italian parentage had stabbed him in the leg with a hatpin, his manner had remained suave and his language guarded.

'You ought not to have taunted her about her physical misfortunes, my boy,' he said disapprovingly. 'She can't help wearing spectacles.'

'But she can. That's the whole point. Her eyesight's perfect. The beastly things are made of plain glass, and she only put them on to impress Lord Emsworth.'

'Her train of thought eludes me.'

'She said they made her look older.'

'Ah yes, I see what she meant. Chet Tipton never objected to her functioning without the headlights, but perhaps she feels that my brother will be more critical. And I don't suppose my sister Hermione would approve of a secretary who looks about eighteen.'

'More like seventeen.'

'Yes, possibly more like seventeen. It's an odd thing, but all girls look seventeen to me nowadays. You'll find that yourself when you get to my age. So she took umbrage?'

'She wasn't too pleased.'

'These redheads are always easily stirred. But surely that was merely a trifling tiff, to be cleared up with a kiss and an apology, not the sort of thing to put a girl permanently off the man she loved?'

'There was more.'

'Tell me more.'

'Well, you see, there's this house of mine ... When you knew my father, did you ever stay at his house in Sussex?'

'Great Swifts? Dozens of times. Big barracks of a place.'

'Exactly. And costs the earth to keep up. My father left it to me, and I want to sell it.'

'I don't blame you.'

'So that I can buy a partnership in a publishing firm. I don't think I've much future at the Bar, but I know I would be sensational as a publisher.'

'There's money in publishing.'

'You bet there is, and I want some of it.'

Gally sipped his whisky thoughtfully. It was unpleasant to

have to discourage his young friend's fresh enthusiasms, but he felt it was only kind to warn him that what he was contemplating was far from being the dead snip he seemed to suppose it. England, he knew, was full of landed proprietors anxious to unload their holdings but unable to find takers.

'It may not be too easy to sell it. People these days haven't much use for a big place like that.'

'Oofy has.'

'Who?'

'Oofy Prosser, one of the fellows at the Drones. He's just got married and his wife wants a country house not far from London. She's seen Great Swifts and is crazy about it.'

'That sounds promising. He is rich, this Prosser?'

'Got the stuff in sackfuls. His father was Prosser's Pep Pill; I'm sure I can stick him for at least twenty thousand pounds if the deal goes through.'

Gally's doubts vanished. He had erred, he felt, in supposing the thing not to be a snip.

'Well, as my brother Clarence is so fond of saying, Capital, capital, capital!' Gally paused. He had noted a look of gloom on his companion's face, and it surprised him that he should be despondent when his prospects were so glittering. 'If you don't think it capital, *why* don't you think it capital?'

'Because there's a snag. Oofy insists on having the place done up before he'll part with a cheque. It's rather run down.'

'It was a little that way in your father's time. Buckets in most of the rooms to catch the water coming through the roof and the whole outfit a good deal bitten by mice. I begin to see your difficulty. Will it cost a lot to have it done up?'

'I think I could manage with about seven hundred pounds. But so far I've only been able to save two hundred.'

'Nobody you could touch for the rest?'

'Not a soul. Well, that was the position of affairs when this thing at the Drones happened.'

'You're going too fast for me. What thing at the Drones?'

'The sweep. They had a sweep there.'

'On the Derby?'

'No, on which member of the club would be the next to get married. I suppose it was Oofy's marriage that gave them the idea.'

'A very sound idea. We had a similar sweep at the Pelican years ago, only there it was on who would be the next to die.'

'Rather gruesome.'

'Oh, we didn't mind that at the Pelican. The suggestion was enthusiastically welcomed. The favourite, of course, was old Charlie Pemberton, who was pushing ninety and was known to have had sclerosis of the liver since his early days in the Federated Malay States. I remember how elated your father was when he drew his name out of the hat. He thought he had it made. But, as so often happens, the race went to a dark horse. Buffy Struggles, poor fellow. Got run over by a hansom cab the very day after the drawing. The rankest possible outsider. But I'm interrupting your story. This sweep, you were saying?'

'Well, of course I entered for it.'

'Of course,' said Gally, surprised that any other action should be considered possible. 'How much were the tickets?'

'Ten pounds.'

'Ten *pounds*? Shillings, you must mean.'

'No, pounds. It happened to be at a time when there was an unusual lot of money about. So I put up my tenner, and Sandy gave me the devil. She said I was just throwing it away. She had been a bit austere a few weeks previously when, hoping to bump up my little savings, I speculated on the races and dropped twenty quid.'

Gally nodded. He thought he could see where the narrative was heading.

'And your ten went down the drain and she said "I told you so"?'

'No, I had the most amazing luck. There were only two entries really in the running – Austin Phelps, the tennis player, you've probably heard of him, his name's always in the papers, and Tipton Plimsoll, an American fellow. He's engaged to a girl called Something Wedge.'

'Veronica Wedge. My niece. So you know our Tipton?'

'No, we've never met. We don't even know each other by sight. He's mostly in America and hardly ever comes to the club. He's in America now, but I understand he's coming over here very soon and the wedding will take place directly he arrives.'

'That's right. It's fixed for early in September. Big affair. It'll be at Blandings, with the whole county at the reception.'

'Oh? Well, naturally, when I drew the Plimsoll ticket and heard next day that Phelps's engagement had been broken off for some reason, I thought I was on velvet.'

'And aren't you?'

'It depends on how you look at it. I'm bound to collect the sweep money, which amounts to over five hundred pounds, but I've lost Sandy.'

Gally shook his head.

'I don't get it. I'd have thought she would have flung her arms round you and looked up at you with adoring eyes and murmured "My hero!"'

'You don't know all.'

'How the hell can I if you don't tell me?'

'I'm trying to tell you.'

'Well, get on with it.'

III

Sam refreshed his drink. He was an abstemious young man as a rule, but this morning, possibly because of the disturbances in his love life, possibly because the mere presence of Galahad Threepwood nearly always turned the thoughts of those with whom he forgathered in the direction of alcohol, he felt impelled to indulge. He took a deep draught and resumed.

'She couldn't forgive the stand I took about the syndicate.'

Gally stirred in his chair, exasperated. An accomplished raconteur himself, he chafed when others were obscure. He was thinking that if this was his young friend's customary way of telling a story, it was madness on his part to suppose that anything of his, no matter how strong its kitten interest, would have a chance of acceptance by a discriminating organ like *Wee Tots*. His monocle flashed fire.

'What syndicate? Which syndicate? What do you mean, the syndicate?'

'I was approached by a syndicate,' said Sam, suddenly becoming lucid, 'who offered me a hundred pounds for my Plimsoll ticket.'

Gally started.

'You weren't ass enough to take it?'

'No.'

'Good boy,' said Gally, relieved. 'I thought for a moment you were going to tell me you did.'

Sam scowled at an inoffensive fly which was stropping its back legs on the syphon.

'It might have been better if I had,' he said morosely. 'That was what Sandy and I split up about. She wanted me to close with the offer. Her view was that a sure hundred was money in the bank, while an uncertain five wasn't.'

Gally nodded sagely.

'Women are notoriously deficient in sporting blood. They resent one having a flutter and going for the big stakes. I remember, when I was a kid, someone gave me ten bob on my birthday and influenced by a hot tip from the local hairdresser when he was cutting my hair I planked the entire sum on the nose of a long-priced outsider for the Grand National. You never heard such a fuss as the female members of my family made when the story broke. I couldn't have got nastier notices if I'd been caught burgling the Bank of England. My selection wasn't placed, unfortunately, which made it worse. So what happened?'

'Oh, we argued for hours, and when I remained firm and absolutely refused to take the syndicate offer, she blew her top.'

'Girls with her shade of hair are sadly apt to. I've often wondered why Nature, widely publicised as being infinite in its wisdom, should have made the grave mistake of creating redheads, always so impulsive and quick on the trigger. If she had been a brunette or a platinum blonde, this tragedy would never have occurred. So she gave you back the ring?'

'She threw it at me. You may have noticed the slight abrasion on my left cheek.'

'And now she's returned your letters. All because of your larger vision. All because you very properly saw that more was to be gained by taking a chance. You say you argued for hours. Had her arguments any sense in them?'

Sam had been sorely hurt, but he was fair and could give credit where credit was due.

'Well, yes, I suppose they had in a way. When she was working for his uncle, she saw a lot of this fellow Plimsoll, and she said he was always getting engaged and nothing ever came of it. She said it would be the same with your niece. Apparently girls who get engaged to him have second thoughts.'

'Veronica won't.'

'What makes you so sure of that?'

'The fact that since Sandy knew him his uncle has died, leaving him millions. My sister Hermione will see to it that her ewe lamb doesn't get ideas into her head. You can take it as certain that whatever false starts Tipton Plimsoll may have made in the matrimonial race in the past, this time the wedding is going to come off.'

'Well, that's good, of course, but it doesn't alter the fact that I've lost Sandy.'

'Are you sure she's the right girl for you?'

'Quite sure. No argument about that.'

'Well, I'm not saying you're wrong. I've found her charming, and I suppose she can't help having that feminine streak of caution. The best of girls always want to play it safe. Yes, I think she's the mate for you.'

'But she doesn't.'

'Temporarily, perhaps. But she'll come round. You only have to talk to her quietly and reasonably and she'll be co-operative all right.'

'How can I talk to her? She's at Blandings Castle and I'm in London.'

Gally's eyebrows rose, but such was his personal magnetism that the monocle remained in its place. He stared at Sam incredulously.

'You aren't proposing to remain in London?'

'Where else?'

'My dear boy, have you no spirit, no enterprise? You must take the first train to Market Blandings. I say Market Blandings because I am unfortunately not in a position to invite you to the castle. My sister Hermione is in charge there, and for some reason all my sisters have got the idea that if someone's a friend of mine, he must be a rat of the underworld. No guest of my inviting would last a minute in the dear old place. Hermione would get a grip on his trouser seat and he would find himself flung out on his ear before he had finished unpacking. No, what you do is go to Market Blandings, take a room at the Emsworth Arms and lie in wait. Sandy is always bicycling to Market Blandings to change library books and so on. You're on the watch, and you spring out at her from behind a lamp post and go into your sales talk. Girls like being sprung out at. They take it as a compliment. At your age I was always springing out at girls I'd had some little disagreement with, and it never failed to lead to a peaceful settlement.'

'But suppose she doesn't bicycle to Market Blandings?'

'Then we must arrange a meeting on Visitors' Day.'

'What's that?'

'Thursday of each week is Visitors' Day at the castle. You cough up half-a-crown and Beach, our butler, shows you round. The battlements, the portrait gallery, the amber drawing-room, all that sort of thing. The customers come from Wolverhampton, Bridgnorth and other centres. All you have to do is join the mob and there you are. The thing's in the bag.'

His enthusiasm began to infect Sam.

'It certainly sounds good,' he agreed. 'But how do I get hold of Sandy?'

'I'll bring her along.'

'Where to?'

'Yes, we must fix a meeting place. We'd better make it the Empress's sty.'

'The what?'

'The residence of Empress of Blandings, my brother's prize pig.'

'Oh, I see. How do I find it?'

'Anyone will tell you where it is. It's one of the Blandings' landmarks. So I may expect you shortly?'

'I'll take a train to Market Blandings this afternoon.'

'That's the way I like to hear you talk. Give me a ring on the telephone when you arrive. And now,' said Gally, 'I must be getting along to Barribault's and picking up Clarence.'

IV

Having been carefully informed by Sandy Callender on the telephone the previous evening that he would be calling for him shortly before one and it now being twelve fifty-four, Lord Emsworth was naturally astounded to see Gally. He was sitting in the lounge when Gally reached Barribault's Hotel, his long lean body draped like a wet sock on a chair, and he appeared to be thinking of absolutely nothing. His mild face wore the dazed look it always wore when he was in London, a city that disturbed and bewildered him. Unlike his younger brother, to whom it had always been an earthly Paradise, he was allergic to England's metropolis and counted each minute lost that he was obliged to spend there. He rose like a snake hurriedly uncoiling itself and his pince-nez flew from his nose and danced at the end of their string, their invariable habit when he was startled.

'God bless my soul! Galahad!'

'In person. Weren't you expecting me?'

'Eh? Oh yes, of course, yes. You're looking very well, Galahad.'

'You, too, Clarence. Your travels have given you a sparkle.'

'Have you lunched?'

'What, at my own expense with you all eagerness to fill me to the brim at yours? Not likely,' said Gally. 'Let's go in, shall we, and as we fortify ourselves for the drive home you can tell me about your American adventures – what shows you saw, what bars you were thrown out of and so on, and I'll give you the latest news from Blandings.'

Quite a number of his acquaintances, most of them looking like men whom the police were anxious to interview because they had reason to believe that they might be able to assist them in their enquiries, accosted Gally as he went through the grill-room, and he had a good deal of stopping and passing the time of the day to do. It was consequently not for some little while that he and Lord Emsworth were at their table, dealing with their orders of sole mornay and able to take up the thread of their conversation again.

Gally was the first to speak.

'Well, Clarence, what did you think of America?'

'Extraordinary country. You know it well, don't you?'

'Oh yes, I was always popping in and out of it in the old days. You found it extraordinary, you say?'

'Very. Those tea bags.'

'I beg your pardon?'

'They serve your tea in little bags.'

'So they do. I remember.'

'And when you ask for a boiled egg, they bring it to you mashed up in a glass.'

'You don't like it that way?'

'No, I don't.'

'Then the smart thing to do is not to ask for a boiled egg.'

'True,' said Lord Emsworth, who had not thought of that.

'Though the way things are going now over there, you're lucky if you're able to afford boiled eggs.'

'Eh?'

'Didn't you read in the papers about the crash on the American Stock Exchange?'

'I did not see any papers while I was in New York. They left one outside my door every morning, but I never read it. Has there been a crash on the Stock Exchange?'

'And how! Fellows jumping out of windows in droves.'

'That's America for you. One day you're a millionaire, the next you're selling apples.'

'Selling apples?'

'That's right.'

'Why apples?'

'Why not apples?'

'True. Do you think Constance's husband – I forget his name – is selling apples?'

'I don't imagine so. I remember him telling me his money was mostly in Government bonds. How was the wedding, by the way? Did you get Connie off all right?'

'Yes. Oh yes. They are spending the honeymoon at a town called Cape Cod.'

'I know it well. Cape Cod, the Forbidden City. But something in your eye tells me you don't want to talk about Connie and her nuptials, you want to be brought up to date on the latest happenings at Blandings. Let me think. Well, I suppose the first thing you'll want to hear is how the Empress has been getting on in your absence. You will be relieved to learn that she's as robust as ever, her health all that her friends and well-wishers could desire. Rosy cheeks and sparkling eyes. Under the ministrations of Monica Simmons she has flourished like a green bay tree. You'll be glad to see her again.'

'Yes, yes, oh yes indeed. And it is wonderful to think that Constance will not be there to look disapproving and make clicking noises with her tongue when I go off to the sty. You've no idea how I am looking forward to settling down at Blandings without . . . well, of course nobody could be fonder of Constance than I am, but . . .'

'I get your meaning, Clarence. No need to be apologetic about it. You know and I know that Connie was a Grade A pest.'

'I wouldn't say that.'

'I would.'

'But she was very autocratic.'

'Very. Bossy is perhaps the word.'

'Odd how all our sisters are like that.'

'I've always said it was a mistake to have sisters. We should have set our faces against it from the outset.'

'Constance . . . Dora . . . Julia . . . Hermione . . . How they oppressed me! None of them would ever leave me alone. They were always wanting me to *do* things, always saying I must keep up my position.'

'That's what you get for being the head of the family. We younger sons escape all that sort of thing.'

'Hermione, of course, was the worst of them, but fortunately she was not very often at Blandings, while Constance was there all the time. You never attended the annual school treat, did you, Galahad?'

'Too much sense.'

'Constance always made me wear a top hat for it.'

'I'll bet you were a sensation.'

'And a stiff collar. Yes, I must confess that, devoted as I am to Constance, it will be a wonderful relief to be free from feminine society. The peace of it! By the way, who was that who spoke to me on the telephone yesterday? A strange female voice.'

'You can hardly expect me to keep tab on all the strange female voices that ring you up on the telephone. You know what a dog you are with the other sex.'

Lord Emsworth allowed this innuendo to pass, probably feeling that his reputation needed no defending. Since the death of his wife twenty-five years ago he had made something of a life work of avoiding women. In sharp contradistinction to Gally, who liked nothing better than their society and in his younger days had always been happiest when knee deep in ballet girls and barmaids, he had taken considerable pains to keep them at a distance. He could not hope, of course, to evade them altogether, for women have a nasty way of popping up at unexpected moments, but he was quick on his feet and his policy of suddenly disappearing like a diving duck had had excellent results. It was now pretty generally accepted in his little circle that he was not a ladies' man and that any woman who tried to get a civil word out of him did so at her own risk.

'She was speaking from Blandings. She said you would be coming here today to pick me up. She told me her name . . . now what did she say her name was?'

'Callender. Sandy Callender. She's your secretary.'

'But I have no secretary.'

'Yes, you have.'

'I'm sure you're mistaken, Galahad.'

'No, I'm not. She's your secretary all right. Hermione engaged her.'

Lord Emsworth was a mild man, but he could be roused to wrath.

'Meddlesome and officious!' he cried, his eyes gleaming militantly behind their pince-nez. 'High-handed impertinence! What business has Hermione to engage secretaries for me? When did she do this?'

'Shortly after her arrival at Blandings.'

The sole lay untasted on Lord Emsworth's plate, the hock unsipped in his wine glass. His pince-nez had gone adrift again and his nude eyes glazed at Gally with a horror that touched the latter's heart.

'Hermione's not at Blandings?' he quavered.

Gally patted his hand sympathetically. He knew how he felt.

'I've been wondering all this time how to break it to you, Clarence. I was planning to do it gently, but perhaps the surgeon's knife is best. Yes, Hermione has moved in and is firmly wedged into the woodwork. Egbert's there, too, of course. And Wilfred Allsop.'

'And that tall half-witted girl of theirs?'

'If you are alluding to your niece Veronica, no. She's in London. I brought her with me this morning and left her at Dora's. I gather she's stocking up with clothes against the day when young Plimsoll returns from America and makes her his bride. I'm afraid this has been something of a blow to you, Clarence.'

Lord Emsworth nodded dismally, limp among the ruins of his golden dreams. The prospect of having his sister Hermione substituted for his sister Constance had affected him rather as the announcement that for the future they might expect to be chastised with scorpions instead of, as under the previous administration, with whips must have affected the Children of Israel.

Nobody who knew her would have denied that Constance was an able disciplinarian, but they would have been obliged to concede that she could not be considered in Hermione's class. Hermione began where she left off.

'Oh dear, oh dear!' he whispered with bowed head, seeming to be addressing what remained of his sole mornay.

For perhaps a fleeting second Gally hesitated before speaking. It pained his kindly heart to witness his brother's distress, but having adopted the policy of the surgeon's knife he felt that the worst must be told even if it led to the stricken man having what in the land from which he had just returned is known as a conniption fit.

'I wonder, Clarence,' he said, 'if you remember a girl called Daphne Littlewood? And don't think I'm changing the subject, because she is definitely germane to the issue.'

There were very few things that Lord Emsworth ever remembered. This was not one of them.

'Daphne Littlewood? No, I do not.'

'Tall, dark, handsome girl with a formidable personality, not unlike Connie in appearance. In fact, except that she has different coloured eyes and hair, she could go on and play Connie without make-up. She married a rather celebrated historian named Winkworth. She's a widow now with a small and repulsive son and runs a fashionable girls' school. They think a lot of her in educational circles, so much so that she was made a Dame in the last Birthday Honours, a thing that's never likely to happen to you or me. I often wonder who had the idea of calling these women Dames. Probably an American. There's nothing like a dame, he told them, and they agreed with him, and so the order came into being. But I'm wandering from my subject. You've really forgotten Daphne?'

'Completely.'

'Strange. Twenty years ago the bookies were taking bets that you'd get engaged to her.'

'Impossible!'

'That's how the story goes.'

'It is inconceivable that I should have contemplated such a thing.'

'You say that now, but you know what your memory is like. For all you know, you may have wooed her ardently – sent her flowers, written in her confession book, pressed her hand in a conservatory during a dance ... No,' said Gally on reflection, 'I doubt if even in your prime you would have been as licentious as that. Well, anyway, that's who Daphne Winkworth is, and you'll find her at Blandings when we get there.'

'What!'

'With her son Huxley. Hermione invited them.'

'Good God!'

'I was afraid it would upset you, and I'm sorry to say that that's not all. The worst is yet to come.'

Gally paused. He was very fond of Lord Emsworth and hated to upset him, and he knew that what he was about to say would make his eyes, like stars, start from their spheres and also cause his knotted and combined locks, if you could call them that, to part and each particular hair – there were about twenty of them – to stand on end like quills upon the fretful porpentine. He shrank from saying it, but it had to be said. Impossible to allow the poor dear old chap to arrive at Blandings unwarned.

'Hold on to your chair, Clarence, for you're going to get a nasty shock. Has Hermione brought Dame Daphne Winkworth to Blandings because they're old friends? No. Because she enjoys the society of little Huxley Winkworth? No. Then why, you ask.

I'll tell you. It's because she remembers that old romance and hopes it may flare up again. I'm not absolutely certain of my facts, mind you, and it may be that I am alarming you unnecessarily, but from something Egbert let fall when I was talking to him last night I received the distinct impression that she's planning to marry you off this season.'

'What!'

'And Daphne, I gather, is all for it. She feels that little Huxley needs a father.'

Lord Emsworth had sunk back in his chair and was looking like the Good Old Man in old-fashioned melodrama when the villain has foreclosed the mortgage on the ancestral farm. There was not a great deal of flesh on his angular form, but what there was was creeping. Over in a corner of the grill-room a luncher was dealing with madrilene soup. It quivered beneath his spoon, but not so wholeheartedly as Lord Emsworth was quivering.

He knew Hermione. His sister Constance had always been able to dominate him and force him into courses against which his whole nature rebelled, like wearing a top hat and a stiff collar at the school treat, and Hermione had twice Constance's determination and will to win. If Galahad was right, the peril that threatened him was appalling and never before had his diving duck technique been so sorely needed. But would even the elusiveness of the diving duck be enough to save him?

'You can't be sure, Galahad,' was all he could find to say.

'I told you I wasn't, but Egbert's remarks seemed to me capable of only one interpretation, and I strongly urge you, old man, to be alert and on your guard. Only ceaseless vigilance can save you. Don't let her get you alone in the rose garden or on the terrace by moonlight. If she starts talking about the dear old days, change the subject. On no account pat little Huxley on the head and take him for walks. And above all be wary if she asks you to read her extracts from the *Indian Love Lyrics* after dinner. The advice I would give to every young man starting out in life, and that includes you, though of course it's some time since you started, is to avoid the *Indian Love Lyrics* like poison. I remember poor Puffy Benger, a great pal of mine in the Pelican days, getting irretrievably hooked just because in a careless moment he allowed a girl to lure him into reading *Pale Hands I Loved Beside The Shalimar* to her. And I myself ... Ah,' said Gally, breaking off as he saw the waiter approaching the table. 'Coffee at last. You'll probably need a drop of brandy in yours, Clarence.'

CHAPTER 4

I

It was a little past two o'clock when Gally helped a still stupefied Lord Emsworth into the car, adjusted his legs, which always tended to behave like the tentacles of an octopus when he rode in any conveyance, and started on the homeward journey, easing his way through the London traffic with practised skill. At five, Beach, ably assisted by two footmen, served tea in the amber drawing-room of Blandings Castle, and the company awaiting the wanderer's return settled down to keep body and soul together with buttered toast, cucumber sandwiches and cake. Lady Hermione Wedge officiated at the tea pot. Colonel Egbert Wedge stood supporting his shoulderblades against the mantel-piece over the fireplace. Dame Daphne Winkworth sat very upright on what looked an uncomfortable chair, and her son Huxley perched on a footstool as near as he could get to the gate-leg table where the food was. Wilfred Allsop was not present. He was making a point, when possible, of avoiding Dame Daphne's society. Hers, as Gally had said, was a formidable personality. It had been so even in her youth, and many years of conducting a large school for girls had increased its intensity, giving her an imperious air calculated to intimidate all but the toughest. The thought that before many weeks had passed he would become a member of her staff, permanently under that eye of hers, never failed to induce in Wilfred a sinking feeling.

Sandy Callender came in with a slip of paper in her hand.

'The post office has just telephoned this telegram, Lady Hermione,' she said.

'Oh, thank you, Miss Callender. It is from Tipton, Egbert,' said Lady Hermione as the door closed behind Lord Emsworth's conscientious secretary. 'He has arrived in London and will be coming here tomorrow. Tipton,' she explained to Dame Daphne, 'is the charming young American who is marrying Veronica.'

'Splendid chap,' said Colonel Wedge, whose spirits always rose when he thought of his future son-in-law's millions.

'Yes, we are devoted to dear Tipton. Veronica, of course, adores him.'

'Love at first sight,' said Colonel Wedge. 'Very romantic.'

'He has been in New York, looking after his business interests. He inherited a great deal of money from an uncle.'

'Chester Tipton. Chet, they called him. Galahad used to know him.'

'I wonder if Clarence and he met when he was over there.'

'We must ask him. Ah, that must be Clarence now.'

A tooting had made itself heard from the direction of the front door, and presently footsteps sounded outside. It was not, however, Lord Emsworth who entered, but Beach. His presence surprised Lady Hermione.

'Was that the car, Beach?'

'Yes, m'lady.'

'Then where is Lord Emsworth?'

'His lordship desired me to say that he would be delayed a few moments, as he has gone to see his pig, m'lady,' said Beach and, his mission accomplished, withdrew.

Dame Daphne seemed puzzled.

'Where did he say Clarence had gone?'

'To see his pig,' said Lady Hermione, speaking the final word as if it soiled her lips.

'Prize pig. Empress of Blandings it's called,' Colonel Wedge explained. 'Clarence is crazy about it.'

'That pig needs exercise,' said Huxley, speaking thickly through a mouthful of cake. He was a small, wizened, super-cilious boy with a penetrating eye, who had inherited some of the qualities of both his parents – from his mother that air of hers of calm superiority, from his father the sardonic manner which had made him so unpopular in the Common Room of his college at Cambridge. 'Too fat. I'm going to let it out of the sty and make it run.'

And with the feeling that there was no time like the present, he left the room. It had occurred to him that at this hour Monica Simmons might be off somewhere having her cup of tea, and her absence was vital to his plans. He had a wholesome fear of that well-muscled girl, and her statement at their last meeting that if she caught him hanging around the Empress's boudoir again, she would skin him alive had not failed to make an impression on him. It was only when he was halfway down the stairs that he remembered that Lord Emsworth was at the sty, and he decided to give the thing up for the moment. It would, he saw, be necessary to bide his time.

'Crazy,' said Colonel Wedge, continuing his remarks. 'Let me tell you an incident that happened when we were here a year or two ago. I came back late one night from a Loyal Sons Of Shropshire dinner in London and went for a stroll in the grounds to stretch my legs after the long train journey, and I was pass-ing the Empress's sty when something I had taken for a suit of overalls hanging on the rail suddenly reared itself up, and it was Clarence. Gave me no end of a start. I asked him what he was doing there at that time of night – it was about twelve o'clock – and he said he was listening to his pig. And what was the pig doing, as I said to Hermione when I talked it over with her later? Singing? Reciting Gunga Din? Not at all. It was just breathing and Clarence was listening to it – courting lumbago, as I told him.'

There had been a frown on Lady Hermione's face as this anecdote proceeded. She was not pleased with her husband for telling a story which might well make Lord Emsworth's destined bride dubious as to the advisability of linking her lot with a man who went out at midnight to listen to pigs breathing. It seemed to her that Dame Daphne was pursing her lips as she might have pursed them in her study at school, had she been informed by an undermistress that Angela and Phyllis had been found smoking cigarettes behind the gymnasium.

'All it was doing,' said Colonel Wedge, driving home his point in case it might have been missed, 'was breathing. You remember what I said to you, old girl? "Old girl," I said to you, "we've got to face it, Clarence is dotty."'

'Nothing of the kind,' said Lady Hermione sharply, and would have gone on to add that what her brother needed was a wife who would put a stop to all this fussing over a ridiculous pig, when Lord Emsworth made his belated appearance.

'Ah, Hermione,' he said. 'Ah, Egbert. Quite, quite.'

Lady Hermione regarded him austerely. Considering that he was returning from travels which had involved facing all the perils of New York and two ship's concerts, at one of which he had had to take the chair, her greeting might have been more affectionate.

'So here you are at last, Clarence. We had almost given you up. You remember Daphne Winkworth who used to be Daphne Littlewood?'

'Oh, quite. Yes, quite,' said Lord Emsworth.

He spoke with splendid fortitude. There was nothing in his manner or his voice to show that the sight of this woman was making him feel like the hero of a novel of suspense trapped in an underground den by the personnel of the Black Moustache gang. Your English aristocrat learns to wear the mask.

'Daphne is staying with us till her school re-opens.'

'Quite.'

Feeling possibly that if not checked he would go on saying 'Quite' for the rest of the evening, Lady Hermione asked him coldly if he would like some tea and with a final 'Quite' and a 'Tea? Tea? Yes, that would be capital, capital' he sat down and began to sip. Colonel Wedge offered him a hospitable cucumber sandwich.

'Glad to see you again, Clarence,' he said. 'You've caught me just in time. I'm off tomorrow.'

A quick gleam of hope shone on Lord Emsworth's darkness.

'Hermione, too?' he said, feeling that things were looking up.

'Good Lord, no. Hermione isn't coming with me. I shall only be away a day or two. My godmother in Worcestershire, it's her birthday the day after tomorrow, and I always have to be with her for that. Sort of a royal command.'

'Oh?' said Lord Emsworth, his hopes shattered.

He was feeling bewildered. Eyeing Dame Daphne furtively over his cup, he found it incredible that even twenty years ago, when he was younger and sprightlier than he was today and presumably capable of feats of daring now beyond him, he could have contemplated getting engaged to so forbidding a woman.

And the thought of actually marrying her made him feel that instead of the cucumber sandwich at which he was nibbling he was swallowing butterflies. He was willing to respect Dame Daphne Winkworth, to wish her continued success in her chosen career and to recommend her seminary to parents with daughters requiring education, but that was as far as he was prepared to go.

He was roused from the coma into which he had fallen by the sound of Dame Daphne's voice. She was saying that she had letters to write. With an unusual glimmering of the social sense he rose and opened the door for her.

'Strange,' he said, returning to his chair. 'Galahad assures me that she and I were acquainted many years ago, but I can honestly say I didn't know her from Eve. What did you tell me her name used to be?'

'Never mind her name,' said Lady Hermione tartly. 'Clarence, you really are impossible.'

'Eh?'

'Going off like that instead of coming here when you arrived.'

'But I wanted to see my pig.'

'No manners whatever. I could see that Daphne was offended. Anyone would have been. I hope you will take the trouble to be more polite to Tipton.'

'Eh?'

'A telegram has come from Tipton saying that he will be here tomorrow.'

'Who is Tipton?'

'Oh, Clarence! Tipton Plimsoll is the man who is marrying Veronica.'

'Who—' Lord Emsworth began, but was able to save himself in time. 'Yes, yes, of course. Your daughter Veronica, you mean. Quite.'

'Did you see anything of Tipton when you were in New York?' asked Colonel Wedge.

An 'Eh? What? No, I didn't' was trembling on Lord Emsworth's lips, when recollection flooded in on him. Plimsoll. Tipton Plimsoll. Of course, yes. It all came back to him.

'No, we didn't meet,' he said, 'but he rang me up one night on the telephone. Nice fellow, I thought. Rather a husky voice, but very civil. Too bad he's lost all his money.'

II

It was not often that Lord Emsworth's *obiter dicta* attracted any close attention. People when he spoke were inclined either not to listen to him at all or, if his remarks did reach their ears, to dismiss them as unworthy of their notice. But not even Gally, telling the latest good story to an admiring circle at the Pelican Club, could have gripped his audience more surely than he with these few simple words had done.

There fell upon the room a silence of the kind usually described as stunned. Eyes widened, jaws dropped. Then the Wedges, colonel and wife, spoke simultaneously.

'Done *what*?' cried the colonel.

'Lost his *money*?' cried Lady Hermione.

'Yes, didn't you know?' said Lord Emsworth, mildly surprised. 'I'd have thought he would have told you. He's completely destitute. He's selling apples.'

Lady Hermione clutched her forehead, Colonel Wedge his moustache.

'Apples?' said Lady Hermione in a low voice.

'How do you mean, apples?' said Colonel Wedge.

Lord Emsworth saw that he would have to do some careful explaining.

'According to Galahad, that is what everybody in America is doing now. I could not quite follow what he was telling me, but as far as I could gather there has been what is called a crash on the Stock Exchange. What that is I'm afraid I don't know, but apparently it is something that causes people to lose money, and when they have lost all their money, they sell apples. Oddly enough, though most people like them, I have never been very fond of apples. Still, they are said to keep the doctor away, so no doubt there is a market for them. I suppose your friends tell you how much to charge. I wouldn't know myself, but Tipton has probably found someone who understands these things. One would sell them by the pound, I imagine, but—'

'Clarence!'

'Eh?'

'Where did you hear this?'

'Hear what?'

'About Tipton losing his money.'

'He told me himself. I remember the conversation quite distinctly. It took place, as I say, on the telephone. All these New York hotels have telephones in the bedrooms. You order your meals through them. A very obliging housemaid told me that. She said that if I wanted let us say breakfast, all I had to do was to pick up the telephone and ask for Room Service, and she was perfectly right, too. I tried it several times and always with success. Did you know that when you order tea in America, they bring it to you in little bags?'

Lady Hermione did not strike her brother with a bludgeon, but this was simply because she had no bludgeon.

'Clarence!'

'Eh?'

'Stop *rambling*!'

'Yes, tell us about this conversation you had with Tipton,' said Colonel Wedge.

'I *am* telling you,' said Lord Emsworth, aggrieved. 'As I was saying, it took place on the telephone. It was very late at night, and I had gone to bed, and suddenly the telephone rang and a voice said "Is that Lord Emsworth?" No, I'm wrong. It said "Hello" and *then* it asked if I was Lord Emsworth. Of course I was, so I said so and it said it was sorry to disturb me at this time of night. "Quite all right, my dear fellow," I said. As a matter of fact, I wasn't asleep. Somebody else had woken me a short while before, another mysterious voice. It wanted to know if I was the Oil of Emsworth, and when I said I was, it rang off. Rather odd, I thought, but I suppose that sort of thing is happening all the time in America. Very strange country.'

'Clarence!'

'Eh?'

'Will you *please* stop dithering and get on with your story.'

'My story? Ah yes. Yes, yes, quite. Where had I got to? Ah yes. This voice – the second voice – said it was sorry to disturb me at this time of night and I said "Quite all right, my dear fellow" or it may have been "Perfectly all right, my dear fellow. By the way, who are you?" I said, and he said he was Tipton Plimsoll. "I've lost all my money," he said, and I said I was sorry to hear that, and he asked me if I would lend him twenty dollars. I forget what this is in our currency, but something quite small, so I said of course I would. I should mention that he had begun by telling me that he was the man who was engaged to my niece Veronica and that he had actually stayed at the castle, though I have no recollection of it. Well, to cut a long story short, I said of course I would, and he thanked me profusely and burst into song.'

It was some minutes since Lady Hermione had clutched her forehead. She repaired this omission.

'*Song?*'

'Yes, he began singing. Something, if I remember, about there being a rainbow in the sky, so let's have another cup of coffee and let's have another piece of pie. I wasn't at all surprised. I suppose it was a long time since he had had a square meal, and pie is very filling. They eat cheese with pie in America, which no doubt is all right for those who like it, but I wouldn't care to do it myself. Well, I asked him if he would be calling for the money in the morning, but he said no, he needed it at once. They're like that over there. Hustle, bustle, do it now. He said would I send it by messenger, and I said certainly, and I heard him asking someone called Garroway what was the address of the prison where he was.'

'*Prison?*'

'This Garroway seems to have been a knowledgeable chap, for he told him all right. Galahad used to know a policeman named Garroway, but he died years ago, so it can't have been him. Or he? I remember being rapped on the knuckles by that governess we had when we were children, Hermione, some name like Biggs or Postlethwaite, because I couldn't get that he/him thing right. Yes, apparently he was in custody.'

Lady Hermione had stopped clutching her forehead, probably feeling that it was using up energy and getting her nowhere. She was looking like a cook who on the night of the big dinner party suddenly discovered that the fishmonger has not sent the lobsters. Her immediate impulse was to scream, but she forced herself to speak quietly, and if her voice bore a close resemblance to a voice from the tomb, the most censorious critic can hardly blame her.

'Clarence, is this a joke?'

'It can't have been much of a joke for Plimsoll. Nobody likes having to plead for money.'

'I mean, are you making up all this?'

Lord Emsworth was justly offended. It was difficult for a man as lean and limp as he was to bridle, but he came as near to bridling as was within the scope of his powers.

'Of course I'm not making it up. Why would I make it up? And how could I if I wanted to? Dash it, do you think I'm capable of making up a story like that? I'm not Shakespeare.'

'But how can he have been in prison?'

The question surprised Lord Emsworth.

'Well, lots of fellows do go to prison. Galahad in his younger days frequently spent the night at Bow Street and if I'm not mistaken once nearly did fourteen days without the option of a fine. He was arrested so often that he tells me he got to know most of the policemen in the West End of London by their first names. Extraordinary names some of them had, too. One of them was called Egbert. Why, bless my soul, Egbert, that's your name, isn't it? Shows what a small world it is.'

Too small, Lady Hermione was thinking, to be large enough to contain with anything like comfort her brother Clarence and herself. Lord Emsworth in one of his rambling moods never failed to affect her powerfully. She hoped she was a charitable woman, but the best she could find to say about the ninth Earl at this juncture was that he did not wear a monocle.

'Good God!' said Colonel Wedge, and this seemed to sum the situation up.

It was growing dark now and as always when the light began

to fade his study and his Whipple *On The Care Of The Pig* called to Lord Emsworth. He edged towards the door, and such was the preoccupation his tale had caused that he was through it and down the stairs before his sister or his brother-in-law had observed his going. Years of sliding away from the other sex had given him a technique second to none.

III

In the room he had left, silence, for some moments, hung like a pall. It was as if his simple narrative of night life in New York had robbed its occupants of speech. Lady Hermione's vocal cords were the first to recover.

'Egbert!'

'Yes, old girl?'

'Do you think this is true?'

'Must be, I'm afraid.'

'You know how Clarence gets things muddled up.'

'He does, I agree. As a rule, I write off anything he tells me as just babble from the padded cell. Normally, I wouldn't take Clarence's unsupported word if I saw the countryside flooded and he told me it had been raining. But in this case I don't see how we can doubt. I mean to say, Tipton told him himself.'

'Yes.'

'And touched him for twenty dollars.'

'Yes.'

'Well, there you are, then. Obviously he had been speculating on the Stock Exchange and the crash wiped him out. He isn't the first millionaire that's happened to, and I don't suppose he'll be the last.'

A gloomy silence fell. Colonel Wedge cleared his throat

'What steps do you propose to take, old girl?'

'Veronica must be told.'

'Of course. Can't have her going blindly into marriage and having the bridegroom reveal to her in the vestry that he hasn't a bean.'

Lady Hermione frowned. She considered that her husband was showing a lack of tact. These military men often do.

'Money has nothing to do with it,' she said. 'If it were simply a matter of Tipton not being as rich as we had supposed, I would have nothing to say. But Clarence says he was in prison.'

'I wonder what they jugged him for.'

'Vagrancy probably or begging in the streets. What does it matter? The point is that we cannot allow Veronica to marry a man with a prison record.'

'So you'll write to Vee?'

'I shall go and see her.'

'Yes, that's the best plan.'

'Ring for Beach and tell him to tell Voules to have the car ready as quickly as possible. He must drive me to London tonight.'

'You'll get there pretty late.'

'Too late, of course, to see her, but I will talk to her in the morning and tell her she must write to Tipton breaking the engagement.'

'Do you think she will?'

'Of course she will. I shall see to that. Veronica always does what I tell her.'

'That's true,' said Colonel Wedge, who resembled his daughter in this respect.

He stepped to the wall and pressed the bell.

CHAPTER 5

I

The little country town of Market Blandings is one at which Shropshire points with pride, and not without reason. Its decorous High Street, its lichened church, its red-roofed shops and its age-old inns with their second storeys bulging comfortably over the pavements combine to charm the eye, and this is particularly so if that eye has been accustomed to look daily on Halsey Court, London W.1.

To Sam the place had appealed aesthetically immediately on his arrival, and on the following afternoon, as he sat with pad and pencil in the garden of the Emsworth Arms, he found its spell was being of great assistance to him professionally. It is a fact well known to all authors that there is nothing like a change of scene for stimulating the powers of invention. At Halsey Chambers Sam had had no success as a chronicler of the adventures of Pinky-Poo the kitten, but now he found the stuff simply flowing out. It was not long before he was able to write 'The End' with the satisfactory feeling that, provided the editor was not suffering from softening of the brain, always an occupational risk with editors, a cheque from *Wee Tots* was to all intents and purposes in his pocket.

His task done, his thoughts, like those of every author who

has completed a testing bit of work, turned in the direction of beer. At dinner on the previous night and again at lunch he had tried out that of the Emsworth Arms and found it superb. Rising, he replaced pad and pencil in his room and made for the bar. And at that precise moment Beach the butler, looking hot and exhausted, tottered into it.

His duties at the luncheon table concluded and no further buttling being required of him until the dinner hour, Beach had started ponderously down the long drive of Blandings Castle and carried on through the great gate at the end of it and into the high road. Something approximating to a heat wave was in progress and the sun was very sultry, but though the poet Coward has specifically stressed the advisability of avoiding its ultra-violet ray, it was his intention to walk to the Emsworth Arms, a distance of fully two miles, and in due season to walk back again.

It would have gratified Huxley Winkworth had he known that this athletic feat was the direct result of his critique of the previous morning. His words had stung Beach at the time, for there had been a tactlessness in their candour calculated to wound, but he was a fair-minded man and realised on reflection that the child, though one might frown on his mode of expressing himself, might possibly have been right. His figure *was* perhaps a little too full and in need of streamlining. The sedentary life of a butler is apt to take its toll.

Of his misadventures on the way – the beads of perspiration, the laboured breath, the blister on the right foot – it is not necessary to speak. The historian passes on to the moment when, arriving at the Emsworth Arms, he limped into the bar and licking his lips surreptitiously requested the barmaid to draw him a mug of the beer which Sam had found so palatable. He felt that he had earned it.

The barmaid's name was Marlene Wellbeloved and she was the niece of George Cyril Wellbeloved, Lord Emsworth's former pigman. Beach had never been fond of George Cyril, considering him a low proletarian and worse than that a man with no respect for his social superiors. Word had reached him that on several occasions he had been referred to by this untouchable as 'Old Fatty' and 'that stuffed shirt', and the occasion when the other had addressed him with the frightful words 'Hoy, cocky' was still green in his memory. Nothing in the way of chumminess could ever exist between this degraded ex-pigman and himself, but for Marlene he had a tolerant liking, and when after a few desultory exchanges he took out the silver watch he had won in the darts tournament to see how the time was getting along and she said, 'Oo, Mr Beach, can I look at that?' he readily consented. He unhooked it from his waistcoat and laid it on the counter, well pleased with her girlish interest.

Her reactions were all that could have been desired. She uttered two squeaks and a giggle.

'Why, it's beautiful, Mr Beach!'

'A very handsome trophy.'

'And you really won it playing darts?'

'I was so fortunate.'

'Well, I think it's lovely.'

It was as she was saying You must be terribly good at darts, Mr Beach, and Beach was deprecating her praise with a modest gesture of the hand that Constable Evans of the Market Blandings police force entered the bar. He had parked his bicycle outside and was coming in for a quick one before resuming his rounds. On seeing Beach, he temporarily forgot his mission. At the station house that morning he had heard a good one from his sergeant and he wanted to pass it along.

'Hi, Mr Beach.'

'Good afternoon, Mr Evans.'

'Got a story for you.'

'Indeed.'

'Not for your ears, Marlene. Come outside, Mr Beach.'

They went out together just as Sam reached the doorway. A collision was unavoidable.

'Pardon *me*, sir,' said Beach.

'My fault. Entirely my fault. Sorry, sorry, sorry,' said Sam.

He spoke with a gay lilt in his voice, for he was in buoyant and optimistic mood. It was not only the circumstances of having finished his story and seen the last of a kitten he had never been fond of that induced this sense of well-being. His conversation with Gally at Halsey Chambers had stimulated him, as conversations with Gally so often stimulated people. It had left him convinced that he had only to meet Sandy and inaugurate a frank round-table talk and all misunderstandings, if you could call what had passed between them a misunderstanding, would be forgotten. He would say he was sorry he had called her a ginger-haired little fathead, she would say she was sorry she had thrown the ring at him, they would kiss again with tears as the late Alfred, Lord Tennyson had so well put it and everything would be all right once more.

There was no possible doubt in his mind that Gally had been correct in describing the thing as in the bag, and the world was looking good to him. He was loving everyone he met. He had caught only a fleeting glimpse of the obese character with whom he had collided in the doorway, but he was sure he was an awfully nice obese character, once you got to know him. He liked the looks of Constable Evans and also those of Marlene Well-beloved, whom he now approached with a charming smile and a request that she would let him have a stoup of the elixir for which the Emsworth Arms was so justly famous.

'Nice day,' said Marlene as she filled the order, for she was a capital conversationalist. A barmaid has to be as quick as lightning with these good things. They promote a friendly atmosphere and stimulate trade.

'Beautiful,' said Sam with equal cordiality. 'Hullo, has somebody been giving you a watch? Your birthday is it, or something?'

Marlene giggled. A most musical sound, Sam thought it. In the mood he was in he would have been equally appreciative of a squeaking slate pencil.

'It's Old Fatty's. He won it in the darts tournament.'

'Old Fatty? You mean the gentleman I was dancing the rumba with just now?'

'My Uncle George always calls him Old Fatty. Uncle George is terribly funny.'

'I'll bet he keeps one and all in stitches. What's it doing on the counter?'

'He was showing it to me. He went out because Constable Evans wanted to tell him a dirty story.'

'What was the story? You don't happen to know?'

'No, I don't.'

'I must get him to tell it to me some time. Yes,' said Sam, picking it up, 'it's certainly a handsome watch. Well worth winning even at the expense of having to play darts, which to my mind is about the lousiest pastime in the—'

'World' he would have concluded, but the word died on his lips. The door of the Emsworth Arms bar faced the road and was always kept open in fine weather, and passing it, wheeling a bicycle, was a red-haired girl at the sight of whom all thoughts of beer, watches and barmaids were wiped from his mind as with a sponge. He bounded out, calling her name, and she looked round startled. Then as she saw him her eyes widened and leaping on her bicycle she rode off, gathering speed as she went. And Sam, breathing a soft expletive, ran after her, though with little hope that anything constructive would result.

As he ran, he was dimly aware of a sound like a steam whistle in his rear, but he had no leisure to give it his attention.

II

The steam-whistle-like sound which had made so little impression on Sam had proceeded from the lips of Marlene Wellbeloved. It had taken her a few seconds to run to the door and come on the air, for astonishment had held her momentarily paralysed. Hers until now had been a placid existence, and nothing like this theft of valuable watches beneath her very eyes had ever marred its even tenor. The bar of the Emsworth Arms was not one of your Malemute saloons where anything may happen when a bunch of the boys start whooping it up. Its clients were of the respectable stamp of Beach the butler, Jno. Robinson, proprietor of the station taxi cab, and Percy Bulstrode the chemist. It was the first time that Dangerous Dan McGrews like the customer who had just left had swum into her ken.

She was, accordingly, deprived of speech. Then, her vocal cords in mid-season form again, she expressed her concern and agitation with an EEEEEEEEEEEE!! which probably made itself heard and excited interest in many a distant parish.

It certainly interested Beach and Constable Evans, chuckling over the sergeant's story some dozen yards away. Her voice came to them like a bugle call to a couple of war horses. They had seen

Sam emerge and start running along the road, but had thought nothing of it, attributing his mobility to an appointment suddenly remembered. When, however, they realised that his departure had been the cause of Marlene Wellbeloved going EEEEEEEEEEEE!!, reason told them that there was something sinister afoot. Level-headed girls like Marlene do not go EEEEEEEEEEEE!! without solid grounds for doing so. With one accord they ran towards her, the constable in the lead, Beach, who was not built for speed, lying a length or two behind.

'Smatter?' asked P.C. Evans, always a man of few words. A trained observer, he noticed that Marlene was wringing her hands, and he found the gesture significant. Coming on top of that EEEEEEEEEEEE!!, it seemed to P.C. Evans that it meant something.

'Oh, Mr Beach! Oh, Mr Beach!'

'What is it, Miss Wellbeloved?'

'That feller's gone off with your watch!' cried Marlene, her hands continuing to gyrate. 'He put it in his pocket and ran off with it!'

The effect of these words on the two men differed substantially. They froze Beach into a statue of dismay, for his watch was very dear to him and the bereavement made him feel like one of those nineteenth-century poets who were always losing dear gazelles. He had not experienced such a sense of desolation and horror since the night when a dinner guest at the castle had asked for a little water to put in his claret. It made him wonder what the world was coming to.

Constable Evans, on the other hand, had found in her statement all the uplifting properties of some widely advertised tonic. Where Beach mourned, he rejoiced. The cross which all English country policemen have to bear is the lack of spirit and initiative in the local criminal classes. A man like New York's Officer Garroway has always more dope pushers and heist guys and fiends with hatchet slaying six at his disposal than he knows what to do with, but in Market Blandings you were lucky if you got an occasional dog without a collar or Saturday-night drunk and disorderly. It was months since Constable Evans had made a decent pinch, and this sudden outbreak of crime brought out all the best in him. To leap on his machine and begin pedalling like a contestant in a six-day bicycle race was with him the work of an instant. He did not even stop to say 'Ho', his customary comment on the unusual.

It was not long before he sighted the man wanted by the police. Sam had soon given up the chase, realising the futility of trying to overtake on foot a cyclist who had had fifty yards' start. He was standing now in the middle of the road, his lips moving in a silent soliloquy which, if audible, would have had no chance of passing the censors even in these free-speaking days.

The sunny mood in which he had begun the day had changed completely. Five minutes before, he had been the little friend of all the world and could have stepped straight into a Dickens' novel and no questions asked, but now he viewed the human race with a jaundiced eye and could see no future for it. When Constable Evans came riding up, he thought he had never beheld a police officer he liked the looks of less. The man seemed to him to have not a single quality to recommend him to critical approval.

Nor did the constable appear to be liking him. It would have taken a very poor physiognomist to have read into his glance anything even remotely resembling affection. He had a face that seemed to have been carved from some durable substance like granite, and it was with a baleful glitter in his eye that he lowered his bicycle to the ground. As he advanced on Sam, a traveller in the East who knew his tigers of the jungle would have been struck by his resemblance to one of them about to leap on its prey.

'Ho!' he said.

The correct response to this would of course have been a civil 'Ho to you,' but Sam was too preoccupied with his gloomy thoughts to make it. He stared bleakly at Constable Evans. He was at a loss to know why this flatty had thrust his society on him, and he resented his presence.

'Well?' he said briefly, speaking from between clenched teeth. 'What do *you* want?'

'You,' said the constable even more briefly. 'What are you doing with that watch?'

'What watch?'

'This watch,' said Constable Evans, and deftly removed it from the right-hand pocket of Sam's coat by the chain which dangled from it.

Sam stared as, when a child, he had so often stared at a conjurer who had just produced from a borrowed top hat two rabbits and a bowl of goldfish.

'Good Lord!' he said. 'That belongs to the fat man at the Emsworth Arms.'

'You're right it belongs to the fat man at the Emsworth Arms.'

'I took it away by mistake.'

Constable Evans was a man who did not laugh readily. Even at the sergeant's anecdote, droll though it was, he had merely smiled. But this drew a quick guffaw from him, and having guffawed he sneered. Another man would have said, 'A likely story!' He merely said, 'Ho!'

Sam saw that explanations were in order.

'What happened was this. The girl behind the bar was showing it to me, and I suddenly saw someone – er – someone I wanted to have a word with pass the door, so I ran out.'

'With the watch in your pocket.'

'I must have put it there without knowing.'

'Ho!'

Remorse for having inadvertently deprived a good man of what was no doubt a treasured possession had calmed Sam down a little. He still felt hostile to the human race and would have been glad to do without it, but he could see that he had put himself in the wrong and would have to make apologies. He clicked his tongue self-reproachfully.

'Idiotic of me. I'll take it back to the owner.'

'*I'll* take it back to the owner.'

'Will you? That's very nice of you. He'll be amused. You'll have a good laugh together.'

'Ho!'

The monosyllable intensified the dislike which Sam had been feeling from the first for this intrusive bluebottle.

'Can't you say anything except Ho?' he snapped.

'Yus,' said Constable Evans. He was not as a rule a quick man with a repartee, but it was not often that he was given an opening like this. With the insufferably complacent air of a comedian who has been fed the line by his straight man he proceeded. 'Yus, I *can* say something except Ho. I can say "You're pinched",' he said, and laid a heavy hand on Sam's shoulder.

It was not the moment to lay hands on Sam's shoulder. He had been finding it difficult enough to endure the conversation of one who seemed to him to combine in his single person all the least attractive qualities of a race – the human – which he particularly disliked, and to have his collarbone massaged by him was, if one may coin a phrase, the last straw. With a reflex action which would have interested Doctor Pavlov his fist shot out and there was a chunky sound as it impinged on the constable's eye with all the weight of his muscular body behind it. It sent him staggering back, his foot tripped over a loose stone and he fell with a crash loud enough for two constables. And Sam, leaping at the bicycle, flung himself on it and rode off at a speed which Beach in his hot youth might have equalled but could not have surpassed. Had he been alive forty years before and a member of the choir attended by Beach, and had his voice by some lucky chance not broken before the first Sunday in Epiphany, thus enabling him to enter for the contest in which the butler had won his spectacular triumph, the race in all probability would have ended in a dead heat.

III

If you start two hundred yards or so from Market Blandings on a bicycle you have stolen from one of the local police force and continue to pedal along the high road, you come before long to the little hamlet of Blandings Parva, which lies at the gates of Blandings Castle. It consists of a few cottages, a church, a vicarage, a general store, a pond with ducks on it, a filling station (its only concession to modernity) and the Blue Boar Inn. The last named was where Sam's trip came to an end.

It was on foot that he completed its final stages, for some time before he reached Blandings Parva the thought had crossed his mind that the sooner he got rid of his Arab steed the better. It is never wise to remain for long in possession of a hot bicycle, particularly one formerly the property of a member of the constabulary. Some quarter of a mile before journey's end, accordingly, he propped the machine against a stile at the side of the road and was able to enter the premises of the Blue Boar in the guise of a blameless hiker. He took a seat in the cool, dim tap-room and started to review the situation in which he found himself.

It fell, he immediately perceived, into the category of situations which may be described as not so good. Try to gloss over the facts though he might, he could not reach any conclusion other than that he was a fugitive from justice and one jump, if that, ahead of the police. Totting up the various crimes he had committed – watch stealing, bicycle stealing, resisting an officer in the execution of his duty and causing him bodily injury – he had the feeling that if he got off with a life sentence, he would be lucky.

The problem of what to do next was one beyond his power of solution. It called for a wiser head than his, and most fortunately there was just such a head within easy reach.

'I wonder if you could let me have a piece of paper and an envelope,' he said to the landlord. 'And is there someone who could take a note for me to Mr Galahad Threepwood at the castle?'

The landlord said his son Gary would be happy to, if sixpence changed hands.

'I'll give him a shilling,' said Sam.

He was not a rich man and a shilling was a shilling to him, but if a shilling would provide for him a conference with one for whose ingenuity and resource he had come to feel a profound respect, it would in his opinion be a shilling well spent.

CHAPTER 6

I

A night's rest and a strengthening cocktail before lunch had quite dispelled any fatigue Gally might have been feeling as the result of his yesterday's motoring. His superb health, fostered by tobacco, late hours and alcohol, always enabled him to recuperate quickly, and he could be alert and bubbling with energy after activities which would have sent most teetotallers tottering off to their armchairs, to lie limply in them with their feet up.

Sam's telephone call just before lunch, announcing his arrival at the Emsworth Arms, had completed his sense of well being, and he was about to seek Sandy out and tell her of the treat in store for her, when as he passed the door of Lord Emsworth's study it flew open and its occupant came out, his face contorted, his pince-nez flying in the breeze, his whole demeanour that of a man who has been pushed too far.

'Galahad,' he cried passionately, 'I won't stand it. I shall assert myself. I shall take a firm line.'

'Take two if you wish, my dear fellow,' said Gally equably. 'This is Liberty Hall. What are you planning to take firm lines about?'

'This Callender girl. She's driving me mad. She's an insufferable pest. She's worse than Baxter.'

These were strong words. It had always been Lord Emsworth's opinion that the Efficient Baxter, now happily in the employment of an American millionaire and three thousand miles away in Pittsburgh, Pennsylvania, had, when it came to irritating, harrying and generally oppressing him, set a mark at which all other secretaries would shoot in vain.

'She's worse than that Briggs woman.'

Here, too, was an impressive statement. Lavender Briggs, who had resigned her portfolio and gone to London to conduct a typewriting agency, may not have been as intolerable as Rupert Baxter, but she had come very close to achieving that difficult feat.

'She covers my desk with letters which she says I must answer immediately. She keeps producing them like a dashed dog bringing his dashed bones into the dining-room. Where she digs them out from I can't imagine. Piles and piles of them.'

'Fan mail, do you think?'

'And what she has done to my study! It stinks of disinfectant and I can't find a thing.'

'Yes, I saw her tidying it up.'

'Messing it up, you mean. It's hard,' said Lord Emsworth, quivering with self-pity. 'I go to America to attend a sister's wedding, and when I come back expecting to have a little peace at last, what do I find? I find not only that another sister has come to stay but that she has introduced into my home a spectacled girl with red hair whose object seems to be to give me a nervous breakdown.'

Gally nodded sympathetically. There was nothing he could do to soothe, but he put in a mild word on Sandy's behalf.

'It's just zeal, Clarence. You get it in the young. She's a trier.'

'I find her trying,' Lord Emsworth retorted, one of the most brilliant things he had ever said. It was so good that he repeated it, and Gally gave another sympathetic nod.

'I can understand that her ministrations must be hard to bear,' he said, 'but put yourself in her place. She's a young girl eager to make good. She's told by her agency or whatever they call those concerns that they've found a job for her at Blandings Castle, and her eyes widen. "Isn't that where the great Lord Emsworth hangs out?" she says. "Quite correct," they say. She quivers from head to foot and a startled cry escapes her. "Hell's bells!" she says. "Then I'll have to spit on my hands and pull up my socks and leave no stone unturned or my name will be mud. That boy will expect good service." What you've got to realise, Clarence, is that you're a godlike figure to young Sandy. She has heard about you in legend and song. You awe her. She looks on you as a cross between a Sultan of the old school and a grandfather.'

'Grandfather?' said Lord Emsworth, stung.

'Great-grandfather,' said Gally, correcting himself. 'Well, if she has given you all that homework to do, you'd better buckle down to it.'

'I'm going to see my pig.'

'I'll come with you. I often say there is nothing so bracing as a good after-luncheon look at the Empress. Well known Harley Street physicians recommend it. But you'll catch it from her if she finds you've been playing hooky.'

'I do not allow myself to be dictated to by my secretary,' said Lord Emsworth haughtily.

As they made their way to the buttercup-dabbled meadow in a corner of which the Empress's self-contained flat was situated, Gally enlivened their progress with the story of the girl who said to her betrothed, 'I will not be dictated to!' and then went and got a job as a stenographer, while Lord Emsworth, who never listened to stories and very seldom to anything else, continued to explain why he found Sandy Callender such a thorn in the flesh. They had reached their destination and were gazing with suitable reverence on the silver medallist's superb contours, when a voice hailed them and, turning, they perceived a long, thin young man approaching. To Lord Emsworth, though they had frequently met, he appeared a total stranger and he merely blinked enquiringly, but Gally, having a better memory for faces, recognised him as Tipton Plimsoll and gave him a cheery greeting. He had always been fond of Tipton, sometimes going so far as to feel that, if that famous club had still existed, he would have been perfectly willing to put him up for membership at the old Pelican.

'Well, when did you get here, Tipton?' he said.

'Hello, Mr Threepwood. I've just arrived. Hello, Lord Emsworth. They told me in the house they thought you might be out here. You don't happen to know if Vee's around?'

The name conveyed nothing to Lord Emsworth.

'Vee? Vee?'

'She's in London,' said Gally.

'Oh, shoot. When do you expect her back?'

'I really couldn't say. I understand she's buying clothes, so I doubt if you can hope to see her for some little time. Still, you've always got me. Did you have a good trip?'

'Swell, thanks.'

'You're looking very bobbish.'

'I'm fine, thanks.'

It seemed to Lord Emsworth that for a man who had so recently been reduced to beggary by losses on the Stock Exchange this Tipton, whom with a powerful effort of the memory he had now recognised, was extraordinarily buoyant, and he honoured him for his courage and resilience. He was reminded of a Kipling poem the curate had recited at a village entertainment his sister Constance had once made him attend – something about if you can something something and never something something, you'll be a man, my son, or words to that effect.

'How was the coffee, Tipton?' he said.

'Pull yourself together, Clarence,' said Gally. 'You're dithering.'

'I am doing nothing of the sort,' said Lord Emsworth warmly. 'We had a most interesting conversation on the telephone one night in New York, and he told me that he was going to have a cup of coffee and a piece of pie.'

'Oh, sure, yes, I remember,' said Tipton. 'And talking of that, I owe you twenty dollars.'

'My dear fellow!'

'I'll give you a cheque when I get back to the house.'

Lord Emsworth was horrified.

'No, really, you must not dream of it. I am amply provided with funds and you cannot possibly afford it. Let us forget the whole thing. Tipton,' he explained to Gally, 'has lost all his money on the Stock Exchange.'

Gally looked grave. As has been said, he liked Tipton and wished him well, and being familiar with his sister Hermione's prejudice against penniless aspirants for her daughter's hand he feared that this was going to affect his matrimonial plans to no little extent. Like so many mothers, Lady Hermione expected a son-in-law to ante up and contribute largely to the kitty.

'Is this true?' he asked, concerned.

Tipton laughed amusedly.

'No, of course it isn't. I'm afraid I misled Lord Emsworth that night in New York. I've never lost a nickel in the market. All I wanted was twenty bucks to get self and friend out of the pokey.

Somebody had got away with my roll, leaving me without a cent, and a cop told me bail could be arranged if somebody would loan me the needful. So I thought of Lord Emsworth.'

Illumination came to Gally, and with it a renewed feeling that this young man would have been just the sort of new blood the Pelican would have welcomed.

'Oh, you had been pinched?'

'That's right.'

'Drunk and disorderly?'

'That's right.'

'I see.' A wave of nostalgia flooded over Gally as his thoughts went back to the time when he, too, had lived in Arcady. 'I was always getting pinched for d. and d. myself in my younger days. This was especially so when I supped at the old Gardenia – pulled down now, I regret to say, to make room for a Baptist chapel of all things. I was more or less of a marked man there. The bouncers used to fight for the privilege of throwing me out, and there seldom failed to be a couple of the gendarmerie waiting in the street as I shot through the door, on me like wolves and intensely sceptical of my sobriety. I always felt I was slipping in those days if it didn't take two of them to get me to the police bin, with another walking behind carrying my hat. How are the prisons in New York? I have visited that great city constantly, but oddly enough I was never arrested there. Much the same as on this side, I imagine. The place not to get jugged in is Paris, where similar establishments have no home comforts whatsoever. I remember on one occasion, after a rather sprightly do at the Bal Bullier—'

He was unable to complete what would no doubt have been a diverting anecdote full of inspiring hints for the younger generation, for at this moment a stalwart figure in smock and trousers came striding up. Monica Simmons back from lunch. She greeted her employer with a hearty bellow which echoed over hill and dale.

'Heard you'd arrived, Lord Emsworth,' she boomed. 'Glad to be back, I shouldn't wonder. No place like home, I often say. How do you think the piggy-wiggy's looking?'

'Capital, capital,' said Lord Emsworth. 'Capital, capital, capital.'

He spoke with genuine enthusiasm. There had been a time when both he and Gally had entertained the gravest doubts as to Monica Simmons's fitness for her high position, due to this habit of hers of referring to the Empress as the piggy-wiggy. As Gally had said, it was the wrong tone and seemed to show that she was too frivolous in her outlook to hold so responsible a post. The girl, he pointed out, who carelessly dismisses a three-times silver medallist at the Shropshire Agricultural Show as a piggy-wiggy today is a girl who may quite easily forget to give the noble animal lunch tomorrow. And according to Augustus Whipple in his monumental work a pig cannot afford to skip meals. If it does not consume daily nourishment amounting to fifty-seven hundred calories, these to consist of proteins four pounds five ounces, carbohydrates twenty-five pounds, it becomes a spent force.

But that was all in the past. The term piggy-wiggy no longer made him wince. Monica Simmons had proved herself a worthy daughter of the agricultural college from which she had graduated and more than equal to the tremendous task of keeping Empress of Blandings up to bursting point.

Nor did her conception of her duties stop at providing her charge with calories. Her next words showed that she had its welfare at heart in other directions.

'Oh, by the way, Lord Emsworth,' she said, 'I nearly forgot to ask you. Who would that boy be? A small boy with a face like a prune run over by a motor bus.'

Lord Emsworth was baffled. He had no solution to offer. It was left to Gally to supply the information. The description, he said, fitted Dame Daphne Winkworth's son Huxley like the paper on the wall and could scarcely have been improved upon by the most meticulous stylist.

'But why do you bring him up?' he asked. 'How has he thrust himself on your attention?'

'He keeps hanging round trying to let the Empress out of her sty.'

'He does that?' cried Lord Emsworth, appalled.

'I caught him at it yesterday and again this morning.'

'The next time he does it, give him a good hard knock.'

'I'll rub his face in the mud.'

'And Sandy Callender will rub yours in the mud, Clarence, if you don't go back and attend to your correspondence,' said Gally. 'Come along. The party's over.'

II

Left alone with Monica Simmons and scanning her with a critical eye, Tipton found a difficulty in detecting those glamorous qualities in her which appeared to make so strong an appeal to Wilfred Allsop. He willingly conceded that if attacked by a mad bull or a gang of youths with switch knives and brass knuckles he would be happy to have her at his side, for the muscles of her brawny arms were obviously strong as iron bands, if not stronger, but as an arouser of the softer emotions he could not see her with a spyglass. He was thinking, indeed, as so many men have thought on meeting their friends' loved ones, that given the choice between linking his lot with hers and going over Niagara Falls in a barrel he would greatly prefer the latter form of unpleasantness.

However, being aware that Wilfred held other views, he prepared to do all that was within his power to further his interests, employing more direct methods than his friend had done. Wilfred, he had gathered from his observations in their mutual cell, had been conducting his wooing on remote control or Patience-on-a-monument lines, and it was a policy of which he thoroughly disapproved. In matters of the heart he was solidly in favour of laying cards on the table and talking turkey. Only so could business result.

'Fat pig, that,' he said by way of easing into the deeper topic he had in mind.

'The fattest in Shropshire, Herefordshire and South Wales,' said Monica proudly.

'Not on a diet, I notice.'

'No, sir, you don't catch this piggy-wiggy slimming. She believes in getting hers and to hell with what it does to her figure. You're the fellow who's marrying Veronica Wedge, aren't you?'

'That's me. Plimsoll is the name. Tipton Plimsoll.'

'Monica Simmons at this end.'

'I thought as much. Willie Allsop was speaking to me of you not long ago.'

'Oh, was he?'

'And in the highest terms, I don't mind telling you. He gave you a rave notice. He couldn't have gone overboard more completely if you had been the current Miss America.'

When it came to blushing, Monica Simmons was handicapped by the fact that her face was obscured by the mud inseparable from her chosen walk in life. It is virtually impossible to retain that schoolgirl complexion unimpaired if you are looking after pigs all the time. Even more closely than Sandy Callender when tidying up Lord Emsworth's study she resembled one of those sons of toil buried beneath tons of soil of whom Gally had spoken. Nevertheless, probing beyond the geological strata Tipton thought he could discern a pinkness. Her substantial foot, moreover, had begun to trace coy arabesques on the turf. These phenomena encouraged him to proceed.

'In fact,' he went on, laying the whole deck of cards on the table and talking turkey without reserve, 'he loves you like a ton of bricks, and his dearest wish is that you will consent to sign your future correspondence Monica Allsop.'

It was impossible for a girl constructed on Monica's lines to leap like a startled fawn, but she quivered perceptibly. A sound not unlike the Empress's grunt proceeded from her, and her eyes rounded to about the dimensions of standard golf balls. It was some moments before she could speak. When she did, the words came out in a husky whisper.

'I can't believe it!'

'Why not? All pretty straightforward, it seems to me. What's your problem?'

'He's so far above me.'

'Couple of inches shorter, I'd have said.'

'Intellectually, I mean.'

'Who ever told you Willie Allsop had an intellect?'

'He looks so spiritual.'

'So do I, but you can't go by that. He may look spiritual, but you can take it from me that he's a regular guy all right. I've seen him when he was going good, and he's well worth watching. But putting that aside for the moment, what I want to know is what his rating is with you. Where does he stand in your book? How would you react if he asked you to marry him? Would you feel he had the right idea, or would you give him the horse's laugh and say "Drop dead, you little squirt"?'

Beneath the mud Monica Simmons flushed hotly. It was plain that an exposed nerve had been touched.

'He is not a little squirt!'

'Well, that's what he says he is. It was precisely how he described himself when he was talking to me about you. "She's so majestic, and I'm such a little squirt" were his exact words. But you appear to think otherwise, so am I to infer that he'd really have a chance of bringing home the bacon?'

'If you mean would I accept him if he asked me to marry him, yes I would. I'd jump into his arms.'

'Well, I'm not sure I'd advise that. I don't want to seem personal, but you're on the solid side and he's kind of flimsy. You might fracture something. Still, the point, the thing we've been trying to get at, is that your views on the subject of centre-aisleing coincide with his, so that's all right. I'll go and tell him.'

'Will you really?'

'Right away.'

'Oh, Mr Plimsoll!'

'Call me Tipton.'

'Oh, Tipton!'

'Or, rather, Tippy.'

'Oh, Tippy, you're an angel.'

'I'm like Officer Garroway, a buddy of mine whom you haven't met,' said Tipton. 'I started out in life as a Boy Scout, and I can't seem to shake off the habit of doing my day's good deed. And now to find Willie.'

III

It was no easy task to do this, for Wilfred Allsop had been detained on the terrace by Dame Daphne Winkworth. Dame Daphne liked to become acquainted with her staff and she had kept him answering personal questions for a full hour, after which he had gone to his room to bathe his forehead. When he emerged, feeling somewhat better though still weak, the first person he met was Tipton, who had almost decided to give up the search.

There took place, of course, something in the nature of a joyous reunion. It was their first meeting since they had parted with mutual civilities outside the New York police station, and each was thinking how greatly the other's looks had improved in the interim. Tipton's face then had seemed to Wilfred to be an unwholesome yellow in colour and to flicker a good deal like an early silent motion picture, and so had Wilfred's to Tipton. Even now neither could have entered a beauty competition with any real confidence of success unless Officer Garroway had been the sole other contestant, but there had been a distinct change for the better.

When two friends meet after a separation, the conversation tends as a rule to begin with enquiries from both regarding old Joes and Jacks and Jimmys whom they have seen or not seen anything of lately, but as Tipton Plimsoll and Wilfred Allsop had met only once and the only acquaintance they had in common was Officer Garroway, a few exchanges on the subject of that golden-hearted city employee were enough to cover these preliminaries and Tipton was almost immediately at liberty to get down to those brass tacks to which he always liked to get down as soon as possible.

'Well, Willie,' he said, going straight to the *res*. 'I've just been having a chat with the Simmons broad. We had quite a visit.'

An austere look came into Wilfred's face. He had had to complain before of Tipton's freedom of speech when alluding to the girl he worshipped. It was the other's only fault, but a grave one.

'Would you mind not referring to Miss Simmons as a broad,' he said coldly.

'Sorry. Slip of the tongue. I should have said I've been talking to your little serving of peaches and cream, and I have some rather interesting news to impart. It appears that you are her dream man.'

'What!'

'That's what she told me. You're ace high with her. She didn't actually say she would die for one little rose from your hair, but that was the impression she conveyed. What she said was that if you asked her to marry you, she would jump into your arms. I don't see what more you want than that.'

Wilfred stared, gulped and tottered.

'You aren't kidding?'

'No, I'm not, and nor was she. All you've got to do is walk up to her, wipe some of the mud off her face, clasp her in your arms, and you're home.'

The programme, as outlined, plainly attracted Wilfred. Nevertheless he hesitated.

'Clasp her in my arms?'

'And kiss her. Having of course cleaned her up a little first. She needs thoroughly going over with soap and hot water.'

Wilfred shook his head.

'I couldn't do it.'

'Why not?'

'I haven't the nerve.'

Tipton smiled indulgently.

'The very words I said to a girl called Prudence Garland when she urged me to propose to Vee.'

'You mean my cousin Prue?'

'Is she your cousin? Everybody seems to be your cousin.'

'She's my Aunt Dora's daughter. She's married to a man named Lister. Bill Lister. They run a sort of roadhouse place near Oxford.'

'Yes, I remember they wanted me to put money into it, but I was light on my feet and kept away. Well, she was staying here when I first met Vee, and one day she drew me aside and said "You're in love with Vee, aren't you, Mr Plimsoll?"'

'To which you replied?'

'I didn't reply, because I was busy falling off a wall at the time. We were sitting on the wall of the terrace, and her words gave me such a start that I overbalanced. Returning to my seat, I said I was, and she said Well, why don't you ask her to marry you, and just like you I said it couldn't be done, because I hadn't the nerve. And do you know what she suggested?'

'What?'

'She said that that could be readily adjusted if I had a good quick snort by way of a send-off.'

'And you did?'

'I did, and it altered the whole set-up. It made a new man of me and I approached the matter in hand in an entirely different spirit.'

'You became the dominant male?'

'With bells on.'

'And asked Vee to marry you?'

'Ordered would be a better word. I just gave her her instructions.'

'What did you actually say?'

'By way of leading into the thing? "My woman!", if I remember rightly. Yes, that was it. "My woman!" I thought for a moment of saying "My mate!", but decided against it because it seemed to me to have too nautical a ring. But you don't need to worry about the dialogue. That's a side issue. It's the clasping in arms and kissing that puts the act across. And I'll tell you what I'll do for you, Willie. In the glove compartment of my car there is a well-filled flask. It's yours. Slip it in your pocket and about five minutes before the kick-off drain its contents. You'll be surprised.'

For an instant Wilfred Allsop's face lit up, as that of the poet Shelley whom he so closely resembled must have done when he suddenly realised that 'blithe spirit' rhymes with 'near it', not that it does, and another ode was as good as off the assembly line. Then it fell. He fingered his chin dubiously.

'Can I risk it?'

'No risk involved. It's good Scotch.'

'I was thinking of Dame Daphne Winkworth.'

'Who's she?'

'She runs the school where I'm going to teach music.'

'Of course, yes. You mentioned her that night in New York. But how does she come into it?'

'She's staying here. She would fire me like a shot if she caught me drinking. And while drumming the elements of music into the heads of a bunch of goggle-eyed schoolgirls isn't what I'd call an ideal form of employment, it's a job and carries a salary with it. Do you think I ought to take a chance?'

'You'll never get to first base if you don't. When were you planning to contact Miss Simmons?'

'Tomorrow morning, I thought.'

'I'll tell her to expect you then.'

'Though I'm still nervous about Ma Winkworth.'

'Relax. I'll see that she isn't around. I'll get hold of her and keep her talking.'

'You're a true friend, Tippy.'

'I like to do my bit. That's settled, then. Shall we just run through the scenario to make sure you've got it straight?'

'It might be as well.'

'Walk up.'

'Walk up.'

'Clasp in arms.'

'Clasp in arms.'

'Kiss.'

'Kiss.'

'And say "My woman!" It's as easy as falling off a log. You can't miss.'

CHAPTER 7

I

It is never pleasant for a girl to find that she is being followed, and if she has to be followed she would always prefer it not to be by a man who has recently called her a ginger-haired little fathead. Sandy, as she passed through the front door of the castle on her return from Market Blandings, was seething with indignation, resentment and a number of other disagreeable emotions. She was also conscious of a choking sensation. The sight of a Sam Bagshott where no Sam Bagshott should have been had taken her breath away and she was still in the process of recovering it.

The front door opened on a spacious hall, and as she entered it a footman appeared at the other end. He was carrying a coiled-up red rope, and this he hooked to a ring in the wall. He then carried it to the opposite wall and hooked it there. After which, he hung up in prominent positions two printed notices, both on the brusque side. One said:

KINDLY KEEP IN LINE

the other:

NO SMOKING

He then dusted his hands and stepped back with the air of a man who has done a good day's work.

Surprise at these peculiar goings-on made Sandy momentarily forget Sam and his adhesiveness. She would come back to him later, but in the meantime she wanted to know what all this was about. The footman, when she put this question to him, smiled the indulgent smile of the expert illuminating a novice.

'Visitors' Day, miss.'

'Today?'

'No, miss, tomorrow. Premises thrown open to the public every Thursday. Mr Beach shows them round.'

'Do a lot of them come?'

'This hot weather seems to bring them out like flies. Three charabangs and a girls' school last week.'

'I didn't get here till the Friday, so I missed them.'

'You were lucky,' said the footman, his eyes bleak. He seemed to be brooding on past horrors. 'Draw that rope tight, Thomas,' he added as another footman entered bearing a sign that read:

KINDLY DO NOT FINGER OBJECTS OF ART

'Last Thursday a couple of hussies climbed over it and sat on that fender as bold as brass.'

A sudden disquieting thought struck Sandy like a blow. Only now did that phrase 'Premises thrown open to the public' come home to her.

'Can *anyone* come on Visitors' Day?'

'Anyone that's got half-a-crown, miss,' said the footman, giving the rope another pull.

There was a thoughtful look on Sandy's face as she made her way to the library, to which she planned to give a thorough straightening and tidying. And indeed she had been provided with food for thought. No doubt Gally would have told Sam about Visitors' Day, and if she knew her Gally would have pointed out to him how admirable an opportunity it provided for invading the castle. And once Sam was in the castle a meeting between them, he being the thrustful young man he was, would be inevitable. He might refrain from smoking, and he might not finger objects of art, but the one thing of which she was certain was that he would not kindly keep in line. It would take more than a mere butler and two footmen to restrain him from roaming at large about the place until he found her.

And she recoiled from the thought of being found by him. She did not want to see him even in the distance. All she asked of him was to stay out of her life. She did not conceal from herself that his absence from it had left a gap in her heart like the excavation for the foundation of a skyscraper, but that could not be helped. Time would presumably fill it up again, and even if that did not happen a man who had called her the things he had called her at their last meeting was obviously a man she was better without.

Reaching the library, she went about her work, but she did it absently. She dusted books, she tidied papers, but her thoughts were not with them. Her mind was concentrated on the problem of how this distasteful encounter could be avoided. It was as she removed from the coal scuttle a letter addressed to her employer which had somehow managed to find that unusual resting place that the solution came to her, and she hurried to Lord Emsworth's study.

Her arrival there startled Lord Emsworth. He peered at her in quick alarm. She looked to him like a girl who had come to bring him some more letters demanding his instant attention. Unless his eyes deceived him, it was a letter she was holding in her hand. He feared the worst, and her words, when she spoke, were music to his ears.

'I wonder if you could possibly spare me for a day or two, Lord Emsworth,' she said. 'My father is very ill.'

This would have struck old friends like Gally and Tipton Plimsoll as peculiar, knowing as they did that the late Ernest Callender had passed away shortly before her eighth birthday, but Lord Emsworth, lacking this knowledge, tut-tutted courteously.

'I am sorry,' he said. 'Too bad. Quite.'

'Will it be all right if I go away for a few days?'

'Certainly, certainly, certainly, certainly,' said Lord Emsworth with perhaps a greater enthusiasm than was tactful. 'Stay away as long as you like. My brother-in-law Colonel Wedge is catching some sort of a train this afternoon, got to go to Sussex or somewhere. You could drive into Market Blandings in the car. An excellent idea. Yes, quite.'

'Thank you very much.'

'Not at all, not at all.'

'I'll go and pack my things. Oh, by the way, I found this letter in the coal scuttle in the library. I think you should answer it at once.'

Lord Emsworth took the letter gloomily. He was saying to himself that he had thought as much. If Sandy Callender's come, he would have said if he had been more poetic than he was, can letters to be answered at once be far behind?

II

Gally on returning to the house had wandered off to the smoking-room and begun to glance through the illustrated weekly papers. But their pages, filled mostly with photographs of Society brides who looked like gangsters' molls and the usual gargoyles who attend Hunt Bails, failed to grip him, and the thought having occurred to him that another chat with one whose conversation he always enjoyed might offer greater entertainment, he made his way to Lord Emsworth's study. And he had just reached the door when Lord Emsworth came popping out like a cuckoo from a cuckoo clock.

'Oh, Galahad,' he said. 'The very man I was looking for.'

To Gally's surprise he seemed, despite the fact that Blandings Castle had been filling up so much of late, in excellent spirits. On their way to the sty he had been moody and peevish and, when speaking of his current secretary, inclined to wallow in self-pity, but now he was not merely cheerful but exuberantly cheerful.

'Galahad,' he cried, as sunnily as if there had been no Lady Hermione, no Colonel Wedge, no Dame Daphne Winkworth, no little Huxley Winkworth and no Sandy Callender in the house, 'the most wonderful thing has happened. I have never been so pleased in my life.'

'Don't tell me they've made you a Dame?'

'Eh? No, not so far as I know. You told me yourself that such a thing was most unlikely. But you have heard me speak of Augustus Whipple?'

'The chap who wrote that book you're always reading? *Put Me Among The Pigs*, isn't it called?'

'*On The Care Of The Pig*.'

'That's right. Banned in Boston, I believe.'

'Eh?'

'Let it go. What about Augustus Whipple?'

'Miss Callender has just found a letter from him.'

'In the wastepaper basket?'

'No, actually in the library coal scuttle, oddly enough. I cannot imagine how it got there.'

'Sherlock Holmes used to keep his tobacco in the toe of a Persian slipper.'

'I don't think I have ever seen a Persian slipper.'

'Nor have I. It is my secret sorrow. Tell me about this letter from old Pop Whipple. Does he want an exclusive interview with the Empress?'

'He wants to come here and see her. He had heard so much about her, he says, and would like to take some photographs. He writes from the Athenaeum Club.'

'That morgue?' said Gally, who did not think highly of the Athenaeum. There was not a bishop or a Cabinet Minister there whom he would have taken to the old Pelican and introduced to Plug Basham and Buffy Struggles. He might be wronging the institution, but he doubted if it contained on its membership list a single sportsman capable of throwing soft-boiled eggs at an electric fan or smashing the piano on a Saturday night. 'I lunched with him there once.'

Lord Emsworth gasped, astounded.

'You mean you *know* Augustus Whipple?'

'Well, I've met him.'

'Why have you never told me?'

'I suppose the subject didn't come up. It was when I was thinking of writing my memoirs. I wanted some first-hand facts about an uncle of his who grew a second set of teeth in his eightieth year and used to crack Brazil nuts with them. Not at all a bad fellow. Whipple, I mean, not the uncle, who perished of a surfeit of Brazil nuts at the age of eighty-two. Are you going to have him to stay at the castle?'

'Of course. It will be a pleasure and a privilege.'

'The old shack's certainly filling up.'

'I have written a telegram explaining that I have only just seen his letter and inviting him to come here for as long as he wishes. I shall give it to Voules to send off. He is going to Market Blandings to take Egbert to his train.'

'Why don't you phone it?'

'I never seem able to make myself understood when I telephone the post office. There is an idiotic girl there who keeps saying "Pardon? Woodger mind repeating that?" No, I'll give it to Voules.'

'Give it to me. I'm going to the great city. There's a man there I want to see.'

'Why, thank you, Galahad. That will be capital.'

It was in mellow mood that Gally some minutes later set off down the drive, his hat jauntily on one side and his little legs twinkling. He was not actually singing a gipsy song as he trudged along, but it would have been unwise to have betted against his starting to do so at any moment, for this Whipple business had, he perceived, solved all the problems confronting him in his capacity of Sam's guardian angel. Reviewing the position of affairs, he summed it up as looking pretty smooth. He was well pleased with the way everything seemed to be turning out for the best.

The afternoon had now cooled off to some extent, but it was still warm enough to bring visions of the Emsworth Arms beer rising before the mental retina, and they rose before his. At the Emsworth Arms there was a large shady garden running down to the river, where you could sit and quaff beneath a spreading tree, your thirst agreeably stimulated by the spectacle of perspiring oarsmen toiling under the sun in boats often laden with a wife, two of her relations, three children, a dog and a picnic basket: and he was just thinking how extraordinarily well a foaming tankard would go down in these delightful surroundings, when he was aware of a voice saying 'Hoy!' and perceived a small boy at his side. The landlord of the Blue Boar's son Gary had proved faithful to his trust.

'Got a letter for you, Mr Threepwood,' he said. He had never met Gally socially, but like everyone else for miles around he knew him by sight.

Gally took the letter, mystified. The sepia maelstrom of the child's thumb had soiled it a good deal outwardly, but its contents were legible, and he found them disturbing. Sam had written briefly, confining himself to broad outlines rather than going into details, but he had made the main facts clear. He was not, it appeared, at the Emsworth Arms in Market Blandings but at the Blue Boar in Blandings Parva and for some reason he was in sore straits and would be glad of a word of advice from the addressee as to what to do for the best. Now, he implied though not actually saying so, was the time for all good men to come to the aid of the party.

No one had ever made a plea of this kind to Galahad Threepwood and found him unresponsive. The beer at the Blue Boar would, he knew, be vastly inferior to that of the Emsworth Arms, but he had always been a man able to take the rough with the smooth and he did not hesitate. A bare five minutes had elapsed before he crossed the Blue Boar's threshold.

III

In Sam's greeting of him there was a touch of the shipwrecked mariner sighting a sail, for the interval between dispatching the note and seeing this friendly face had given him time for a further review of his situation. It had left him even more apprehensive than he had been at the beginning, and he had been distinctly apprehensive then. The day was warm, but his feet were cold. A bird twittering in the bushes outside sounded to his sensitive ear exactly like a police whistle.

Gally listened attentively as he poured out his tale. His manner, as it proceeded, gave no suggestion that he was shocked and horrified, nor was he. Of the broad general principle of hitting the police force in the eye he had always thoroughly approved. You could not, in his opinion, do it too much and too often. He could, however, see that his young friend had placed himself in a somewhat equivocal position. Steps would have to be taken through the proper channels if he was to be extricated from it and fortunately he was able to take such steps.

'Tell me that bit about Sandy again,' he said. 'You say you saw her. Did she see you?'

'Yes.'

'And instantly, after one glance, streaked over the horizon?'

'Yes.'

'I don't like that.'

'I don't like it myself.'

'Not too promising, her attitude. It gives the impression that she didn't want to speak to you.'

'I thought of that, too.'

'This will have to be corrected. You then hared after her?'

'Yes.'

'With the watch in your pocket?'

'Yes.'

'The cop followed you and seemed anxious to effect a pinch?'

'Yes.'

'And you slugged him?'

'Yes.'

'Now I have it all straight. Your position, as I see it, is more or less that of the hart that pants for cooling streams when heated in the chase. You're a marked man. You can't go back to the Emsworth Arms.'

'I suppose not.'

'It isn't a question of supposing. Show your face there for a single instant and you haven't hope of escaping arrest. The arm of the law will grab you before you can say What-ho. You need a hide-out, and you will be glad to hear that I can provide one.'

Sam shook visibly.

'You can?'

'Most fortunately I am able to. For the next few days, till the hue and cry has died down, you must come and stay at the castle.'

'What!'

'You heard.'

'But didn't you tell me you weren't allowed to invite people to the castle?'

'I did. But it will be my brother Clarence who invites you, not I. He is at this very moment ordering the vassals and serfs to get busy bringing the red carpet up from the cellar and dusting it off in preparation for your arrival. But I was forgetting that you are not abreast of the latest developments. Let me briefly bring you up to date. I happened to run into Clarence just now and found him wreathed in smiles. His favourite reading, I must mention, is a book on pigs by a fellow named Whipple. He pores over it incessantly, savouring its golden words like artichoke leaves. He is never happier than when curled up with it. He must know it by heart, I should think. All straight so far?'

'If you mean Do I follow you, yes. But I don't see—'

'Whither all this is tending? It won't be long before it dawns on you. Shall I proceed?'

'Do.'

'Questioned, he revealed that young Sandy Callender had found a letter from this Whipple asking if he can drop in some time and have a look at Empress of Blandings. You can readily imagine how it affected Clarence. He started strewing roses from his hat and dancing the Can-Can all over the premises. My cup runneth over, he said, and he handed me a telegram to send to Whipple urging him to pack a toothbrush and come running. He gave him to understand that Blandings Castle was his for as long as he cared to stay. Now do you begin to get it?'

'No.'

'You don't see how this solves all your little difficulties and makes your path straight?'

'No.'

'Not very quick at the uptake, are you? Your father would have grasped it in a second. All you have to do is present yourself at the front door and say "Yoo-hoo, I'm Whipple" and you're in like Flynn, as the expression is. After which, getting hold of young Sandy and making her see the light will be a simple task. Extraordinarily fortunate, Whipple having taken it into his head to write to Clarence at just this time. Providential, I call it. One feels that one is somehow being *protected*.'

He had chosen a bad moment for placing his proposition before Sam, for the latter was in the very act of refreshing himself from his mug of beer. It was not until he had choked and gasped for a considerable space and been slapped a number of times on the back that he was able to speak. When he did, there was incredulity in his voice.

'You're crazy! What happens when Whipple turns up?'

'He won't.'

'Not when he gets that telegram?'

'He won't get it. What will reach him will be a regretful bob's-worth saying it's impossible to have him at the castle at the moment, as Clarence is in bed with German measles. I sent it off before I left.'

'Well, suppose there's somebody at the castle who knows me?'

'There isn't. You surely don't imagine I didn't think of that. You've never met my sister Hermione or her husband or Dame Daphne Winkworth, and you told me Tipton Plimsoll didn't know you by sight. Nothing to cause anxiety there.'

'How about Sandy?'

Gally was shocked.

'A nice girl like Sandy wouldn't dream of giving you away. I'm not saying she won't split a gusset when she finds how we have outmanoeuvred her, but her lips will be sealed. No, I can see no possible objection to what I suggest.'

'I can. I wouldn't do it for a thousand pounds. The mere thought of it makes my toes curl. I shall spend the night at this pub and after I've seen Sandy tomorrow I shall go back to London.'

Gally sighed.

'There's something wrong with the younger generation,' he said with a sad shake of the head. 'One notices it on all sides. No dash, no enterprise, none of the up-and-doing spirit. Any member of the old brigade would have leaped to the task with his hair in a braid. You won't reconsider?'

'No.'

'You would be under the same roof as the girl you love.'

'For perhaps five minutes. At the end of that period I can see the Lady somebody you spoke of, the one who grabs people by their trouser seats, attaching herself to mine and starting heaving. No, I am always willing to oblige when feasible, but there are limits.'

'What if that copper finds you here and pinches you?'

'It would be unpleasant, I admit.'

'Well, then.'

'But I'd prefer it to going to Lord Emsworth and saying "Yoo-hoo, I'm Whipple".'

Gally shrugged his shoulders resignedly, as Napoleon might have done if he had asked his army to advance and been told by them that they were not in the mood.

'Oh well,' he said, 'if you won't, you won't. But I still consider your objections finicky. Then we'll just have to carry on with the Visitors' Day programme.'

IV

The car which was to take Colonel Wedge to Market Blandings station and start him off on the first leg of his journey into Worcestershire stood at the front door of the castle with chauffeur Voules at the wheel. It was a good car as cars went, but it paled into insignificance beside the superlative Rolls which had been parked a little farther along the drive. Colonel Wedge, coming out of the house, eyed this ornate vehicle with respectful admiration.

'Whose car is that, Voules?' he asked.

'Belongs to Mr Plimsoll, sir.'

Colonel Wedge could make nothing of this.

'To Mr *Plimsoll*?'

'Yes, sir. The gentleman arrived in it just now.'

The colonel continued bewildered. After what he had heard of the state of Tipton's finances, he would have expected him to arrive on roller skates. And it was as he stood blinking and trying to digest this piece of information that Tipton appeared in person, coming out of the house with an oblong object in his hand that seemed to be, as indeed it was, one of those cases in which jewellers put jewels.

'Oh, there you are, Colonel,' he said. 'I've been looking for you all over. Wanted to show you a necklace I picked up in London for Vee. I was hoping to give it to her directly I hit the joint, but darn it, they tell me she's not here. Great disappointment.' He opened the case. 'I think she'll like it, don't you?' he said, for he knew his loved one's fondness for bijouterie. Veronica Wedge was one of those girls who if they have not plenty of precious stones on their persons, feel nude. Her aim in life was to look as like a chandelier as possible.

Colonel Wedge did not reply at once. A strange breathlessness had gripped him as he saw the contents of the case. He was no expert on jewellery, but if this necklace had not set its purchaser back what is technically known as a packet, he would be dashed.

'But—' he began, and paused, uncertain how to put it. You cannot ask your daughter's fiancé straight out how he is fixed as regards money in the bank. At least you can, but if you do, you risk the raised eyebrow and the frosty stare. 'But can you afford it, my dear fellow?' he asked, feeling that was a delicate way of approaching the subject.

Tipton was puzzled. He had been rich long enough for people to take his extravagances for granted.

'Why, sure,' he said. 'It only cost eight thousand pounds. They knocked off a bit for cash.'

It was established earlier in this narrative that Blandings

Castle was a solidly constructed building, a massive pile with no tendency as a rule to wobble on its foundations, but to Colonel Wedge as he heard these words it seemed to be behaving like one of those Ouled Nail dancers he remembered having seen when a subaltern in Cairo. The same uninhibited twists and twiggles. Though not an unusually intelligent man, he was bright enough to gather that the Wedge family had done a remarkably foolish thing, in their haste depriving themselves of a son-in-law who drove around in five-thousand-guinea cars and thought nothing of paying eight thousand pounds for necklaces. They had, in short, goofed to precisely the same extent as the celebrated Indian who threw a pearl away richer than all his tribe. Veronica's letter breaking the engagement must even now be on its way to the castle, and the thought of what would happen when Tipton opened it and read the contents made Colonel Wedge look and feel as if he had received a crushing blow on the solar plexus.

'Not feeling well, Colonel?' asked Tipton, concerned.

'A touch of my old malaria,' the colonel managed to say.

'You get it often?'

'Fairly often. It comes on suddenly.'

'Too bad. Nasty thing to have.'

'Quite,' said Colonel Wedge, unaware that he was infringing Lord Emsworth's copyright material.

There remained one faint hope, that the letter, if written, had not yet been dispatched, and he was examining this hope and not thinking very highly of it, when Wilfred Allsop appeared at the head of the steps.

'Phone, Uncle Egbert,' he said. 'Aunt Hermione on the phone for you,' and few shots out of guns had ever travelled more briskly than did Colonel Wedge *en route* for the instrument.

'Hullo, old girl,' he panted, having reached and clutched the receiver.

'I am coming home the day after tomorrow, Egbert. You will have left for Worcestershire by then, I suppose.'

'I'm leaving this afternoon.'

'Don't stay there longer than you can help.'

'I won't. How about that letter?'

'Letter?'

'The one you were going to get Vee to write.'

'Oh, that? Have you been worrying about it? There was no need. You know what a sensible girl Veronica is. She quite saw that it was the only thing to do.'

'You mean she's written it?'

'Of course. I posted it just now. What did you say, Egbert?'

Colonel Wedge had not spoken. The sound to which she referred had been merely his hollow groan at the death bed of that hope. It had always been a sickly little thing, plainly not long for this world, and at these five words it had coughed quietly and expired.

'Nothing,' he said. 'Nothing. I am just clearing my throat.'

He debated within himself whether or not to break the bad news, and decided against it. Time enough for the old girl to learn the awful truth when she returned to the castle. Let her have one more day of happiness. 'Well, I suppose I'd better be getting along,' he said. 'Voules is waiting to take me to the train. When do you think that letter will get here?'

'Tomorrow morning, I imagine. Why?'

'I was just wondering.'

'Tipton will find it when he arrives.'

'He has arrived.'

'Oh, has he? Does he seem terribly depressed, poor fellow?'

A vision of Tipton gloating over that necklace, his face split by an outsize in grins, rose before Colonel Wedge.

'No,' he said. 'No, not terribly.'

'How brave of him. I hope the letter will not upset him too much.'

'So do I,' said Colonel Wedge. 'So do I.'

A passer-by, seeing him as he came away from the telephone, would probably have supposed that the conversation just concluded had been one of no great importance, for there was nothing in his bearing to hint at the blow he had received. His backbone was rigid, his upper lip had not ceased to be stiff, nor did his moustache droop. Where Othello, with much less on his mind, had allowed his subdu'd eyes to drop tears as fast as the Arabian tree their med-cinable gum, he contrived to preserve an outward serenity. The British Army trains its sons well.

Nevertheless, his mind was in a whirl, the only thought in it that could possibly be called coherent being a wild regret that he had ever been misguided enough to believe in any statement made by his brother-in-law Clarence. Rashly he had forgotten the lesson that everyone who came in contact with the ninth Earl of Emsworth had to learn, that nothing he said was ever to be taken as making the remotest sense. The rule to live by was to ignore his every utterance.

He was still thinking bitterly about his relative by marriage as he came out of the front door. Tipton had disappeared, but his place had been taken by Gally. He was talking to Voules and seemed to be telling him a humorous story, for while the chauffeur was not actually smiling, chauffeurs not being permitted by their guild to do that, one noted a distinct twitching of the muscles around the lips.

'Ah, Egbert,' said Gally. 'You just off?'

At the sight of him something had seemed to explode inside Colonel Wedge's head like a firecracker. It was an inspiration.

'Could I have a word with you, Galahad?' he said.

'Say on,' said Gally.

Colonel Wedge had no intention of saying on in the hearing of Voules, though he could see by the way the latter's ears were sticking up that he was perfectly willing to act as a confidant. He drew Gally aside to a spot where even the most clairaudient chauffeur, all eagerness to gather material for his memoirs, would be left out of the conversation. Privacy thus secured, he embarked on his narrative.

He told it well. At first perhaps there was a disposition on his part to diverge from the straight story line in order to insert acid criticism of Lord Emsworth, but he quickly overcame this tendency and placed the facts so clearly before Gally that the latter had no difficulty in grasping them and realising the full gravity of the situation.

He felt that he did not need to look into a crystal ball to foresee what would happen when Tipton read that letter. His first move, one presumed, would be to ask Veronica for an explanation, and one could readily guess what explanation Veronica, the dumbest blonde in Shropshire and its adjoining counties, would give. 'But I thought you had lost all your money, Tip-pee,' she would say, rolling her lovely eyes, and it would be all over except for returning the presents, countermanding the bridesmaids, telling the caterer his services would not be required and breaking it to the bishop and assistant clergy that they would have to look for employment elsewhere. Those wedding bells, in short, would not ring out and Sam's sweepstake ticket would become a mere worthless scrap of paper, no good to man or beast. It would not be too much to say that Gally was appalled. In his consternation he even removed his monocle and started to polish it, a thing he never did except when greatly stirred.

'Egbert,' he said, 'that letter must not be allowed to reach Tipton.'

'Exactly the idea that occurred to me,' said Colonel Wedge. 'And what I was going to suggest was that you should intercept it. You see,' he hastened to explain, 'I can't do it myself, because I shan't be here. I've got to go to my godmother's.'

'You can't give her a miss?'

'She would never forgive me.'

'Then, of course, my dear fellow, I shall be delighted to place my services at your disposal.'

In the twenty-five years in which Colonel Egbert Wedge had been married to Lord Emsworth's sister Hermione quite a good deal of his wife's conversation had dealt with the moral and spiritual defects of her brother Galahad, but though he had prudently kept his opinion to himself, she had never been able to shake him in his view that Gally was the salt of the earth. He had always been devoted to him and never more so than at this moment.

'Good heavens, what a relief! You're sure you can manage it?' he said, though he hardly knew why he had bothered to ask the question. If good old Gally said he would intercept a letter, that letter was as good as intercepted. 'It'll mean getting up at some unearthly hour.'

Gally waved his apologies aside.

'That's all right. If larks can do it, I can do it. So you can go off and suck up to your godmother with a light heart. And you ought to be starting, or you'll miss your train.'

'I'm just waiting for that girl.'

'What girl?'

'That secretary of Clarence's. Her father has been suddenly taken ill and she has to go away for a few days. Ah, here she is,' said Colonel Wedge as Sandy came down the steps. Her face was grave, as any girl's might be who was on her way to a parent's sick bed.

'I hope I have not kept you waiting, Colonel.'

'Not at all, not at all. Plenty of time.'

'I'm afraid I shall miss Visitors' Day, Gally.'

'Yes, I gathered that. I'm sorry to hear about your father.'

'Thank you, Gally. I knew you would be.'

'What's the matter with him?'

'The doctors are baffled. Hadn't we better be starting, Colonel?'

'Yes, carry on, Voules.'

The car drove off. Gally, a thoughtful frown on his face, continued to polish his monocle.

CHAPTER 8

I

There is nothing that keys up the system like an eloquent pep talk, and Wilfred Allsop awoke next morning full of optimism and the will to win. 'My woman' he was murmuring as he shaved, 'My woman' he was saying to himself over the coffee and eggs at breakfast, and the words were still on his lips as he approached the Empress's sty some hour or two later with Tipton's flask in his pocket. Only when he reached his destination did there come to him the discouraging thought that things might not be going to go so neatly in accordance with plan as he had anticipated. The sty was there, the Empress was there, but of Monica Simmons there was no sign. He did not know what were the duties of a pig girl, but whatever they might be they had taken her elsewhere. To keep the record straight, one may mention that she was down at the pump in the kitchen garden, washing her face. A girl who is expecting an emotional scene with the man she loves naturally wishes to be at her best.

If there is one thing that damps a lover's spirit, it is the absence from the scene of action of the party of the second part who is so essential to a proposal of marriage, and this unforeseen stage wait had the worst effect on Wilfred's morale. The effervescent mood in which he had started out suffered a severe setback. He could feel his courage ebbing with every moment that passed. For the first time that day 'My woman' seemed to him a silly thing to say to anyone.

It was a moment for prompt action. He had taken one draught from the Tipton flask and had supposed that that would be sufficient but now he saw that the prudent course would be to take another. The old saying about spoiling ships for ha'porths of tar crossed his mind, together with the one that says that if a thing is worth doing, it is worth doing well. Convinced that he was on the right lines, he raised the flask to his lips, and he was leaning against the rail of the sty, his head tilted, when out of the corner of his eye he became conscious of a moving object not a dozen yards away and recognised it as Dame Daphne Winkworth's son Huxley, who, though Wilfred was not aware of it, had come to ascertain how chances were for letting the Empress out of her sty. He was a child with a one-track mind, and the desire to do this and see what happened had become something of an obsession with him.

To say that Wilfred was appalled would in no way be over-stating the case. Huxley, he knew instinctively, was one of those boys who tell their mother everything. To be found fortifying himself from a flask by Huxley was precisely the same thing as being found by Dame Daphne in person. Quick thought was called for, and he thought quickly. Reaching behind him, he dropped the flask in the sty. It fell into the Empress's bran mash, which, he was relieved to see from a rapid glance, completely covered it. Feeling slightly restored, though still far from nonchalant, he turned to face the child, prepared to meet his charges, if any, with stout denial. All his life he had put great trust in stout denial, and it had always served him well.

Huxley, like Tipton, believed in getting down to brass tacks.

He was not the boy to beat about bushes. He said, without preamble: 'I saw you drinking!'

'No, you didn't.'

'Yes, I did.'

'No, you didn't.'

'Yes, I did. Let me smell your breath.'

'I will not let you smell my breath.'

'Suspicious,' said Huxley. 'Highly suspicious.'

There was a pause, occupied by Wilfred in perspiring at every pore. Huxley resumed the conversational exchanges.

'Do you know what alcohol does to the common earth-worm?'

'No, I don't. What does it do?'

'Plenty,' said Huxley darkly. He was silent for a moment, seeming to be musing on the tragic end of earth-worms he had known. 'Mother says you're going to teach music at her school,' he resumed at length. 'Are you?'

'I am.'

'She won't like it if you spend your whole time drinking.'

'I do not spend my whole time drinking.'

'The hags aren't allowed to drink.'

'What do you mean, the hags?'

'The teachers. I call them the hags.'

'Try calling them the ladies of the staff.'

'Crumbs!' said Huxley, apparently not thinking well of the suggestion. He laughed an eldritch laugh. 'It's funny, isn't it?'

'What's funny?'

'You being a lady of the staff. Will they call you Ma'am?'

'Ah, shut up.'

'Or Miss?'

'I'm not keeping you, am I?'

Huxley said no, he was at a loose end. He returned to the aspect of the matter on which he had touched originally.

'Mother would sack you if she knew you were an alcoholic.'

'I am not an alcoholic.'

'She once sacked a hag for having a glass of sherry.'

'Very properly.'

'I shall have to tell her you were mopping it up.'

'I deny it categorically.'

'Let me smell your breath,' said Huxley, coming full circle, as it were.

Wilfred groaned in spirit. There was something about this child's conversational methods that gave him the illusion that he had fallen into the hands of the police. He did not know what future Dame Daphne Winkworth was planning for her son, but she would, he felt, be wise to have him study for the Bar. The boy seemed to him to possess all the qualities of a keen cross-examining counsel, the sort that traps a witness into damaging admissions and thunders an 'I suggest—' or a 'Then am I to understand – ?' at him. And he was asking himself how long he would be able to hold his own in this battle of wills, when a hand reached past him and attached itself to the stripling's left ear, drawing from him an 'Ouch!' of anguish.

It was not merely the sight of Huxley in such close proximity to the Empress that had caused Monica, returning from her ablutions at the kitchen garden pump, to come galloping to the sty. She had also seen Wilfred Allsop, and the last thing she desired was to have a small boy a spectator of the tender scene which she hoped would shortly take place. If you have to have a small boy looking on when you have a tender scene, you might just as well not have a tender scene at all.

Accordingly, having grasped his ear and twisted it for the third time, she proceeded to lead Huxley across the meadow. She opened the gate at the end of it and pushed him through. Then, with a brief word to the effect that if she ever found him near the sty again she would strangle him with her bare hands, she came back to the man she loved.

Tumultuous emotions were stirring in Wilfred's bosom as he watched them go. Behind him he could hear the golloping sound of the Empress tucking into her bran mash, and at another and less tense moment he might have experienced some anxiety as to what the Scotch he had added to it would do to her if it acted so disastrously on earth-worms. But now his thoughts were not on the Empress. There is a time for worrying about pigs and a time for not worrying about pigs.

His morale, lowered by those long minutes of waiting and further weakened by his chat with Huxley, had, he was glad to find, become completely restored. The few mouthfuls he had had time to imbibe from Tipton's flask had done their beneficent work. Once more he was feeling strong and masterful, and when she came back, he was ready for her. He strode up, he clasped her in his arms, he kissed her.

'My woman!' he bellowed in a tone somewhat reminiscent of a costermonger calling attention to his brussels sprouts. Tipton had been perfectly right. It was, as he had said, as easy as falling off a log.

II

Visitors' Day at the castle always found Lord Emsworth ill at ease. It gave him the same apprehensive feeling as did the annual school treat, except that on Visitors' Day he did not have to wear a top hat. He was amiable and on the whole fond of his fellow men, but he preferred them when they remained aloof. It disturbed him when they came surging into his demesne, especially when their unions had been blessed and they brought their children with them. Children, unless closely watched, were apt to sneak off to the Empress's sty and do things calculated to wound that supreme pig's sensibilities. He would not readily forget the day when he had found her snapping feverishly at a potato on the end of a string, the vegetable constantly jerked from her lips by an uncouth little pip-squeak from Wolverhampton named Basil.

It was to prevent the repetition of any such horror that today, having seen the first char-a-banc arrive, he had set out for the sty armed to the teeth with a stout hunting crop, the blood of his Crusading ancestors hot within him. If Basil were playing a return date and had not undergone a spiritual change for the better since his last visit, he was in for an unpleasant surprise. By the time his host had finished with him he would know that he had been in a fight.

Avoiding the front door, for to go there would have meant passing through the hall where the personnel of the char-a-banc were keeping in line, not smoking and not fingering objects of art, he came out through a side entrance, and he had not gone far when his progress was arrested by Sam, who was trying to find the rendezvous which Gally had suggested. The three people he had so far asked to direct him to the Empress's sty had proved to be strangers in these parts themselves.

Sam, like Lord Emsworth, was not without his feeling of uneasiness on this Visitors' Day. The thought that Constable Evans, too, might have taken it into his head to have a look at the castle and its objects of art was not one that made for peace of mind. He had not liked meeting that zealous officer the first time, and something told him that it would be even more unpleasant meeting him again. It was difficult to shake off the feeling that he might appear at any moment round any corner, the handcuffs clinking in his pocket.

He also found Blandings Castle and its surroundings intimidating. To adjust himself to its impressive magnificence was not a simple task for one accustomed to the homelier atmosphere of Halsey Chambers, Halsey Court, London W.1. Basil from Wolverhampton had taken the place in his stride, but it overawed Sam. It made him feel as if his hands and feet had swollen in a rather offensive manner and that his clothes had ceased to fit him.

This meeting with Lord Emsworth, accordingly, braced him like a tonic. His self-confidence functioned once more. If Blandings Castle could accept this seedy old man in his patched flannel trousers and battered fishing hat, he told himself, it could scarcely raise its eyebrows at one who in comparison was almost dapper.

'Good afternoon,' he said. 'I wonder if you could tell me how to get to the sty of the pig they call Empress of Blandings?'

Lord Emsworth's mild eyes glowed. It had always pained him when visitors on Visitors' Day trooped about the castle's interior goggling at pictures, tapestries, amber drawing-rooms and the like and never thought of going to see the one sight that mattered. He beamed at Sam, well pleased at having found a kindred spirit.

'I am going there myself,' he said, and his voice had a cordial ring. 'So you are a pig lover, too?'

Sam considered the question. He had never given much thought to pigs and, if asked, would probably have described himself as able to take them or leave them alone, but his companion had used the word 'too', seeming to indicate that these animals stood high in his estimation, so he felt it was only civil to reply in the affirmative. He did so, and was rewarded with a look of approval that convinced him that he had said the right thing.

'We go through the kitchen garden. It is the shortest way. Is this,' Lord Emsworth asked as they moved off, 'your first visit to Blandings?'

Sam said it was.

'Are you American?'

'No.'

'I thought you possibly might be. So many people are nowadays. I have just returned from America.'

'Oh yes?'

'I went to attend my sister's wedding. I stayed at an hotel in New York. Are you fond of boiled eggs?'

'Yes, I like boiled eggs.'

'So do I. But in America they serve them mashed up in a glass. It is one of the many curious aspects of the country. I objected strongly, but it did no good. Every time I asked for a boiled egg, up it came in a glass.'

'I suppose the solution would have been not to have asked for a boiled egg.'

'Exactly what my brother Galahad said. It would, he said, be the smart thing to do. But that's all very well, because suppose you want a boiled egg. It puts you in a bit of a fix.'

Sam was astounded. Unconsciously he had been picturing the proprietor of this super-stately home of England as a formidable figure on the lines of the old gentleman with the bushy eyebrows in *Little Lord Fauntleroy*, a book which twenty years ago he had read with considerable zest. The shock of finding that the patched and baggy object at his side owned the entire works was as great as that experienced by Colonel Wedge on the night when he had mistaken Lord Emsworth for the pigman's discarded overalls. It held him speechless until they had nearly reached the sty.

As they approached it, Lord Emsworth uttered an exclamation.

'Bless my soul, there's Wellbeloved.'

'I beg your pardon?'

'My former pigman,' said Lord Emsworth, indicating the figure slouched over the rail of the sty. 'He is in retirement now. I believe some relative of his left him a public house in Wolverhampton. He must have come in the char-a-banc from there. Ah, Wellbeloved,' he said. 'Come to have a look at the Empress?'

George Cyril Wellbeloved turned, revealing himself as a man with a squint and a broken nose, the former bestowed on him at birth, the latter acquired in the course of a political discussion at the Goose and Gander in Market Blandings in which he had espoused the Communist cause.

'Hullo,' he said.

He spoke curtly. Between the manner of a pigman dependent on his weekly wage and that of the owner of a prosperous public house in Wolverhampton there is always a subtle but well-marked difference. In George Cyril's case it was more well-marked than subtle, for he could not forget that twice during their mutual association Lord Emsworth had dismissed him from his service and dismissed him with contumely. These things rankle. To be sacked once, yes, a man expected that, it was part of the wholesome give and take between employer and employed, but twice was a calculated insult.

'Fat lot of having a look at the Empress I've been able to do,' he said morosely. 'She's dug in in her shed and won't come out,' he said, and Sam saw that at one end of the sty there was a wooden shelter, presumably where the silver medallist retired to sleep or to meditate.

'Strange,' said Lord Emsworth.

'Sinister, if you ask me. I'd say she was sickening for something.'

'Nonsense. Try chirruping.'

'I have tried chirruping, and the more I chirrup, the less she emerges. She's like the deaf adder in Holy Scripture. I don't know if you're familiar with the deaf adder. It comes in a bit in the Bible I used to learn at Sunday School. Like the deaf adder, it says, what don't pay a ruddy bit of attention to the charmer, though he charms till his eyes bubble. Try chirruping, indeed!' said George Cyril disgustedly.

'You can't have chirruped properly. Chirrup again.'

'Not me, cocky, I've got a sore lip. You have a go.'

'I will.'

When it came to communicating with pigs, Lord Emsworth had resources denied to other men. It so happened that there had come to Blandings Castle a year or so ago a young fellow anxious to marry one of his nieces, a young fellow who on leaving England under something of a cloud had found employment on a farm in Nebraska. He had forgotten his name, but he had never forgotten his teachings. In however deep a reverie a pig might be plunged, this young fellow had said, passing on the lore he had learned on the Nebraska farm, it could always be jerked out of it by what he described as the Master Call, and this he had taught to Lord Emsworth. It consisted of the word 'Pig-hoo-ey', the 'Hoo' to start in a low minor of two quarter-notes in four-four time, building gradually from this to a higher note until at last the voice soared in full crescendo, reaching F-sharp on the natural scale and dwelling for two retarded half-notes, then breaking into a shower of accidental grace-notes.

It had taken Lord Emsworth some little time to master the technique, but he had succeeded eventually. So now, cupping his lips with both hands in order to increase the volume, he observed:

'PIG-HOO-EY!!!'

and Sam, who had not been expecting it, leaped like a lamb in springtime. The ejaculation seemed to him for a moment to have taken the top of his head off.

But he had not suffered in vain. Even before his ears had stopped ringing there came from the interior of the shelter a sound of stirring and rustling, as if a hippopotamus were levering itself up from its bed of reeds. Grunts became audible. The mild, kindly face of the Empress peered out, and a moment later it was possible to see her steadily and see her whole.

But not on Lord Emsworth's part with the pride and pleasure with which he was wont to see her. Something was plainly wrong with the silver medallist. She weaved, she tottered, she took a few uncertain steps towards the trough, then slowly sank to the ground and lay there inert.

'I told you so,' said George Cyril Wellbeloved. 'You want to know what that is, chum?' he went on with relish. 'That's swine fever.'

On Lord Emsworth the spectacle had had a paralysing effect. If the phrase were not copyright, one might say that his heart stood still. But his spirit remained unimpaired. He glared militantly.

'Don't be a fool, Wellbeloved!'

George Cyril gave him a rebuking look.

'I suppose you know what happens when you call your brother a fool,' he said austerely. 'You're in danger of hell fire, that's what you're in danger of. You'll find it in the Good Book. "If thou sayest to thy brother, Thou fool..."'

'You're not my brother!' said Lord Emsworth, at the same time thanking God.

George Cyril Wellbeloved would have none of this quibbling.

'For purposes of argument I am. All men are brothers. That's in the Good Book, too.'

'Get out! Get off my property immediately!'

'Okey-doke. George Cyril Wellbeloved does not remain where he's not wanted, though it's a moot point whether you're legally entitled to chuck the paying public out on Visitors' Day. However, we'll waive that. You'd better go and phone the vet,' said George Cyril over his shoulder as he took a dignified departure. 'Not that he'll be able to do a ruddy bit of good.'

Lord Emsworth was already on his way to telephone the veterinary surgeon, his long legs flashing as he raced to the house, and Sam, left alone, stood gazing at the invalid. And as he gazed the sun came out from behind a cloud and something glinted in the empty trough. It looked like a flask. He climbed the rail and found that it was a flask, and instantaneously all things were made clear to him. He realised now why from the first the Empress's aspect had struck him as vaguely familiar. He had seen men come into the Drones Club smoking-room on the morning after Boat Race night looking just like that. Oofy Prosser practically always looked like that. When Lord Emsworth returned, he was happy to be able to calm his fears.

'It's all right,' he said.

'All *right*?' Lord Emsworth could not believe the ears which exercise had reddened. 'If it's swine fever—'

'It isn't. Look at this.'

'What is that?'

'An empty flask. I found it in the trough.'

'God bless my soul, how did she get hold of it?'

'I wonder. But obviously all that's the matter is that she's been on the toot of a lifetime. That pig is plastered. You probably remember the old poem which begins "The pig at eve had drunk its fill"?'

'No. No, I do not.'

'Well, that's what must have happened. She just needs time to sleep it off. It's a pity we're so far from London. There's a chemist in the Haymarket who fixes the most wonderful pick-me-up. He could have put her right in no time. Still, a good sleep will probably do the trick. You'll see her turning cartwheels tomorrow.'

Lord Emsworth drew a deep breath. He gazed at Sam adoringly. He was not as a rule fond of his juniors, but he could recognise merit when he saw it and it was plain to him that here was something special in the way of juniors, one whom he could take to his bosom and make a friend of. And the thought that this young man, so sound on pigs, so sympathetic in every way, would be fading out of his life when Visitors' Day was over horrified him. He wanted to see him constantly, to have interminable talks on pigs with him, to wake up in the morning with the heartening feeling that he would find him at the breakfast table.

'Are you making a long stay in these parts?' he asked.

Sam, thinking of Constable Evans, said Well, that depended.

'You are not on a walking tour? Not got to get anywhere special?'

'No.'

'Then I wonder if you would care to be my guest at the castle for a few weeks? Or as long as you like, of course?'

If Sam had been able to speak, he would probably have said 'There *is* a Santa Claus! I do believe in fairies!' but this totally unexpected invitation had wiped speech from his lips. When he was able to utter, he said:

'It's awfully kind of you. I'd love it.'

'Capital! Capital, capital, capital!'

'Ah, there you are, my dear fellow,' said the cheery voice of Gally from behind them. 'So you've met Augustus Whipple, have you, Clarence?'

III

Lord Emsworth's pince-nez flew from their base. He shook from fishing hat to shoe sole. 'Whipple? Whipple? Whipple?' he gasped. 'Did you say Whipple?'

'Yes, this is Gus, as the boys at the Athenaeum call him. I suppose you weren't expecting him so soon. But that's what he's like. Never lets the grass grow under his feet and is always like lightning off the mark. Do it now is his slogan. Hullo, what's the matter with the Empress?'

'She is the worse for liquor, Galahad, I am sorry to say. Somebody carelessly dropped a flask of whisky in her bran mash.'

'What a lesson this is to all of us to keep off the sauce. We must try to get her to join Alcoholics Anonymous. Well, I'm glad there's no cause for alarm. A raw egg beaten up in Worcester sauce will probably work wonders. Still, I suppose you ought to have the vet take a look at her.'

'I have already telephoned him. He is on his way.'

'Then I'll take Whipple to your study and you can join us there after you've seen him.'

'Yes, yes, capital. This is a proud moment for me, Mr Whipple,' said Lord Emsworth, and Sam contrived to produce a weak smile. He was not yet equal to giving tongue, and he continued silent as Gally led him to the house. Fortunately Gally, as always, was able to provide conversation enough for two.

'Quick thinking, my boy, quick thinking,' he said complacently. 'I've always been a quick thinker. My resourcefulness was a matter of frequent comment at the old Pelican. "Galahad Threepwood," they used to say, "may not be much to look at, but you seldom find him at a loss." I remember once in those days glancing out of a window and seeing a bookie I owed money to at the front door. I saw that instant precautions would have to be taken, for my financial position was such that it would have inconvenienced me greatly to have been obliged to make a cash settlement at the moment. Only seconds elapsed before inspiration descended on me. When he hammered at my door, I was ready for him. "Have a care, Mr Simms," I shouted. He was Tim Simms, the Safe Man. "Keep away. I've got scarlet fever." He was incredulous, and said so. So I opened the door and he gave one look and was down the stairs in two strides. Most luckily one of my female acquaintances had happened to leave a lipstick in the sitting-room the day before, and I had been able to apply it to my cheeks. I caught a glimpse of myself in the mirror after he had left, and I can tell you it frightened *me*.'

'Listen,' said Sam.

'I know what you are going to say,' said Gally, checking him with a raised hand like a policeman directing traffic. 'You are all eagerness to ascertain why after your intransigent attitude of yesterday I decided to overrule your veto and tell Clarence you were Augustus Whipple. My dear boy, it was essential. You are not aware of it, but young Sandy with a snakiness which redounds little to her credit had slipped a fast one over on us. On some trivial pretext she had got leave from Clarence to go away for a day or two, thus rendering your prospects of a conference with her null and void. It became imperative, accordingly, to think up some way of introducing you into the house as a permanent guest, so that you would be on the spot when she came back, and this, as we have seen, I have been able to accomplish.'

'Listen,' said Sam, and again the raised hand checked him.

'I know you have some fanciful objection to being Augustus Whipple, but I think you will have to admit that the advantages outweigh the disadvantages. You're in the house, safe from Constable Evans, and when young Sandy returns, chuckling to herself as she thinks how she had outsmarted us, she will find you here and hit the ceiling. Weakened by the shock, she will be as dust beneath your chariot wheels. Yes, I think I am entitled to take a few bows for the way I have handled this rather delicate situation. There was talk at one time of my going into the diplomatic service, and I sometimes feel it was a pity I didn't. Well, here we are in Clarence's study. I must apologise for there being so little dust about. That's Sandy's fault. Take a seat and make yourself comfortable.'

Sam sat down and fixed him with an uncordial eye.

'Would you mind if I now slipped a word in edgeways?' he said coldly.

'Of course, my dear fellow. Go ahead. But I want no thanks.'

'Would it interest you to know that half a minute before you came muscling in on us with your "Yoo-hoo, it's Whipple!" Lord Emsworth had invited me to stay at the castle for as long as I wanted to?'

It was not easy to dislodge the monocle from Gally's eye, but this piece of information did it. He stared incredulously.

'Are you pulling my leg?'

'I am not.'

'But what on earth made him do that?'

'He was grateful to me for assuring him that the Empress had not got swine fever.'

'And he really asked you to stay?'

'He did.'

Gally retrieved his monocle and replaced it in its niche. His manner was pensive.

'This opens up a new line of thought,' he said. 'It might perhaps have been better on the whole if I had not introduced the Whipple motif. It's a pity you didn't tell me that before.'

'When did I have a chance to?'

'True. Well, it's done now and nothing more to be said.'

'I can think of a few things.'

Gally looked pained.

'You must not allow yourself to become bitter, my boy. No doubt you are feeling disturbed and upset, but I can't see that you have much to complain of. You were in imminent danger of getting the local police force on the back of your neck, and the one thing you needed most sorely was a hide-out. Now you have one. What are those beautiful lines of someone's about the sailor being home from the sea and the hunter home from the hill? That's you. You're in, aren't you?'

'Under a false name.'

'What of that? There's nothing low or degrading about an alias. Look at Lord Bacon. Went about calling himself Shakespeare.'

'And I'm supposed to be an authority on pigs.'

'You have some objection to being an authority on pigs?'

'Yes, I have, considering that I don't know a damn thing about them except that their tails wiggle when they eat. What do I do when Lord Emsworth starts talking pig to me?'

'No need for concern. Clarence will do all the talking. An occasional low murmur is all he'll expect from you. But hist!'

'What do you mean, hist?'

'Seal your lips. I think I hear him coming.'

Gally was right. A moment later, Lord Emsworth bustled in, wreathed in smiles.

'Ah, here you are, Mr Whipple,' he said. 'Capital, capital. I will ring for tea.'

'Tea?' said Gally. 'You don't want tea. Filthy stuff. Look what it did to poor Buffy Struggles. Did I ever tell you about Buffy? Someone lured him into one of those temperance lectures illustrated with coloured slides and there was one showing the liver of the drinker of alcohol. He called on me next day, his face ashen. "Gally," he said, "what would you say the procedure was when a fellow wants to buy tea?" "Tea?" I said. "What do you want tea for?" "To drink," he said. I told him to pull himself together. "You're talking wildly," I said. "You can't drink tea. Have a drop of brandy." He shook his head. "No more alcohol for me," he said. "It makes your liver look like a Turner sunset." Well, I begged him with tears in my eyes not to do anything rash, but I couldn't move him. He ordered in ten pounds of the muck and was dead two weeks later. Got run over by a hansom cab in Piccadilly. Obviously if his system hadn't been weakened by tea, he'd have been able to dodge the vehicle. Summon Beach and tell him to bring a bottle of champagne. I can see from Whipple's face that he needs a bracer.'

'Perhaps you are right,' said Lord Emsworth.

'I know I'm right. The only safe way to get through life is to pickle your system thoroughly in alcohol. Look at Freddie Potts and his brother Eustace the time they ate the hedgehog.'

'Ate what?'

'The hedgehog. Freddie and Eustace were living on the Riviera at the time and they had a French chef, one of whose jobs was to go to market and buy supplies. On the way to Grasse that day, as he trotted off with the money in his pocket, he saw a dead hedgehog lying by the side of the road. Now this chef was a thrifty sort of chap and he saw immediately that if he refrained from buying the chicken he'd been sent to buy and stuck to the money, he'd be that much up, and he knew that with the aid of a few sauces he could pass that hedgehog off as chicken all right, so he picked it up and went home with it and served it up next day *en casserole*. Both brothers ate heartily, and here's the point of the story. Eustace, who was a teetotaller, nearly died, but Freddie, who had lived mostly on whisky since early boyhood, showed no ill effects whatsoever. I think there is a lesson in this for all of us, so press that bell, Clarence.'

Lord Emsworth pressed it, and Beach, resting in his pantry from the labours of the afternoon, was stirred to activity. Heaving himself up from his easy chair in a manner which would certainly have led Huxley Winkworth, had he seen him, to renew those offensive comparisons of his between him and Empress of Blandings rising from her couch, he put on the boots which for greater comfort he had removed and started laboriously up the stairs. His face as he went was careworn, his manner preoccupied.

In the nineteen years during which he had served Lord Emsworth in the capacity of major-domo it had always been with mixed feelings that Beach found himself regarding the weekly ceremony of Visitors' Day at Blandings Castle. It had its good points, and it had its drawbacks. On the one hand, it gratified his sense of importance to conduct a flock of human sheep about the premises and watch their awe-struck faces as he pointed out the various objects of interest: on the other all that walking up and down stairs and along corridors and in and out of rooms hurt his feet. It was a fact not generally known, for his stout boots hid their secret well, that he suffered from corns.

On the whole, however, the bright side may be said to have predominated over the dark side, the spiritual's pros to have outweighed the physical cons, and as a general rule he performed his task with a high heart and in an equable frame of mind. But not today. A butler who has been robbed of his silver watch can hardly be expected to be the same rollicking cicerone as a butler who has undergone no such deprivation. He had woken with his loss heavy on his mind, and as he led his mob of followers about the castle he was still brooding on it and blaming himself for not having kept a sharper eye on that fellow with whom he had collided in the entrance of the Emsworth Arms bar. He might have known that no good was to be expected from a man with a twisted ear.

On his departure for America to take up his duties in the offices of Donaldson's Dog Joy Inc. of Long Island City, the country's leading purveyors of biscuits to the American dog, Freddie Threepwood, Lord Emsworth's younger son, had bequeathed to Beach his collection of mystery thrillers, said to be the finest in Shropshire, and in three out of every ten of these the criminal, when unmasked, had proved to be a man with a twisted ear. It should have warned him, Beach felt, but unfortunately it had not, and it was with a feeling of dull depression that he entered the study.

The next moment, this dull depression had left him and he was tingling from head to foot as if electrified. For there, apparently on the best of terms with his lordship and Mr Galahad, sat the miscreant in person. His head was bent as he scanned some photographs which Lord Emsworth was showing him, but that twisted ear was unmistakable.

It is probable that if Beach had not been a butler a startled cry would at this point have echoed through the room, but butlers do not utter startled cries. All he said was:

'You rang, m'lord?'

'Eh? Ah. Oh yes. Bring us a bottle of Bollinger, will you Beach.'

'Very good, m'lord.'

'And while it is coming, Mr Whipple,' said Lord Emsworth, 'there are some photographs of the Empress in the library I would like you to see.'

He led Sam from the room, and Gally was surprised to see that Beach, instead of following them, had remained behind and was approaching his chair in a conspiratorial manner. 'Could I have a word, Mr Galahad?'

'Certainly, Beach. Have several.'

'It is with reference to the gentleman,' said Beach, choking on the last word, 'who has just left us. Who is he, Mr Galahad?'

'That was my brother Clarence. You know him, don't you? I thought you'd met.'

Beach was in no mood for frivolity.

'The other gentleman, sir,' he said austerely.

'Oh the other one? That was Augustus Whipple, the author.'

The name was familiar to Beach. Lord Emsworth occasionally had trouble with his eyes and when so afflicted sometimes asked Beach to read him passages from *On The Care Of The*

Pig, which Beach had always been happy to do, though no part of his duties. At the mention of it now he stared a pop-eyed stare.

'Whipple, Mr Galahad?'

'That's right. He wrote that pig book my brother's always reading. He's coming to stay here.'

'Sir!' said Beach, reeling.

Gally looked at him, surprised.

'What do you mean "Sir" and why does your jaw drop? Don't you like the idea?'

'No, Mr Galahad, I do not. The man is a criminal.'

'What on earth makes you think that?'

'He stole my watch yesterday at the Emsworth Arms, Mr Galahad.'

'Beach, I believe you've been having a couple.'

'No, sir. If I might tell you what transpired.'

Gally listened attentively to the twice-told tale. He thought Beach got even more drama out of it than Sam had done. When it was finished, he shook his head.

'Your story sounds very thin to me, Beach. On your own showing you only had a fleeting glance at the fellow.'

'Long enough to see his ear, Mr Galahad.'

'His what?'

'He had a twisted ear.'

Gally laughed indulgently.

'And you're making this extraordinary accusation purely because Whipple also had one? Good heavens, you can't go by that. Shropshire is stiff with men with twisted ears. I believe they form clubs and societies. Anything further?'

'Yes, sir, his age.'

'I don't get you.'

'He is not old enough to have written the book his lordship admires so much.'

'You find his appearance juvenile?'

'Yes, sir.'

'He tells me everybody does. He says it always surprises his fans to see how young he looks, but the explanation is very simple. For years he has been doing bending and stretching exercises every morning before breakfast. He also avoids all fried foods and never misses his Vitamins A, B and C twice a day. This keeps him fighting fit. He does seem young, I grant you that. But, dash it, Beach, you can't go about accusing respectable authors of nameless crimes just because their ears are a bit out of the straight and they aren't as elderly as you would like them to be. These cases of mistaken identity are very comomn. There was a man at the Pelican who was the living image of one of the Cabinet Ministers, which made it very awkward for the latter, as the Pelican chap was always getting thrown out of restaurants, frequently wearing a girl's hat. Didn't my nephew Freddie bequeath you all those mystery stories of his when he went to America?'

'Yes, sir.'

'You read them a good deal?'

'Yes, sir.'

'Well, there you are. They've inflamed your imagination and you see sinister characters everywhere. I believe Agatha Christie suffers in the same way. You mustn't let yourself get worried. Just accept the fact calmly that the bloke who was in here just now is Augustus Whipple all right and buzz off and get that Bollinger.'

Beach was so constructed that he could never be said actually to buzz off, his customary mode of progression being modelled on that of an elephant sauntering through an Indian jungle, but as he made his way to the cellar his pace was even slower than usual. A whirling mind often has this effect on the pedestrian, and his was whirling as it had seldom whirled before. He was convinced that the man to slake whose thirst he was fetching Bollinger was the man who had robbed him of his watch, but, if this was so, how had he come to be on such intimate terms with his lordship and Mr Galahad?

It was not an easy jigsaw puzzle to unravel, and he delivered the refreshments to the study in a sort of trance. He was still in the same condition when he returned to the pantry and took his boots off again. Shakespeare would have described him as perplexed in the extreme. Erle Stanley Gardner would have drawn inspiration from him for *The Case Of The Bewildered Butler*. He himself, if questioned, would have said that his head was swimming.

At times when the head swims, all butlers have the means of restoring its equilibrium ready to hand. Port is what works the magic. Beach kept a bottle in the pantry cupboard, and he now reached for it. And he was about to remove the cork, when the telephone rang.

He picked up the receiver and spoke in his usual measured tones.

'Lord Emsworth's residence. His lordship's butler speaking.'

The voice that replied was high and reedlike. Gally would have called it the typical voice of a member of the Athenaeum Club.

'Oh, good afternoon,' it said. 'This is Mr Augustus Whipple.'

CHAPTER 9

I

Visitors' Day had come and gone. The 'Kindly Keep in Line' and 'No Smoking' signs had been taken down, as had the one that urged the public not to finger objects of art. The chars-a-banc had left. George Cyril Wellbeloved had returned to Wolverhampton. Beach's feet had ceased to pain him. Except that the Empress had a severe hangover and was feeling cross and edgy and inclined to take offence at trifles, Blandings Castle might have been said to be back to normal.

At four o'clock or thereabouts on the following afternoon Lady Hermione Wedge alighted from the London train and stepped into the car which Voules the chauffeur had brought to Market Blandings station to meet her. Sandy Callender, who had travelled by the same train but in a humbler compartment at the other end of it, boarded the station taxi cab (Jno. Robinson, prop'r). And simultaneously Constable Evans of the local police force, mounting the bicycle which had now been restored to him, started to pedal castlewards to give Beach his watch.

The day seemed to be working up for a thunderstorm and her journey had left Lady Hermione a little tired, but relief made her forget fatigue. It was worth undergoing a certain amount of physical discomfort to feel that her child had been extricated from a most undesirable entanglement. Her thoughts, as Voules stepped on the gas, dwelt tenderly on Veronica, than whom no daughter could have been more co-operative, more alive to the fact that Mother knew best. Her attitude when taking down dictation from a parent's lips had been irreproachable. She could not have raised fewer objections if she had been a dictaphone. Once only had she spoken, and that was to ask how many s's there were in 'distressed'. 'Two, darling,' Lady Hermione had said, though actually there are three.

When you have a Voules at the wheel, it does not take long to get from Market Blandings station to Blandings Castle, and Lady Hermione found herself in her boudoir in good time for a cup of tea. She rang the bell, and Beach put on his boots, presented himself, booked the order and withdrew, to reappear after a brief interval accompanied by a footman bearing a laden tray. The footman – Stokes was his name, not that it matters – completed his share of the operations and melted away, and Lady Hermione, having poured herself a steaming cup and begun to sip, became aware that she still had Beach with her. He was standing in the middle of the room with something of the air of a public monument waiting to be unveiled, and his presence surprised her. It was not like him, when he had delivered the goods, to continue to hover around, and she bit into her cucumber sandwich with some annoyance, for she wished to be alone.

'Yes, Beach?' she said.

'Might I have a word, m'lady?'

Lady Hermione did not reply 'Have several' as Gally had done, contenting herself with inclining her head. She did this stiffly, her manner seeming to suggest that she was prepared to listen but that what he had to say had better be good.

The butler did not fail to sense this distaste for chit-chat.

'If you prefer it, m'lady, I could return later.'

'No, no, Beach. Is it something important?'

'Yes, m'lady. It is with reference to the gentleman who arrived yesterday as a guest at the castle,' said Beach, choking on the operative word as he had done in his interview with Gally.

Lady Hermione stiffened dangerously. An autocratic chatelaine, she resented guests arriving at the castle without her knowledge. She could scarcely believe that her brother Clarence would have had the temerity to invite a friend to stay unless he had first asked her permission, so she came – one might say leaped – to the conclusion that the mystery guest must be a crony of her brother Galahad, and her frown grew darker. One knew what Galahad's cronies were like. The dregs of civilisation. A silver ring bookmaker was the least disreputable chum he would be likely to have added to the Blandings circle.

'Who is this man, Beach?' she demanded tensely.

'He gives his name as Augustus Whipple, m'lady.'

Lady Hermione's indignation subsided a good deal. Nobody could associate for long with Lord Emsworth without becoming familiar with the name Whipple, and she knew the author of *On The Care Of The Pig* to be a man of some standing in the best circles, a member of the Athenaeum Club, which she understood to be a most respectable institution, and an occasional adviser to the Minister of Agriculture. Clarence, she presumed, had invited him, and though she still felt that in doing so without consulting her he had been guilty of a solecism, she cooled off quite noticeably.

'Oh, Mr Whipple?' she said, relieved. The vision she had had of one of Gally's friends wearing a loud checked suit and addressing her as 'ducky' in a voice hoarsened by calling the odds at

Sandown Park or Catterick Bridge faded. 'I shall be interested to meet him. Mr Whipple is a very well-known author.'

'If this *is* Mr Whipple, m'lady.'

'I don't understand you.'

'I suspect him of being an impostor,' hissed Beach. It is difficult, even if one wants to, to avoid hissing a sentence so well provided with sibilants, and he did not want to.

His statement ought not to have startled Lady Hermione as greatly as it did. She should have been used to impostors by this time. They had been in and out of Blandings Castle for years. A thoughtful writer had once said of the place that it had impostors the way other houses had mice. Nevertheless she uttered a sound which in a woman of less breeding might have been classified as a snort, and the buttered toast she was holding fell from her hand.

'An impostor!'

'Yes, m'lady.'

'But what grounds have you for saying such a thing?'

'It seemed to me peculiar that shortly after his arrival another gentleman should have rung up from London on the telephone saying that he, too, was Mr Augustus Whipple.'

'What!'

'Yes, m'lady. He was enquiring after his lordship's state of health. He informed me that he had received a telegram stating that his lordship was suffering from German measles. It renders one suspicious of the *bona fides* of the gentleman now in residence at the castle.'

'It certainly does!'

'I must confess to finding the whole situation mystifying.'

Lady Hermione was not mystified. Not, she might have said had she been capable of such vulgarity, by a jugful. As clearly as if the information had been written in letters of fire on the wall of the boudoir she saw behind this superfluity of Whipples the hand of her brother Galahad.

'Oh!' she said, and never had that monosyllable come closer to being the 'Ho!' of Constable Evans of the Market Blandings police force. Her eyes were gleaming balefully. She looked like a cook who has encountered an intrusive black beetle in her kitchen. 'Will you find Mr Galahad and say I would like to see him. No, never mind, I will go and see him myself.'

II

Gally was in the billiards room when she found him, practising cannons with an expert hand. He laid down his cue courteously as she entered. He was not glad to see her, for it was his experience that her presence, like that of her sisters Constance, Dora and Julia, nearly always spelt trouble, but he did his best to infuse a brotherly warmth into his greeting.

'Hullo, Hermione. So you're back? Rotten day for travelling. You must have stifled in that train.'

There was nothing in Lady Hermione's manner to suggest that her feelings towards him were not friendly, or as friendly as they ever were. It was her intention to lull him into a false security before unmasking him and bathing him in confusion.

'It was rather stuffy,' she agreed. 'Do you think there's a storm coming up?'

'I shouldn't be surprised. How was Veronica?'

'She seemed very well.'

'I miss her bonny face.'

'I'll tell her. She'll be flattered. And how are you, Galahad?'

'Oh, ticking over much as usual.'

'And Clarence?'

'He's fine.'

Lady Hermione gave a little laugh.

'I'm talking as if I had been away a month. I suppose nothing has been happening since I left?'

'Nothing sensational. We have another guest.'

'Really? Who is that?'

'Fellow of the name of Whipple.'

'You don't mean Clarence's Whipple, the man who wrote that pig book he's always reading?'

'That's the chap. Clarence had a letter from him asking if he could come and take some photographs of the Empress, so of course he invited him to stay.'

'Of course. Clarence must be delighted.'

'Seventh heaven.'

'I don't wonder. There can't be many men like Mr Whipple.'

'Very few so pigminded.'

'I was not thinking of that so much as of his extraordinary gift for being in two places at the same time. I always think that makes a man so interesting.'

'Eh?'

'Well, you can't say it's not remarkable that he should be at Blandings Castle and still able to ring up on the telephone from London. I wonder how he does it. With mirrors, do you think?'

Gally was not easily disconcerted and only the fact that he removed his monocle and began to polish it showed that her words had stirred him to any extent. Replacing the monocle, he said:

'Odd, that. Very curious.'

'So I thought when Beach told me. He took the call.'

'From Whipple?'

'Speaking from his London branch, not the Shropshire one.'

'He must have got the name wrong. One often catches names incorrectly on the telephone. What did this fellow say?'

'That he was Augustus Whipple and that he was calling to ask how Clarence was, as he had had a telegram saying that he was in bed with German measles. Quite a mystery, isn't it?'

Gally pondered for a moment. Then his face brightened.

'I think I see the solution. Simple when you give your mind to it. It was Visitors' Day yesterday and Beach had to work like a beaver all the afternoon showing the mob around the joint. He's not so young as he was and it took it out of him a lot. When it was over, he was at a low ebb and in need of a restorative. So what happens? He limps off to his pantry, reaches for the port bottle, incautiously overdoes it and becomes as soused as a herring, totally incapable of understanding a word said to him on the phone. The name he mistook for Whipple was probably Wilson or Wiggins or Williams, and what Wilson or Wiggins or Williams was saying was that *he* had got German measles. It's the only explanation.'

Many years previously in their mutual nursery Lady Hermione, even then a force to be reckoned with, had once struck her brother Galahad on the head with her favourite doll Belinda, laying him out as flat as a Dover sole. She was wishing she could put her hands on a doll now. Or she would have been prepared to settle for a hatchet.

'I can think of another,' she said, 'and that is that for some reason at which I cannot attempt to guess you have sneaked one of your impossible friends into the castle. I should say one more of your impossible friends, because this is not the first time it has happened. Who is this man?'

'You want me to come clean?'

'If you will be so good.'

'He's a chap called Sam Bagshott.'

'Wanted by the police, no doubt?'

'Oddly enough, yes,' said Gally with a touch of admiration in his voice. This exhibition of woman's intuition had impressed him. 'But that was due to an absurd misunderstanding. He's a most respectable fellow really. Son of my old pal Boko Bagshott. And he's here because he's jolly well got to be here. It's imperative that he confers with the Callender girl, whom he loves but by whom he has been given the air, and she's away and nobody knows when she'll be back. Obviously he must stay put and await her arrival.'

'Oh, must he? I disagree with you. If you think he is going to remain here another day, you are very much mistaken. I shall tell Beach to see that his things are packed and that he is out of the place in the next half-hour.'

Gally continued tranquil.

'I wouldn't.'

'And if I were not a very tolerant and easygoing woman, he would not be given time to pack.'

'I still maintain that you would be making a mistake.'

'I suppose that remark has some sort of meaning, but I cannot imagine what.'

'It will flash on you in a moment. I must begin by mentioning that I had a chat with Egbert before he left.'

'Well?'

'He said you had gone to London to get Veronica to write to Tipton breaking the engagement.'

'Well?'

'It bewildered me. I should have thought an up-and-coming

young multi-millionaire would have been the son-in-law of your dreams. Aren't you fond of multi-millionaires?'

'Tipton is not a multi-millionaire. He has lost all his money speculating on the Stock Exchange.'

'You astound me. Who told you that?'

'Clarence.'

'And you really look on Clarence as a reliable source?'

'In the present case, yes. He had the information from Tipton himself.'

'It didn't occur to you that Clarence, acting true to the form of a lifetime, might have got everything muddled up? Let me brief you as to the real position of affairs. Tipton hasn't lost a penny, but like many a better man before him he was in chokey and needed bail. He hadn't the price on him, somebody in the course of the evening having pinched his wallet, so he rang Clarence up at his hotel, said he had lost all his money and could Clarence oblige him with a loan of twenty dollars. That's the whole story. If you have any lingering doubt in your mind as to Tipton's solvency, let me tell you that when he blew in the day before yesterday he was at the wheel of a Rolls Royce and waving an eight-thousand-pound necklace, a little gift for Vee which he had picked up in London. I was not privileged to see his underclothing, but I should imagine it consisted of thousand-dollar bills. Fellows like Tipton always wear them next the skin.'

Some people on receiving a shock turn pale, others purple. Lady Hermione did both. The colour faded from her cheeks, then rushed back. There was a settee near where she stood. She sank on to it bonelessly, staring as if she were seeing some horrible sight – some sight, that is to say, even more horrible than a brother with a black-rimmed monocle in his right eye. Her breath came in short gasps, and Gally hastened to supply aid and comfort. He was a humane man and had no wish to see a blood relation keeling over in an apoplectic fit.

'It's all right,' he said. 'You can stop swooning. Egbert asked me to intercept Veronica's letter before it could reach Tipton, so I got up at the crack of dawn and did.'

The relief that flooded over Lady Hermione was so stupendous that she could not speak. The whole world, even Gally, seemed beautiful to her. Having gurgled for a while, she said:

'Oh, Galahad!'

'I thought you'd be pleased.'

'Where is it? Give it to me.'

'I haven't got it.'

Lady Hermione, who had been lying back, sat up with a jerk.

'You've lost it?' she cried, the apoplectic fit threatening to return.

'No, I've not lost it. I've given it to Sam. Whether or not he hands it on to Tipton depends on you. Accept him as an honoured guest and give him that sunny smile of yours from time to time, and you'll be as right as rain. But the slightest relaxation of old-world hospitality on your part and Tipton's mail will be augmented by a communication from the girl he loves. You had better begin practising being the ideal hostess without delay, for both Sam and I have high standards and you mustn't fall short of them,' said Gally, and feeling that this was about as telling an exit line as could be found on the spur of the moment he replaced his cue in the rack and left the room.

It was only when he reached the smoking-room which was his objective and saw Sam sitting there, on his face the dazed look of one who has recently concluded a long conversation on pigs with Lord Emsworth, that a sudden thought struck him. His sister Hermione was a woman for whom as an antagonist he had a great respect, and he knew that she was not one meekly to accept defeat. She might be down, but she was never out. It was highly probable that Sam, all unused as he was to the methods of jungle warfare prevailing in Blandings Castle and little thinking that that was the first place his hostess would search, would have put that letter somewhere in his bedroom. Precautions, he saw, must be taken immediately, for he knew the search would not be long delayed.

'Sam,' he said, 'what did you do with that letter I gave you?'

'It's in my room.'

'As I thought. Just as I had suspected. Go and get it.'

'Why?'

'Never mind why. I want it, and let us hope it's still there. Ah,' he said, when Sam returned, 'all is well. Prompt action has saved the day. Give it to me.'

'What are you going to do with it?'

'I am going to enclose it in a stout manila envelope and tuck it away in a drawer of Clarence's desk. Even Hermione,' said Gally with pardonable complacency, 'won't think of looking there.'

III

In predicting that Lady Hermione would shortly be instituting a search of Sam's room Gally had not erred. Even as he was speaking she had registered a resolve to explore its every nook and cranny. Her first move after Gally had left her had been to telephone her daughter Veronica and explain the facts relating to Tipton's financial status, and when Veronica had uttered a squeal similar in volume to that of George Cyril Wellbeloved's niece Marlene and stammered, 'But, Mum-mee, what about my letter?' she had assured her that she must not feel uneasy about that because Mother had everything under control and Tipton would never see it. She then set out in quest of her nephew Wilfred Allsop, whom she proposed to enrol as an assistant in her investigations. She found him in the hall, meditatively tapping the barometer that hung there, and brusquely commanded him to stop tapping and accompany her to her boudoir.

Except for observing that according to the barometer, which had been very frank on the point, there was going to be the dickens of a thunderstorm any minute now, Wilfred had nothing to say as they went up the stairs. From childhood days the society of his Aunt Hermione had always occasioned him the gravest discomfort, making him speculate as to which of his sins of commission or omission she was about to drag into the light of day and comment on in that forthright manner of hers. Even though his conscience at the moment was reasonably clear, he could not help a twinge of apprehension as they reached the boudoir and she curtly bade him take a seat. He did not like her looks. It was plain to him that she was on the boil. If ever he had seen a fermenting aunt, this fermenting aunt was that fermenting aunt.

To his relief he found that it was not he who had caused her blood pressure to rise. When she spoke, she was, as aunts go, quite civil, not actually cooing to him like a turtle dove accosting its loved one but with nothing in her manner reminiscent of the bucko mate of an old-fashioned hell ship addressing an able-bodied seaman whose activities had dissatisfied him.

'Wilfred,' she said, 'I want your help.'

'My *what*?' said Wilfred, amazed. He could imagine no situation to which this masterful woman would not be equal without outside support. Unless, of course, she was doing a crossword puzzle and had got stumped by a word of three letters begining with E and meaning large Australian bird, in which event his brain was at her disposal.

'You must treat what I say as absolutely confidential.'

'Oh rather. Not a word to a soul. But what's all this about?'

'If you will be good enough to listen, I will tell you. A serious situation has arisen. Have you met this Augustus Whipple who came here yesterday?'

'Seen him at meals. Why?'

'He is not Augustus Whipple.'

'The story that's going the rounds is that he is. Uncle Clarence keeps calling him Mr Whipple.'

'I dare say, but he is an impostor.'

'Good Lord! Are you sure?'

'Quite sure.'

'Then why don't you boot him out?'

'That is what I am about to tell you. I am helpless. He has got a letter from Veronica.'

'She knows him?'

'Of course she does not.'

'Then why the correspondence?'

'Oh, Wilfred!'

'It's all very well to say "Oh, Wilfred!" in that soupy tone of voice, but you're making my head go round. If Vee doesn't know him, how do they come to be pen pals? I don't get it.'

'The letter was written to Tipton.'

'To Tippy?'

'Yes.'

'Let's get this straight. You say the letter was written to *Tippy*?'

'Yes, yes, YES!'

With a wide despairing gesture Wilfred knocked over a small

table containing a vase of roses and a photograph of Colonel Wedge in the uniform of the Shropshire Light Infantry.

'Well, if you think that makes it all clear, you're very much in error. I fail absolutely to understand where Tippy comes into the thing. I simply can't see—'

'Wilfred!'

'Hullo?'

'Stop *talking*! How can I explain if you persist in interrupting me?'

'Sorry. Carry on. You have the floor. But I still say you're making my head go round.'

'It is all quite simple.'

'Says you!'

'What?'

'I didn't speak.'

'You said something.'

'Just a hiccup.'

'Oh? Well, as I said, the whole thing is quite simple. Veronica happened to be feeling depressed and nervous for some reason, and in this mood of depression she felt that she was making a mistake in marrying Tipton. So she wrote him a letter breaking off the engagement. She now of course bitterly regrets it, but the letter was posted.'

'When?'

'Two days ago.'

'Then Tippy must have had it by now.'

'I keep telling you this man has got it. He intercepted it and is—'

'Holding you up?'

'Exactly.'

'What does he want? Money?'

'No, not money. But he will give the letter to Tipton if I do not allow him to stay on at the castle.'

'And you don't want him?'

'Of course I do not want him.'

'Well,' said Wilfred, breaking the bad news, 'it looks to me from where I sit as if you'd jolly well got him. He has you by the short hairs. You can't afford to let Tippy see that letter. Once let his eye rest on it and bim go your hopes and dreams of a millionaire son-in-law.'

An uneasy silence followed. It was broken by Wilfred saying that in his opinion his cousin Veronica ought to lose no time in putting in an application for a padded cell in some not too choosy lunatic asylum. The remark roused all the mother in Lady Hermione.

'What do you mean?' she demanded hotly.

'Writing a letter like that! She must have beeen cuckoo.'

'I told you she was depressed.'

'Not half as depressed as she'll be when Tippy walks out on her. I repeat that she ought to have her head examined.'

Lady Hermione was finding her nephew's manner, so different from his customary obsequiousness, extremely trying, but this was no time for rebuking him. It seemed to her that if these slurs on her daughter's intelligence were to be rebutted, it would be necessary to reveal the true facts. Reluctantly she did so.

'Veronica is not to be blamed. I was under the impression, misled by your Uncle Clarence, that Tipton had lost all his money. I naturally could not allow her to marry a pauper. One has to be practical. So I advised her to break off the engagement.'

'Oh, I see. Didn't she object?'

'She seemed a little upset at first.'

'I'm not surprised. She's nuts about Tippy.'

'But she is a sensible girl and saw how out of the question the marriage would be.'

'It'll be out of the question all right if Tippy sees that letter.'

'He will not see it. I am going to search this man's room and find it and destroy it.'

Wilfred goggled. Years of association with her had left him with no doubt as to his Aunt Hermione being a pretty hardboiled egg, but he had never suspected her of quite such twenty-minutes-in-the-saucepan-ness as this. He had always supposed that her hardboiled eggery expressed itself in words not deeds. A gurgling sound like the wind going out of the children's toy known as the dying duck showed how deeply he had been moved.

'Search his room?'

'Yes, and I want you with me.'

'Who, me? Why me?'

'I shall need you to stand outside the room and give me warning if you see anyone coming. I think you had better sing.'

'Sing?'

'Yes.'

'*Sing?*'

'Yes.'

'Sing what?'

Lady Hermione had often heard of secret societies where plotters plotted plots together, but she wondered if any plotter in any secret society had ever had so much difficulty as she was having in driving into the head of another plotter what he, the first plotter, was trying to plot. It was with an effort that she restrained herself from uttering words which would have relieved her but must inevitably have alienated the only possible ally on whose services she could call. She contented herself with a wide despairing gesture similar to her nephew's.

'What does it matter what you sing? I am not asking you to appear on the concert platform. You will not be performing at Covent Garden. Sing anything.'

Wilfred mentally ran through his repertoire and decided on that thing about having another cup of coffee and another piece of pie which Tipton had taught him in the course of their revels in New York. He liked both words and music, the work, he had been given to understand, of the maestro Berlin, author and composer of *Alexander's Ragtime Band* and other morceaux.

'Well, all right,' he said, though not with any great enthusiasm. 'And what will you do then?'

'I shall make my escape.'

'Down the water pipe?'

'Through the french window and out on to the lawn. The man has been given the Garden Suite,' said Lady Hermione bitterly. She would have resented an impostor being housed even in a garret and the Garden Suite was the choicest locality that Blandings Castle had to offer. It was where you put guests like the Duke of Dunstable, for whom the best was none too good.

His aunt's statement that he was to play a prominent part in this cloak-and-dagger enterprise had caused Wilfred Allsop to look like a nephew on whose head the ceiling has unexpectedly fallen, and that is how he was looking as she proceeded.

'The first thing to do is to get the man out of the way.'

'What!'

'Go and tell him that your Uncle Clarence is waiting to see him at the Empress's sty.'

'A very sound idea,' said Wilfred, much relieved. Her use of the expression 'get out of the way' had misled him for a moment. He had feared that she was going to suggest that he waylay this synthetic Whipple and set about him with a meat axe. He would not have put it past her. The lengths to which she appeared prepared to go seemed to him infinite, and he had been feeling like Macbeth talking things over with Lady Macbeth. It was with a heart lighter than he had supposed it would ever be again that he rose and set off in quest of Sam.

Sam was still in the smoking-room when Wilfred found him, and he received his message without pleasure. In the short time in which he had known him he had conceived a great liking for Lord Emsworth and would have been glad whenever the latter wished to chat with him about the Brontë country or the Land of Dickens or indeed about anything except pigs, but something told him that it would be upon these attractive animals that his host would touch when they met. However, it being impossible to ignore the summons, he started out for the sty, taking the short cut through the kitchen garden which they had taken on the previous day, and Constable Evans, standing at the window of Beach's pantry with a glass of port in his hand, had an excellent view of him as he passed. For an instant he stood staring, then with a brief 'Ho' he laid down his glass and sallied out in pursuit. No leopard on the trail could have flung itself into the chase with greater abandon. It was his first chance in months of making a pinch that amounted to anything and he was resolved to seize it.

The first thing Sam noticed on arriving at the sty was a complete shortage of Lord Emsworths and he could make nothing of it, for Wilfred had distinctly told him that his host was awaiting him there. Some mistake, he assumed, and glad of the respite he lit a cigarette. And he had scarcely done so when there was a flash and a roar and the storm which had been threatening all the afternoon broke with a violence which probably came as a surprise to the barometer Wilfred had tapped in the hall. It had predicted dirty weather, but it could hardly have anticipated anything on this scale. To Sam, whose nervous system was not at its best, what was in progress seemed to combine the outstanding qualities of the Johnstown flood and the Day of Judgment.

It was a moment to seek shelter, and most fortunately there was shelter within easy reach. At the junction between the kitchen garden and the meadow where the Empress had her headquarters there stood what looked like – and indeed was – a potting shed. Its interior, he presumed, would be stuffy and probably smelly, but these disadvantages were outweighed by the fact that it would be dry, and dryness was what he wanted – or, as he would have said when writing a review for one of the higher-browed weeklies, desiderated. He was inside it in a matter of seconds and was congratulating himself on the promptness with which he had acted, when the door slammed behind him and he heard the shooting of a bolt. It surprised and disconcerted him.

'Hoy!' he cried, and from outside a voice spoke, the cold, metallic voice of a policeman who has effected a fair cop.

'You're pinched,' it said.

Silence followed. It had been Constable Evans's original intention on seeing Sam enter the shed to go in after him and take him into immediate custody, but second thoughts had led to a change of plan. Better, he felt, to wait till he could bring up reinforcements. He could not forget that this particular malefactor packed a wicked wallop, and he had no desire to be on the receiving end of it again. So having shot the bolt and said, 'You're pinched' he hastened back to Beach's pantry to telephone the police station to send a car and an assistant, preferably a large and muscular one.

It was some slight consolation to Sam to feel that he must be getting soaked to his underlinen.

CHAPTER 10

I

It was the boast of Jno. Robinson, its proprietor, that the station taxi, though a little creaky in the joints and inclined to pant when going up hill, never failed to get its patrons to their destination sooner or later, and it had got Sandy to hers without mishap. Her first move on arrival, like a conscientious secretary, was to go and report to Lord Emsworth, whose jaw dropped slightly when he saw her, for he had been hoping that she would have been away rather longer. She then went to the small room opening off the library where she worked.

She was not long without company. Musing on life in a deck chair on the front lawn, Gally had seen her drive up, and though reluctant to stir from his comfortable seat he felt it imperative to seek her out and put her in touch with recent developments at the castle. He also proposed to chide her for sneaking off as she had done. She had behaved, he considered, with a low cunning which he deplored. He had always been a man who disliked having a fast one put over on him, and he was prepared to be somewhat stern with Sandy.

Sandy, for her part, was prepared to be somewhat stern with him. On seeing Sam emerge from the Emsworth Arms bar she had been sure that Gally was responsible for his being there, and it was at him even more than at Sam that her resentment was directed. Their meeting, consequently, was marked by a certain frostiness on both sides. She greeted him with a cold 'Good evening', and he said, 'Take that lemon out of your mouth, Mona Lisa. I want a word with you.'

Sandy continued haughty. Her full height was not much, but she drew herself to what there was of it.

'If it's about Sam—'

'Of course it's about Sam.'

'Then I don't want to hear it.'

A less courageous man than Gally might have quailed at the iciness of her tone, but it left him undaunted.

'What you want and what you're going to get,' he said, 'are two substantially different things. Sam has told me all about that Drones Club sweepstake and the offer from the syndicate and how you tried to get him to sell out for a hundred pounds when he had only to sit tight and let nature take its course in order to clean up on a really impressive scale, and frankly I was appalled. Your mutton-headedness stunned me.'

'I don't consider that I was mutton-headed, as you call it.'

'Then your standards must be very high.'

'I had a good reason for wanting him to sell out. I knew what Tipton was like.'

'He's rather like a string bean, but I don't see how that enters into it.'

'I'm not talking about what he looks like. The sort of man he is, I mean.'

'And what sort is that?'

'Susceptible. Always falling in and out of love. When I was working for his uncle, he got engaged to a whole series of girls, and every time the engagement was broken off. I supposed that this latest one would follow the usual pattern.'

'Often a bridesmaid but never a bride, you felt? You were mistaken. His passion for Veronica is the real thing. When he fetched up here the day before yesterday, it was with the love light in his eyes and an eight-thousand-pound necklace for her in his trouser pocket. He'll be a married man in next to no time. The date is set, the caterer notified, the bishop and assistant clergy lined up at the starting gate waiting for the flag to fall.'

'And suppose she breaks off the engagement? Tipton's girls always do.'

'Not this one. Sam's on a certainty. If ever there was a Today's Safety Bet, this is it. My advice to you, young Sandy, is to admit you were wrong and kiss and make up. When you see him—'

'I shan't see him.'

'Oh yes, you will. He's here now.'

'I know he is. At the Emsworth Arms.'

'Not at the Emsworth Arms, at the castle.'

'What!'

'Passing for the moment under the name of Augustus Whipple.'

'What!'

'You do keep saying "What", don't you? Yes, on my advice he assumed the name of Whipple, for I felt it would endear him to Clarence, as indeed it has. And that brings me to another talking point. If ever you entertained doubts as to the wholeheartedness of his love, reflect that simply in order to be near you and plead his cause he has placed himself in a position where he has to listen to Clarence talking pig to him from morning to night. He's suffering agonies, and all for you. So be guided by me, young Sandy, and fling yourself into his arms and murmur "Oh, Sam, can you ever forgive me?" or "Oh, Sam, let the past be forgotten" or, of course,' said Gally, always ready to make concessions, 'any other gag along those lines you may prefer. I'll leave you to think it over.'

His story had shaken Sandy. It had been well said of Galahad Threepwood in his Pelican Club days that few could equal him at telling the tale. He was credited by his associates with the ability to talk the hind leg off a donkey, and the passage of the years had in no way diminished his spellbinding qualities. Half an hour ago the idea of ever speaking to Sam again in this world or the next would have seemed to Sandy so bizarre as not to deserve consideration, but now she was beginning to feel that that idea of flinging herself into his arms might have something in it.

Like so many girls with similarly coloured hair, she had a low boiling point and was easily stirred to sudden furies, but they resembled those of the storm outside, which after a sensational start had already begun to calm down, in being soon over. Looking out of the window, she saw that the Niagara of a few minutes back was now a gentle trickle and the thunder and lightning had ceased altogether. It was as if the forces of Nature felt that they had made their point and could relax, and she found herself in harmony with their softened mood.

Ever since the morning when Sam had spoken his mind to her on the subject of ginger-haired little fatheads and she had thrown the ring at him she had tried to keep resentment alive, but she had never really liked the idea of not speaking to him again in this world or the next. She had told herself that he was the obstinate pig-headed type whom no girl of sense would dream of marrying and that the severance of relations between them was the best thing that could have happened, but all the while a voice within her had kept reminding her that, even though pig-headed, he was unquestionably a lamb, and lambs are not so easily come by in these hard times that you can afford to throw them carelessly away. Remorse, in short, had gnawed her, causing her to feel almost precisely as Colonel Wedge and his wife Hermione had felt on discovering that they had rashly given the bum's rush to a prospective son-in-law who oozed dollar bills at every pore.

On only one point had Gally left her dubious, and that was the likelihood of Tipton Plimsoll becoming a married man. She had seen so many of his false starts when she had been working for his Uncle Chet that she could not believe that any betrothal of his could possibly culminate in a wedding. Recalling his long line of fiancées, all of whom had come and gone with a quickness that deceived the eye, she was unable to picture him lined up with this latest one at the altar rails. It would be necessary, there-fore, even while flinging herself into Sam's arms, to make it quite clear to him that her views on the syndicate's offer had in no way changed. On this she was resolved to be firm. Lamb or no lamb, he would have to accept her ruling.

She had reached this point in her meditations, when some-thing long and string-bean-like bounded in with a 'Hi!' that rattled the window pane and for the first time since she had left her native America she beheld Tipton Plimsoll.

Her presence at the castle had astounded Tipton. Looking out of the smoking-room window, he had seen the station taxi drive up and a girl whom his experienced eye classified as quite a dish alight from it. Her appearance had seemed to him oddly familiar, but it was only when she raised her head while handing Jno. Robinson his fare that he recognised her as one of his closest and most esteemed buddies.

He was exuberantly glad to see her. He had always been devoted to Sandy. Her place in his life had been that of a kindly sister in whom he could confide whenever he fell in love with someone new and needed the services of a confidante. She had given him encouragement when he required it and sympathy when he required that, which usually happened a few weeks after he had become engaged, for his fiancées had a disconcerting knack of writing to tell him they were sorry but they had just married elsewhere, adding in a postscript that they would always look on him as a dear friend.

'Sandy Callender as I live and breathe!' he cried. 'I couldn't believe it when I saw you getting out of that cab. I didn't even know you were on this side. What on earth are you doing here?'

'I'm Lord Emsworth's secretary. Gally Threepwood got me the job. I met him in London just when his sister was looking around for someone to work for Lord Emsworth. Well, it's wonderful seeing you again, Tipton. How are you?'

'Pretty spruce, thanks.'

'That's good. I hear you're engaged again.'

Tipton lost some of his joyous effervescence. Not meaning to wound, she had said the wrong thing.

'Don't say "again",' he protested, 'as if it was something I did every hour on the hour.'

'Well, isn't it?'

Tipton was forced to concede that there was a certain amount of justice in the question.

'Well, yes,' he admitted, 'I have got tangled up with a girl or two—'

'Or three or four or five.'

' – in my time, but that was just kid stuff. This is the real thing. This is for keeps. You remember those other babes I got starry-eyed about?'

'Doris Jimpson, Angela Thurloe, Vanessa Wainwright, Barbara Bessemer...'

'All right, all right. No need to call the score. What I was going to say was Do you know what was wrong with them?'

'They married somebody else.'

'Yes, that, of course, but they wouldn't have done for me even if they had gone through with it. They were either the smart hardboiled type, always wisecracking and making one feel like a piece of cheese, or the intellectual kind that wanted to mould me. I couldn't keep up with them. We weren't batting in the same league. But Vee, she's different. I've never been a brainy sort of guy, and what I want is a wife with about the same amount of grey matter I have, and that's how Vee stacks up. Do you remember Clarice Burbank?'

'Was she the Russian ballet one?'

'No, that was Marcia Ferris. Clarice was the one who made me read Kafka. And the reason I bring her up is that Vee would never dream of doing a thing like that.'

'She probably thinks Kafka's a brand of instant coffee with ninety-seven per cent of the caffeine extracted.'

'Exactly. She's just a sweet simple English girl with about as much brain as would make a jay bird fly crooked, and that's the way I want her.'

'Well, that's fine.'

'You bet it's fine.'

'When is the wedding to be?'

Tipton looked cautiously over his shoulder, as if to assure himself that they were alone and unobserved.

'Can you keep a secret?'

'No.'

'Well, try to keep this one, because if it gets out, all hell will break loose. Before I left for America, Vee and I fixed the whole thing up. We decided that a big Society wedding was a lot of prune juice and we wanted no piece of it. We're going to elope. I'm off to London tomorrow, and a couple of days after that we'll be married at the registrar's.'

'What!'

'Yes, sir, right plumb spang at the registrar's.'

'You mean that two days from now—'

'I'll be picking the rice out of my hair, if registrars throw rice when they marry you.'

Sandy was breathing emotionally. How wrong, she felt, how terribly misguided she had been in urging Sam to accept the syndicate's offer, and how thankful she was that it was not too late to tell him so.

'I think that's wonderful, Tippy,' she said, speaking with some difficulty and raising her voice a little so as to be audible over the soft music which was filling the room. 'I'm sure you're doing the right thing.'

'Me, too.'

'Who wants a lot of bishops and assistant clergy?'

'Just how I feel. Let the bishops bish elsewhere and take the assistant clergy with them.'

'I know you'll be happy.'

'I don't see how I can miss.'

'As happy as I'm going to be.'

'Don't tell me you're thinking of jumping off the dock, too?'

'One of these days. In your wanderings about Blandings Castle have you happened to meet a character called Whipple?'

'I've seen him around. Husky guy with a cauliflower ear. Is he the one?'

'He's the one.'

'He looks all right to me.'

'To me also. You don't know where he is, do you?'

'Sure. I heard Willie Allsop telling him old Emsworth wanted to see him down at the pig sty. You'll find him in the pig sty, you can tell him by his hat,' quoted Tipton blithely.

'Thanks, Tippy,' said Sandy, equally blithely. 'I'll be on my way.'

II

It is never easy for a young man to be carefree and at his ease when, after having had difficulties with the police, he finds himself immured by them in a smelly shed, and Sam, sitting on a broken wheelbarrow and breathing in the scent of manure and under-gardeners, did not come within measurable distance of achieving this frame of mind. He would have been only too happy to look on the bright side, if there had been a bright side, but as far as he could discern there was not. He viewed the future with the gravest misgivings.

He was not quite sure what was the penalty for the crimes he had committed, but he had an idea that it was something lingering with boiling oil in it, and the thought depressed him. He was also feeling puzzled. Not being a mind reader, he was unaware of Constable Evans's change of plan and he could not imagine why, having uttered those fateful words 'You're pinched', he had faded so abruptly from the scene.

Rightly concluding that speculation on this point was idle, he turned his mind to thoughts of Sandy, but these merely deepened his despondency. Gally, that blithe optimist, seemed to be under the impression that he had only to meet her and their relations would instantly revert to their original cordiality, but he could not bring himself to share this sunny outlook. To begin with, he had called her in his heat not only a ginger-haired little fathead but other things equally offensive to a girl of spirit. She could hardly be expected to forgive that without straining a sinew.

And secondly there was this matter of the prison term that overshadowed his future. In due course, he presumed, he would come up before some sort of tribunal and be sentenced to whatever it was you got for stealing watches and assaulting the police, and few girls care to marry a jailbird, with all the embarrassments such a union involves. It is never nice for a young bride to have to explain to hosts and hostesses that the reason her husband has not come to the party is that he has just started another stretch in Pentonville.

The poignancy of it all swept over him like a wave, and he heaved a sigh. At least, that was what he had intended to heave, but by some miscalculation it came out like the wail of a banshee, and from somewhere outside a startled voice cried 'Oo!', causing hope to stir in a heart that had practically forgotten what the word meant. The voice had sounded feminine, and women, he knew, can generally be relied upon to bring aid and comfort to those in trouble. Poets have stressed this. The lines 'When pain and anguish wring the brow, a ministering angel thou' floated into his mind. Scott had written that, and you could rely on a level-headed man like Scott to know what he was talking about. There was a small window in one wall of the shed, its glass long broken and the vacant space given over to spiders' webs. He approached it, and said:

'Is that somebody out there?' and simultaneously the voice said:

'Is that somebody in there?' and it was as if he had been seated in an electric chair at its most electric. What he could see of the outer world, which was not much, swam before his eyes.

Even when merely saying 'Oo!' the voice had seemed familiar. Now that it had become more talkative, he had no difficulty in recognising it.

'Is that you, Sandy?' he said, and then, speaking diffidently, for he had no means of knowing how such a plea would be received by one in whose estimation he had fallen so extremely low, 'Would you mind letting me out?'

'Why don't you *come* out?'

'I can't. He's bolted the door.'

'Who has?'

'The cop. I'm under arrest.'

'Under what?'

'Arrest. A for apple, R for—'

'Oh, Sam, *darling*!'

Again Sam experienced that electric chair illusion. There was something sticking in his throat that seemed about the size of a regulation tennis ball. He swallowed it, and said in a hushed voice:

'Did you say darling?'

'You bet I said darling.'

'You mean – ?'

'Of course I do.'

'Everything's really all right?'

'Everything. Sweethearts still.'

Sam drew a deep breath.

'Thank God! I've been feeling suicidal.'

'Same here.'

'I wish I had a quid for every time I've thought of shoving my head in the gas oven.'

'Me, too.'

'I'm sorry I called you a ginger-haired little fathead, Sandy.'

'You were one hundred per cent right. I was a ginger-haired little fathead. Wanting you to take that syndicate offer. I must have been crazy.'

'You mean you've changed your mind?'

'I'll say I have. I've seen Tipton and he's going to elope with Veronica Wedge the day after tomorow. He's practically married already. But we mustn't stand here talking. I'll let you out, and then you can tell me what on earth all this cop-arrest stuff is about.'

It took Sam only a few moments to do this after the door had opened, and Sandy listened with growing concern.

'Oh, Sam!' she wailed and flung herself into his arms as Gally had recommended, and Gally, coming up as she did so, surveyed them with fatherly approval.

'Satisfactory,' he said, 'but there's no time for that sort of thing now. You're on the run, my boy, so start running. Constable Evans should be with us at any moment, and you'll look silly if he finds you here. He will approach, I presume, when he does approach, via the kitchen garden, so make for the front entrance and work your way to the billiards room or the smoking-room or wherever else you see fit so long as it offers sanctuary. Sandy and I will wait here to receive him. You are possibly wondering,' he said after Sam, recognising his advice as good, had taken it, 'how I happened to pop up out of a trap like this at the centre of things. Very simple. I was trying to find our young friend to tell him I thought you were favourably disposed to a reconciliation, and I looked in at Beach's pantry to ask if he had seen him. Constable Evans was there, speaking on the telephone, and Beach informed me in an undertone that the zealous officer had locked Sam in the shed by the pig sty and was calling up his reserves. One guesses what was in his mind. At their previous meeting Sam had – rightly or wrongly – plugged him in the eye and he shrank from having it happen again. No doubt it was his prudent intention, when his assistant arrived, to let him go in first and see what would develop. If eyes are to be plugged, your cautious constable always prefers them to be the other fellow's. And talking of eyes, I think it would be a graceful act and one which would help to make Sam's day if you were to dispense with those ghastly spectacles of yours.'

'Don't you like them?'

'No, I don't.'

'Nor does Sam. He said they made me look like a horror from outer space.'

'He flattered you. Take them off and jump on them.'

'Right,' said Sandy, and did so.

'And now,' said Gally, having viewed the remains with satisfaction, 'if you glance to your left, you will see Evans and friend heading our way, prowling and prowling like the troops of Midian in the well-known hymn. I think perhaps you had better let me do the talking. It was an axiom in the old Pelican days that in all matters involving the boys in blue it was wisest to leave the *pourparlers* to Galahad Threepwood. These conferences with the cops call for delicacy and tact. Good evening, officers. Welcome to Blandings Castle and all that sort of thing.'

The two constables made an intimidating pair. A pen portrait of Officer Evans has already been given and it need only be said of Officer Morgan, his brother-in-arms, that he resembled him so closely as to create in the mind of anyone encountering them in each other's company the illusion that he was seeing double. Only the former's rich black eye served to distinguish him.

'Pleasant after the storm, is it not?' said Gally. 'So you're out for a country ramble? Taking it easy among the buttercups and daisies, eh? Having a good loaf, are you?'

Constable Evans, resentful of the implication that the police force of Market Blandings lived for pleasure alone, replied that this was far from being the case. He and his colleague, he said, had come to make an arrest, and Gally raised his eyebrows.

'Not my brother's pig, I trust?'

'No, sir,' said the constable shortly. 'Man wanted for theft from the person and obstructing the police in the execution of their duty.'

'Any clue as to his whereabouts?'

'He's in that shed.'

Gally adjusted his monocle and looked in the direction indicated. He was plainly puzzled.

'That shed?'

'Yes, sir.'

'The one over there?'

'Yes, sir.'

'The one with the tiled roof?'

'Yes, sir.'

Gally shook his head.

'I think you're mistaken, my dear fellow. This lady and I were peeping in there only a moment ago, and the place was empty. Well, when I say empty, we noticed an old wheelbarrow and two or three flower pots and, if I remember rightly, a dead rat, but certainly no fugitive from justice. What gives you the impression that he's there?'

'I locked him in myself.'

'In that shed?'

'Yes, sir.'

'Or are you thinking of some other shed?'

'No, sir, I am not thinking of some other shed.'

'Well, it's all very mysterious,' said Gally. An idea seemed to strike him. 'He wasn't a midget, was he?'

'No, sir.'

'I thought he might have been hiding behind one of the flower pots, which would have accounted for our not seeing him. Then I must confess myself baffled. How he managed to get out of that shed is beyond me. Door locked, no other exit. It's the sort of thing Houdini used to do. I wonder ... no, that can't be right. I was thinking he might have been one of those Indian fakirs who dematerialise themselves and reassemble the parts elsewhere, but then he wouldn't have bothered to unlock the door, and it was open when we looked in. The whole thing's inexplicable. I doubt if we shall ever get to the bottom of it.'

A dark flush had appeared on Constable Evans's granite face. He was by no means an unintelligent man, and with a swiftness which Lady Hermione herself could not have exceeded he had reached the conclusion that Gally was responsible for the disappearance of his quarry. But he did not dare to put his conviction into words. Gally, whatever his moral defects, was an inmate in good standing of Blandings Castle, and a respect for Blandings Castle had been instilled into him from his Sunday School days. There was nothing to do but say 'Ho!', so he said it. Constable Morgan, a man of deep reserves, said nothing, and after a few more sympathetic comments on a mystery which in his opinion, he said, would rank for ever with those of the *Marie Celeste* and The Man In The Iron Mask, Gally resumed his progress to the house, apparently unaware of the long lingering looks which both officers of the law were directing at his retreating back.

'Too bad,' he said as he and Sandy went on their way. 'One's heart bleeds for Constable Evans and his strong silent friend whose name did not crop up in the course of our conversation. I can readily imagine what a disappointment this must have been to them. I have known a great many policemen in my time, and they all told me that nothing gave them that disagreeable feeling of flatness and frustration more surely than the discovery, when they went to make an arrest, that the fellow they were after wasn't there. It must be like opening your Christmas stocking as a child and finding nothing in it. Still, one must not forget that these setbacks are sent to us for our own good. They make us more spiritual. Tell me,' said Gally, abandoning a painful subject, 'about you and Sam. What I saw gave me the impression that your hearts were no longer sundered. Correct?'

'Quite correct.'

'Excellent. What was it the poet said about lovers' reconciliations?'

'I don't know.'

'Nor do I, but it was probably something pretty good. I suppose you're feeling happy?'

'Floating on air.'

'Great thing, young love.'

'Nothing to beat it. Were you ever in love, Gally?'

'Very seldom out of it.'

'I mean really in love. Didn't you ever want to marry someone who was the only thing that mattered to you in the whole world?'

Gally winced a little. She had reopened an old wound.

'Yes, once,' he said briefly. 'Nothing came of it.'

'What happened?'

'My old father didn't approve. She was what was called a serio on the music halls. Sang songs at the Oxford and the Tivoli. Dolly Henderson was her name. He put his foot down. Painful scenes. Raised voices. Tables banged with fists. Not sure a father's curse wasn't mentioned. I was shipped off to South Africa, and while I was there she married someone else. Chap named Jack Cotterleigh in the Irish Guards.'

'Poor Gally!'

'Yes, I must say I didn't like it much. But it was a long time ago, and nobody's going to ship Sam off to South Africa. By the way, I take it that when you were fixing things up with him, you waived your objections about the syndicate?'

'You bet I did.'

'Sensible girl. You won't regret it.'

'I know I won't. Tipton's getting married the day after tomorrow. At the registrar's.'

'You don't say? Is that official?'

'He told me himself. Dead secret, of course.'

'Naturally. Though I wish I could tell Clarence. It would relieve his mind to know that the big wedding is off.'

'Why?'

'No wedding, no speech and, above all, no top hat. Clarence has always been allergic to top hats. Strange how tastes differ. I like them myself, particularly when grey. There were days in my youth when the mere sight of a bookie whose account I had not settled would make me shake like a leaf, but slap a grey top hat on my head and I could face him without a tremor. And now, I suppose,' said Gally, as they came into the house, 'you will be wanting to go in search of Sam?'

'I thought I might.'

'Well, try to cheer him up. For some reason he has seemed to me nervous and depressed since he got here. As for me, I think I'll go and have a talk with Clarence. I always find his society stimulating.'

III

Gally was humming the refrain of one of Dolly Henderson's songs as he made for Lord Emsworth's study. Odd, he was thinking, how after thirty years he could still have that choked-up feeling when he thought of her. Oh well, what had happened had probably been all for the best. Pretty rough it would have been for a nice girl like Dolly to be tied up with a chap like him, he felt, for he had never had any illusions about himself. His sisters Constance, Julia, Dora and Hermione had often spoken of him as a waster, and how right they were. His disposition was genial, he made friends easily and as far as he could recall had never let a pal down, but you couldn't claim that as a life partner he was everybody's cup of tea. And people who knew them had described Dolly and Jack as a happy and devoted couple, so what was there to get all wistful and dreary about?

Nevertheless, all this marrying and giving in marriage that was going on around one did rather encourage melancholy thoughts of what might have been. Tipton was marrying Veronica, Sam was marrying Sandy, Wilfred Allsop, so Tipton informed him, was marrying that large Simmons girl. Good Lord, he told himself with a sudden twinge of alarm, for all he knew Clarence might have relaxed his vigilance and be in danger of marrying Dame Daphne Winkworth. Once this sort of thing started, you never knew where it would stop.

And it was as this disquieting thought flitted through his mind that the door of the study opened and he saw Dame Daphne coming out of it. She disappeared along the corridor and the next moment he was bustling into the study, all brotherly concern.

'Ah, Galahad,' said Lord Emsworth, glancing up from his pig

book, 'I was hoping you might look in. A most peculiar thing has happened.'

Gally was in no mood to hear whatever it was that had struck his brother as peculiar.

'Are you crazy, Clarence?' he said. 'Have you forgotten what I told you?'

'Yes,' said Lord Emsworth, who always did. 'What was it you told me, Galahad?'

'On no account to allow yourself to be alone with the female whom, but for the luck of the Emsworths, you might have married twenty years ago. Your old girl friend Dame Daphne Winkworth. How could you be so criminally rash as to hobnob with her?'

'But, my dear fellow, how could I help it? She came in. I could hardly forcibly eject her.'

'What were you talking about?'

'Oh, various things.'

'The dear old days?'

'Not to my recollection.'

'Then what?'

Lord Emsworth searched a treacherous memory. Recalling what anyone had talked about two minutes after the conclusion of the conversation was always a taxing task for him.

'Was any mention made of the *Indian Love Lyrics*?'

'I don't think so. She was speaking, now that I remember, of someone called ... now what was he called? ... yes, I have it, someone called Allsop. The name was strange to me. Have you ever heard of an Allsop?'

'You have a nephew of that name.'

'Are you sure?'

'If you don't believe me, look in Debrett. Wilfred Allsop. What was she saying about Wilfred?'

'As far as I could make out, she is not going to employ him as a music master at her school. She did not like him getting intoxicated.'

'Intoxicated?' Gally was surprised. Even at the old Pelican it had been unusual for members to get into that condition in the middle of the afternoon. He felt that there must be more in his nephew Wilfred than he had suspected. 'Blotto, do you mean? Pie-eyed?'

'So she said. It appears that her son ... I forget his name ...'

'Huxley.'

'Of course yes, Huxley. It appears that Huxley was passing along the passage leading to the Garden Suite and Wilfred Allsop was standing there singing drunken songs. And only yesterday the boy had found him drinking heavily by the pig sty. He of course told his mother, and she has cancelled Wilfred Allsop's appointment. I am not sure that I altogether blame her. She seemed to fear that I might be offended, but I quite see her point of view. I have never been the headmistress of a girls' school myself, but if I were, I should certainly think twice before engaging an alcoholic music master. Such a bad example for the pupils.'

'And that was all? She didn't go on to more tender and sentimental subjects?'

'Not as far as I recall. We talked about pigs. She is interested in pigs. I was surprised how interested she seemed to be.'

Gally's monocle sprang from its place. He called loudly on the name of his Maker.

'The thin end of the wedge! Clarence, you must get this woman out of the house and speedily, or you haven't a hope of avoiding matrimony. It's the case of Puffy Benger all over again. The same insidious tactics. With Puffy the girl started by talking to him about his approach putts – he was a keen golfer – and little by little and bit by bit she went on till she had him reading *Pale Hands I Loved Beside The Shalimar* to her, and that was the end. I tell you solemnly that unless you act promptly and firmly and heave this woman out on the seat of her pants while there is yet time, you're a dead snip for the wedding stakes. She's closing in on you, Clarence, closing in on you.'

'You appal me, Galahad!'

'That's what I'm trying to do. Well, there you are. You have been warned,' said Gally, and stumped out, feeling that he had done all that man could do to save a loved brother from the fate that is worse than death.

Closing the door, he remembered that at the start of their interview Clarence had said something that had aroused his curiosity, though at the time more urgent matters had prevented him giving his mind to it. Something about something being peculiar or something peculiar having happened or something. He opened the door and poked his head in.

'What was that you said just now?' he asked.

'Eh?' said Lord Emsworth, who appeared dazed.

'The peculiar thing?'

'Eh?'

'Pull yourself together, Clarence. You said a peculiar thing had happened.'

'Oh, that?' said Lord Emsworth, coming out of his trance. 'It was nothing really, but it struck me as odd. I was looking through my desk, trying to find the annual report of the Shropshire, Herefordshire and South Wales Pig Breeders' Association, which Miss Callender must have hidden away somewhere with

her infernal tidying up, and I came on a manila envelope.
I opened it, and inside it was another envelope addressed to
Tipton Plimsoll. I couldn't imagine how it had come there. So
I rang for Miss Callender and asked her to take it to Tipton.
I hope the delay in delivering it will not have caused him any
inconvenience.'

CHAPTER 11

I

Sandy, meanwhile, though she would have preferred to stay talking to Sam in the billiards room in which he had taken refuge, had gone to her office in the small room off the library to resume her work. She was a conscientious secretary and had always felt that as she was paid a salary, she should try to earn it. It was this defect in her character that so exasperated Lord Emsworth. His ideal secretary would have been one who breakfasted in bed, dozed in an armchair through the morning, played golf in the afternoon and took the rest of the day off.

But though she had sat down at her desk full of zeal and though there was still plenty to be done in the way of cleaning the Augean stables of her employer's correspondence, she found a strange difficulty in concentrating on the task in hand. And she had fallen into a trance as deep as any of Lord Emsworth's, when the bursting open of the door brought her back to the present, and after blinking once or twice she was able to identify her visitor as Gally. It seemed to her that he was agitated about something, and her diagnosis was perfectly correct. It was not easy to make Gally lose his poise. Throughout his long life a great number of people ranging from schoolmasters and Oxford dons to three-card trick men on race trains had attempted the feat, but always without success. It had been left for his brother

Clarence to succeed where so many had failed. He spoke without wasting time on preliminaries.

'That letter? Have you got it?'

'What letter? I've got about a hundred, and all of them ought to have been answered weeks ago.'

'The Tipton letter Clarence gave you.'

'Oh, that one? No. I haven't got it. I gave it to Beach to give to him.'

'Death, damnation and despair!' said Gally.

He bounded from the room as rapidly as he had bounded into it. Mystified, Sandy returned to her work and was reading a communication from Grant and Purvis of Wolverhampton, who sold garden supplies and were at a loss to understand why they had received no answer from Lord Emsworth to theirs of the eleventh ult, when he reappeared.

'I thought Beach might still have it,' he said, 'but he hasn't. He gave it to Tipton a quarter of an hour ago. Curses on his impetuosity. May his next bottle of port be corked.'

No secretary, however conscientious, could have kept her mind on her work with this sort of thing going on. Sandy abandoned Grant and Purvis of Wolverhampton and their petty troubles.

'For heaven's sake, Gally,' she said, 'what's the matter? What's all this about Tipton's letter? What's wrong with him getting his mail?'

Gally, as a raconteur, had a tendency at times to elaborate his stories in a manner that tried the patience of his audience, but in his reply to her query he was admirably succinct, confining himself to the bare facts, and as these facts emerged the colour faded from Sandy's face and she stared at him with horror in her eyes.

'Oh, Gally!' she said.

He nodded a sombre nod.

'You may well say "Oh, Gally!" I wouldn't have blamed you if you'd said "Oh, hell!" The whole infernal mess is my fault. It shows what comes of trying to be clever. I thought it was such a bright idea to slip that letter in among Clarence's papers. The odds against him ever looking through them were at least a hundred to one, but, as so often happens, the good thing came unstuck. However, all is not yet lost.'

Sandy stared.

'How can you say that? What can you possibly do?'

'I can get hold of Tipton and tell him the tale and convince him that there is nothing in that letter to cause him concern.'

'If you can do that, you're a genius.'

'Well, we know that already. I'll go and find him now.'

The proposed search, however, proved unnecessary. Scarcely had he reached the door when it flew open and the object of it appeared in person.

'Ah, Tipton,' he said. 'Come on in. We were just talking about you.'

Tipton's demeanour had undergone a great change since Sandy had last seen him. Then the dullest eye would have recognised him as a young man sitting on top of the world. Now it was equally apparent that he had fallen off and come down with a bump. His brow was furrowed, his eyes dull, his mouth drooping. He was looking, in short, just as Sandy had seen him look when he had come to her for sympathy after being reduced to the status of a dear friend by Doris Jimpson, Angela Thurloe, Vanessa Wainwright, Barbara Bessemer, Clarice Burbank and Marcia Ferris.

'Oh, hello, Mr Threepwood,' he said, evincing no joy at seeing him. 'I didn't know you were here.'

'I am,' Gally assured him, 'and I may tell you I know all about that letter you have in your hand. Sandy and I were discussing it before you came in.'

'You were? Who told you about it?'

'Oh, various people. I have my spies everywhere. May I look at it?' said Gally, twitching it from his grasp without going through the formality of waiting for permission. He skimmed it in silence, his brows knitted, and when he came to the end gave a short, contemptuous laugh.

'As I expected,' he said. 'An obvious fake.'

Tipton's mouth, which emotion had caused to fall open like that of a mail box, opened an inch or two further. Gally's conversation often had this effect on people.

'You mean it's a forgery?' he asked with a sudden gleam of hope. This was something he had not thought of.

Gally shook his head.

'Not exactly that. The hand is the hand of Veronica, but the voice is the voice of her blasted mother.'

'You mean she made Vee write it?'

'Of course she did. It sticks out a mile. She probably stood over the poor girl with a horsewhip. Hermione dictated every word of this letter. Sift the evidence. On the second page the phrase "incompatibility of temperament" occurs. Do you suppose that that half-witted girl ... pardon the word half-witted ...'

'Don't apologise,' said Sandy. 'Tipton likes her that way.'

'So do I. So do we all. It's part of her charm. It's what endears her to everyone. If a girl as beautiful as she is had any brains, the mixture would be too rich. Where was I?'

'You broke off on the word "half-witted".'

'Ah yes. What I was going to say was that it is unbelievable that

Veronica not only knows what incompatibility of temperament means, but is able to spell it. I yield to no one in my appreciation of her many excellent qualities, but her best friend would have to admit that she is about as dumb a brick as ever had a wind-swept hair-do, completely baffled by anything over two syllables. Look, too, at that "distressed" on page one. Is it conceivable that she would have put two s's in it if she had not had a mother to guide her? And another thing. Mark how wobbly the writing is. She was finding it hard to bring herself to push the pen. See that blotch that looks as if a wet fly had walked across the paper? An obvious tear drop. She might allow herself to be coerced into taking dictation, but she was dashed if anyone was going to stop her weeping bitterly. What we have before us, in short, is a communiqué from a girl whose heart is breaking with every word she is forced to write, but one who all her life has done what Mother told her to. I have watched Veronica ripen from infancy to womanhood, and if there was a single moment during those years when Hermione allowed her to call her soul her own, it escaped my notice. Ignore this letter is my advice to you, Tipton, my boy. Wash it completely from your mind.'

He probably had more to say, for he was a man who always had more to say, but Tipton rose to a point of order.

'But it doesn't make sense.'

'What doesn't?'

'Her mother twisting Vee's arm and making her write the thing. She was tickled to death when we got engaged.'

'Ah, but that was before you started going about the place telling everyone you had lost all your money. Hermione heard it from my brother Clarence, and it radically altered her views on your suitability as a son-in-law. I have no doubt that Veronica loves you for yourself alone, but Hermione doesn't.'

Tipton had begun to bloom like a flower beneath the rays of the sun, or perhaps it would be better to say like a string bean under those conditions.

'Then you think – ?'

' – That Veronica's sentiments towards you have not changed? I'm sure of it. I am vastly mistaken if you are not still the cream in her coffee and the salt in her stew, as the song says. Five will get you ten if you care to bet against it. Go and get her on the phone now and coo to her, and see if she doesn't coo right back at you. And when the voice off stage asks you if you want another three minutes, take them and blow the expense. There's a telephone in the library,' he would have added, but Tipton had already flashed from the room.

Sandy closed the door behind him. She looked at Gally with awe.

'So now I know what telling the tale means!'

'A very minor effort,' said Gally modestly. 'You should have caught me in my prime. One loses something of one's magic over the years. Still I think I accomplished my objective, don't you?'

'As far as Tippy is concerned, yes. But what happens when he gets her on the phone and she says she doesn't love him?'

'She won't. I cannot picture any niece of mine not loving someone as rich as he is.'

'You don't think it's only his money that's the attraction, do you?'

'Certainly not. They're soul mates. She has about as much brain as a retarded billiards ball, and he approximately the same. It's the ideal union and I am gratified that I have been able to do my little bit to push it along. Curious what a glow it gives one to see the young folk getting together. Which reminds me. I want to see Tipton about Wilfred Allsop.'

'What about him?'

'He's lost his job, and I am hoping to persuade Tipton to find him another.'

'You'll persuade him.'

'You think so?'

'Not a chance of him resisting when you start to tell the tale. You ought to have been a confidence man, Gally.'

'So others have told me,' said Gally complacently. 'I have always had that ability to touch the human heart strings. Why, in my early days, when I was at the top of my form, I have sometimes made bookies cry.'

II

The library was empty when he reached it, and he presumed that Tipton, having concluded a satisfactory talk with Veronica, had decided to join her in London without delay and had gone to the garage to get his car. The place to catch him would be on the drive outside the front door, and he made his way thither.

It was now getting on for the hour of the evening cocktail and a man less dedicated than Gally to the service of his fellows might have given up the idea of interviewing Tipton on Wilfred Allsop's behalf and hurried indoors. But where it was a matter of doing someone a good turn he was always willing to face privations. He hoped, however, that Tipton would not keep him lingering here too long, for already he was conscious of a dryness of the thorax which only a prompt martini could correct, and at this moment, as if having divined his thoughts by extrasensory perception, the man he wanted came bowling up in his Rolls Royce.

A glance at him was enough to tell Gally that his recent telephone conversation with Veronica Wedge must have taken place in what reporters of conferences between foreign ministers describe as an atmosphere of the utmost cordiality, for his grin was the grin of a young man without a care in the world and he alighted from the car with a lissom leap that told its own story.

'Hello, Mr Threepwood,' he carolled. 'I'm just off to London.'

'To see the little woman?'

'That's right.'

'I take it, then, that the two bob or whatever it was that you spent on that telephone call was not wasted. You found Veronica in genial mood?'

'You betcher.'

'And the wedding will proceed as planned?'

'Curtain goes up the day after tomorrow. Apparently you have to let these registrar birds have a day's notice.'

'That's to give them time to get over the shock of meeting the bridegroom.'

'I suppose they get all sorts?'

'Yes, it must be a wearing life. How about your witness?'

'That's all laid on. I'm taking Willie Allsop with me. He's up in his room, packing.'

'Ah? Well, before he arrives I should like to talk to you about Wilfred. Are you aware that he has lost his job?'

'I hadn't a notion. You mean the Winkworth woman isn't going to hire him as a music teacher?'

'No, she has cancelled the appointment and he is at liberty. It appears that she was tipped off that he had been singing drunken songs in the corridor.'

A grave look came into Tipton's beaming face. He shook his head.

'She wouldn't like that.'

'She didn't!'

'She's strongly opposed to anyone hoisting a few.'

'We all have our faults.'

'So what's Willie going to do?'

'Precisely what I wanted to see you about. I was thinking that you might come to the rescue and find him something.'

'Who, me?'

'You control a number of lucrative businesses, do you not?'

'Yes, I guess I do.'

'Such as – ?'

'Well, there's Tipton's Stores.'

'What could he do there?'

'Only go around in white overalls telling customers where to find the cleansers and detergents.'

'You can't think of anything better?'

'There's the ranch Uncle Chet left me out in Arizona. But can you see Willie as a cowboy?'

'Not vividly. But didn't your Uncle Chet own a music publishing concern in London? I seem to remember him saying something to me about it.'

'Good Lord, I'd quite forgotten. Sure he did. Aunt Betsy used to write songs, and the only way he could get them published was to buy out the publishers. It cost him a couple of million, but he said it was worth it just to keep harmony in the home. It's a very good firm, and I believe he'd got most of his money back when he passed on.'

'Then that's where Wilfred finds his niche. Unless you have any objections?'

'No kick from me. A guy who can play the piano like Willie can't go wrong in a music business. I'll see to it directly I hit London.'

'Excellent. Be large-minded when you're fixing his salary. Don't forget he wants to get married. And an idea strikes me. You're taking Wilfred to London. Why not take Miss Simmons, too, and make it a double wedding?'

The suggestion plainly appealed to Tipton. It was, he agreed, a thought.

'But what will Lord Emsworth say when he finds she's stood him up?'

' "Bless my soul!" no doubt, or something like that. No need to worry about Clarence. These shocks are good for him. They keep him alert and on his toes. It's something to do with the stimulation of the adrenal glands. And have no anxiety about the Empress's well-being. She'll be all right. Beach will give her her calories. He's done it before and can carry on perfectly well till Clarence signs up a professional. Go and sound out La Simmons and see how she feels about it. You'll probably find her with Wilfred.'

Tipton was convinced. He bounded off and in an incredibly short space of time was back with the news that all was well.

'I sold her the idea in sixty seconds flat. She's gone off to pack a suitcase.'

'Splendid. Then as I am becoming more and more conscious of the parched feeling that steals over one at this time in the evening, I will leave you. With, may I say, my best wishes and heartiest congratulations and all that sort of apple sauce. An uncle by marriage's blessing on you, Tipton, if you care to have it.'

III

As Gally made his way to the drawing-room, where the cocktails were, he was feeling that mellow glow which comes to men of good will when they have done the square thing by their fellows. It was always his policy, if he could manage it, to strew a little happiness as he went by, and there could be no gainsaying that in the last half-hour or so he had strewn it with a lavish hand. There were those of his acquaintance who had sometimes spoken with bitterness of his habit of playing the guardian angel – or, as they were more inclined to put it, of making a pest of himself by meddling in other people's affairs, but in this case he felt that he had meddled to good purpose.

As a rule his evening cocktail was a thing Gally liked to linger over, but this was only when he was in congenial company. Today he found himself alone. The drawing-room was empty when he entered it, and after a quick one of a purely medicinal nature he trotted off to enjoy another talk with Sandy Callender. She would, he knew, be interested to hear how his interview with Tipton had come out.

'Well, young Sandy,' he said, bustling into her office, 'your faith in me was justified. Tipton, as you anticipated, was as corn before my sickle. I played on him as on a stringed instrument. He's giving Wilfred a good job and Wilfred and the Simmons are going to London with him to make a double wedding of it. A nice smooth bit of work, if you ask me. And what have you been doing in my absence? Sweating away and earning your weekly envelope, I trust?'

'No, I had a slack period.'

'Sitting and thinking of Sam, no doubt?'

'As a matter of fact, I was listening to the six o'clock news on the radio.'

'Anything of interest?'

'Not much. Austin Phelps has got married.'

'I hope he'll be very very happy. Who the hell is Austin Phelps?'

'The tennis player, my good child. You must have heard of Austin Phelps. The Davis Cup man.'

'Oh, that chap? Yes, I've heard of him. Goes around shouting "Forty love" and "Love fifteen" and all that sort of thing. Phelps?' said Gally, his brow wrinkling. 'Austin Phelps? There's something about him I'm trying to remember, something apart from tennis. Somebody was mentioning him to me only a day or two ago in some connection. Was he divorced recently? Did he plunge into the Thames to save a drowning child? Or win a by-election in the Conservative interest? Or get arrested for drunk driving? Maddening how these things slip from one's mind. Phelps? Phelps? Austin Phelps? Ah, perhaps you can tell me, Sam.'

On Sam's face, as he came into the room, there had been the purposeful look of a man about to converse with the girl he loves. It faded as he saw Gally. He was very fond of that deplorable character, but there are times when the best of friends are superfluous.

'Tell you what?'

'All you know about a man called Austin Phelps.'

'He plays tennis.'

'I am aware of that. But what is there about him that gives me the idea that he is somehow significant? Has he a side line of any sort?'

'I don't believe so. Just keeps on playing tennis as far as I ...

Oh, I know what's in your mind. The Drones Club sweep. Don't you remember I told you he was the second favourite? Tipton Plimsoll and he were running neck and neck for a while, but he had some trouble with his girl and the engagement was broken off. Luckily for me.'

'Good God!' said Gally, his monocle parting from its moorings, and simultaneously there proceeded from Sandy a cry or scream or wail similar in tone and volume to that of a stepped-on cat, and Sam soared some six inches in the direction of the ceiling. That cry or scream or wail or whatever it was had affected him much as if some playful hand had given him a hotfoot. Returning to terra firma, he touched the top of his head to make sure it was still there and stood gaping.

' W – ?' he said. He had intended to say, 'What's the matter?' but the sentence refused to shape itself.

Gally looked at Sandy. Sandy looked at Gally.

'Shall I tell him, or will you?'

'I'll tell him,' said Sandy. 'I'm afraid you're going to get a shock, darling.'

Sam braced himself to receive it. He had been at Blandings Castle only a short while, but it had been long enough to enable him to know that anyone enjoying its hospitality must expect to get shocks. A few possibilities flitted through his mind. The house was on fire? Empress of Blandings had taken to the bottle again? Augustus Whipple was a pleasant visitor? Constable Evans had arrived with a search warrant? There was a wide area of speculation, and he was prepared for bad news in any form.

In any form, that is to say, except the one in which it came.

'Austin Phelps is married,' said Sandy, and it was as though he had been playing for the Possibles in that England trial game and one of the Probables had hurled himself on some particularly tender portion of his anatomy. He tottered and might have fallen had he not clutched at Gally, who said 'Ouch!' and disengaged himself.

'It can't be helped,' said Sandy. 'It's just one of those things. You mustn't take it too hard, angel.'

Sam, as he looked at her, felt his heart swell. He was conscious of a sudden increase of a love which had always been substantial. What a helpmeet, he was saying to himself, what a life partner. Not a word of reproach had she said for his folly in refusing the syndicate's offer. Was there another woman in the world's history who would not have touched on that at least briefly? Would Helen of Troy in similar circumstances have been able to restrain herself? Would Cleopatra? Would Queen Victoria? He very much doubted it, and advancing on her he took her in his arms and kissed her reverently. It was some time before either of them became aware that Gally was speaking.

'I'm sorry,' said Sam, feeling that an apology was due. 'I missed that. You were saying – ?'

Gally, momentarily shaken out of his customary calm, was himself again. His monocle was back in its place, and he was once more the Galahad Threepwood whom years of membership in the old Pelican Club had trained to resilience.

'I was expressing my contrition for having allowed this wallop to ruffle me,' he said. ' 'Twas but a passing weakness. I can now think clearly again. Obviously there is only one thing to be done. Our course is plain. We approach Clarence. How much money were you telling me you had managed to save? Two hundred pounds, was it not? And you require seven. Right. Clarence shall make up the deficit.'

If somebody had told Sam that he was looking like a startled sheep, he would probably have been offended. Nevertheless, that was how he was looking, for he was wondering if he could have heard aright. He had still to learn – what the female members of this man's family had discovered in their nursery days – that there were few things of which Galahad Threepwood was not capable.

'You're going to try to touch Lord Emsworth?' he gasped.

Gally frowned.

'I dislike that word "try". It suggests a lack of confidence in my powers.'

'But you can't ask him to lend a stranger like me five hundred pounds!'

'You are perfectly right. I shall make it a thousand. You will need a margin. One always does when one is doing up a house. No sense in trying to run the thing on too slender a budget. And don't forget that you are not a stranger. You are the author of the book which has been his constant companion for years. He loves you like a son.'

Sam remained unconvinced. He had always had a sturdy distaste for being a borrower.

'I don't like the idea of cadging money from Lord Emsworth.'

'I'll do the cadging. No need for you to appear in the negotiations at all.'

'I still don't like it. Do you, Sandy?'

'Yes,' said Sandy simply.

'Of course she does,' said Gally. 'She's got sense. She knows that when you want a thousand quid, you can't be finicky, you have to go to the man who's got a thousand quid, no matter what your scruples. And, dash it, my dear fellow, it isn't as if we are asking Clarence to make you a birthday present of this paltry little sum. You'll be able to pay him back when you sell the house. But I think I know what's really bothering you. You're thinking that being the author of *Put Me Among The Pigs* isn't quite enough to sway him, that something else is needed to give him that extra push which will send him racing for his fountain pen and cheque book, and possibly you're right. Anyway, it's best to be on the safe side. See you later,' said Gally, and with the impulsiveness which was so characteristic of him he dashed briskly from the room.

It was some moments before Sam spoke. When he did, it was in a low, rather trembling voice that showed that life in Blandings Castle had begun to take its toll of him.

'Sandy!'

'Right here, my king.'

'Have you known Gally long?'

'Quite a time.'

'Has he always been as jumpy as this?'

'More or less.'

'Where do you think he's gone?'

'Who can say? I should imagine he had a sudden inspiration of some kind. His sudden inspirations always make him quick on his feet.'

'Well, I wish they wouldn't. He made me bite my tongue.'

'Of course, there's another angle.'

'What's that?'

'He may just have thought we would like to be alone together for a while.'

'And how right he was,' said Sam, instantly forgetting his troubles and problems.

It was a quarter of an hour before Gally returned. There was always something about him that reminded those with whom he mixed of a wire-haired terrier. He was looking now like a wire-haired terrier which after days of fruitless searching for a buried bone has at last managed to locate it. He had the same air of quiet triumph.

'Sorry to keep you waiting,' he said.

'Quite all right,' said Sandy. 'We found lots to do.'

'You billed?'

'And cooed. Shall I tell you something, Gally? Sam's a lamb.'

'I dare say, but we need not dwell on that now. What concerns us at the moment is the lurking-in-sheds side of him.'

Sam winced.

'I would rather you didn't mention that word "shed" in my presence,' he said. 'It does something to me.'

'And how do sheds enter into it?' said Sandy. 'What, if anything, are you talking about?'

'I'll tell you. You are probably wondering why I left you so abruptly. I went to find that blot on the body politic Huxley Winkworth.'

'What on earth for?'

'I found him in the morning-room. He was cataloguing his collection of lepidoptera, and we had a long talk.'

'About lepidoptera?'

'About letting the Empress out of her sty. You don't know it, but it is the young thug's dearest wish to do this and see what happens. Several times he has attempted it, but on each occasion he was foiled by the vigilance of Monica Simmons. Staunch and true, steadfast at her post, she was always there to baffle him.'

'Lucky she was. Lord Emsworth would have a stroke if the Empress got loose.'

'Exactly. It would shake him to his foundations. Well, as I say, I found the child busy among the beetles and I put it to him squarely. Now, I said, was his moment. Monica Simmons had gone to London, the angel with the flaming sword was no longer on the spot and the coast was clear. Grasp this opportunity, I said, for it may never come again. I had little difficulty in selling him the idea. Sandy will tell you that I am a man not without a certain persuasive eloquence. To come to the point, he thought well of the scheme and assured me that he would attend to it directly he had completed his cataloguing. He estimated that it would take him about another twenty minutes. So there you are.'

He paused as if waiting for a round of applause, but Sam showed no enthusiasm.

'You'll probably take a low view of my intelligence,' he said, 'but how do you mean "there we are"?'

Gally stared at him incredulously.

'Don't tell me you haven't got it? I'll bet Sandy has.'

'Of course. Sam lurks in the shed, Huxley sneaks up on his nefarious errand, Sam pops out and grabs him. He takes him to Lord Emsworth and tells the tale and Lord Emsworth is so grateful that he can deny him nothing. Then you go to Lord Emsworth and ask him to lend his benefactor a thousand pounds and he says "Capital, capital, capital" and there's your happy ending. Right, professor?'

'Right to the last drop. You'd better be getting along, Sam, and taking up your station.'

Sam displayed even less enthusiasm than before.

'You want me to go and sit in that blasted shed?'

'You've grasped it.'

'There's a dead rat there.'

'It'll be company for you.'

'And what's more I'm not at all certain there aren't live rats, too. When I was there before, I kept hearing a very sinister rustling. I won't do it.'

'Of course you will, my pet,' said Sandy briskly. 'Think what it means to us.'

'Yes, I know, but—'

'Sam! Sammy! Samuel, darling!'

'It's all very well to say Sam, Sammy, Samuel darling—'

'For my sake! The woman you love!'

'Oh, all right.'

'That's my brave little man.'

'But I do it under protest,' said Sam with dignity.

'Odd,' said Gally, as the door closed, 'that a single visit should have left him so prejudiced against that shed. You wouldn't think to look at him that he was the neurotic type. But you often find these fellows with tough exteriors strangely sensitive. It was the same with Plug Basham that time Puffy Benger and I put the pig in his bedroom.'

'Why did you do that, if you don't mind me asking?'

'To cheer the poor chap up. For several days he had been brooding on something, I forget what, and Puffy and I talked it over and decided that something must be done to take him out of himself. He needs fresh interests, I said to Puffy. So we coated a pig liberally with phosphorus and left it at his bedside at about two in the morning. We then beat the gong. The results were excellent. It roused him from his despondency in a flash and gave him all the fresh interests he could do with. But the point I'm making is that it was years after that before he could see a pig without a shudder. He took the same jaundiced view of them that Sam has taken of potting sheds. And Plug was an even tougher specimen than Sam. Curious. Oh, hullo, Beach.'

The butler had loomed up in the doorway, a portentousness in his manner that showed that this was no idle social call.

'Were you looking for me?'

'No, sir. For Mr Whipple.'

'Why do you want Mr Whipple?'

'Constable Evans and Constable Morgan are anxious to interview him, Mr Galahad. They are waiting in my pantry.'

It was a sensational announcement, and it caused Sandy, the
weaker vessel, to give a gasp that reminded Gally of the death
rattle of an expiring soda syphon. Gally himself, true to the tradi-
tions of the old Pelican Club, remained calm.

'You mean they're back?'

'Yes, sir.'

'You amaze me. I thought we'd seen the last of that comedy
duo. What brought them?'

'I informed Constable Evans on the telephone that the person
I allude to was in residence at the castle, Mr Galahad. You will
recall that I expressed to you my belief that he was a criminal
and an impostor.'

'I remember that you did gibber along the lines you have indicated, but I thought I had reasoned you out of that silly idea.'

'I have returned to it, sir.'

'Well, you're wrong, of course, and those constables are going
to blush hotly when they realise what asses they've made of
themselves, but if they want Whipple, they'll find him down at
the lake. He went to have a swim before dinner.'

'Thank you, Mr Galahad. I will notify the officers.'

The door closed. Gally uttered an impatient snort.

'What a curse zeal is! It's what makes Clarence disapprove of
you so much. Beach has been zealous since he was a young
under-footman. Never lets well alone. There have been lots
of complaints about it. Well, this means we'll have to cut the
Sam–Huxley sequence.'

'I was thinking the same thing myself.'

'Not that it matters. I can bend Clarence to my will perfectly adequately without it.'

'And the lamb Sam? What do we do about him?'

'We get him away.'

'So I should think, with this troupe of bloodhounds after him.'

'There's nothing to keep him here now that you and he have ironed out your little difficulties. Go and pick him up at the shed and take him to the garage and let him select the best car he sees there and drive to London. And tell him that speed is of the essence.'

'So he's stealing cars now as well as bicycles?'

'Yes, he's getting into the swing of the thing capitally. What are you waiting for?'

'I'm not waiting. I'm just going.'

'Well, go. And I,' said Gally, 'will be off to see Clarence.'

CHAPTER 12

I

With an interview of major importance before him, the prudent man does not act precipitately. Someone younger and less experienced might have hastened immediately to Lord Emsworth's study without pausing to prepare himself, but Gally knew that on these occasions a stimulus is required if one is to give of one's best. His first move, accordingly, after Sandy had left him, was to make for the drawing-room. The cocktails there would, he feared, by now be mostly ice water, but there was no time for the leisurely glass of port in Beach's pantry which he would have preferred, and he had always been a man who could rough it when he had to.

The martini which he proceeded to pour proved an agreeable surprise. It did not bite like a serpent and sting like an adder, but it was not without a certain quiet authority, and he had taken it into his system and was feeling much invigorated, when the door opened and his sister Hermione appeared.

Anyone who had seen Lady Hermione as little as ten minutes ago would have been astounded by her demeanour as she entered the room, for ten minutes ago she had been in the poorest of shapes. The failure of her expedition to the Garden Suite had left her shaken, and running over the details of the disaster in her mind as she sat in her boudoir she was still quivering. She seemed to hear once again her nephew Wilfred's sudden outburst of song, and she shuddered as she recalled it. That horrible noise had set every nerve in her body a-tingle. It would be too much, perhaps, to say of a woman of her strong character that she had the heeby-jeebies, but she was certainly emotionally disturbed. A psychiatrist, seeing her, would have rubbed his hands gleefully, scenting lucrative business.

But now her agitation had subsided and she was calm again. Smug, too, thought Gally as he eyed her. Acquaintance with her from their nursery days had made him expert at analysing her various moods, and he did not like the current one at all. Her air seemed to him the air of a sister who had that extra ace up her sleeve which makes all the difference. Nevertheless, he greeted her with a cordial 'Hullo, there' and prepared himself for whatever might be going to befall by taking another martini and water.

The action drew from her a sniff of disapproval.

'I thought I should find you near the cocktail shaker, Galahad.'

'You wanted to see me?'

'Yes, there are several things I have to say to you.'

'Always glad of a chat.'

'I doubt if you will like this one.'

'Have you come to tell me that Dame Daphne Winkworth has tied a can to Wilfred?'

'I beg your pardon?'

'She isn't taking him on as a music master.'

'Indeed? No, I had not heard. But it was not Wilfred that I wanted to talk about.'

'Then would you mind saying what you do want to talk about? I'm a busy man and I have a hundred appointments elsewhere. I can't give you more than five minutes.'

'Five minutes will be ample.'

Lady Hermione sat down, and the smugness of her manner became more pronounced. Gally, who had been trying to think who it was that she reminded him of, suddenly got it. The Fat Boy in Pickwick. She had only to say 'I want to make your flesh creep', and the resemblance would be complete.

'A few minutes ago Veronica rang me up on the telephone.'

'Oh yes?'

'She was radiantly happy. She had just been having a long talk with Tipton.'

'Oh, yes?'

'And to cut a long story short—'

'Always a good thing.'

' – He told her he had read that letter—'

'The one you dictated?'

' – And was sure she had not meant a word of it. And of course she said she hadn't. They are getting married at the registrar's the day after tomorrow. I very seldom approve of these runaway weddings, but in this case I think they are quite right. I'm afraid their decision affects you a good deal.'

'You mean about Sam Bagshott?'

'Is that his horrible name? I had forgotten. Yes, about Sam Bagshott.'

'What do you plan to do?'

'What do you expect me to do? I shall tell him to leave the castle immediately, and then I shall go to Clarence and explain what has happened.'

'I see.'

'Where is he?'

'In his study, I imagine.'

'Not Clarence. This man Bagshott.'

'Oh, Sam? He was in that little room off the library just now. The one Sandy Callender works in.'

'Thank you. There is no need for you to come, Galahad,' she said some moments later, pausing outside the library door.

'You wouldn't care to have me as a bodyguard?'

'I don't understand you.'

'Sam, when stirred, is apt to plug people in the eye.'

'I don't think I am in any danger.'

'Have it your own way. But be on the alert. The thing to do is to watch his knees. They will tell you when he is setting himself for a swing. Keep your guard up and remember to roll with the punch.'

'Thank you. Goodbye, Galahad,' said Lady Hermione coldly.

She went in and Gally, closing the door behind her, turned the key in the lock and trotted briskly away. His schedule called for quick action. He was sorry to have had to inconvenience his sister, but it was imperative that she remain in storage until the conclusion of his business talk with his brother Clarence. And the inconvenience would after all be slight. There were comfortable chairs for her to relax in and several thousand good books to curl up with if she wanted something to help her pass the time. It was with no burden on his conscience, such as it was, that he set out for Lord Emsworth's study.

His route lay through the spacious hall where the 'No smoking' and 'Kindly keep in line' signs had been, and as he descended the stairs he was aware of a measured voice speaking from that direction. It seemed to be urging someone to come to the castle with all possible speed, and reaching the hall he saw Beach at the telephone. The conversation, whatever its import, had apparently concluded, for the butler, with a polished 'Thank you, sir. I will inform Dame Daphne,' was hanging up the receiver.

'What was all that about, Beach?' he asked.

'I was telephoning the doctor on behalf of Master Winkworth, Mr Galahad.'

'He's ill, is he? Nothing trivial, I hope?'

'He has sustained a wounded finger, sir. The Empress bit him.'

'What!'

'Yes, sir. I have no information as to how it occurred.'

'I can fill you in. His one aim in life is to let the Empress out of her sty, and he must have sneaked off to do it, little knowing that she had a bad hangover and was spoiling for a fight with someone. She went on a bender yesterday.'

'Indeed, Mr Galahad? I was not aware.'

'Yes, she mopped the stuff up like a vacuum cleaner and today is paying the price. One pictures the scene. Huxley steals up and no doubt chirrups. The Empress winces. He continues to chirrup. She approaches the gate, cursing under her breath. He puts his finger in to raise the latch, and she lets him have it. I don't blame her, do you?'

'No, sir.'

'You take the broadminded view? You feel, as I do, that he was asking for it and deserved everything that was coming to him? I thought you would. Best possible thing that could have happened, in my opinion. It will teach him a lesson. I shouldn't wonder if this didn't prove a turning point in his life, and if anybody's life needs all the turning points it can get, it's his. The occasion, as I see it, is one for sober rejoicing. But I mustn't stay here chatting with you, much as I enjoy it. I have a business appointment. You don't happen to know if the constables found Mr Whipple, do you?'

'No, sir. The officers have not yet returned.'

'Well, give them my love when they do. Charming chaps, charming chaps,' said Gally.

He resumed his progress to the study. Opening the door, he halted on the threshold, staring, a startled 'Lord love a duck!' on his lips.

II

The sight that met his monocle was one well calculated to cause alarm and concern. Something had plainly occurred to upset the even tenor of his elder brother's life. Roget, searching in his Thesaurus for adjectives to describe Lord Emsworth as he drooped bonelessly in his chair, would probably have settled for stunned, flustered, disturbed, unnerved and disconcerted. Gally, who had a feeling heart, was disconcerted himself as he saw him, though, looking on the bright side, as was his habit, he felt that whatever had happened must have done his adrenal glands a world of good.

'Strike me pink, Clarence,' he exclaimed, 'what's bitten you?'

Lord Emsworth, though stunned, flustered and disturbed, was able to see that he was under a misapprehension.

'It was not I who was bitten, Galahad, it was Daphne Wink-worth's son, I keep forgetting his name.'

'Yes, so Beach was telling me. But I'm surprised that you're taking it so hard. I should have thought you'd feel it was just retribution and the wages of sin and all that.'

'Oh, I do. Yes, quite.'

'Then why are you looking like the wreck of the *Hesperus*?'

Gally's sympathetic attitude was helping Lord Emsworth to become calmer. A kindly brother in whom one can confide always works wonders on these occasions.

'Galahad,' he said, 'I have just been through a most painful experience.'

'Don't you mean Huxley has?'

'It has left me shaken. Have you ever been face to face in a small room with an angry woman?'

'Dozens of times in my younger days. One of them spiked me in the leg with a hatpin. Yours didn't do that to you, did she?'

'Eh? Oh, no.'

'Then you're that much ahead of the game. Who was your angry woman? It couldn't have been Hermione, for I happen to know that she is occupied elsewhere, so I take it it was the divine Winkworth. Am I right?'

'Yes, she burst in on me with the news about her son's finger, and do you know what she said? You will scarcely credit this, but she said the Empress was a savage and dangerous animal and must be destroyed. The Empress!'

'Gadzooks! Didn't you explain to her that the poor soul had a morning head?'

'I was too flabbergasted. I stared at her for quite a while, unable to speak. Then I fear I was rather rude.'

'Excellent. What did you say?'

'I'm afraid I told her not to be a fool.'

'You couldn't have done better. And then?'

'A violent argument followed, in the course of which I became still ruder. In the end she said she would not stay another day in the castle and flounced off.'

'What-ed off? Oh, flounced? I see what you mean.'

'I think what caused her particular annoyance was that while we were talking I telephoned the vet to ask if there was any danger of infection to the Empress.'

'A very sensible precaution.'

'It appeared to infuriate her. We both became very heated. I ought to have shown more restraint. I shouldn't have offended Daphne.'

'Why not? It was the consummation devoutly to be wished. Dash it, Clarence, you were in deadly peril from this woman. Already she had told you she was interested in pigs, and from there to getting you to the altar rails would have been but a step. Your attitude seems to me to have been exactly right. If poor Puffy Benger had had your courage and resolution, he wouldn't today be the father of a son with adenoids and two daughters with braces on their teeth. You have removed the Winkworth from your life. The shadow has passed. You have won through to safety.'

'Bless my soul, I never thought of that.'

'If you feel like doing the dance of the seven veils all over the castle, I shall have no objection. But you still have a careworn look. Why is that?'

'I was thinking of Hermione.'

'What about Hermione?'

'She will have something to say, I fear.'

'Well, when she says it, show the same splendid firmness you did in dealing with Ma Winkworth. Who's Hermione? A woman you have frequently seen spanked by a Nanny with a hairbrush. If she starts getting tough, remind her of that and watch her wilt. A fig for Hermione, if I may use the expression. Her views on the matter in hand don't amount to a hill of beans.'

Lord Emsworth's mild eyes glowed.

'You're great comfort, Galahad.'

'I try to be, Clarence, I try to be.'

Lord Emsworth fell into a meditative silence, but Gally's assumption that he was thinking of his sister and inwardly rehearsing things to say to her – probably out of the side of his mouth – was incorrect. When he spoke, it was of the Empress.

'What I cannot understand, Galahad, is how that boy was allowed to approach the sty. Miss Simmons positively assured us that she would be on the alert to see that he didn't. If I remember, she said in so many words that she would rub his face in the mud if he attempted to come near the Empress.'

Gally saw that the time had arrived to tell all.

'I'm afraid I have some bad news for you, Clarence. Miss Simmons is no longer with us. She's gone to London to get married.'

'What!'

'Yes, she's marrying Wilfred Allsop. You're losing a pig girl but gaining a niece.'

Lord Emsworth's eyes, no longer mild, shot fire through his pince-nez.

'She had no right to do such a thing!'

'Well, you know, love conquers all, or so I read somewhere. I suppose she couldn't resist the urge.'

'But who will look after the Empress?'

He had brought the conversation round to the exact point which Gally desired.

'Why, who but Augustus Whipple?' he said. 'I'm sure he will be delighted to act as understudy till you can fill the part elsewhere.'

Lord Emsworth blessed his soul.

'But, Galahad, do you think he would?'

'Of course he will. There are no limits to what Gus Whipple will do to oblige people he's fond of, and I know he feels that you and he have started a beautiful friendship. He will have to return to London shortly, but while he's still here you can rely on him. A nice chap, don't you think?'

'Capital, capital. Quite. But why should he have to return to London?'

Gally glanced over his shoulder. The study door was closed. He could not be overheard.

'This is all very hush-hush, Clarence.'

'What is?'

'What I am about to tell you. Whipple has got to go to London to try to raise some money. I know you will let this go no farther, but the poor fellow's heavily in debt, and what makes it worse is that the debt is one of honour. He got into a poker game at the Athenaeum the other night, and you don't need me to tell you what that means at a place like the Athenaeum, where they play for high stakes. Many a bishop there has come away without his apron and gaiters after an all-night session. Whipple lost his shirt. He gave IOUs to half a dozen of the members, and if he welshes on them, they'll kick him out of the club without a pang of pity.'

Lord Emsworth's pince-nez were bobbing at the end of their string like adagio dancers.

'You shock me, Galahad! How much does he need?'

'A thousand pounds. What you would consider a mere trifle, but to him a colossal sum. Let us hope he will succeed in borrowing it somewhere.'

'But, Galahad! Why didn't he tell me?'

'Why you?' Gally paused, astounded by a bizarre thought that had come to him. He looked at Lord Emsworth incredulously. 'You don't mean you would lend him the money?'

'Of course I will. The man who wrote *On The Care Of The Pig*! I'll write a cheque immediately.'

Gally's face lit up. He rose from his chair, patted his brother twice on the shoulder and sat down again, plainly overcome.

'Well, that would certainly be the ideal way of putting everything right. It never occurred to me to think of you. But there's just one thing. You had better make the cheque payable to me. Whipple is a very proud man and though I know he's extremely fond of you, you are after all a comparative stranger to him. He might refuse to accept money from you, but if an old friend like me offered it to him, that would be different. You see what I mean?'

'Quite, quite. Very considerate of you to think of it. Now where is my cheque book? It should be somewhere, if Miss Callender hasn't hidden it with her infernal tidying—'

He broke off. Lady Hermione was entering the study.

III

Lady Hermione, like her brother Clarence, was looking stunned, flustered, disturbed, unnerved and disconcerted, so much so that Roget, had he been present, would have got the impression that these things run in families. Her face had taken on a purple tinge and her stocky body seemed to vibrate. Gally, who was given to homely similes, thought she was madder than a wet hen, and he was right. Only an exceptionally emotional hen when unusually moist could have exhibited an equal annoyance.

It was Lord Emsworth whom she had come to see, but it was to Gally that she first addressed herself.

'How dare you lock me in the library, Galahad?'

Gally started.

'Good heavens! Did I?'

'I might have been there still, if Beach had not heard me calling and let me out.'

'You're sure it wasn't Beach who locked you in? He has a very subtle sense of humour.'

'Quite sure. I happened to try the door just after you had left, and it wouldn't open.'

'Probably just sticking.'

'It was not.'

'Doors do.'

'This one didn't. It was locked.'

'Then,' said Gally, generously accepting the blame, 'I'm afraid it must have been me, but if I did it it was purely inadvertently. You know how you turn keys absent-mindedly. I'm terribly sorry.'

'Bah!' said Lady Hermione.

Lord Emsworth had been listening to these exchanges with growing impatience. Though there was no actual written rule to that effect, it was an understood thing that his study was a sanctuary into which the most thrustful sister must not penetrate. Sisters who wished to confer with him were supposed to do it in the library or the amber drawing-room or somewhere out in the grounds. It was the one flicker of spirit the downtrodden peer had ever been known to show. So now he intervened in the debate with something which if not truculence was very near it.

'Hermione!'

'Well?'

'I am having an important talk with Galahad.'

'And I am going to have an important talk with you. I have just seen Daphne. She is furious. She says you were very rude to her.'

Lord Emsworth was now definitely truculent. The mere mention of that name plumbed hidden depths in him and sent his blood pressure soaring into the higher brackets.

'She does, does she? What did she expect me to be, coming in—'

'Flouncing in,' said Gally.

'Yes, flouncing in and telling me I must have the Empress destroyed just because she bit that beastly little boy—'

'Who started it,' said Gally.

'Exactly. He was trying to let the Empress out of her sty, and goodness knows what might have happened if he had succeeded. The meadow is full of holes and ditches. She might have broken a leg.'

'Two legs,' said Gally.

'Yes, two legs. Apart from the nervous strain. The least thing upsets her and makes her refuse her food. It might have been days before she would have taken her proper meals, and if she does not consume daily nourishment amounting to fifty-seven hundred calories, these to consist of protein four pounds five ounces, carbohydrates twenty-five pounds—'

For an instant it might have seemed that the afternoon's thunderstorm had broken out again, but it was merely Lady Hermione banging the top of the desk. She had absent-mindedly, as Gally would have said, possessed herself of a heavy ruler, and she was using it with a lot of wrist work and follow through.

'Will you stop babbling about that insufferable pig of yours! I did not come here to talk about pigs. You must apologise to Daphne.'

Flame flashed from Lord Emsworth's pince-nez. Just so had it done when he was dismissing George Cyril Wellbeloved from his employment for the second time.

'I'm blowed if I apologise!'

'Well spoken, Clarence. The right spirit. It is men like you who have made England what it is.'

It was not Lady Hermione who said this, it was Gally, and she gave him a look which would have shrivelled anyone but an ex-member of the old Pelican Club.

'I don't want your opinion, Galahad.'

'I can applaud, can't I?'

'No.'

'Well, I shall. As I did, I remember, when I saw you being spanked by our mutual Nanny with a hairbrush.'

Lady Hermione winced, as if the old wound still troubled her. She was silent for a moment, but it was not in her redoubtable character to let ancient memories silence her for long. With another look of a kind which no sister should have directed at a brother she resumed her observations.

'Daphne says that unless you apologise she will leave.'

'She must suit herself about that.'

'If Daphne leaves, I leave. For the last time, will you apologise to her and have that pig destroyed?'

'Of course I won't.'

'Then I shall take the first train to London tomorrow.'

'Voules can drive you in the car.'

'I do not wish to be driven in the car. I shall go by train, and before I go I have something to say which may interest you. Has Galahad told you of the amusing practical joke he has been playing on you?'

'Eh? What? No.'

'You should have, Galahad. It spoils a joke to keep it up too long. This man he has passed off on you as Augustus Whipple is not Augustus Whipple at all.'

'What!'

'He is some loathsome friend of Galahad's whom he has sneaked into the castle for some purpose of his own.'

'I can't believe it!'

'Perhaps you will when I tell you that almost immediately after he arrived Beach took a telephone call from the real Augustus Whipple, speaking from the Athenaeum Club in London. Goodbye, Clarence. I shall probably not be seeing you in the morning.'

The door closed behind her, and Lord Emsworth, after blinking some six times in rapid succession, said:

'Galahad—'

'Clarence,' said Gally, in his enthusiasm cutting him short, 'you were superb. A colossal feat. We tip our hats respectfully to the man who can look Dame Daphne Winkworth in the eye and make her wilt, but when immediately afterwards he crushes Hermione and sends her, too, flouncing off, words fail us and we can only bow before him in silence, recognising him as a hero and a daredevil the like of whom one seldom sees. And you will reap your reward, Clarence. You have won for yourself a full, happy life alone with your pig, a life entirely free from sisters of every description. And you deserve every minute of it. But I interrupted you. You were going to say something, I think? Was it about that absurd charge of Hermione's?'

'Er – yes.'

'I thought so. You are wondering if there was any truth in it. My dear fellow, can you ask?'

'But how very odd that Beach should have spoken on the telephone to someone claiming to be Augustus Whipple.'

'Not really, when you come to think of it. I can explain that. I explained it to Hermione, but she wouldn't listen. You know how Visitors' Day always takes it out of Beach. Exhausting work showing people about the place. He was half asleep when he answered the phone. Got the name wrong. That sort of thing's always happening. There was a girl I knew in the old days who was madly in love with a man called Joe Brice. Telephone goes one morning, voice says, "Hullo, Mabel or Jane or Kate or whatever her name was, this is Joe Brice. Will you marry me?" Naturally she says he can bet his Old Etonian socks she will and she asks where they can meet. He mentions a bar in the Haymarket, and she goes there and a chap called Joe Price, whom she hardly knew, leaps at her and folds her in a close embrace, and when she hauls off and socks him on the side of the head with a crocodile bag apparently filled with samples of ore from a copper mine, he gets as sore as a gumboil and reproaches her bitterly. "You told me only an hour ago you would marry me," he says. Took her quite a while to straighten the thing out, I believe. Oh, hullo, Egbert. You back?'

The words were addressed to Colonel Egbert Wedge, who had come into the room at this moment looking travel-stained but less tired than might have been expected after his long journey from Worcestershire.

'Just got here,' he said. 'I caught an early train. I stopped off for a quick one at the Emsworth Arms. Oh, Gally, that letter I was telling you to expect. Did you get it?'

'I got it.'

'Good,' said Colonel Wedge, greatly relieved. He might have known, he felt, that he could rely on Gally. 'What's become of Hermione? Beach told me she was here.'

'She left a few minutes ago.'

'Then I'll catch her in our room. She's probably gone to dress. Oh, Clarence,' said Colonel Wedge, pausing at the door, 'this'll interest you. While I was having my quick one in the Emsworth

Arms bar, a fellow came in whose face I thought I knew, and he turned out to be Whipple, the chap who wrote that book you're always reading.'

'What!'

'Yes. I asked him what he was doing in these parts, and he said you had invited him to the castle but couldn't have him at the moment as you were in bed with German measles, so as he wanted badly to have a look at the Empress he had put up at the Emsworth Arms. There must be some mistake somewhere, because you don't look as if you had German measles. You'd better give him a ring and find out what it's all about. Well, I think I'll be going along and having a bath. I'm caked with dust and cinders.'

Lord Emsworth spoke in a low, quivering voice.

'One moment, Egbert. You say you are personally acquainted with Mr Whipple?'

'I've met him two or three times at the Athenaeum. Old General Willoughby takes me to lunch there occasionally.'

'Thank you, Egbert.'

A long silence followed the Colonel's departure. Lord Emsworth broke it, and there was infinite reproach in his voice.

'Well, really, Galahad!'

It had often been said at the old Pelican Club that there was no situation, however sticky, which would not find Galahad Threepwood as calm and cool as a halibut on a fishmonger's slab, and he proved now that this was no idle tribute. Where a lesser man with an elder brother looking at him as Lord Emsworth was looking would have blushed and twiddled his fingers, he preserved his customary poise and prepared to tell the tale as he had seldom told it before.

'I know just how you're feeling, Clarence,' he said. 'You're as sore as a sunburned neck, and I don't blame you. I blame myself. I ought not to have been guilty of this innocent deception, but it was a military necessity. This chap – his name's Sam Bagshott and he's the son of the late Boko Bagshott, whom you probably don't remember though he was a bosom friend of mine – is in love with young Sandy Callender and there had been a rift within the lute and it was essential that he clock in at the castle and heal it. This I am glad to say he has now done thanks to you extending your hospitality. And I wanted to tap you for that thousand quid because he needs it in order to marry her. In fact, from start to finish I acted from the best and soundest motives, but don't think I don't see your point of view. You naturally jib at the idea of parting with a thousand of the best and brightest – though it would only be a loan and you'd get it back with interest – to someone you hardly know. And you are perfectly justified in taking this attitude. Don't dream of parting. I was wrong to ask you. Keep the money in the old oak chest. It's a pity, though, because if you did feel like paying out, you would be sitting on top of the world. You've got rid of the Winkworth, you've got rid of Hermione, and this way you'd be getting rid of Sandy, too. I beg your pardon, Clarence? You spoke?'

Lord Emsworth had not spoken. What had proceeded from his lips had been a strangled cry. His pince-nez were gleaming with a strange light.

'Galahad!'

'Hullo?'

'Do you mean that if I lend this fellow Boko Bagshott—'

'Sam Bagshott. Boko's the father.'

'Do you mean that if I lend this Sam Bagshott a thousand pounds, he will take Miss Callender away from here?'

'That's right. But, as you say, there's no earthly reason why you should – except of course that if you don't she'll be here as a fixture. No doubt you say to yourself that you are quite competent to give her the sack, but are you? I doubt it. She would cry buckets and your gentle heart would be melted. And as you could hardly expect a young girl to stay here unchaperoned, that would mean begging Hermione to return, and one presumes that Hermione would bring the Winkworth with her and there you would be, back where you started.'

Lord Emsworth drew a deep breath.

'I will give you that cheque, Galahad. I will write it immediately.'

Gally was astounded.

'You will?'

'Quite.'

'Capital, capital, capital,' said Gally. 'Thank you, Clarence,' he added a few moments later as he took the oblong strip of paper with its invigorating signature.

He rose. He glanced at his watch. There would, he was glad to see, be just time before the dressing-for-dinner gong sounded for a quick visit to Beach's pantry. He looked forward to it with bright anticipation. Not only would there be port there but in all probability an added attraction in the person of Constable Evans, with whom it was always a privilege and a pleasure to exchange ideas.

THE END

'Had P.G. Wodehouse's only contribution to literature been Lord Emsworth and Blandings Castle, his place in history would have been assured. Had he written of none but Mike and Psmith, he would be cherished today as the best and brightest of our comic authors. If Jeeves and Wooster had been his solitary theme, still he would be hailed as The Master. If he had given us only Ukridge, or nothing but the recollections of the Mulliner family, or a pure diet of golfing stories, Wodehouse would never the less be considered immortal. That he gave us all those and more – so much more – is our good fortune and a testament to the most industrious, prolific and beneficent author ever to have sat down, scratched his head and banged out a sentence.'

Stephen Fry

We hope you have enjoyed this book. With over ninety novels and around 300 short stories to choose from, you may be wondering which Wodehouse to choose next. It is our pleasure to introduce...

UNCLE FRED

Uncle Dynamite

Meet Frederick Altamount Cornwallis Twistleton, Fifth Earl of Ickenham. Better known as Uncle Fred, an old boy of such a sunny and youthful nature that explosions of sweetness and light detonate all around him.

Cocktail Time

Frederick, Earl of Ickenham, remains young at heart. So his jape of using a catapult to ping to silk top hat off his grumpy half-brother-in-law, is nothing out of the ordinary but the consequences abound with possibilities.

UKRIDGE

Ukridge

Money makes the world go round for Stanley Featherstonehaugh Ukridge – looking like an animated blob of mustard in his bright yellow raincoat – and when there isn't enough of it, the world just has to spin a bit faster.

MR MULLINER

Meet Mr Mulliner

Sitting in the Angler's Rest, drinking hot scotch and lemon, Mr Mulliner has fabulous stories to tell of the extraordinary behaviour of his far flung family. This includes Wilfred, whose formula for Buck-U-Uppo enables elephants to face tigers with the necessary nonchalance.

Mr Mulliner Speaking

Holding court in the bar-parlour of the Angler's Rest, Mr Mulliner reveals what happened to The Man Who Gave Up Smoking, what the Something Squishy was that the butler on a silver salver, and what caused the dreadful Unpleasantness at Bludleigh Court.

MONTY BODKIN

The Luck of the Bodkins

Monty Bodkin, besotted with 'precious dream-rabbit' Gertrude Butterwick, Reggie and Ambrose Tennyson (the latter mistaken for the late Poet Laureate), and Hollywood starlet Lotus Blossom, complete with pet alligator, all embark on a voyage of personal discovery aboard the luxurious liner S. S. Atlantic.

JEEVES

The Novels

Thank You, Jeeves

Bertie disappears to the country as a guest of his chum Chuffy – only to find his peace shattered by the arrival of his ex-fiancée Pauline Stoker, her formidable father and the eminent loony-doctor Sir Roderick Glossop. When Chuffy falls in love with Pauline and Bertie seems to be caught in flagrante, a situation boils up which only Jeeves (whether employed or not) can simmer down . . .

Jeeves and the Feudal Spirit

A moustachioed Bertie must live up to 'Stilton' Cheesewright's expectations in the Drones Club darts tournament, or risk being beaten to a pulp by 'Stilton', jealous of his fiancée Florence's affections . . .

Much Obliged, Jeeves

What happens when the Book of Revelations, the Junior Ganymede Club's recording of their masters' less than perfect habits falls into potentially hostile hands?

Aunts Aren't Gentlemen

Under doctor's orders, Bertie moves with Jeeves to a countryside cottage. But Jeeves can cope with anything – even Aunt Dahlia.

Jeeves in the Offing

When Jeeves goes on holiday to Herne Bay, Bertie's life collapses; finding his mysterious engagement announced in *The Times* and encountering his nemesis Sir Roderick Glossop in disguise, Bertie hightails it to Herne Bay. Then the fun really starts . . .

The Code of the Woosters

Purloining an antique cow creamer under the instruction of the indomitable Aunt Dahlia is the least of Bertie's tasks, for he has to play Cupid while feuding with Spode.

The Mating Season

In an idyllic Tudor manor in a picture-perfect English village, Bertie is in disguise as Gussie Fink-Nottle, Gussie is in disguise as Bertram Wooster and Jeeves, also in disguise, is the only one who can set things right . . .

Ring for Jeeves

Patch Perkins and his clerk are not the 'honest bookies' they seem, but Bill, the rather impoverished 9th Earl of Rowcester, and his temporary butler Jeeves. When they abscond with the freak winnings of Captain Biggar, Jeeves's resourcefulness is put to the test . . .

Stiff Upper Lip, Jeeves

Bertie Wooster visits Major Plank in an attempt to return a work of art which Stiffy had told Bertie had been effectively stolen from Plank by Sir Watkyn Bassett. Thank goodness for Chief Inspector Witherspoon – but is he all he seems?

Right Ho, Jeeves

Bertie assumes his alter-ego of Cupid and arranges the engagement of Gussie Fink-Nottle to Tuppy Glossop. Thankfully, Jeeves is ever present to correct the blundering plans hatched by his master.

Joy in the Morning

Trapped in rural Steeple Bumpleigh with old flame Florence Craye, her new and suspicious fiancé Stilton Cheesewright, and two-faced Edwin the Boy Scout, Bertie desperately needs Jeeves to save him . . .

JEEVES

The Collections

Carry on, Jeeves

In his new role as valet to Bertie Wooster, Jeeves's first duty is to create a miracle hangover cure. From that moment, the partnership that is Jeeves and Wooster never looks back . . .

Very Good, Jeeves

Endeavouring to give satisfaction, Jeeves embarks on a number of rescue missions, including rescuing Bingo Little and Tuppy Glossop from the soup . . . Twice each.

The Inimitable Jeeves

In pages stalked by the carnivorous Aunt Agatha, Bingo Little embarks on a relationship rollercoaster and Bertie needs Jeeves's help to narrowly evade the clutches of terrifying Honoria Glossop . . .

The World of Jeeves

A complete collection of the Jeeves and Wooster short stories, described by Wodehouse as 'the ideal paperweight'.

BLANDINGS

Something Fresh

The first Blandings novel, featuring the delightfully dotty Lord Emsworth and introducing the first of many impostors who are to visit the Castle.

Pigs Have Wings

Can the Empress of Blandings avoid a pignapping to win the Fat Pigs class at the Shropshire Show for the third year running?

Leave it to Psmith

Lady Constance Keeble, sister of Lord Emsworth of Blandings Castle, has both an imperious manner and a valuable diamond necklace. The precarious peace of Blandings is shattered when her necklace becomes the object of dark plottings, for within the castle lurk some well-connected jewel thieves – among them a pair of American crooks, Lord Emsworth's younger son Freddie, desperate for money to establish a bookie's business, and Psmith, hoping to use a promised commission to finance his old school friend Mike's purchase of a farm to secure his future happiness.

Service with a Smile

When Clarence, Ninth Earl of Emsworth, must travel to London for the opening of Parliament, he grudgingly leaves beloved pig, the Empress of Blandings, at home. When he returns, he must call upon Uncle Fred to restore normality to the chaos instilled during his absence ...

Summer Lightning

The first appearance in a novel of The Empress of Blandings, the prize-winning pig and all-consuming passion of Clarence, Ninth Earl of Emsworth, which has disappeared. Suspects within the Castle abound ... Did the butler do it?

Full Moon

When the moon is full at Blandings, strange things happen. Including a renowned painter being miraculously revivified to paint a portrait of the beloved pig The Empress of Blandings, decades after his death ...

Uncle Fred in the Springtime

Uncle Fred believes he can achieve anything in the springtime, however disguised as a loony-doctor and trying to prevent prize pig, the Empress of Blandings from falling into the hands of the unscrupulous Duke of Dunstable, he is stretched to his limit ...

A Pelican at Blandings

Skulduggery is afoot, involving the sale of a modern nude painting, which in Lord Emsworth's eyes, resembles a pig. Inundated with unwelcome guests, Clarence is embarking on the short journey to the end of his wits. Fortunately Galahad Threepwood is on hand to solve all the mysteries ...

The World of Blandings (Omnibus)

This wonderfully fat omnibus (containing three short stories and two full novels) spans the dimensions of the Empress of Blandings herself, surely the fattest pig in England ...

Blandings Castle

The Empress of Blandings, potential silver medal winner in the Fat Pigs Class at the Shropshire Agricultural show, is off her food. Clarence, absent-minded Ninth Earl of Emsworth, is engaged in a feud with Head Gardener McAllister. But first of all, the vexed matter of the custody of the pumpkin must be resolved. This collection also includes Mr Mulliner's stories about Hollywood.

And Some Other Treats...

What Ho!

Introduced by Stephen Fry, this is a bumper anthology, providing the cream of the crop of Wodehouse's hilarious stories, together with verse, articles and all manner of treasures.

The Heart of a Goof

From his favourite chair on the terrace above the ninth hole, the Oldest Member reveals the stories behind his club's players, from notorious 'golfing giggler' Evangeline to poor, inept Rollo Podmarsh.

The Clicking of Cuthbert

A collection of stories, including that of Cuthbert, golfing ace, hopelessly in love with Adeline, who only cares for rising young writers. But enter a Great Russian Novelist with a strange passion, and Cuthbert's prospects might be looking up ...

Big Money

Berry Conway, employee of dyspeptic American millionaire Torquil Patterson Frisby, has inherited a large number of shares in the Dream Come True copper mine. Of course they're worthless ... aren't they?

Hot Water

In the heady atmosphere of a 1930s French Château, J Wellington Gedge only wants to return to his life in California, where everything is as it seems ...

Laughing Gas

Joey Cooley, golden-curled Hollywood child film star, and Reginald, six-foot tall boxer Earl of Havershot, are both under anaesthetic in the dentist's when their identities are swapped in the fourth dimension.

The Small Bachelor

It's Prohibition America and shy young George Finch is setting out as an artist – without the encumbrance of a shred of talent. Will George triumph over the social snob Mrs Waddington and successfully woo her stepdaughter?

Money for Nothing

Two households, both alike in dignity, in fair Rudge-in-the-Vale, where we lay our scene ... Will the love of John Carmody and Pat Wyvern survive the bitter feud between their fathers, miserly Lester Carmody and peppery Colonel Wyvern?

Summer Moonshine

Poor Sir Buckstone Abbott owns in Walsingford Hall one of the least attractive stately homes in the country, so when a rich continental princess seems willing to buy it, he's overjoyed. But will the deal be completed?

The Adventures of Sally

When Sally Nicholas inherits some money, her life becomes increasingly complicated; with a needy brother, a handsome fiancé, who is not all he seems, and a naive generosity of spirit, Sally must turn to doting, clueless Ginger Kemp to set things right ...

Young Men in Spats

Meet the Young Men in Spats – all innocent members of the Drones Club, all hopeless suitors, and all busy betting their sometimes non-existent fortunes on highly improbable outcomes. That is when they're not recovering from driving their sports cars *through* Marble Arch ...

Piccadilly Jim

It takes a lot of effort for Jimmy Crocker to become Piccadilly Jim – nights on the town roistering, and a string of broken hearts. When he eventually succeeds, Jimmy ends up having to pretend he's himself, possibly the hardest pretence of all . . .

A Damsel in Distress

The Earl of Marshmoreton just wants a quiet life pottering around his garden, supported by his portly butler Keggs. However when his spirited daughter Lady Maud is placed under house-arrest due to an unfortunate infatuation, and American George Bevan determines to claim her heart, the Earl is allowed no such reprieve . . .

The Girl in Blue

Young Jerry West has a few problems, including uncles with butlers who aren't all they seem, and a love for the woman he is not due to marry . . . When his uncle's miniature Gainsborough, *The Girl in Blue*, is stolen, Jerry sets out on a mission to find her . . . Will everything come right in the process?

Join the P G Wodehouse community!

Visit the official website:
www.wodehouse.co.uk

Become a fan on facebook:
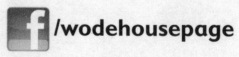 **/wodehousepage**

Join the P G Wodehouse Society:
www.pgwodehousesociety.org.uk